Helen J. Ro[illegible]ary fiction with charac[illegible]h.

Before she[illegible]olfe worked in I.T. unt[illegible]ied journalism and writi[illegible] for Women's Health & Fitness magazines as w[illegible]wsletter content and media releases for a not-for-profit organisation. In 2011 the fiction bug bit and Helen has been writing fiction ever since.

Helen J Rolfe lives in Hertfordshire with her husband and two children.

Find out more at www.helenjrolfe.com, and follow her on Twitter @HJRolfe.

Also by Helen J. Rolfe

The Friendship Tree

Handle Me with Care

What Rosie Found Next

The Chocolatier's Secret

Helen J. Rolfe

Published by Fabrian Books

For Christine, who was brave enough to put me first, and to my parents for opening their hearts. This one's for you.

Chapter One

Andrew

Andrew Bennett stared at the computer screen. 'After all this time,' he said out loud, even though he was alone. Julia Mason's name was right there in front of him, and he didn't even need to click on her Facebook message to read what she had to say. There was only one word: 'Why?'

After what she'd done to him, he'd wanted to ask her the very same question for the last thirty years.

He heard Gemma on her way up the stairs, probably with a cup of tea. She'd been up before him this morning and whoever was first out of bed usually did the honours. He shut the laptop, unable to concentrate on the online work he needed to do, and headed to the bedroom. He kissed his wife and took his tea into the bathroom, all the while trying to process memories of the past.

He showered, ate a bowl of cereal for breakfast and left the house on Myrtle Close to take the ten-minute walk to Magnolia Creek Chocolaterie, the business he owned and ran. As he walked he tried to shake off thoughts of Julia Mason, the girl who'd broken his heart in the cruellest way possible. He thought about his wife, Gemma, the woman who had his heart now. They'd met at LJ Bennett Chocolates eleven years ago. Owned and run by his father, Louis Bennett, the business was a lucrative, successful chocolate shop that thrived in the heart of the city. Andrew had learned from his father, from the ground up, and as part of the business they'd run workshops. There had been a hen do one day and Gemma was one of the participants – Andrew, especially knowing the amount of champagne likely to be consumed and with no desire himself to get involved, had delegated the workshop to a female employee – and when he'd returned to the shop after running an errand, Gemma had literally fallen into his arms, drunk and more than a little unsteady on her feet. He'd been thirty-four years old at the time, and from that moment on he was smitten.

Andrew and Gemma married three years later, and now all they wanted was a family. Eight years his junior, Gemma had age on her side, or so they thought when they'd started trying for a baby two years ago. She'd only been thirty-five then and they'd both been convinced it would happen easily enough. But after falling pregnant quickly, a miscarriage had shattered their dreams. Since then, she'd conceived three more times, yet none of those pregnancies had gone the distance. Only two days ago she'd called him at the chocolaterie to tell him she'd miscarried again and Andrew was beginning to feel powerless to help her. Added to that, his father, Louis, was on dialysis for kidney failure and with Andrew running the business, Gemma was the one who flitted between her own part-time job at the local school, the chocolaterie and home to be with Louis or take him to the hospital sessions. All of this was putting a strain on their marriage and both of them knew it.

Andrew continued along the main street of Magnolia Creek, allowing the sun to gently warm his back. He loved this time of the morning, before most people got out of bed, before Magnolia Creek welcomed its first tourists of the day, before school kids bustled down the streets and up to the little school at the top of the hill. This morning held a welcome freshness after the stifling heat of summer that had seen temperatures into the forties all last week. In truth he was looking forward to the approaching autumn and winter seasons, which would bring with them plenty of requests for their signature hot chocolate in the café upstairs.

Apart from family, chocolate was Andrew Bennett's life. He loved creating new recipes, intricate designs. If only everything in his life was that easy.

He unlocked the rear entrance to the chocolaterie, which led through to the office, the main kitchen where he switched on the lights and a segregated room where they held workshops and parties. He'd worried these premises would be too compact in the summer months, become unbearable when the heat bore down on the whole of Melbourne. Chocolate needed an ideal temperature – not too hot, not too cold. Gemma called it the Goldilocks Temperature. But the air conditioning had worked a treat, and the heaters would warm the place up when the cooler months were upon them.

Andrew switched on the tempering machines, which had been on standby overnight, maintaining the melted chocolate so it was ready to begin using quickly in the morning. He sat on the wooden stool at the bench in the kitchen and checked the list he'd made last night. Through the day yesterday, as with every other day, when stocks ran low it was noted down; if they had an online order for a customer – Magnolia Creek Chocolaterie supplied one of the big Melbourne department stores – it was added to the list as well. He pulled on the brown apron embellished with Magnolia Creek Chocolaterie in silver writing on the front, and he set to work. This was something he could throw himself into so he didn't have to think about his marriage and how it had once been so perfect, so dream-like; so he didn't have to think about Julia Mason and what she'd done all those years ago. He was forty-six years old and ever since he was fifteen, he'd wondered what had driven her to treat him that way when they'd been a couple very much in love. But he guessed it wouldn't be long, now Julia was in touch with him online, before he got the answers to his questions. He laughed at the irony. Technology was great in some ways; in others, it could turn your whole world upside down.

Andrew let the smell of chocolate envelop him. This was his comfort, and despite working with chocolate every day, he never lost an appreciation for its beauty. As he worked he let the familiarity and his passion calm his mind. He visualised the process, the finished product, the love he'd felt since the day he started working in the family business. The job of a chocolatier was fiddly, it required patience. What it didn't need was him losing concentration as memories of the past resurfaced, and taking his anger out on the stuff and ending up with inedible rubbish that anyone off the street could've made rather than someone with over twenty years' experience.

He watched the silky-smooth, tempered dark chocolate pour out of the spout into the vat below, wishing he could lose his own thoughts of the past in the depth and beauty of the mixture. He pressed the floor pedal to stop the flow, put a jug beneath the spout and released his foot to fill it halfway. Over at the benchtop he filled a piping bag with the dark mixture, twisted the top to secure the contents, snipped the bottom of the bag and piped chocolate discs onto the laid out transfer sheet of cocoa butter circles covered in multicoloured roses.

This was what he loved. This was what always kept him sane. No matter what else was going on in his life, his work had a way of grounding him.

His hands took control, his fingers applied the right amount of pressure to the bag to get the perfect shape and finish. Already he could see the green and red cheerful pattern from the transfers topping the dark, glossy chocolate and creating the perfect contrast. When he'd piped twenty, he set the tray onto a high shelf and piped a second batch onto another sheet. These chocolates were one of their biggest sellers, and once they were cooled they would be packaged up for sale in the shop.

Come midday, it was all systems go and the place was awash with activity. Emilio, an experienced chocolatier Andrew had plucked from competitors when he attended a conference in the city, put the finishing touches to dark chocolate truffles for the counter in the shop, and local girl Stephanie was working the floor out front, having taken well to her part-time job, which also involved designing packaging for their products. Andrew filled an online order, continued with the list of chocolates needed for replenishing the shelves in the shop, served locals and visitors ice cream they had supplied by a local farm in the Yarra Valley. Chocolate tempered in the machines to produce the rich, silky mixture to work with. There was mixing, moulding and decorating, and Andrew finished off the seashells he'd made earlier by sprinkling sea salt over the top to create the heavenly range that sold so well.

By the time Andrew left the chocolaterie, the sun had begun its descent, sweeping a golden evening glow across the mountain ash trees of the surrounding bushland. The chocolaterie had been manic today with the last of the tourists enjoying the final weeks of Melbourne's summer, and it had served as a distraction from the questions circulating in his mind about Julia and what had happened.

When he arrived back at the house, he planted a kiss on his wife's cheek. It was good to be home. He wrapped his arms around Gemma as she cuddled in close to him. As far as he knew, she hadn't cried after the last miscarriage. She'd simply taken herself off for a bubble bath, as she'd done every other time, like a ritual, but not one you wanted to get used to.

Gemma sighed exhaustedly before looking up at him and taking his face in her hands. She stood on tiptoes and kissed his lips – a soft brush to let him know they were still Andrew and Gemma, still the rock-solid couple they'd always been, but that life was being unfair to them right now.

She moved over to the stove. 'Your dad came for dinner.'

Some days Louis ate with them, other days he preferred to fix a light meal in the annexe at the foot of their garden, a separate outbuilding that allowed him his coveted independence.

'How is he?'

'He's fine. Not too tired.'

'Are you okay?' He had to ask. Gemma was a rock for everyone else, but he often wondered when she was going to catch a break herself.

'I'm fine.' She patted the handle of a covered pan on the stove. 'Leftover meatballs and sauce.' She patted another. 'Some pasta to go with it.'

Andrew hugged her again until she relaxed in his arms, then he kissed the top of her head before she pulled away to dish him up a serving of dinner. 'Did Dad eat much?' he asked.

'Stop worrying.' She placed a bowl of pasta in front of him and gave his shoulder a reassuring squeeze before turning to pull on the washing-up gloves by the sink.

'Leave it.' He told her twice until she relented and filled a glass of water beneath the tap.

Satisfied she'd leave the clearing up to him, he asked, 'Is he still complaining about swelling in his ankles?'

'He is. I'll mention it when I take him for his dialysis tomorrow.'

'I can take him if you'd rather.'

'No need. I've arranged cover at the school. They're pretty good about family commitments. I'll make sure I pop to the shops and get him the bigger size of slippers too.'

Three times a week they took Louis to the hospital for his dialysis, and while at first it had seemed a minor imposition – it was only a thirty-minute drive each way – now it'd been going on months and it was getting harder. Gemma didn't need to be doing this when she had her own health concerns, and he simply didn't have much time himself, with the shop, especially in peak periods like Easter and Christmas.

'I'll take him next time.' Andrew speared another piece of pasta with his fork. 'Stephanie and Emilio are capable of looking after the shop if I get them started for the day, and they know what needs replenishing, whether there are any orders to fill.'

Gemma came to her husband's side, bent down and kissed the top of his head. 'I'm going for a long bubble bath.'

'You'll wash yourself away one of these days.' His lips briefly met hers and he hooked her blonde, bobbed hair behind her ears so he could see her face properly. 'I love you.'

'I love you too.' She looked deep into his eyes and then stood up. 'Make yourself useful and pour me a glass of wine?'

He knew what she was thinking – there wasn't a lot of point in avoiding alcohol when she wasn't pregnant … again. 'Of course I will.'

Andrew finished his dinner, stacked the plates in the dishwasher and poured Gemma a generous glass of red. By the time he reached the upstairs, she'd sunk deep into the bubbles and he knew she didn't want to talk through anything, not tonight. Sometimes she'd ask him to share the bath with her, other times she'd pat the side of the bath and he'd know she wanted company. But tonight she wanted to be left alone.

Andrew took his own glass of wine into the study and opened up the laptop. He had emails to respond to, orders to double-check, advertising to keep on top of, and he'd accomplished a grand total of nothing this morning. He'd been in such a hurry to shut off Julia's message and every thought it came with. Hopefully by the time Gemma emerged from the bath, they'd be able to snuggle on the sofa and watch a movie, one of her favourite, simple things to do together.

First step was to add some more photographs to the business Facebook page. He'd only started a profile on there because Gemma had told him to get with the times. He had a Twitter account for the business too and had to admit it seemed to bring people in. Only the other day he'd heard Stephanie chatting with a group of young adults in the shop as she arranged the packages on display. The group had told her they'd seen Magnolia Creek Chocolaterie's Facebook page and were interested in having a chocolate-making party for a twenty-first birthday. Stephanie had referred them to him and he'd set up the event.

He grinned, thinking how 'with the times' he was, and how Gemma was right, again.

He'd taken photos of their newly created milk chocolate champagne truffles brushed with gold lustre dust, and he uploaded them beside another photo he'd taken of a steaming cup of their signature hot chocolate and labelled the advertisement, 'winter warmers'. It made his mouth water so he hoped it would do the same for their followers, who had grown to almost three thousand already despite only being open for business for five months.

He replied to a couple of messages, one requesting a kid's birthday party and the other enquiring about mail-order chocolates, and then decided to move on to Twitter and post the same photograph of the hot chocolate cup there to cover all bases.

When he had finished everything he needed to do for the business, he knew he couldn't ignore his personal life any longer. It was time he replied to Julia's message and found out exactly what was going on.

Perhaps now, after all this time, he'd find the answers he'd needed for over three decades.

Chapter Two
Molly

Molly had been a midwife in England for three years and as a student she'd observed her fair share of emergencies, and still, every time she was called to another, she felt the familiar adrenaline surge for the job she loved. This patient, a nineteen-year-old single mother called Sophie, was terrified. Her baby was posterior and had refused to budge for hours. Now though, it had turned on its own and it was time.

'Okay, Sophie. It's time to push,' said Molly, loud enough to be heard above the groans and the tears from the labouring mother.

'I can't do it, I can't!'

Molly could see Sophie was exhausted. She had nobody with her in the labour room, nobody waiting outside as far as Molly knew, and she was so young.

'I know this is hard, Sophie, but you can do this. You're almost there, the head's out.'

Sophie dug her elbows into the bed below her, and with one final push her baby boy came into the world. Molly cut the cord and lifted the baby onto his mother's tummy.

'It's a boy,' Sophie cried, tears streaming down her face.

'Do we have a name?' Molly asked, marvelling at mother and baby. She never tired of seeing this joy.

'Max.' Sophie sniffed. 'His name's Max.'

'It suits him. Is there anyone I can call for you?' She felt sure there must be a queue of people waiting to get in to see this little one and offer their congratulations.

Sophie's eyes were fully focused on her baby: his delicate features, the scrunched up fist moving against her breast as he suckled, eyes tightly shut as though he wasn't quite ready to see the big wide world.

'It's just me and Max now,' said Sophie. 'And to think … they wanted me to have an abortion. God, look at him. How could they ask me to do that?' Molly knew better than to make judgements and she let Sophie carry on talking. 'The father isn't in the picture.'

She said it with such finality, and Molly was left wondering whether the father knew about the baby at all.

'He's at university studying to be a doctor,' Sophie went on, 'and I don't think he needs this. Our families were both dead set against it.' The new mum gazed down at her baby and stroked the downy head of dark hair. 'I was supposed to go to university myself. My parents think I'm wasting everything I've ever worked for by having a baby. But you know what? They couldn't be more wrong. I worked hard before all this, and now I have Max, I've even more reason to carve out a decent future. For both of us.'

Molly carried out the necessary checks and left mother and baby alone as she went out to the nurses station.

'Happy news?' asked Freya, her colleague and friend.

'Mother and baby doing very well.' Molly pretended to be engrossed in the form-filling she was required to do. Sometimes she felt as though she were better acquainted with paperwork than the babies themselves. But her mind was elsewhere. Her mind was – if such a thing could happen – back in 1985, the year she was born. Of course she didn't have any idea what the scene was like, but in August of 1985, she was born to a mother who hadn't kept her like Sophie was keeping Max. She'd given her up for adoption.

Molly's parents, Margaret and Jeff Ramsey, had struggled to conceive Molly's older brother, Isaac, and after a pregnancy fraught with problems, they'd decided to adopt to complete their family. Molly had always known she was adopted. She couldn't even remember being told, it was simply a fact she'd grown up with, like knowing the grass was green and the sky was blue. The information had easily blended into her happy childhood with her parents and older brother. But two years ago, Molly's job as a midwife had piqued her curiosity. Every day she witnessed elated mothers, jubilant fathers, and on the not so good days, she saw pain when the worst happened and babies died before they'd even taken their first breath outside the womb. It was all those moments rolled into one that had set the wheels in motion for Molly to find out what had happened all those years ago.

Via an agency, Molly successfully traced her birth mother and was given an address for her. She kept the address for nearly four weeks before she decided to do anything about it, and then she sent a letter. It was a simple letter stating her name as it was now and the year they'd lost contact – the only information needed to identify herself to this woman but nobody else.

Molly waited, and she waited. The counsellor had told her some birth mothers would struggle with painful memories, so much so, it could either take a very long time to reply, or may deter them from contact at all. Molly tried hard to be patient, but as the weeks and then months went on and the reply still didn't come, she couldn't wait any longer. She took matters into her own hands. Feeling she'd waited long enough, Molly visited her birth mother's home address in a tiny village not far from her own home in Lower Weston, Bath.

One snowy day in January, Molly met her birth mother for the first time and lost her again in the space of five minutes. She wasn't invited inside the home. She was kept on the doorstep, as though her presence would alter everything if she stepped over the threshold, and her birth mother told her she couldn't do this. Molly had asked about her birth father but was told nothing, only that the memories were too painful. Her birth mother begged her over and over not to come again until Molly had turned, covered her ears like a small child and run away crying down the street, only stopping when she was so out of breath she couldn't go on any longer.

And to this day, Molly hadn't contacted her birth mother again.

Chapter Three

Andrew

Andrew ran a hand through his dark hair that had faded over the years since he'd met Julia Mason. It was flecked with grey now, and he knew one day he'd look exactly like his father, his silver hair masking any trace of the colour it had been before.

He heard laughter coming from downstairs, laughter from Gemma and Louis as though they'd known one another all their lives. It warmed him to hear Gemma happy though, if only for a moment. There hadn't been much time for that lately, and since Julia's message half an hour ago in reply to his, all Andrew had been able to do was sit on the edge of the bed and stare at the curtains blowing in the breeze from the open window. He'd shut the computer down and run away from it since the brief exchange over Facebook messenger, as though the machine would spill out more secrets if he didn't get away from it right now. Their exchange had been short and to the point but no less weighty in its content, and since then he'd shunted between anger, disbelief and sadness. He was so confused. He had no idea how to feel.

How the hell was he going to explain any of this to his wife? Should he tell her? Should he simply ignore it and carry on with his life as though he hadn't made the shocking discovery?

Thirty-one years ago, two loved-up teenagers had the world at their feet, together, or so they'd thought. And then, all of a sudden, Julia had stopped phoning and she never came to his house again. Julia Mason had ceased all contact with Andrew Bennett and until this day, he'd never understood why. It wasn't as though Andrew hadn't moved on, of course he had. He hadn't thought about Julia in years until he and Gemma had started trying for a baby and the significance of past events plagued his thoughts and his dreams at night.

Andrew heard Gemma's footsteps as she trotted up the stairs, and he bent down to pull off his socks. When he looked up, Gemma was standing at the door, glass of wine in hand. Her blonde hair and tanned skin captured the beautiful girl he'd fallen in love with from the first moment they met.

'The chicken pasta bake is cooking,' she said. 'Dinner in an hour?'

He held out his hand and she walked over to him. 'Come here, you.' His hands on her hips, he pulled her into him gently and rested his head against her chest. She was the anchor in his world right now when everything else, including his feelings, seemed to have been set adrift.

Gemma laughed in an attempt not to spill the red wine all over the cream rug on the bedroom floor. She ran her hand through his hair. He couldn't help but grin. She'd always liked his hair. 'Your dad's downstairs,' she admonished.

'I wasn't suggesting we do anything.' He reached up and cupped her cheek and looked into baby blue eyes as he ran a thumb across her bottom lip. He was sure his marriage was solid, but right now he didn't know whether Gemma was strong enough to know the details of Julia's message. He was still trying to make sense of it himself, and his wife was in a world of hurt from the most recent miscarriage and each one that had come before. He could see it in her eyes, in the way she acted as though everything was fine when it was anything but.

He stood, took Gemma's hand, and her smile was back as he led her downstairs to join Louis again. An hour later the conversation was flowing along with the red wine, and Andrew refused to let anything ruin the precious moment, at least not tonight. There'd be plenty of time for that later.

Generous serves of pasta bake were scooped out of the glass dish onto plates for Gemma and Andrew, a crisp green salad added to each portion. For Louis, Gemma served lean basil chicken with the salad, following the diet plan given to them by the hospital. Since Andrew's mother died six years ago, Louis had lived in the annexe. When they'd moved to Magnolia Creek, an annexe had been a prerequisite and the three of them now happily coexisted in Myrtle Close. They often shared meals with one another, spent time together whenever it suited, and it was the perfect solution with Louis' health a constant concern. It also meant Louis was there to talk business, and some of Andrew's favourite times were with his father sitting at the kitchen table as they were doing right now, talking over new flavours and variations of chocolates, seasonal trends and customer orders that were helping his business to grow.

'I'm telling you, toffee would work well with mango,' Andrew insisted as he topped up his glass of wine, enjoying himself as they waxed lyrical about their joint passion. 'It's fresh and fun.'

'It'd work well, but why not try something different?' Louis hadn't eaten much at dinner, but Andrew was pleased to see the colour back in his cheeks when they talked shop.

‘What do you suggest?’

‘What about dark chocolate with a lemon infusion?’ said Louis. ‘Or a variation with cardamom, now we’re coming into autumn.’

Gemma stacked their plates on top of one another and took them over to the sink. ‘I think someone’s missing the chocolatier business,’ she called over her shoulder to Louis.

‘Do you miss it, Dad?’ Andrew ran hot water into the oven dish, added a squirt of washing up liquid and told Gemma he’d let it soak and tackle it later. ‘You know you’re welcome in the chocolaterie anytime.’

‘I know, son. I try not to interfere, but maybe I’ll walk down tomorrow. Sometimes all I need is the intoxicating smell of a kitchen full of chocolate and it’s enough to put a smile on my face. If you set me up with a chair in the corner of the kitchen, I’d be a very happy man.’

Andrew and Gemma exchanged a fond look as Louis lost himself in his memories. Louis was in his early seventies now and although he hadn’t wanted to retire, the job had become too physical for him. Some people romanticised the life of a chocolatier, but it was hard work and long hours. You had to love it to do it well. Luckily for them, Louis’ love had been passed down a generation to Andrew, who loved nothing more than talking about the chocolaterie with his father, coming up with new flavour ideas, suggesting changes to the range they sold in the shop. Louis’ encouragement went further than anyone could ever realise.

‘Are you okay, Dad?’ Andrew asked as he returned to the table and picked up his wine.

‘I’m a bit tired. I’m old.’

‘Here we go.’ Andrew laughed. ‘Trying for the sympathy vote again?’

Louis grinned at him, the youthful part of his mind held in the sparkle of his eyes.

‘The test results will be in soon,’ Andrew said, all joking aside. ‘I’ll take you to your dialysis next time, give Gemma a break.’

‘You two shouldn’t have to run around after me.’

‘Nonsense.’ Andrew and Gemma laughed when they said the same word at the same time. Louis was forever apologising for being a burden, and as hard as it was to manage sometimes, he really wasn’t.

‘Can the other staff manage the shop?’ Louis asked.

‘Course they can. I’ve learnt to delegate.’

Louis’ laugh was weaker than usual. ‘You always had a problem with letting anyone else do anything for you.’

‘I take after you.’ Andrew’s smile faded. ‘And talking of not letting others do anything for you, I wish you’d reconsider the live transplant.’

Andrew had been tested and found to be a compatible match for a live donation of one of his own kidneys, but Louis was adamant he didn’t want Andrew to take any risk for him. This was his fight, he said. And to be fair, Louis was holding his own so far and every day there was a chance he’d move further up the transplant list.

Louis shook his head. ‘No, son. Let’s wait and see what the doctors say.’

Andrew already had a sneaky suspicion the news wasn’t going to be good and a transplant would be Louis’ only chance. The waiting list was long and a live transplant from a family member was the best option. And although the whole process wasn’t going to be easy on any of them – the operation itself, the recovery time, extra staffing costs, not to mention a business in its infancy that Andrew would worry about the whole time he wasn't there – he was prepared to do it. He'd do anything for the father who'd been by his side his whole life.

Louis pulled a box from the sideboard near the kitchen table. 'Enough morbid talk for one night. How about a chocolate?' He opened the gold packaging to reveal some family favourites from the chocolaterie. 'Stephanie packages up the rejects for me – poorly shaped chocolates, some whose decorations aren't quite right – and drops them over each day after her shift. The poor girl doesn't realise my diet is restricted. I'd hate to be rude and tell her I can't eat them, but I also hate seeing such beautiful creations go to waste.'

'Thanks, Dad.' Andrew felt content he had staff he trusted and liked. It would help if his father ever agreed to the operation that would alter his life. He smiled at Gemma as he chose a milk chocolate heart not quite as symmetrical as it should've been. When they'd first got together and Gemma stayed with him night after night, he'd leave in the early hours of the morning – he'd be up at least two hours before she'd have to get showered and dressed to head out for her job as a teacher – and every morning he'd leave a chocolate on the pillow next to her. She'd loved it at first, and he'd thought it the most romantic thing in the world until she told him to cut it out, he was making her put on weight by starting the day with a chocolate fix. 'That's my job,' he'd told her, and he'd taken her in his arms and made love to her to 'burn off those calories'.

Andrew looked at Gemma and at Louis, all smiles around the table despite the setbacks and challenges they were constantly faced with. They were rock-solid, a family who stayed together. He wasn't about to let his former girlfriend's lies destroy his marriage.

Somewhere out there in the big, wide world he had a daughter, who'd been a six-pound, seven-ounce baby given up for adoption. She'd grown into a young woman who wanted answers, but he couldn't let it blow their world apart.

He wouldn't.

When he and Gemma had suffered the pain of all those miscarriages, Andrew had wondered whether it was the universe and karma having their say. He'd thought karma was punishing him for what he and Julia had done to their baby, karma getting revenge even though he'd been pushed out of the equation. How wrong he had been. He was the fourth side to the triangle, and to try to make sense of the misshapen world he'd suddenly found himself spiralling into was something he simply didn't know how to do. He was the side that didn't exist. There was the adoption triangle familiar to many, the naturally occurring three sides of the puzzle: the birth mother, the adoptee and the adoptive mother.

Where the hell did he fit into that?

Chapter Four

Molly

The rain lashed at the windows of the hospital and the thunder rolled for the fourth time in a row.

'There's one hell of a storm brewing,' said Freya. 'Not sure I can be bothered with the pub tonight. You up for it, Molly?'

Molly's hand stilled on the paperwork she hadn't even dealt with, her mind on a completely different birth. 'Not if all you're going to talk about is your holiday to Malta.'

'You know what they say?'

Molly had a feeling she knew where this was heading.

'If you can't beat 'em, join 'em.'

'Now how did I know you were going to have another dig?' Molly grinned.

'You're missing out,' said Freya. 'I'll hold your hand personally, I promise.'

Molly's fear of flying had meant missing out on this trip to Malta, as well as the previous two trips her girlfriends at the hospital had organised. Last year they'd skied in Andorra, two years ago it'd been a holiday soaking up the sun in Turkey. Molly thought of all the kids born to celebrities who dragged them across the globe right from when they were in nappies. Maybe if she'd been on a plane as a little girl, if it was as regular as catching a bus or a train, she wouldn't have let stories of pilot error or terrorist attacks fuel her fear.

'Hopefully I'll join you next year,' said Molly.

‘I’ll hold you to that. Are you still in the support group, or whatever it’s called?’

‘It’s a Facebook group.’ She smiled. Up until now she’d missed out on holidaying with friends, but with Isaac getting married in America in July, Molly had even more reason to work through this. Sometimes she swore he’d met and got engaged to Claire, from Connecticut, just so he could force his sister to face her fear.

A couple of months ago, Molly had discovered and signed up to join a Facebook group founded by an Australian guy called Ben. The online group was there for support and advice for anyone who had a fear of flying. Some people on there were time wasters and the admins of the group were pretty sharp at blocking them, others were in a lot deeper than her and couldn’t see their fear ever being conquered. But some members had recently taken their first flight and posted pictures of the places they’d been, and she hoped it wouldn’t be long before she could do the same.

Josie, the senior midwife, answered the phone at the nurses station and warned of a new patient coming in. ‘Could you check on Mrs Antrim, Molly? She’s having trouble breastfeeding.’

‘Sure thing.’ Molly set her paperwork aside. Midwifery wasn’t only about caring for the mother during labour, but also being there afterwards as support. Confident and strong anyway, Molly’s job made her even more so. After all, no mother wanted a midwife who didn’t look or sound like they knew exactly what they were doing. They wanted to know their midwife would take control of a situation. Mind you, there was a balance. During her training she’d heard bolshy midwives say it was nonsense to find breastfeeding a struggle. They'd get the baby, get the boob, shove them together and bam.

As Molly talked to Mrs Antrim, whose baby girl Annabel had, by now, latched on and was suckling at her breast, she wondered what those first few days in the hospital would've been like for her own birth mother. Since the day she'd turned up on her birth mother's doorstep, Molly had checked the post constantly, willing the opening letterbox to drop some kind of hope onto the doormat. But nothing.

The rest of Molly's day passed in a busy blur, and as visiting hours came to a close and the department quietened, she heard a voice behind her.

'I need to see her,' said the man. 'My girlfriend, I think she's here. At least, it's the only place she can be.'

Molly recognised the signs: Anxious Father Syndrome. She came out from behind the desk. 'Come and sit down.' She led him to the three chairs lined up opposite the nurses station. 'Now tell me, what's her name?'

He seemed relieved to be supported by the plastic chair. 'Her name's Sophie and she's having my baby.'

'Can you give me her surname?' Molly wasn't about to confirm or deny, even though she suspected this was the boyfriend studying to be a doctor.

'Philpott,' said the man.

'And you are?'

'Allan. She broke up with me. She thinks I can't handle being a dad, not yet. But I can. I want to.'

Molly pressed her hand on top of his in a reassuring gesture. 'Let me see if I can find something out for you, see if she's here.'

'Thank you.' He put his head in his hands as Molly went to see Sophie. As she walked along the corridor and smiled at the orderly wheeling an empty trolley past her, Molly wondered again what the scene in 1985 had really been like. Had her mother been all alone like Sophie? Had her birth father been at the hospital desperate to see her, like Allan was here to see his newborn now?

She smiled at Sophie. Sophie had laid Max in the cot next to her bed but couldn't quite let go enough to close her eyes and sleep.

'There's someone here to see you,' said Molly.

'Who?'

'Allan.'

Sophie sat up in bed, fully awake now. 'How did he know?'

'I've no idea. But I think he'd really like to see you. Both of you.'

Sophie shook her head and the tears began to fall.

Molly sat on the edge of her bed. 'What's wrong?'

'I can't let him see me. I can't let him see Max.'

'Why ever not?'

'Because then he'll want us,' Sophie sobbed. 'We were only seeing each other casually. I never meant to get pregnant. I don't want to be with Allan any more, I don't love him enough.'

Molly found it hard to supress her opinions sometimes, and this was one of those times. 'But he's the father. He has a right to see his baby.'

Had she overstepped the mark?

Sophie lay back and stared at the ceiling. 'I said no. I won't see him and when I leave here later today, I'll be taking Max away for good.'

It wasn't Molly's place to judge, but that didn't make her job any easier. After she told him, Allan shouted at her. It wasn't his fault, he was upset. Molly tried her best to diffuse the situation. Freya came to help, and an orderly escorted Allan out of the ward. Molly had no idea now what would become of him, of Sophie, of Max, but the look in that father's eyes stayed with her for the rest of the day. She even took on another patient and let Freya deal with Sophie when it was time for her to leave the hospital with her newborn. It was usually one of her favourite parts of the job. But she couldn't watch it this time.

At the end of the shift, Molly headed to the pub with Freya, Georgia and the rest of the group. She ordered a mulled wine as the rain of the day turned to snow and a cheer went up around the table. A conversation about snowball fights and snowmen-building competitions ensued, and Molly let her drink warm her right through as she watched the snow highlighted from the yellow glow of the streetlamp outside the mullioned window. She thought some more about Allan and his reaction when she'd told him he couldn't see his baby. Some men walked away, she'd seen it often enough, but not all of them did. Not all of them were given a choice.

Molly laughed and chatted with her friends, but she was distracted wondering about her own birth father and whether he'd ever regretted what happened all those years ago, whether he'd tried to see her like Allan had tonight with a steely look of determination from someone who cared more than they were allowed to. Nothing could be as painful as having her biological mother stand on a doorstep and tell her to go away. So perhaps now it was time for the truth. And whatever the outcome, at least she'd know everything, once and for all.

As the snow began to line the ledges of the windows outside, Molly made her decision. Come morning she hoped to see the blanket of winter, the scene she loved when all around her fell silent and everything looked brand new, a fresh start, with not even a single footprint in the snow that had fallen overnight. And tomorrow she'd be ready to take the next step.

She was going to find her birth father.

Chapter Five
Gemma

Gemma Bennett loved weekends as much as the next person. She loved time with friends, in the city with the hustle and bustle of Melbourne and its eclectic mix of people, away from the quietness of Magnolia Creek. But these days, meeting up with best friends from university didn't hold the same clout as before, and she wasn't looking forward to today quite as much as she should've been.

She stepped off the train into the heat of the afternoon and walked across the pedestrian footbridge to the other side of the Yarra River, grateful she'd worn a loose-fitting cotton dress with the summer temperature still lingering in the thirties.

'Hey you.' Darcy was already at the seafood restaurant they'd chosen and waved over to Gemma as she arrived.

'I thought I'd be the last one here.' Gemma opened her arms to hug her friend, feeling guilty she hadn't really wanted to come along today. There was no sign of Carmen or Sofia, both of whom lived closer to the city than Gemma and Darcy.

Darcy checked her iPhone and left it on the table. 'Sofia texted to say her twin boys were tag-team crying, and Carmen's still pumping out milk to leave in a bottle for her husband to do the next couple of feeds.'

Gemma couldn't imagine how busy it was having young kids, but she wished she knew. 'I've ordered the most gorgeous mobile from the gift shop in town,' she gushed, willing herself to show enthusiasm for her friend and her five-week-old baby. 'The only one left had been on display for a while and had faded in the sunshine.'

Darcy put a hand over Gemma's as she rambled.

'I'm fine,' Gemma insisted.

'I know you are,' said Darcy. 'But I also see how hard it must be for you. Don't shut us out, but *do* tell us to shut up if you need to.'

Gemma dismissed the suggestion with a wave of her hand. 'I'm sure it won't come to that.' She smiled when she saw Carmen approaching the table.

'Carmen!' They greeted their friend in unison.

All four women had been a tight-knit group since their university days and the only thing separating them now was time and distance. And non-existent babies, which Gemma knew were driving a wedge, even if she was determined not to let it happen.

Carmen hugged her friends, and when Sofia came bustling into the restaurant, all four of them disturbed the peace in the venue as their voices fought one another to catch up with everything since they'd last seen each other. And for now, Gemma knew she was really happy to see these girls.

'How's Joshua doing?' Gemma could do baby conversation; she'd done it plenty of times before. And her friends knew not to ask her anything about her attempts. She'd told them as much last time they met up, before Joshua was born. They'd had a picnic on the banks of the Yarra with babies in tow, and she'd broken down and sobbed when she held Darcy's ten-month-old, crying into her soft, downy hair while her friends reassured her they were all there for her. She'd asked them to steer clear of any conversation about her getting pregnant, because the last thing she wanted was for them to start keeping things from her for fear of upsetting her. She wanted them to be as they always were, even if it meant being oblivious to some of the goings on in her life. And that was why she wasn't going to tell them about her latest miscarriage.

Carmen, her belly still swollen from baby number two and her breasts aching – her explanation, not Gemma's observation – said, 'Well, he's finally sleeping for four or five hour stretches at night. Which is a godsend.'

'I'll bet.' Gemma dipped the complimentary bread into olive oil, trying to pick up some of the balsamic vinegar beneath.

The conversation got round to university days, and Gemma enjoyed the turn in topic as they reminisced about the last holiday they'd all been on together up to the Blue Mountains, when heavy snow had delayed their return for two days.

'How's Andrew?' Sofia asked. Gemma had guessed the question would come up sooner or later.

'He's good.' Gemma sipped her orange juice. Nobody else was drinking, but Gemma had caught the train to the city today and suddenly she wished at least one of the others were having a few drinks. She needed to kick back and relax. But Sofia was driving, Carmen was breastfeeding and didn't feel it would be right, and Darcy said if she had one she'd want many more and her daughter Tegan turned two tomorrow so she would be in Full Mummy Mode, policing a party for ten rambunctious kids.

'And how's the chocolate business? Booming?' This from Darcy.

Gemma smiled. 'It's early days, but it seems to be going really well. You know what Andrew's like, he loves his work.'

'He loves his woman too,' Sofia remarked with a cheeky grin.

Gemma let herself smile. She and Andrew were still so in love, but their idyllic existence had been marred with the stress of trying to start a family, muting the special and tender moments, even though she did her best not to let it.

'What was it?' Darcy laughed. 'Chocolates on the pillow? Talk about cliché!'

Sofia's hands covered her heart. 'And then the big chocolate he made asking you to marry him. Gosh. Tyler doesn't have a romantic bone in his body. You're so lucky.'

And she was. Of course she was. She had a man who loved her, and when they left the restaurant full of food and satisfied with a friendly catch-up, she felt better than she'd felt all week. She had a lot to be thankful for, and she was determined to focus on the positives rather than the pressures they faced right now.

'I'll collect your present soon,' Gemma told Carmen as they said goodbye. 'I'm really sorry I didn't have it earlier.'

Carmen hugged her friend and squeezed both of her hands. 'It's fine. Honestly. And it'll give us a good excuse to get together again soon, right?'

'It certainly will.' Gemma hugged each of her friends goodbye.

'Don't squeeze too tight,' laughed Carmen. 'My boobs might explode.'

Gemma looked down and couldn't help but laugh. Carmen's shirt was stretched tighter than it had been earlier. 'You're a machine!'

'What can I say? I should've been a cow.' She hugged Gemma again, and Gemma was more than glad she'd come. She never wanted to lose these women, and she wouldn't let herself push them away no matter how hard it was with babies popping up in every family except hers.

*

Gemma arrived home in Magnolia Creek and from the station she walked down Main Street. She passed the fire station and waved at Owen Harrison – they'd got to know him well when he'd renovated the annexe ready for Louis, and nothing had been too much trouble. Gemma raised a hand to Bella across the street and finally greeted Mal when she reached Magnolia Gifts. He'd been sweeping away leaves from the doorway but looked up when she approached.

'Hey, Mal. Any news on the mobile I ordered?' She loved how quickly they'd established a presence in town and how they were on a first name basis with most of its residents already.

'As a matter of fact, we got a delivery this afternoon.' Mal indicated for her to follow him into the shop. 'Emily's out back, I'll get her to find it for you.'

Gemma hadn't met his sister Emily. She knew of her, but they'd never actually exchanged a greeting. The girl was quiet as anything. Last week Gemma had seen her walk past the fire station on her way to catch a train and when Gus, one of the CFA crew, had said hi to her, she'd gone the fiercest red and not a sound had come out of her mouth.

‘Here you go, Mrs Bennett.’ Emily’s voice came from behind the box containing the mobile as she appeared in the shop.

‘Thanks, Emily.’ She took the box, and Emily scurried away without so much as another word.

Gemma reached Magnolia Creek Chocolaterie and poked her head in the door, called a hello over to Andrew, who was busy up a ladder stacking a top shelf with empty gold and silver boxes they’d had made to advertise their brand, and then headed home where she wrapped the present ready to give to Carmen, trying to remember the resulting high should she ever doubt the need to have an afternoon in the company of friends.

Gemma turned her mind to preparing dinner and took out the pre-prepared meat mixture from the fridge, grabbed the lasagne sheets from the cupboard, plus all the ingredients she needed to make the béchamel sauce. She hummed away as she worked the flour and the milk together in a pan. She grated a generous helping of cheese – a mixture of cheddar and mozzarella – and knowingly smiled. Andrew and Louis had always wanted as much of the cheesy topping as they could get. Like father, like son. Except now, with Louis’ restricted diet, he wouldn’t even be able to enjoy this. She’d steam a piece of white fish for him later and serve it with roasted summer vegetables. She’d have been happy to follow the same or at least a similar diet to her father-in-law but right from diagnosis, he’d insisted they keep up some semblance of normality.

She assembled the various layers, and as she finished with the béchamel sauce, the fly screen at the back of the house creaked open and there was Louis’ familiar knock at the wooden kitchen door. Always the same … the popular door knock pattern of five knocks, a short pause, then another two knocks.

'Come in,' she called chirpily, sprinkling the cheese across the top of the lasagne.

'Do you want me to leave this open?' Louis asked, patting the wooden door. 'The cool change is through.'

'Yes, please,' Gemma called over her shoulder as she slotted the dish into the oven and set the timer. She opened the window above the sink and immediately felt the welcome breeze. They had air conditioning in the house, but she tried not to switch it on unless she really had to.

'Something smells good.' Louis opened the door wide and fixed it in place with a doorstop.

Gemma grinned. 'I'm not sure what's worse for the waistline.' She stole a pinch of grated cheese she'd deliberately left on the plate. She'd only had a light seafood lunch and was hungry again already. 'This or chocolate.'

'They're both good and bad for you. You can't win.' Louis lowered himself onto one of the six mahogany chairs at the kitchen table. 'I could murder a big slice of whatever you've got cooking.'

Gemma smiled kindly. 'Your dinner will be delicious, I promise.' She opened a bottle of French red wine but didn't offer it to Louis. He hadn't drunk wine in a long while, and it made her sad thinking about some of the long evenings when they'd indulged together and talked late into the night. She poured a glass for herself and joined Louis, taking a seat opposite. 'The test results should be back tomorrow when we go for your dialysis session.'

'Good, good.'

'Did you manage to sleep this afternoon while I was out?'

He nodded. 'A little.'

Gemma lifted her glass but managed to miss her mouth and slop wine onto the table. She tutted and went to get a cloth and, trying to wipe up the spill, knocked the glass again and deftly caught it in her other hand.

Louis laughed, his old, crinkled face like a painting she wished she could capture. 'Were you on the booze this afternoon with your friends?'

'No!' She laughed along with him as she wiped the side of the glass and tried again, this time successfully, to sip her wine. 'See, managed it perfectly that time.'

This was the Louis she always wanted to remember, the Louis who always came to mind when she talked about him. The man in front of her now, laughing at something so inconsequential. Sometimes, especially since he'd become sick, she'd gone out to the annexe only to walk away and leave him to it when she'd spied him through the window, sitting in his favourite tartan armchair, staring into space. It seemed like such an old man thing to do, and it was out of character for her father-in-law, but she'd never once asked him about it. She'd assumed it was all part and parcel of the kidney disease and had never wondered whether there was anything else bothering him. But now she was curious and wished he'd open up to her.

Perhaps, in time, he would.

Chapter Six
Molly

Back at her flat a few streets away from the hospital where she worked, Molly sat at the kitchen table with a cup of tea and opened up her iPad. Without bothering with the News Feed, she was straight into the Facebook support group. Somehow, over the last few months, she and Ben, the founder of the group, had hit it off, and while most of their correspondence had been in comments on the group page at the start, they had started to private message one another. At first their conversations had only focused on flying, but soon they were chatting about anything and everything. Molly told him about her brother's upcoming wedding, Ben talked about his travels, and last week she'd even shared the story of her adoption and all about her birth mother. Sometimes it was easier to tell a stranger your secrets than reveal them to those close to you. Ben was impartial, a good sounding board, and they were separated by a computer screen.

Neither Molly nor Ben had shared many specifics like their ages, addresses, other details that didn't matter so much in the virtual world. All she really knew was that Ben was an Australian who, once he'd got over his fear, had found the world at his feet and was enjoying travelling around, currently in Ireland seeing the sights such as the Guinness factory and Temple Bar.

Molly wrote now and told him about her decision to trace her birth father.

Molly: Do you think I'm a bit crazy to be doing this?

Ben: Yes.

Molly: Really?

Ben: Yes.

Molly: Stop saying yes!

Ben: Okay.

Molly: Please, I need an opinion. Am I crazy to dig up the past?

Ben: In everything you've said about your search for answers, in looking for your birth mother, finding her and having her reject you (sorry if it sounds harsh but I'm no typist so don't have the dexterity to tiptoe around the facts), why have you never once mentioned the birth father?

Molly: Ah, so you can type well enough to use fancy words like 'dexterity'?!?

Ben: Don't avoid the question.

Molly: I'm not.

She didn't type anything for a moment because the day she'd met the man, Allan, at the hospital had affected her more deeply than she'd realised.

Molly: Truthfully, I'm starting to wonder what part he played in all of this. He could've been some arse who walked away. Then again, maybe he didn't even know about me.

Ben: It must be frustrating ... the not knowing part, I mean.

Molly: I'm not sure I could handle rejection all over again. It hurt so much the first time.

Ben: I don't doubt it. But if you were curious about your birth mother, why not find out about the birth father? Do you know anything about him?

Molly: His name is on my original birth certificate.

Ben's reply took a couple of minutes to come through.

Ben: I know we've never met and probably never will, but I've spent enough time in this group to get to know some of the members pretty well. You seem like a determined young lady (all adjectives used are subject to change if we ever should meet!) and you seem the sort of girl who would rather know and deal with the consequences than never know at all. Am I making sense?

Molly: Kind of.

Ben: Well ... you have a name. Start the easy way ... our good friend, Google. I'll do it if you like – give me the name and I'll see what dirt I can dig up about this man.

Molly: I don't think that'll be necessary.

Ben: Go for it ... clear up the emotional mess afterwards. Maybe this man has the right to have the chance to get to know you. (Btw I'm cringing here in case you're angry at me for being so blunt.)

Molly: I'm not angry.

Ben: Oh God, do you think this makes me the male version of a feminist?

Molly: Yep, I can just see you burning your boxers in a protest!

Ben: How do you know I wear boxers? I could be a Y-fronts man!

Molly: Don't bother to flirt ... it'll never happen. We live in different countries.

Ben: Plenty of people have long distance relationships.

When the buzzer to the flat sounded she hurriedly typed, 'Gotta go, hot date for dinner …'

She pushed the button beside the door to release the lock on the main entrance downstairs, conscious this wasn't the first online exchange to leave her wondering what Ben looked like in real life. His profile picture was of a glass of Guinness, and before that it was a croissant from his travels to Paris and before that a photo of him as a baby. She'd asked him about it once and he'd claimed he wasn't exactly photogenic.

When there was a knock at the door of the flat, Molly knew she'd have to stop wondering about Ben for the time being and whether he could turn out to be some crazy online predator or not. Still, she was definitely having fun with him, whoever he was.

'How's it going, sis?' Isaac lived around the corner, and they saw each other at least every couple of weeks.

'Good, thanks.' She hugged him. 'Claire not joining us?'

'Next time. She's got a lot of work on at the moment and she wants to leave with impeccable references.'

'I'm sure she will.' Claire was doing a two-year stint with an insurance company, working as a marketing assistant, and when she left in a few months to return to America, taking Isaac with her, she'd need to find a new job.

Molly pulled on her leather jacket. 'You finish early tonight?'

‘What can I say?’ He waited for Molly to lock the flat door behind them. ‘I haven’t eaten a Chinese in a fortnight, I’m having withdrawal symptoms.’

‘Sounds about right.’ Molly laughed as they went down the stairs.

‘I’ll work some more tonight at home.’ Isaac was an estate agent and alternated working between the Bristol office and the Bath office and other days from the study in the semi-detached house he shared with Claire.

‘I’ll drive if you like,’ he offered. ‘You can have a couple of drinks.’

‘Sounds perfect to me.’

The local Chinese was a firm favourite, and when they were seated and had ordered their meal, Molly sipped on her beer as Isaac told her about the nightmare of a day he’d had.

‘Sixteen people in the bloody chain, Molly. Sixteen. And one idiot pulls out and the whole thing collapses, and now fifteen people are up shit creek.’

Molly took a prawn cracker from the basket in the centre of the table. ‘It’s a stupid system.’ She often wondered how anybody got a foot on the property ladder. And even if they did, it seemed pretty easy to fall off or be pushed off.

‘I’m off to Center Parcs with Claire next weekend.’

‘Jealous,’ said Molly. ‘Love it there.’

‘Hey, her idea not mine. I’d rather go to an all-inclusive somewhere hot than be bashed around on the rapids, guzzling the entire swimming pool when you go down one of those fast slides.’ Isaac rolled his eyes, but Molly knew he was jesting. They’d been as teenagers with their parents and had loved every second.

‘And how’s Mum coping with the thought of you upping and moving to the other side of the world?’

‘Get to the point why don’t you, Molly.’

The relationship their family had been sure would fizzle out had done nothing of the sort. It had quickly blossomed and before Isaac knew it, he’d fallen for Claire and they were engaged, and she’d made it clear all along that she wanted to live in America near her own family. Long-distance relationships were a touchy subject in their household. Twenty years ago their maternal grandmother had decided to emigrate and follow their Uncle over to Canada. There, she’d started a new life, leaving Molly and Isaac’s mother to sell her house, clear out all the clutter and manage her own feelings of being abandoned. Molly’s mum had been heartbroken and both Molly and Isaac knew it, but when Claire had come onto the scene, Margaret Ramsey had done what all good English people did. She’d maintained the stiff upper lip, the respectable distance from interfering and told her son it was his life and he was free to do as he liked. But Molly hadn’t been fooled. A part of Margaret Ramsey’s life was about to fall away, and Molly had known then that she could never do the same to her mum. Sometimes she wondered how Isaac could.

‘Mum’s fine,’ said Isaac as the waitress brought shrimp spring rolls over to their table and they both tucked in.

‘Or so she says.’

He bit into a spring roll and changed the subject. ‘How was your day? Deliver lots of gorgeous babies?’

‘It was okay.’

‘Just okay?’

‘Stressful.’ She watched Isaac, ready to gauge his reaction. ‘I’ve been thinking.’

‘Sounds dangerous.’

‘I’m considering tracing my birth father.’ There, she’d said it.

The last spring roll paused on its way to Isaac’s mouth, and then made the rest of its journey as he shook his head. They’d always been close, and her brother had struggled to see why she’d ever want any other parents apart from their own mum and dad. But he was tied to them biologically and she wasn’t. She’d reached a point in her life where she wanted, and needed, some answers.

‘And you criticise me for trying to upset Mum,’ was Isaac’s reply.

‘I didn’t say you were trying to upset her.’

‘No, but it’s implied. But you can’t help who you fall in love with, Molly.’

Molly smiled. ‘I don’t suppose you can, and Claire’s great … Mum thinks so too.’

‘Thanks, and I really think she’ll come round eventually. She’ll come and visit and realise it isn’t so bad.’ Isaac smiled back at his sister, although he looked as unconvinced as she was. ‘Do you really think it’s wise to go ahead and search? Remember how you felt last time, when it all blew up in your face?’

With a roll of her eyes, Molly said, ‘I was hurt last time.’ She’d got so drunk the night after she was turned away by her birth mother. Tequila slammers, vodka shots. It made her feel sick to think of it even now. ‘All I know is that if I don’t do this, I’ll never get answers. At least if I search and find him, then I’ll have done everything I can to make sense of who I am.’

When Isaac didn’t speak for several minutes, she asked, ‘What are you thinking?’

Isaac sat back in his seat. ‘You had a great childhood. Why do you feel as though you need more?’

‘It’s hard to explain to someone who isn’t adopted. It’s not about wanting more.’

‘What is it about? I’m doing my best to understand, Molly.’

She sipped her beer. ‘I’m curious. I want to know if I look like someone, I want to know where I get my mannerisms from. It probably sounds ridiculously clichéd, but it’s the only explanation I have. Please don’t take it personally. God, I could end up with another big brother!’

Her attempt at a joke placated him. ‘You should be so lucky.’

‘I am lucky, Isaac. I have you, and I have Mum and Dad. But I’d rather know my background than go through my entire life wondering. Do you remember when I had those hideous migraines in my final year at school?’

‘How could I ever forget? Mum worried herself sick about you.’

‘When I went to the doctor, he asked whether I had a family history of migraines and of course I had no idea. And neither did Mum or Dad.’

‘But everything was fine,’ said Isaac.

‘Don’t you see? It’s the same whatever the ailment – if I turned up at the surgery with a mole that had turned funny, they’d ask if there was a history of skin cancer, if I had heart problems, they’d want to know my background. And if I want kids one day, it’ll be even more difficult. I know from my job that to be forewarned is to be forearmed. Every time I’m asked anything about my health history, I have to say I don’t know.’

‘I never thought of it that way.’

‘Do you see now why I’d like to know something, anything?’

'I'm starting to.' He sighed. 'I'll make sure I hide all the alcohol this time, shall I?'

She grinned at him. 'No need. I'm prepared.' Saying it out loud, however, cast serious doubts in her mind. What could she possibly do to prepare for a stranger, tied to her biologically, who could turn her away, slam a metaphorical, or even physical, door in her face?

Their main courses arrived and Isaac spooned out his Szechuan chicken while Molly dished out her sweet-and-sour pork, and her brother served them both a helping each of the egg fried rice.

'How's Operation Wedding going for you?' Her brother asked.

'Huh?'

'The onlinc support group.'

'Good.' She scooped up the fried rice with her chopsticks, laughing at Isaac's attempt. She'd always been much better at using them than he had. 'Another member made their first flight last week and it went without a hitch.'

'Wow, this Ben bloke should take commission for all these members he cures.'

'You make it sound like he's some freaky god we pray to.'

Isaac finally secured a piece of chicken with his chopsticks. 'As long as he can help get you on a plane by the time I get married, he's got my vote.' He popped the morsel into his mouth before it had a chance to fall. 'I want my little sister to be at my wedding.'

'I know you do.'

They chatted some more about the ghastly UK chain system when it came to buying a house, and they talked again about her plans to trace her birth father.

'It'd mean a lot to me if you said you support me,' she said.

'I've never known you to back down about much, Molly, so I'll be there to pick up the pieces if you need me.' He winked at her.

'I think I'm old enough to not have my big brother looking after me.'

'You need a boyfriend to pick up the slack.' When she giggled, he added a little more seriously, 'I mean it though. If you decide to go through with it, then I'll help you in any way I can. And you know Mum and Dad will too.'

After Isaac dropped her home, Molly filled a glass of water in the kitchen and took it into the bedroom. She lay on her stomach on her bed and logged back on to Facebook, but Ben had only said, 'Catch you later,' in answer to her hurried goodbye, so she shut off the iPad dejectedly. She turned over onto her back, her arm thrown above her head as she looked at the ceiling.

Was she really going to do this? Was she really going to find her birth father?

The question went round and round in her head for a good ten minutes as she lay there looking at nothing, and then the decision was made.

She rolled onto her tummy and pulled the iPad back across the bed. She clicked on Internet Explorer, and when the Google search field appeared at the top of the page, she typed in her birth father's name.

And before she could talk herself out of it, she pressed Enter.

Chapter Seven
Andrew

On his lunch break, Andrew drove around the corner to Magnolia House to deliver a chocolate fountain, glad of the job that kept him so busy and focused. It kept his mind off Julia and the messages they'd exchanged since she'd first contacted him. He'd fired more questions her way, but so far her answers had been short and to the point. It was like trying to squeeze out a dishcloth that had spent all day in the Aussie heat and any time she liked, she could completely dry up and he'd struggle to find out more about the daughter he'd never met.

Andrew had no idea where to go from here. The only thing he knew right now was how to do his job, and how to do it well.

Rosie, PR assistant and wedding coordinator, was chatting with a florist, double-checking the order for the wedding that afternoon – cream carnations with green foliage for the groomsmen and deep, velvety pink lilies for the bride and bridesmaids.

'Sorry.' Rosie apologised for the wait after she'd directed the florist on where to take the flowers. 'There's so much to do on the actual day.'

'You do look a bit frazzled.' He smiled warmly at her.

'I'll be fine as long as everyone turns up when they should and does everything they're supposed to.' She put down a clipboard and tied her chestnut hair up into a ponytail as Andrew opened the rear doors of his van.

It was warm again today, forecast to reach the high thirties by mid-afternoon. People in Magnolia Creek were talking readily about waiting for the cool change, the moment all Melburnians breathed a collective sigh of relief. And from what Andrew understood, residents were still on edge this summer since the bushfires that had swept too close for comfort right after Christmas.

Rosie picked up the clipboard and flipped to the appropriate page as Andrew waited for instruction.

'Right,' she said, 'to confirm … we have one large ultimate chocolate fountain, unlimited milk chocolate and someone to help out for five hours at the function.'

'Correct,' he answered.

'Why are you smiling?'

Andrew laughed, he couldn't help it. 'Well, here you are getting ready for a beautiful wedding with – and I can only assume – at least one white dress, and probably umpteen other things in white.' He glanced around. 'And here I am installing one of the messiest things you could ever have at a function like this.'

'You know, when you put it like that, it sounds pretty crazy!' Rosie laughed as she led the way to the main function room in Magnolia House where the air conditioning was working full pelt to keep the temperature bearable.

'I wouldn't mind betting the bride doesn't come anywhere near this fountain.' Andrew set the box down on the trestle table at the edge of the room and began to unpack. Unexpectedly, he found himself wondering whether his own daughter was married. Had he missed the chance to walk her down the aisle? Maybe she even had her own children by now.

There was so much he didn't know.

‘From memory,’ said Rosie, clutching her clipboard, ‘the bride was the one who wanted this.’

Andrew looked doubtful. ‘Maybe after all the photographs are taken and all the champagne is drunk.’

‘Maybe,’ she said. ‘Are you staying to help out?’

‘Not me. I’ll set it up for you now and run through what’ll happen later, but it’ll be Emilio who comes along for the five hours. He’ll top up the chocolate and make sure it doesn’t run out, and he’ll keep the fountain clean and flowing.’

‘Fabulous. See, no stress when everyone and everything is as they should be.’ Rosie briefed the kitchen staff about the chocolate fountain and the fruit, marshmallows, wafers and mixed lollies to be arranged on the table around it, ready for the guests.

Andrew liked Rosie. She lived in Rosie Cottage with her boyfriend, Owen, and was fairly new to town after house-sitting for his parents and falling for their son. From what Gemma told Andrew – she’d gleaned the gossip from Bella – the path to true love hadn’t gone smoothly, but they were incredibly happy now. Rosie looked to be in her late twenties, around the same age as his daughter. He wanted to put a name to the end of his train of thought but he couldn’t. Julia had told him the bare facts in her message and nothing more. It was the little details that disturbed him the most: the fact he didn’t even know the name of his own child, how he didn’t know what colour her eyes were, her hair colour, her height.

Since Julia had dropped the bombshell that the baby he’d believed to be aborted had grown up with a new family, Andrew had found himself wondering not only what his daughter was like physically, but how she was emotionally. Had she been happy all these years? Had the parents who'd cared for her all her life loved her as much as they would their own flesh and blood?

When he arrived back at the chocolaterie, Andrew checked his watch. Gemma would be with Louis at the hospital now, getting his dialysis, possibly finding out the test results. He tried not to worry, but ignoring the train of thought lead to thinking about Julia's revelation again. His mind was messy, like a circuit board experiment with its tangle of wires connected by alligator clips. Whenever one section switched off, another went on, and sometimes you had no idea at all how to turn it off.

He'd only exchanged a couple of messages with Julia, and all she'd offered in her latest reply was to say this was too painful for her to go into detail and he needed to be patient with her.

Andrew was a patient man. You couldn't do this job if you weren't. But he also felt like shouting from the rooftops, 'What about me? Don't I have a right to talk about it after being kept in the dark for so long?'

Andrew filled the third tempering machine with couverture white chocolate chips. They didn't use this machine every day – the demand for white chocolate was much less than milk or dark – but it was still a reasonable seller. He switched the machine on when Gemma came through to the back of the shop.

He led her into the store room at the back where they kept the ten-kilo bags of the finest dark, milk and white chocolate, and stacked the now half-empty bag of white chocolate chips next to the others.

'How'd it go?' He kissed her on the cheek.

'The results aren't good.' She took his hands in hers. 'The doctors want Louis on dialysis four times a week from now on.'

'Oh, God.' Andrew leant against the wall and breathed deeply.

Gemma was by his side. 'We suspected this. The swelling in his hands and feet has got worse, he's so tired all the time and he gets out of breath if he walks too far.'

Andrew nodded. The news shouldn't have come as a surprise, yet it still shocked him.

'Andrew. I don't know how we are going to do this and run a business. Then there's my job …'

'Do we know how much he's moved up the list for a transplant?'

She shook her head. 'He's only been on it a few months … it could take years. And he doesn't have years.'

Andrew put a hand around the back of her neck and pulled her close, kissed the top of her head. She was close to Louis, as close as he was in many ways.

'I'll talk to him,' said Andrew. 'I'm a match, I'm fit and healthy. There's no other option. This can't be it. I'm not ready to lose him.'

A tear rolled down her cheek and he kissed it away.

'I know there's no other way,' she agreed. 'But both of you enduring operations won't be easy either. I'm worried about the business too. We're just getting started—'

'I've got good staff. We'll manage, I promise. There's no other choice, nothing else we can do. Where is he now?'

'He's sleeping at home. I said I wouldn't be long.' She sniffed, took out a tissue to blow her nose. 'Will you be able to cope with the junior chocolate-making this afternoon?'

He'd forgotten about it entirely. His mind wasn't on the job enough to do it, and they were short staffed with Emilio manning the chocolate fountain at the wedding, but he'd have to manage. 'It's fine, you go and be with Dad and I'll be home at the usual time.'

'The class starts at four o'clock. I usually send the parents up to the café or tell them to take a wander, check out the shops. Or—'

'Relax … I'll be fine. And Stephanie's a dab hand at these workshops, she loves it. You go and take good care of Dad, send him my love.'

What he really wanted to do was lock up and go home to his family, shut up shop until all this was sorted out. But he couldn't. When it was your business, no matter whether you were at death's door, you showed up and ran the place. Word had already started to spread regarding the workshops, and it was exactly what the business needed. Already they had today's kids' workshop plus another two booked tomorrow, a hen party at the weekend and an adult corporate group next week. If he thought too much about the recuperation time following an operation as well as the business needing him, not to mention Gemma, it'd send him into a blind panic. But they were a strong family. They could get through this.

Andrew roped Stephanie in to help with the workshop. She was more than willing; it was a nice break from wrapping and labelling the chocolates. She'd finished packaging up various different chocolates, given them all lot numbers and used the label maker in the office to produce the legally required information for the back of each pack. Now she made labels for all the children in the workshop, allocated aprons for each of them and made sure Andrew had all the props – the poster he liked to show kids that illustrated a brief journey of the cocoa bean until it became the confectionery they knew and loved; the replica of a cocoa bean; the pot of chocolate chips from the packets they bought in bulk.

Andrew fastened his apron. Each child today would be mesmerised by chocolate, keen to learn, ready to get messy and make their own creations to take home. He loved seeing all those little faces light up and their eyes grow as big as the moon. A lightbulb from the circuit board of his mind went on again. Julia had deprived him of the chance to be a dad. He'd never watched his daughter's first steps or heard her first words. He hadn't seen his daughter's face light up when she tasted her first chocolate, he'd missed out on Christmas morning excitement, he'd never hugged her close when she fell and grazed her knee. Julia had taken it all away from him.

Andrew worked hard to battle thoughts of Julia, block out worries of Louis, and thankfully the kids were a great bunch. Sometimes there was one scallywag intent on showing off to his peers, but today they were all calm and eager to learn. When they'd started these classes, Gemma had had to give Andrew a few tips. She was a natural with the kids. Gemma's smile lit up a room and kids instantly warmed to her. She seemed able to effortlessly suss out the little ones and get on their wavelength, making them laugh and have fun as they learnt. She'd make a good mum. A really good mum.

When the kids were decorating enormous chocolate discs with gold lustre paint, hundreds and thousands and crumbled dried fruits, Andrew went to help out upstairs. Some of the parents liked to wait up there, read a book, generally relax until it was time to take their little monkeys home.

He wiped his hands on his apron and rang an order through on the till as Bella, owner of Finnegan's café, came to chat with him.

'You're busy,' she said, taking a seat on the stool at the counter, ordering a signature hot chocolate.

He shut the till and handed his customer their change before starting to make Bella's hot chocolate. 'Are you missing the café?' he asked. Finnegan's had perished in the bushfires and was slowly being rebuilt.

'Like you wouldn't believe.' She looked around her.

He crossed his arms and smiled. 'You're checking out the competition.'

Her red-lipsticked mouth opened to protest, but instead she grinned.

Upstairs in Magnolia Creek Chocolaterie it wasn't just the modest café that drew people in, but also the floor to ceiling windows allowing a view far into the distance, into the bush, the magnificent Dandenong Ranges. When they'd decided to put in a café up here, Andrew had been well aware of the former Finnegan's café. He was anxious to be a real part of the community, and the last thing he'd wanted to do was be a direct competitor. He'd even chatted with Bella and Rodney Finnegan before they opened up Magnolia Creek Chocolaterie and had adjusted what his own café supplied in accordance with what would again be available in Magnolia Creek when Finnegan's café reopened. In doing so, he had commanded Bella's respect in particular, and she was a key member of the community. She even volunteered with Magnolia Creek Fire Brigade, keeping them all organised, and he'd found in her an ally. They'd devised their menu for the upstairs with Bella and Rodney in the forefront of their minds, and they now sold simple snacks of cookies and various flavours of ice cream.

‘It is a magnificent view of the bush.’ Bella thanked Andrew for the hot chocolate. ‘Last time I was in here, with Jane, we tried the tasters.’

‘Ah, they’re new. What did you think?’

Her eyes rolled heavenward as Andrew took an order from another customer. ‘They’re to die for.’

Their most recent offering, the Trio of Tasters, was a set of three espresso glasses, each one filled with a different type of hot chocolate: white, milk and dark. They hadn’t sold many so far, but come autumn and winter Andrew knew they’d entice people in out of the cold, and already Stephanie had produced some posters advertising the new addition to their collection.

‘So how’s Louis?’ asked Bella. ‘I saw Gemma earlier, but she looked crazed.’

Andrew sighed. ‘He’s not good.’ He mixed another serving of the melted chocolate with milk frothed in the machine and took it over to one of the mums reading a book and looking out at the spectacular view.

Andrew kept his voice down low when he returned to Bella. ‘He’s going on to dialysis four times a week.’

‘I’m so sorry, Andrew. Is he anywhere near the top of the transplant list?’

Andrew shook his head. ‘He’s a long way off.’ He hesitated. ‘I said I’d donate to him.’

‘Good on you.’

Andrew shrugged. ‘I bet you’d do the same.’

‘You’re not wrong there. I’d do it for family or for a friend. It’s saving a life. It’s saving a life that’s part of your own.’ When Andrew nodded, she said, ‘But you’re worried about this place?’

'Wouldn't you be?'

'You know, a couple of years ago I would've been petrified that a setback, weeks or months out of action, would've finished us for good, but since the bushfires and losing the café, I realise … I mean, really realise … there's nothing more important than your own life and the lives of those around you. Sure, money helps, money helps a lot, but it isn't the be all and end all.'

She sipped her hot chocolate. 'What does Gemma think?'

'I think Gemma's sick of life dealing us crap.' And life wasn't done yet either. She still had no idea about Julia or the daughter he had, the biological child Gemma would give her right arm to have with him. They'd talked about IVF a few months ago but since then had done nothing about it. Maybe it was time he put his wife and her dreams first.

'She's a fighter, Andrew.' Bella's red lipstick had left its mark on her cup. 'And both of you have become friends. Without Finnegan's up and running for another couple of months, I'm here if you need me. I can work a till, make deliveries and I promise not to eat all your chocolate.'

Tears rarely sprung to Andrew's eyes, but the welcoming from this community heightened his emotions. 'Bella, thank you. You're a true friend.' Whether he accepted Bella's offer or not, he warmed at how they were settling into life here surrounded by people who genuinely cared.

'And if I know Stephanie well enough,' Bella continued, 'she'll leap at the chance to work some extra shifts and earn a bit more pocket money. When I was her age, I was saving for my first car.'

Andrew grinned. 'Me too.'

Bella finished her hot chocolate and went on her way, and by the time Andrew returned downstairs to supervise the cleaning up of the party room, Gemma was back.

'How's Dad?'

'He's asleep again. I tried to get him to eat some crackers or some dry toast, but he's off his food.'

They stood aside as hyper kids left with their creations, party bags and huge smiles.

'Do the parents realise how manic these kids'll be this afternoon?' He smiled.

Gemma stood next to her husband and watched a little girl leave. 'This is what I want.'

Andrew looked at her. 'Six rowdy kids buzzing on sugar and chocolate?'

'I'm serious, Andrew. I keep telling myself it'll be okay, if it never happens for us, it doesn't matter.' Tears filled her eyes. 'But it does.'

He could see the pain she was in and it killed him to know he'd soon be adding to it. But for now he wanted to give her what she wanted, to give her the world. 'Why don't we go and see the doctor, talk about IVF?'

Gemma looked at him. 'I wasn't sure you'd want to go down that route.'

'I think we should try.' He smiled and pulled her hand into his, but the moment was broken when someone dropped their giant chocolate button and it smashed all over the floor. Gemma was straight to the little boy's side. She hugged him and took out a packet of chocolate dinosaurs to give to him. He gasped with glee, the tears dried and he left the shop all smiles.

If only Gemma's heart could be mended as easily.

*

When Andrew arrived home after work, Louis was already in the kitchen.

‘How are you feeling?’ He rested his hand on his dad’s shoulder.

‘I slept for too long, son. But I’m hungry now.’

‘It’s a good sign.’ Andrew nodded over to Gemma, who was spooning out beef and barley stew from the pan on the stove.

She put a bowl of stew in front of Louis. ‘While you’re up I’ll wash your sheets and whip the vacuum around,’ she told him.

‘She’s too good for you,’ Louis teased Andrew, tucking heartily into his stew. It was the most Andrew had seen him eat in ages. It was like watching a child, making sure they got their five a day, calcium to make them strong, enough water.

Gemma left them to it.

‘Dad, this can’t go on,’ said Andrew as the back door shut behind his wife and she followed the path down to the annexe.

Louis ignored him.

‘Dad.’

‘No, Andrew. I won’t let you do it. I won’t let them cut you open when you’re perfectly healthy. It’s asking for trouble. You’re young, you’re fit, you have a wife and a business. It’s too much.’

Andrew went over to the stove and spooned out a bowl of stew for himself. He’d only had a small sandwich for lunch, and for this emotional battle he needed a lot more fuel.

Sitting back at the table, he said simply, ‘You’ll die.’

Louis slurped another spoonful. ‘We’ll all die, son.’

‘And you’ll leave me behind knowing I could’ve had another ten good years with you. More if we’re lucky.’

Louis sighed. ‘It’s not an easy operation. You won’t be back at work for some time.’

‘Emilio and Stephanie are both capable, and Bella has said she’d help out. Secretly I think she’d love to, with the café still not up and running. And Gemma will put in the time when she can.’

‘Of course she will, but she shouldn’t have to.’ His eating slowed as he filled up quicker than Andrew. ‘Gemma needs you and you need her, and your marriage should be your focus, not me.’

Andrew put down his spoon. ‘And we both need you. One day, we want to start a family and when we do, I want our lives to involve you, Grandpa Louis.’

It was the first time he’d seen Louis’ eyes fill with tears since he’d been diagnosed with kidney disease. Up until now he’d taken everything in his stride.

‘Let me do this, Dad. Let me give you one of my kidneys.’ Andrew grinned. ‘Having two is just plain greedy.’

Louis’ face relaxed. ‘I suppose it kind of is when you think about it.’

‘Then it’s settled. We’ll call the hospital and get things moving.’

And in that moment, Andrew and Louis both thought they knew exactly what the future held.

Chapter Eight
Molly

The flat was silent, no more comings and goings and footsteps on the stairs as her neighbour came home from a night out, no more classical music from the man in the flat below as he played his violin. It was almost two a.m. and the moon cast its beam through Molly's bedroom window as she lay on the bed surfing the net. Since she'd decided to search for her birth father two weeks ago and had contacted the adoption agency to set the wheels in motion, she'd been doing as much searching herself as she could. She'd taken the first step into the unknown, and now she wanted to know more, but there was so much information out there. There were men with the same name from all corners of the globe, many with physical characteristics like hers, at an approximate age to make paternity realistic.

Overwhelmed by the enormity of it all, Molly stared out at the moon hanging in the sky suspended between pencil grey clouds and wondered whether her birth father had ever thought about her, ever tried to find her. He might have done, who knew? He could even be living at the end of the street or in the next town. Anything was possible.

And with those thoughts, she finally drifted off to sleep in her clothes, dreaming of answers she needed to find.

*

'Sore neck?' Molly's colleague Freya asked the next day as Molly was coming to the tail end of her shift.

Molly hadn't realised she was rubbing it again. She picked up the notes for the mother-to-be in room six. 'I must've slept funny,' she offered. 'Don't look at me like that.'

'Like what?' Freya laughed. 'Have you got a secret boyfriend we don't know about? Did he keep you up all night?' Freya sighed. 'I wish I was young enough to remember what it was like to be up, doing it all night.'

Molly turned to go to room six. 'You live in la-la land. The only company I had last night was my computer.'

'There's a lot of online dating these days,' Freya called after her.

As Molly pushed open the door and greeted the woman in the early stages of labour, she couldn't help but associate Ben with Freya's reference to meeting people online. She warmed at the thought of chatting with him later.

Ben had been her confidant since she'd got the ball rolling with the search for her birth father and as hesitant as she'd been about doing the search in the first place, her conversations with Ben had helped her to feel in control. The worst had happened anyway – her birth mother wanted nothing to do with her – so if her biological father reacted in the same way, then she'd hurt for a while but she'd pick herself up, dust herself off and get on with it. Either that or she'd find a shot glass, a bottle of tequila and deal with it the same way she had last time.

'Two days to go, ladies!' This from Katy as Molly approached the nurses station at the end of her shift. 'I still can't believe you're not coming to Malta.'

'I'm working on it,' said Molly, truly regretful to be missing out. 'One year I will.'

'I'll hold you to that.'

'See you lot tomorrow.' Molly bid her colleagues farewell, and wrapping her lilac knitted scarf around her neck twice, she made her way out of the department, down to the main entrance and out into the cool early evening air. It was the last week of winter, with spring merely days away, but for now the weather seemed to have conveniently forgotten it was allowed to let the sun shine and the frost disappear. Molly stuffed her hands in her pockets to keep them warm, until her phone rang and forced her to extract them again.

'Molly Ramsey speaking,' she said, not recognising the number.

'Hello Molly, it's Andrea.'

Molly didn't register at first, but then she realised it was the caseworker from the adoption search agency.

'Hi.' Her stomach churned as she waited to hear what came next.

'I have some news for you.'

'Really?'

The smile in Andrea's voice was clear; it was obvious she loved delivering news and satisfying clients like this. 'I have an address for you, some details.'

Molly felt dazed, in shock. She apologised to the man behind her as she stopped right in his path. 'Is he still living in the area?'

'The whole family upped and emigrated to Australia the same year you were born,' Andrea told her.

For some reason it shocked Molly. The year of her birth must have been a time of enormous change for this man. She and Ben had joked around after she'd messaged him about her search. They'd laughed and said her biological father could be a sultan somewhere exotic, they'd pondered whether or not she looked like him, complete with matching facial hair. She wondered how shocked Ben would be to find out the man was a fellow Aussie now.

This was real. Her birth father was out there. And he was a long way away.

'Molly, are you still there?'

She cleared her throat. 'Still here.'

'Do you have a pen handy?'

'Give me a sec.' Molly stopped at the bench beside the main entrance and balanced her phone as she pulled out a pen and an old receipt from Boots. 'Go on.'

Andrea reeled off the address and a few details, and Molly didn't care how cold her fingers were as she scribbled down everything she'd been desperate to hear for the last month. It hadn't been difficult to find him because the family hadn't changed their name, and once they had the link with the family business, it had been easy. The caseworker went on to explain to Molly how best to approach her birth father. This man could know nothing about her, he may have chosen to walk away or he may not have done. Molly was advised to tread carefully. She'd heard the spiel before, and this time it kind of went in one ear, lingered a little bit, then filtered right out the other side.

As soon as Molly got home she called Isaac, relieved when he picked up on the second ring. She hadn't wanted to call him as she walked. She'd wanted to use the time to let the information sink in.

'Molly, this is huge! What are you going to do? It's not like you can turn up on his doorstep now you know he's on the other side of the world.'

He said it as though it was a given, but it was anything but. She breathed long and heavy into the phone. 'I don't know what to do, Isaac.'

'I can't tell you what to do. I'm not in your position and saying I understand would be lying. But you know we are all here for you – me, Mum, Dad, Claire. All of us.'

Molly smiled now. 'Thanks, Isaac.'

'I'm glad about it, in a way.'

'What do you mean?'

'Well, if me getting married wasn't enough to convince you to try and get over your fear of flying, maybe this will give you an extra shove in the right direction.'

'I guess you're right.'

'What does the cult leader think about all this?'

'Don't call him that,' she admonished. 'And I haven't been onto Facebook. I phoned you first.'

'I'm honoured. Listen, I've got to go, meeting a client at a house in Oldfield Park, but call me later if you need me. I'm taking Claire out for dinner for her birthday, but if you need us to come over, or you need anything, let me know.'

'Will do. And wish her a happy birthday from me.'

Molly ran herself a bath and lost herself beneath the bubbles as she tried her best to take things slowly through her mind, allow them to settle. But seconds later, she was up. Dripping water all the way across the landing and with suds running down her legs and dropping onto the carpet, she went back to her bedroom. She had a name, an address, a family business … and she had Google. She had the power to find out everything she needed to know about chocolatier Andrew Bennett.

Everything.

She devoured the information as it appeared in front of her: the history of her biological family, photos of

Andrew himself who, despite flecks of grey, looked as though he'd once had the same deep brown hair as she did. She pored over every detail of his history she could find, wondering what this man was really like. And when she was done, she logged on to Facebook to tell Ben all about it:

Ben: Wow, this is huge! Didn't take long to find him. And he's a fellow Aussie – being there since the eighties qualifies him! So what are you going to do? You could write to him. Would you consider flying over to see him?

Molly: I can't do that. There's my fear of flying for a start. And it could be a very, very bad idea. Look what happened when I turned up at my birth mother's house. She didn't want to know, but at least I didn't have far to get home.

Ben: I'm impressed he makes chocolates for a living.

Molly: Maybe it's where I get my chocolate addiction from.

Ben: Didn't know you had one, but hey, at least I now know the way to your heart.

Molly: Whoa, stranger danger! Internet predator alert! And besides, you live in Australia, I live in England ... never gonna happen.

Ben: I'm crying now.

Molly: No you're not.

Ben: How do you know?

Molly: I just do.

What was she doing? Molly could feel butterflies dancing in her tummy. She didn't even know Ben! This man could be seventy years old for all she knew, married with kids.

Get a grip, Molly, she told herself and looked at Ben's latest reply.

Ben: So what are you going to do? You could write to him.
Molly: I could.
Ben: Something tells me you're not going to.

He was right. And Molly needed, and wanted, his help.

Molly: What I think I really need is for you to work your magic. Help me get over my fear of flying so I can get on a plane.

*

Molly was on the late shift the following day and from the kitchen window in her flat, she looked out to the black clouds congregating in the skies above. She'd need her raincoat and umbrella for the walk to work. But for now, sitting at the small, weathered table, she opened up Facebook to the latest post in the online support group, immediately escaping to the blue skies of Florida along with a member's post. Stacey, a girl who suffered severe claustrophobia and who had never been on a plane before in her life, had taken the dramatic step of attending a fear of flying course with a major UK airline and it'd worked wonders. And now, with the support of her sister, she was standing on Cocoa Beach, the azure waters lapping around her ankles, flip-flops hanging from her fingers of one hand, the other hand shielding her eyes from the sun. Her smile was as big as the ocean, and her status said: 'So happy I joined this group … this would never have been possible without you guys.'

Molly enjoyed a bit of banter with others in the group, one whose boss had taken three colleagues up in a light plane – after they'd signed the declaration exonerating him of all responsibility should they meet an untimely death – and the reactions were funny. Some said it was one way of tackling your fear head on and asked for his number. Some said smaller planes weren't as scary, others disagreed and said they felt safer in a huge plane. 'It's like the London Eye,' said one guy. 'I'm happy to go on that, but you wouldn't get me on a Ferris wheel for any money.'

Molly laughed and wrote her reply. She hated Ferris wheels too. She'd been to Amsterdam once – via ferry of course – with a boyfriend for the weekend and at the top of the Ferris wheel, he'd stood up and rocked the thing backwards and forwards. She hadn't realised how scared she was of heights until then.

The number 'one' appeared on Molly's message icon at the top of the page and she clicked onto it. It was Ben.

Ben: How are you feeling today? Any thoughts on strategy for operation flight time?

Molly: It's all I've thought about. I think I'll do what you suggested to someone the other day ... the guy whose fiancée wants to get married on the Amalfi Coast.

Ben: So you're going to spend time at the airport?

Molly: Seems stupid when you put it like that. I sound like a train spotter ... except plane spotter.

Ben: Molly, nothing about this is 'stupid'.

Molly: Stop using my name, it's freaking me out! You sound all serious.

Ben: Molly, Molly, Molly, Molly ... okay, I'm done. It's a nice name.

Molly: Thanks. The plan is to go to Heathrow airport tomorrow with my friends. They're all off to Malta on holiday.

Ben: It's a good starting point.

Molly: I hope so.

Ben: So come on, where in Australia does this guy live? I could be related to him and then we'd have to stop this online relationship we've got ... it could be bordering on incestuous.

Molly: Uh-uh ... no specifics! Got to be careful with online groups. You could be some weird stalker who gets totally obsessed by me.

Ben: And vice versa ... no specifics from me, or you could begin stalking me!

This is what she enjoyed so much about chatting online with Ben – the most serious topic of all could end up feeling much lighter when he was involved. He could see the serious side of being scared of flying, but his responses were upbeat, helpful, talked about from firsthand experience. She wondered, again, what he looked like. Was he cute?

Molly signed off with Ben wishing her luck when she went to the airport tomorrow. The plan sounded totally insane now, to be going to Heathrow when she wasn't even going anywhere! All she was going to do was look at the airplanes taking off and coming in to land, to watch people calmly (she hoped) getting on and off flights. But she really hoped it was a starting point, one she could work from to get her to where she needed to go.

*

The next day, Molly drove her friends to Heathrow. Freya hauled suitcases from the boot and handed one to Lucy, the other to Katy.

'I still can't believe you've come here to watch planes,' said Katy to Molly.

'I know, sounds crazy, right?'

'It's not crazy.' Lucy smacked Katy on the arm.

'None of us have the same fear as Molly,' Freya interjected, 'so we don't know what it's like. Fears often sound irrational to those who don't share them. *Katy.*'

It didn't matter how Molly's fear had started. It was as real to her as monsters under the bed were to a kid.

'Thanks for that,' said Katy, who had an odd fear of buttons.

Molly grinned. She was glad of Freya's comeback on her behalf. 'You're proper weird, you are, Katy.' She pulled at a button on her shirt and put it closer to Katy, who winced.

'Shut up or I'll make you fly in my place, right now,' Katy assured her.

They made their way into the airport, and Molly tried to take in her surroundings, let the noises of the airport settle around her. Ben's top tips were to imagine being inside each of the aircraft she saw taking off and landing. She should be imagining the noises, sounds of parts of the aircraft adjusting.

Molly tried to remember everything Ben had told her as she waited for her friends to check-in. Once they'd done so, she would be able to spend a couple of hours here watching the planes. She felt like a five-year-old boy obsessed by aircraft! She couldn't help wondering how much fun this would be if Ben were here in person, and she took out her iPhone to message him but then put it back in her handbag. She was here for a reason and she needed to focus.

She watched a flight crew walk by, immaculate, with their uniforms ironed perfectly, the women with their make-up precise, nothing out of place. They were orderly and it instilled a sense of calm, a sense of order for Molly, who hoped that when her time came and she boarded a plane, she would be no different to the millions of ordinary passengers who travelled safely by air each day.

Check-in complete, the girls went to the café and gathered at a table, coffees all round.

'I hope next time we plan a holiday,' Katy began, 'Molly will be coming with us.'

'Hear, hear,' agreed the others.

Molly smiled. 'You know, I think it might be possible, although with thoughts of Australia and America this year, I'm fast running out of money.'

'Well, get saving,' said Lucy. 'We're planning a shopping trip to New York next!'

Molly chatted and laughed with her friends until it was time for them to go through to departures, and then she spent the next couple of hours visiting the Heathrow Academy building on Newall Road where she could watch planes taking off and coming in to land. She'd entered the building with trepidation, but by the end of her time there she was actually quite bored. It really had been uneventful, which she guessed was the point of the exercise. She'd watched twin boys, about four or five years old at a guess, watching avidly out of the window, one of them snatching his mummy's iPhone to take a ridiculous number of photos involving planes. It was refreshing to see an obsession born out of excitement and wonder rather than fear, and by the time Molly drove away from the airport, she knew she was on her way.

Chapter Nine

Gemma

Gemma went with Andrew and Louis to the hospital several times, not only for dialysis, but for further checks to ensure the live transplantation could go ahead. Andrew's X-rays didn't need to be repeated, but he had another ECG and more blood tests to make sure he was fit enough to go through with the operation. The removal of a healthy, functioning kidney was no small undertaking, and over the last few months since the initial decision, Andrew had seen more doctors than Gemma was able to keep track of. He'd seen the renal physician to assess his suitability, the transplant coordinator to ensure all the correct tests had been done and that Andrew was making an informed decision, the surgeon to again assess pre-op fitness and even a psychiatrist to ensure Andrew understood what was happening and that he was doing it for the right reasons.

More than once, Gemma had seen Andrew staring out of the window, or even simply staring at the wall. He looked as if he had the weight of the entire world resting on his shoulders, but whenever she asked him about it, he said he was fine. How could he be? His father was sick, his wife was desperate to conceive and give him a baby and his business was too new to be leaving in anyone else's hands if the recovery time following an operation ended up being longer than expected.

Every time Gemma looked at Andrew and thought how detached he was from the minutiae of their everyday lives lately, it niggled her. He was distant, his mind elsewhere and it was hard work trying to get inside his head and help him through any of this. They'd always been so open and honest in their marriage and in these tough times, she was desperate for him to keep the channels of communication open. Keeping quiet about what was bothering you was where it all went wrong. She'd seen it enough times in kids at school. Children who seemed fine on the surface but deep down had been unhappy for so long it had a risk of affecting them long-term.

Louis was exhausted from his dialysis, Andrew and Gemma were strung out from all the toing and froing to the hospital, and Gemma couldn't dampen down her apprehension. She sometimes wondered what portion of it came from thinking about Louis dying, how much came from stressing about Andrew going under the knife and how much came from everything else in their lives that would have to keep ticking over while the operations took place.

In their journey towards having a family, Gemma and Andrew had decided to let nature take its course, but Andrew, in some mad attempt to keep things normal or to consider her feelings at this stressful time, had gone ahead and made an appointment with a specialist today to discuss IVF. She'd questioned why it couldn't wait. It was a crazy time for them right now, but he'd been insistent. So here they were, apparently eager to get things moving along. Fourteen months ago they'd gone through initial tests, the results of which had revealed no specific reason for their inability to have a baby. But Andrew's determination to move forwards, today of all days, with everything they had coming to them over the next few months, was making Gemma feel pressured, fearful of whether they were in the right headspace for this.

'Andrew, can we afford this?' Gemma clutched a pile of leaflets to her chest – everything from fertility and egg collection to ovulation cycles and embryo transfers – as they left Doctor Baxter's office. Money was always a worry and would continue to be if the business slowed over the next few months with most of their time assigned to a hospital schedule until Andrew was back to himself again. The doctor had given them estimates of the costs involved with IVF, so they weren't surprised, but although Medicare would cover some of it, Gemma already knew the out-of-pocket costs were going to be astronomical.

Andrew hugged his wife close as they reached the little school at the top of the hill. 'We want a family, of course we can afford it.'

'But we've spent so much money setting up the shop. And I'll have to turn down any more workshop bookings while you're in hospital.'

'Try not to worry,' Andrew assured her. 'Everything will work out, you'll see.' He kissed her goodbye before she disappeared into the school and he set off down the hill to the chocolaterie.

*

At lunchtime, after her stint on playground duty, Gemma went to the staffroom. She ate her sandwich and fruit and then put the kettle on to boil for a well-earned cup of tea.

'How's Ellie?' It was Bridget, principal of Magnolia Creek Primary and someone who was already becoming a friend.

'She's doing well. She's a lovely girl and I think with some dedicated time she'll soon settle in.' She dropped a teabag into her cup.

Ellie was an eight-year-old with a heart of gold but with learning difficulties, which meant she'd fallen further and further behind her peers. She had mild autism, which hadn't been picked up until she'd started school, and Gemma was determined her light would shine as brightly as any other child's in the class. Kids weren't moulded like the chocolates at the shop, they weren't labelled with standard ingredients. Kids came in all different shapes and sizes, so did their minds and their personalities, their quirks.

Bridget found a cup and a teabag, and Gemma poured the water for both of them.

'I can see she's blossoming with you,' said Bridget.

Ellie hadn't had the easiest of times. She'd been in and out of foster care for the first couple of years of her life and was eventually adopted when she was four years old. The child needed stability, and Gemma would do her utmost to at least give it to her in the school environment.

'Your qualifications jumped out at me the first time I saw your résumé, Gemma.' Bridget sat down on the sofa beside her. 'We've needed someone like you on the team for a while.'

Gemma beamed. 'I'm so happy to be here.' She'd always wanted to be a teacher, and her high school work experience at a primary school had eventually led to studying a Bachelor of Education (Special Education).

'So tell me, how's the chocolaterie going?' Bridget sipped her tea. 'You and your husband are like angels sent from heaven … you with your teaching skills, him with the heavenly chocolate.'

'You'll start drooling in a minute.'

‘I can’t help it. Bella’s café was bad enough, and those scones she makes are to die for, but a chocolate shop is something else.’

‘Thanks, I’ll be sure to pass on the compliment to Andrew. It’s going well and we love the town.’

‘I have a soft spot for it myself.’

‘Emerald is beautiful too.’ Bridget lived in a pretty country house in Emerald, a thirty-minute drive away at the top of a little hill. It was secluded and surrounded by bush, and on the couple of occasions Gemma had visited her there, she’d loved the tranquillity almost as much as Magnolia Creek.

‘Emerald is home,’ said Bridget. ‘But don’t ever open a chocolate shop there or I’ll have to start one of those crazy boot camps to keep the kilos off!’

Gemma tapped her wedding rings against her mug as they sat.

‘Something troubling you?’ asked Bridget.

‘Why do you ask?’

‘Er … the irritating way you’re doing that.’ She nodded to Gemma’s hands clasped around her mug as the rings tap-tapped again.

Gemma’s hands stilled. ‘Sorry.’

‘Are you worried about Louis?’

Gemma had been juggling her times at school more than she would’ve liked, and Bridget had been utterly fabulous about it all. And now she’d need more time off with the upcoming operations for her husband and father-in-law.

Gemma lowered her voice. ‘We’re worried about Louis, but we’re also trying to have a family.’

Bridget matched Gemma’s hushed tones. ‘Maybe it’s the worry over Louis. Stress can sometimes hamper the baby-making process.’

Gemma's face told the other woman it was far more complicated. 'We've been trying for a while, and I've had a few miscarriages.'

'Gemma, I didn't realise. Trust me to put my great big foot in it.'

'I don't tell anyone because I try to deny there's anything wrong. I tell myself something wasn't right with the baby so this is for the best. I tell myself that next time … next time it'll work and it'll stick, the baby will grow happily inside me for nine months and all this pain will be worth it.' She swiped a single tear daring to start its way down her apple cheek.

Bridget put down her mug and patted Gemma's arm. Thankfully the staffroom was empty now except for them, everyone else having catcn as soon as the bell had gone.

Gemma pulled a tissue from the pocket of her cotton trousers and blew her nose. 'This morning we chatted to the doctor about IVF. Although God knows where we're going to fit it in, with Louis' dialysis, the operations.'

After a moment, Bridget said, 'How's Andrew taking all this?'

'You know, I forget that every time I miscarry, he's losing a child as well. He's desperate to become a dad, I know he is, but he doesn't tell me, not any more.'

'It must be putting a strain on you. I'm here if you need to talk,' she added with a glance at the clock that told them they'd better ready themselves for the end of lunchtime and the start of the school afternoon.

A problem shared was supposed to be a problem halved, but right now Gemma felt as though their family troubles could only be reduced in size if a massive meteorite fell from outer space and landed right in the middle of them.

*

When Andrew arrived home that evening, covered in chocolate and powder from the shop, Gemma was at the stove preparing a soft caramel to use to fill truffles at the shop the next day. As the caramel mixture came to the boil, she removed it from the heat and turned to hug her husband.

'I'm filthy!" He laughed but pulled her into him.

Gemma kept her head resting in the crook of his neck, breathing against his skin. She didn't care if he was dirty. The sweet scent of chocolate intoxicated her, and it was the smell of home, of comfort and security.

Andrew pulled back, and she brushed chocolate powder from the front of her top. He held a hand to the side of her face. 'How was your afternoon?'

'Good, and yours?'

'Busy as always.'

Andrew was his usual calm self, and Gemma wondered how he did it. How was he able to remain so composed rather than fretful about everything happening in their lives all at once? She poured cream into the hot liquid in the pan and stirred it through. Without looking at her husband, she said, 'I know this whole baby-making plan must be taking its toll on you, but please don't stop talking to me. Please.'

He hugged her from behind. 'Of course I won't.'

The cream had disappeared into the liquid by now, but she didn't move. She stayed in his arms. He was still hugging her as she chopped butter into cubes and stirred it until it'd melted.

Louis knocked at the back door like he always did before he came in. 'Not interrupting, am I?' he asked.

'Dad, come in.' Andrew was at his side straight away, but Louis swished his arm away, declaring he wasn't completely useless. At least not yet. It was baby steps with Louis. He'd agreed to let them help by arranging the kidney transplant, but he wasn't about to let them do anything else before he had to, no matter how small.

Gemma made them all a cup of tea and added milk to hers and Andrew's. She tried not to stare at her father-in-law, who seemed to have aged another ten years in the space of twenty-four hours. He looked so tired, the skin sallow and sagging around his eyes, the pallor of his face ghost-like. His fingers were more swollen than usual, and with his breathing came a wheezing sound she hadn't heard before. It seemed to echo around the quiet kitchen today as she watched father and son lift their mugs at the same time, form the same rounded shape with their lips to blow across the scalding liquid. Next to one another, Louis looked like Andrew except the fast forward button had been hit and wound ahead a couple of decades.

'I always thought it'd be my mind to go first,' said Louis.

Gemma sipped her tea. 'Before your kidneys?'

'I don't work, I hate those crosswords or sudoku things Penny would lose herself in for an afternoon. Not using your brain is supposed to be very bad.'

Andrew was quick to correct him. 'You use your brain all the time. It's not like you've been sitting around staring at the TV. You're always chatting, thinking about the chocolaterie, helping me introduce new ideas. Your mind is that of a twenty-year-old.'

'Oh dear, let's hope that's not true!' Louis chuckled.

The laughter warmed Gemma right through as Louis reminisced with his son about some of the best chocolates they'd thought of over the years. It never took them long to get onto their favourite topic in the world.

Everything from the chocolate replica of dog poo for Halloween to the Willy Wonka Golden Ticket they'd made for World Book Day. The laughter reminded Gemma of the first time she'd met Louis and Penny Bennett. Andrew had been asked to look after his parents' house and their dog, Bill, when they went away to Adelaide. Andrew had gone all out with the romance factor, seeing as they'd only been dating for a month, and he'd lit candles, made a roaring log fire, wined and dined her. One thing led to another, and they were almost naked on the rug in front of the fire when Louis and Penny had pushed open the lounge door. They'd flown home a day earlier than Andrew had expected. All four people had frozen, shock on their faces, and Louis and Penny had scarpered from the room as quickly as the passion had disappeared. And then all Andrew and Gemma could hear were his parents absolutely wetting themselves laughing, echoing around the entire house, and before long they were laughing too. It was certainly one way to get quickly acquainted with her in-laws. Gemma had made Louis promise not to mention the way they'd met in any future family gatherings, and so far he'd been a man of his word.

'I never thought I'd have to resort to taking a kidney from my own son,' said Louis when they'd finished talking about the supply of Easter eggs Andrew needed to provide for Magnolia House.

'Dad, we've talked about this. It's the only way.' Andrew could be firm with his father when he wanted to be.

'It's too much to ask.'

'You're not asking, I'm telling.'

'I'm scared, son. Scared for us all.'

Gemma put a hand on his shoulder. 'We're all in this together and we'll be fine.' She was reassuring herself as much as the two of them. 'In this family we stick together and this is no different to anything else that's come our way.'

'This is short-term pain for both of us, Dad,' said Andrew. 'And it could buy you a lot longer with us. We need you around.'

Andrew put his elbows on the table and steepled his fingers together the way he often did when he was concentrating on a big order for the chocolate business and contemplating the logistics of it all. 'It's only a few more weeks to wait, Dad. We've got time to get more plans in place. Then, when it's done, we can all move forward.'

Gemma tipped her cup back to get the remains of her tea. 'How are your feet?' She nodded towards the new navy slippers she'd bought him. Lately his feet had been swollen more than usual, one of the first signs he was deteriorating.

'They feel better today, since I've rested.'

'Do you think you'd still be able to manage short walks down by the lake?'

Louis nodded. 'There's life in me yet. I'll take it slow, but I don't want to miss the beauty of autumn.'

Gemma touched Andrew's knee beneath the table, and he found her hand. He was close to his father. His siblings had both left home and Melbourne years ago. Daryl lived in London, and Kirsten lived in Italy. Both had young families, and although they visited they weren't a huge part of Louis' life any more. Gemma guessed it happened with distance. But Andrew had always been by his side. It wasn't forced, it wasn't like he felt it was his duty, it had happened naturally.

Louis gulped back the rest of his tea. 'I'll leave you kids to it.' Gemma put her arm out to steady him as he got to his feet. 'Thank you.' He didn't decline the help this time but motioned Andrew away when he tried to walk him out to the annexe.

'Breakfast in the morning?' Gemma called after Louis. She usually laid out a proper breakfast at the weekend, with the tablecloth, the best cutlery, a selection of foods adapted especially for Louis: fruit, oatmeal, waffles.

'I'll be here.' Louis smiled over at her before he shuffled out the back door and down the path bordered with lemon trees.

'You know, I can't ever remember Dad being unwell when I was growing up,' Andrew began when Gemma sat down again. 'He must've had common colds like everyone else, but I honestly can't remember a day when he was ever too sick to work, ever too sick to look after us all.'

Gemma's hand stretched across the table to Andrew's. 'It's easier said than done, but both of you need to stay strong and try not to worry.'

'I'm strong, Dad's strong, but I'm scared. I'd never admit it or Dad would back away from the operation, I know he would.'

'This is the best shot at him living a good life for plenty of years to come. You heard the doctor,' said Gemma. 'Live transplants are statistically better than donor kidneys.'

'Let's hope so.' Andrew moved to the sink and poured the dregs of his tea down the plughole. 'Thanks for making the caramel mixture for the shop.'

'No worries,' said Gemma.

They left their mugs in the sink. Gemma turned off the kitchen lights and then followed Andrew upstairs, holding the bottom of his T-shirt. Usually, when he finished work, she'd chat with him as he took a shower, hand him a glass of wine that he'd drink as he tried to keep it out of the line of the jets, but tonight he went into the bathroom without the cheeky look back he usually gave her, without the sexy wink which sometimes led to her jumping in the shower with him. Gemma put a hand to her belly, wondering what it would be like to carry his baby, carry it to term and feel the first flutters and kicks inside her. She longed to raise a child and have this almighty, indestructible bond with them, like the bond between Andrew and Louis.

When Gemma climbed into bed that night, moving closer to Andrew, her hand on his upper arm and her breath on his back, she hoped Andrew would do as he'd promised and keep talking to her, keep their lines of communication open.

And she hoped they were strong enough to fight any more battles to come their way.

Chapter Ten

Andrew

Andrew woke early to the sounds of a kookaburra announcing the beautiful morning in Magnolia Creek. The bird had taken up position on the back fence hidden by the creamy white sprays of a Fiddlewood tree.

Unable to get back to sleep, Andrew saw the opportunity to do some admin work for the chocolaterie. He uploaded the latest photos for the upcoming Easter celebrations to their Facebook page. He'd devised a thick milk chocolate egg with the words Happy Easter piped in looping letters on one half of the shell, and around the edges he'd piped lilac flowers and miniature green leaves. An idea of Louis' had been to make half an Easter egg in really thick milk chocolate and then they'd concocted different designs for eggs to be arranged in the centre of it. They had a gold-lustre egg, a speckled egg, eggs in white and dark chocolate. Their corporate brochure had already been sent out to customers showing these designs, but having Facebook got the ideas out there to families, tourists and corporate clients.

After he'd posted the photos, he responded to a few comments from customers. They were in the early days of building up their customer base out here in Magnolia Creek, but Magnolia House used their products and had turned out to be a bit of a local launch pad for the chocolaterie. They'd already had some big orders from the surrounding suburbs following the success of the chocolate fountain supplied for the wedding, and Andrew hoped there would be more.

He posted an advert for the Easter Egg Hunt he'd been roped into. On Good Friday, the event would be held in the beautiful grounds of Magnolia House and money raised from ticket sales would go to the Magnolia Creek Fire Station, which was a one-hundred per cent volunteer run station. Funds would support training, maintenance on vehicles and allow the station to update their radios and keep everything running smoothly for the entire town's benefit. Andrew was to supply ten thousand eggs plus a raffle prize, which would be a giant milk chocolate Easter egg filled with individually wrapped chocolate bunnies – Louis' idea – and Stephanie had come up with the packaging solution to present it in the best way.

With the admin tasks done for now, Andrew sat back and picked up one of the IVF leaflets he hadn't yet read. The impersonal nature of all the information was hard to get his head around, let alone reach the stage where he wanted to sign up for any of it. But he wanted and needed to do this for Gemma. He wished he could wrap her up and protect her from a world of hurt rather than be the cause of it.

He pinched the top of his nose tightly. Gemma dreamed of a family, he dreamed of a family. How was he going to tell his wife he already had a grown-up child?

Andrew had every intention of going back to join his wife in bed now the kookaburra had moved on to annoy someone else, to cuddle Gemma and whisper in her ear that everything would be fine, but somehow, instead, he opened up Julia's message, and before long he found his fingers gliding over the keys as memories of more than three decades eclipsed everything else.

He didn't hold back. He'd been patient long enough. He asked her straight out what the hell had happened back then. He asked her why she hadn't told him about the baby, why she hadn't let him help. He told her he understood how painful this must be, but he was in pain too. He wanted to know whether his daughter was okay. Was she happy? Did she hate them for what had happened? He wondered what she looked like: did she look like Julia? Did she look more like him? Was she a made-up version of the both of them? 'Please, find it in your heart to tell me what happened all those years ago,' he wrote. 'I at least deserve that.'

He didn't sign his name. He didn't put a smiley face or a kiss, as seemed so popular these days. There was no emoticon to convey how he felt: washed out, drained, no idea which way to turn.

When Gemma called out to say breakfast was ready, he realised how long he'd been staring at the screen, trying to find the appropriate words … words which wouldn't scare Julia away but words that felt fair on the both of them.

He closed down Facebook after his message went off into cyberspace and joined his wife and dad downstairs.

*

Andrew kept his mind on his work the second he left the house, and by mid-afternoon he'd piped chocolate discs of all types – white, milk, dark – and decorated some with crumbled freeze-dried raspberries, some with gold lustre dust, others with sea salt. He piped the caramel mixture Gemma had made into the intricate chocolate cups to make truffles, he approved a special Easter packaging Stephanie came up with and placed an order for some new moulds.

Despite being busy, Andrew had been clock-watching all day, and finally, at six o'clock before he left the shop, he went out to the office at the back to use the computer. It was morning in the UK by now – he'd checked the time difference on his iPhone – and he was desperate to know whether Julia had responded. But when he logged onto Facebook and saw the message symbol with a 'one' beside it, he wasn't sure he wanted to click and find out the answers to all the questions that had poured out of him earlier.

Andrew looked at the screen, the message symbol, and his hands stayed glued to his thighs. He stayed that way when Stephanie came and said goodbye, when Emilio called out to him and said he was heading off for the day. And when they'd both left, he finally had the courage to move the mouse and open up Julia's message:

Julia: I do owe you an explanation, but I think you owe me one too.

What was she talking about? She'd severed all contact with him, gone off and had their baby without telling him, without letting him be a part of it. Who did that? Who, when they were young and in love, could walk away, out of someone else's life entirely?

Andrew: I don't want to argue with you, but I can't see what I did wrong. You let me believe you'd gone ahead and aborted our baby. We were fifteen, I was petrified of going to jail for being underage, but how could you let me go on believing we'd killed our baby? You upped and left. I got your necklace – the locket I gave you on your fifteenth birthday – and you broke my heart the day I got your letter telling me you'd had an abortion. You told me to forget about you as though it were easy.

Andrew kept clicking the refresh icon waiting for Julia's reply to come through. He was desperate for answers.

And then her message came …

Julia: The only letter I know about is the one you sent to me.

Andrew: I never wrote to you.

Julia: You did. You told me you were too young for a baby, too young for all of this and it was best if we both moved on.

Andrew stared at the computer monitor; his fingers hovered over the keys. He had no idea what she was talking about. He'd never written her any letter. And, it seemed … she hadn't written him one either.

Chapter Eleven

Molly

Up until now, the only items on Molly's magnetic board in her bedroom were a Chinese takeaway menu, a photo of the Christmas party at work last year, which was curled at the corner where it wasn't fixed down properly by a pineapple-shaped magnet, and a flyer for the local cinema showing session times. But pinned up now was one of the biggest purchases of her entire life: an airline ticket.

She'd booked the ticket a couple of days ago after clearing leave with her manager. With some of the other midwives on holiday, she couldn't leave right away, but that wasn't necessarily a bad thing. It would give her time to really get her head around this, around what was going to happen. When she'd told Isaac he had tried to sound supportive, but she knew from the sound of his voice that he was worried sick. And who could blame him? This had the potential to blow right up in her face, and it was one hell of a risk to take.

Molly chatted on Facebook with a new member to the group, Ava, whose parents lived in Ireland. With her mother's health rapidly deteriorating, this girl, needed to 'get over it', as she put it, and jump on a plane. Molly chatted with her and a couple of other members, but as soon as Ben put a response against Ava's post, Molly swapped to the messenger section and clicked to write to him.

Molly: Hi.

Ben: Hi yourself.

Molly: I did it.

Ben: You dumped your boyfriend because you realised you're totally and utterly in love with me?

Molly: Ha ha ... very funny. I don't have a boyfriend ... I'm single.

Ben: Now we're talking.

Molly: Focus, Ben.

Ben: Ah, so you bought a ticket to Australia? Am I right?

Molly: I leave March 12. I have to change in Singapore, so it's two flights.

Ben: You'll be fine. Getting on the first flight will be the worst part and once you've done it you'll wonder why you never did it before.

Molly: I really hope you're right.

Ben: I am. Now go and post to the group ... share the good news!

Molly: I will. x

It was only after she'd pressed return and the message was sent that Molly realised she'd added a kiss to her reply. Oh, God. She clicked away from it and ignored the message symbol with the 'one' on it as she typed a post to the group. The responses flew in: 'Oh my God! That's huge!' 'Start small, why don't you? Talk about the biggest flight you could do!' 'Good on ya!' She chatted with other members of the group, noticing Ben hadn't commented at all, and the whole time, in the corner of her eye, she could see the 'one' on the messenger symbol, beckoning her to take a look at his response.

She clicked, biting her lip and grimacing, scared of what she may see.

Ben: xx I knew you'd fallen for me. xx

Molly: As if! I momentarily lost concentration.

Ben: That's what they all say. So how are you feeling about the flight? Did going to the airport help?

Molly: I don't know. It was a start, but it feels like I need another year to gear myself up for this. But I can't wait another year. My birth father is out there and the more I stew about it, the more wound up I get. I need some answers.

Ben: I have a suggestion.

Molly: Go on ...

Ben: Fly with a friend, as support and a distraction.

Molly: I don't think any of my friends could stretch to a ticket to Australia to accompany my sorry arse to the other side of the world.

Ben: How about someone who kind of knows you – or knows enough – and is planning on flying home to Australia with a stopover?

Molly knew where this was going and she waited for him to type more.

Ben: My travelling has come to an end, so I'm heading home. All stalking jokes aside, I'm trying to be a friend here when I think you could use one. I was intending to go via Singapore for a week or two to see an old uni friend. So ... I could accompany you from Heathrow to Changi Airport and then we'll part ways. I won't even know where you're flying to in Australia, so your destination is still top secret. And if we become better friends than we are now (which, I suspect, will happen), we can share more details. If, on the other hand, we loathe one another, we can bid farewell at Changi Airport and never have to see each other again.

Molly couldn't think. There'd been an undeniable flirtation between her and Ben online, but it had never, and would never, go any further when they were both hiding behind a computer screen. Meeting him in the flesh would make it all real.

Then again, she'd never even seen a photograph of him. She was being ridiculous worrying about it at all.

Her computer bleeped.

Ben: Tell me what you're thinking?

Molly: I'm thinking I'm more scared of meeting you than I am of flying right now!

Ben: Great, job done! Let me know your flight details for the first leg to Singapore and I'll see what I can do. A single seat shouldn't be too hard to come by.

Molly messaged over the details before she could change her mind and then shut down her iPad and headed over to her parents' place for dinner. Isaac and Claire would be there too, so she'd be able to tell them all what was going to happen in a few weeks, although Ben was a secret for now. She wasn't sure how she felt about this herself, and she wasn't ready to share anything yet.

'Molly, come in, love.' Jeff Ramsey opened the door and kissed his daughter on the cheek. She grinned when his beard scratched her skin in that familiar way.

Her dad went straight to the fridge to offer her a beer. He wasn't a drinker himself but kept it in the fridge, ready for the kids when they visited. 'Isaac's on his way,' he said, passing her the opened bottle.

'Something smells good. Hello, Mum.' She gave her mum a hug and a kiss.

'Molly, love. Good to see you.' Margaret Ramsey smiled. 'I'm making your favourite.'

Molly clapped her hands together. 'I thought I could smell chicken.'

Margaret pulled the roasting tin from the oven and pushed a two-pronged fork into the skin to check the juices ran clear. Molly spied the stuffing balls browning lightly in the oven, and she lent a hand by stirring the gravy while her Mum checked the vegetables boiling in another pan.

'I have some news,' said Molly. She'd tell Isaac later. It was probably easier to handle her parents' reaction first, and now she was here, she couldn't wait.

'You're doing it, aren't you?' Her mum's oven-gloved hands hovered mid-air, and then she calmly pulled each one off and turned to her daughter. 'You know we'll support you one-hundred per cent.'

This had gone so much further than simply thinking about it and being ready to start the search. Sometimes she felt guilty, especially when her parents were as lovely as hers were, but to explain what she was doing and why was difficult. Outsiders rarely understood the drive of an adoptee wanting to trace their roots, make sense of their place in the world, and as supportive as Jeff and Margaret Ramsey were, Molly knew they'd also worry.

'Mum, sit down a minute. You too, Dad,' she added when he took out the carving knife, ready to cut up the chicken.

When they'd both sat down, she said, 'I already have an address for him.' She heard a sharp intake of breath from her Mum. 'He lives in Australia.'

'Well, I never.' Her dad sat back in his chair, thinking Molly had finished.

'And I've booked a flight to go and see him.'

'What?' Jeff Ramsey's face paled as much as his wife's. 'But you're scared of flying. You're terrified.' He pushed his glasses up the bridge of his nose.

'Remember the Facebook group I told you about?'

'Vaguely.' Her mum was still in shock. 'Wasn't it a group of other people who are scared of flying too?'

Molly nodded.

'So you're cured?' Margaret Ramsey went over to the cooker, turned off the gas beneath the pan of vegetables, ever the multitasker.

'I wouldn't put it quite that way, but I've taken steps I think will enable me to get on the plane.' Should she tell them she was meeting a total stranger? No, best not to. 'I have to do this,' she said instead.

'You were so upset when your birth mother refused to see you.' Margaret shook her head in disbelief.

'I know I was, and it took a long time to get back to normal afterwards.' Molly thought about the drunken night she'd danced away, even smoked three cigarettes, something she never did.

'Something happened at work a few weeks ago,' Molly explained, 'and it started me thinking about tracing him. I figured I've been through the pain of rejection once. It may or may not happen again, but there's only one way to find out.'

'Molly, this seems such a drastic way to go about it.' Jeff, former barrister, always laid things out matter-of-factly, looked at a situation objectively. 'This man may not know anything about you. He may have another family. You could be hurting a lot of people doing this.'

She looked down at her lap and wondered whether, deep down, this could hurt him and her mum. She pulled a piece of white cotton thread from the leg of her jeans – it must have fallen from the new cotton shirt she was wearing. 'I know.' Her voice was small, and she felt her confidence waning. 'I suppose I'm afraid that if I tread lightly it'll be far too easy for him to tell me he doesn't want to see me. I'd rather have everything out in the open. I spent months agonising over whether my birth mother would want to see me, whether she'd explain everything. This time, if it's painful, it'll be short and sharp and I can move on.'

Molly could see her parents close enough together to know they were holding hands beneath the table. The last thing she wanted to do was bring any pain onto them.

Jeff got up and went over to the sideboard where he took out his iPad. 'I'll come with you. You can't do this alone.'

Molly went to his side and covered his hand before he had a chance to tap his password into the device. 'You don't need to come with me.'

'But it's on the other side of the world,' his voice pleaded. Rarely did she see him looking unstuck. He was such a together man until it came to his children. When she'd broken her leg and her wrist falling from the monkey bars at school, he'd been a basket case at the hospital, and it'd been the first time she'd seen him lose composure. A barrister was always pulled together, suited up, a representation of the legal system. It was one of the first times she'd seen a softer side to her dad, and from that moment on she'd looked at him differently. He'd really become a dad that day, not just a father.

'Dad, remember when my mates went backpacking in Europe after university?'

'I remember how upset you were that you wouldn't be going.'

'It was the first time I'd realised I even had the fear. The thought of going up in the air, in this massive machine that could drop to the ground at any second, was terrifying. All the news reports and TV shows about plane crashes, terrorism, searches for black boxes, didn't help either. It hadn't been an issue up until then, but I know my fear has held me back over the years.

'I guess the point I'm trying to make is that people go off to places, to countries they don't know and they do it all the time. Remember Debbie Timmins?'

'Your best friend from primary school?'

'Yes. She bought a one-way ticket to New Zealand on a whim after resigning from her hairdressing job here. She'd never been there before, knew nobody and off she went. Ten years later, she's still living there, settled and happily married. And more importantly, still in one piece. I can do this, Dad. I really can.'

'Please don't do a Debbie Timmins,' said Margaret. Molly saw her pull a tissue from her sleeve and dab it beneath her eyes. 'Please come back to us.'

'At least we're in the digital age, love.' Jeff went to his wife's side and abandoned the iPad. He knew his daughter. When she got something in her head, changing her mind was near impossible. 'We'll be able to email, FaceTime, phone, text.'

Margaret nodded and went back to tend to the dinner. She removed the pan of vegetables from the stove and drained them over the sink, and Molly briskly stirred the gravy – it had thickened a bit too much now, but it was salvageable. She daren't look at her mum. She knew what she was thinking. First Isaac was leaving for America, and now, what if Molly went to Australia and never came back?

Jeff Ramsey carried the enormous oval platter holding the chicken over to the table, and the doorbell chimed to announce Isaac and Claire's arrival. 'Do you want a leg?' he asked, knife and two-pronged fork helping him divide the meat.

'Whatever's going is fine.' Molly poured the gravy into the awaiting gravy boat and delivered it to the table.

'You know plane food is nowhere near as good as this.' Her dad laughed and winked at his wife.

If Molly thought too much about what her trip would do to anyone else, she'd probably never go.

Chapter Twelve

Andrew

With the kitchen naturally cool from the onset of autumn and the accompanying temperatures, Andrew set about making a start with the mini eggs for the Easter Egg Hunt. This was what he loved: his passion and how it oozed all around him and out into the town for everyone to enjoy. He smiled at the thought of children from Magnolia Creek and the surrounding suburbs coming together, the joy on their faces priceless. He gulped at the thought of his own daughter. He'd never held her hand as she looked for Easter Eggs, never had the chance to hide eggs all around the garden for her to find when she woke in the morning.

The tempering machine demanded his attention and Andrew focused once more. He had to. He set the machine to pulse out three and a half grams of milk chocolate into each section of the mould. Then, using the foot pedal, he controlled the pulses as he moved the tray until each of the twenty individual sections was filled. Each would be half an egg fixed together with another half using more melted chocolate.

The gloss on the mixture was perfect, and when he'd filled five trays of twenty egg halves, he moved onto the white chocolate. He had enough moulds to do three lots of those. He used the vibrating grill on the machine each time to get the chocolate evenly spread in the mould shapes and then put them all on a high shelf to set. Next on the to-do list were the Irish Cream white chocolate truffles, a hit at the shop and with Magnolia House, who had ordered a hundred boxes of six for wedding bonbonniere on behalf of a client who'd sampled them a few weeks ago. Andrew worked with the cooled mixture, shaping it into balls. Gemma had made the mixture first thing this morning, waking him with the smell of heaven as it drifted up from the kitchen. The tension at home had eased somewhat with the kidney donation and transplant scheduled for the week after Easter. All three of them had had a chance to get their heads around it and now it was a waiting game. The pressure eased, knowing they wouldn't be doing four dialysis sessions each week for much longer, knowing that once Louis and Andrew recovered they could establish some sense of normality. At least until Andrew dropped a bombshell of his own.

Andrew dipped each ball into the awaiting bowl of dark tempered chocolate. It was a busy job being a chocolatier. Some thought it glamorous, but he was glad, especially today, that he didn't get too many idle moments to reflect or obsess about much else.

*

'How's Dad?' Andrew asked as soon as he arrived home that day. Louis had been strung out after the dialysis session yesterday, but this morning Gemma had reported he'd managed a bowl of oatmeal, so it had to be a good sign.

'He's much better than yesterday.' She leant in to return Andrew's kiss. 'He's in the annexe, and when I went over to take out the rubbish he mentioned going for a walk round the lake.'

'And how are you?' Andrew pulled her close.

'I'm fine.' She plucked a grape from its stalk, then another. 'There's a lot going on right now.'

‘I know.’ Andrew made her giggle when he nicked the grape from her fingers before it could make it to her mouth.

‘You watch it, Andrew Bennett. You be good to me or I won’t help you recuperate after the op!’

He flashed her a smile before going out to the annexe to fetch Louis. The garden was bathed in autumn sunshine and the sweet smell of the dahlia tree wafted towards him as Andrew reached out to move aside the shaggy, tutu-like lavender flowers overhanging the doorway of the annexe. He’d have to cut it back before it took over.

‘Knock, knock,’ Andrew called, rapping lightly on the door.

Louis appeared almost immediately and Andrew was glad to see he looked so well. Today was a good day. Last week Louis had shuffled in the back door to the house with the biscuit barrel tucked under his arm. It must have nearly killed him to ask for help opening it and Andrew took it as a sign his dad had accepted what was happening to him. But accepting it and letting others see it were two very different things.

‘Hello, son.’ Louis stepped out into the dahlia, untroubled that it was encroaching on his own front door. He had a hat on his head, runners on his feet.

‘Like the hat.’

‘I don’t want skin cancer to kill me after my I get my new kidney, so laugh all you like, I’m being careful.’

Andrew took Louis’ arm in his. They went to the end of the garden, admiring the camellias with their glossy green foliage, the deep pinks of the flowers that added colour in autumn and winter. They went out the back gate and slowly up Myrtle Close to the top, along Main Street and down past the lake. They chatted about the shop, how sales were going, the upcoming Easter Egg Hunt.

'It's a magnificent venue for it,' said Louis, looking up at Magnolia House as they walked past. They'd moved slowly, Louis' arm linked through Andrew's all the way, a first for them.

'How are your feet?' Andrew asked. 'Not too sore?'

'They're not bad. Your Gemma bought me these runners, a size up from my usual, and they'll do fine. The swelling seems to have gone down since yesterday.'

'That's good.'

Louis gestured to the sand-coloured low wall running the circumference of the lake. 'Having said that, do you mind if we sit for a moment?'

'Of course not.' Andrew helped Louis down to the level of the wall, glad his father was shorter than him, and a lot lighter, as he was bearing his weight. 'Rest when you need to. There's no need to rush.'

'This Easter Egg Hunt will do wonders for the shop,' said Louis, gesturing to the beautiful lake, the green space sitting to one side.

'It's good to get involved. I feel as though I've lived in Magnolia Creek a lot longer than I actually have.'

'It's got the small town charm for sure,' said Louis. 'I didn't know whether you'd take to it, Gemma either, but you've both settled in fast as anything.'

'Do you miss the big smoke?'

Louis shook his head. 'I thought I would but coming here with you both, I see the beauty in a country I've lived in for many years yet never taken a step back to fully appreciate. Breathing in country air is good for us all, Andrew.'

'It is.'

'Why do I sense a "but"?'

Andrew took a deep breath. 'It's Gemma. I'm worried about her. Oh no, there's nothing wrong,' he added when he saw his dad's face, 'we're having some problems, that's all.'

'Marital problems?'

'Baby problems.'

'Gemma's pregnant?'

'No. Well, she has been … before. She's had four miscarriages since we started trying a while back.'

Louis' face fell. He took off his hat and ran a hand across what grey hair he had left to smooth down. 'Why didn't you tell me any of this? We live – or almost live – in the same house.'

'Gemma didn't want to tell anyone, she didn't want to worry you. You've got enough going on.'

'We've all got problems, Andrew. Every single one of us.'

'You're probably right, but you know Gemma, she always wants to keep people happy. She loves you and I expect she senses how much you'd love a grandchild.' Andrew smiled, almost to himself. 'She also knows you'd spoil them rotten.'

Louis' return smile seemed a split-second too long in coming.

'Are you sure you're up to this walk?' Andrew asked him. 'We can head straight home if you like.'

'Stop worrying. Come on. We'll follow the path and loop back round up to Main Street.'

Andrew helped him up, pulling his arm through his own again, holding his hand in place. They walked past the cottages and the lake and onto the trails leading through the bush. Thankfully this side of the town had got off lightly from the bushfire that swept through at the end of last year. There were still some blackened trees at the edges of the roads towards Magnolia Creek, but none of the residential streets had been affected and the blooms gave no hint of anything sinister.

After a while Andrew broached the other subject on his mind.

'I heard from Julia,' he said.

Louis stopped momentarily. 'Julia?'

'Julia Mason.'

Louis took his arm from Andrew's and continued walking. The path thinned and he walked carefully in front of his son, until it widened again.

'Do you remember her?' Andrew pushed his sunglasses onto the top of his head.

It was shaded on the trail despite some of the trees being lost in the bushfires. Louis removed his hat and carried it hooked onto his fingertips. 'I do.'

Andrew loved how close Louis was to Gemma, and he thought he'd been fond of Julia at the time, but since Julia had got pregnant all those years ago, his father had never mentioned her again. He'd never once asked how Andrew was, how he felt about what had happened. He'd whisked them away to Australia and hadn't even blinked at the disruption it had caused.

'Why did we suddenly emigrate?'

Louis took a while to choose his words. 'You know why. The opportunity came up and we wanted to take it.' His breathing sounded laboured and Andrew pulled him to a standstill so he could focus on one action at a time: talking. 'Son, what a fantastic life we lead now in a country of such beauty.'

Andrew reached out and touched the blackened bark of a gum tree that had suffered in last year's bushfires. The bark flaked beneath his fingers and fell to the ground. 'Did you know most gum trees – eucalypts – can regenerate from seed after fire?'

'I think I did hear that somewhere.' Louis stared at the gum trees bordering the path up to the road.

'They have amazing strength to be practically destroyed by what went before and still start all over again and flourish.' Andrew turned to his father. 'Dad, an opportunity to emigrate doesn't just turn up, it has to be looked for. What I'm curious about is why you wanted to leave England? What happened to give you the nudge to do it?'

Louis sighed and reached out to touch the bark of one of the trees, his feet negotiating the gnarled roots of another tree underfoot and across the path. 'I wanted a fresh start for the whole family.'

'After Julia got pregnant, you mean?'

Louis didn't speak but his face said a thousand things. Except Andrew had no idea what they were.

'Dad, Julia never had an abortion.'

Louis stared at him in shock.

'She had the baby. She gave our baby up for adoption.'

Louis turned and walked slowly over to a tree stump, lowered himself down so he was sitting. 'But I thought …' A look of utter disbelief flooded Louis' face, his hunched-over body giving away the fight with his health.

Andrew sat down next to him and raked a hand through his hair, looked up into the pale blue sky, the clouds tinged with orange as the sun hid behind it. 'All these years I've thought she had an abortion, but she didn't. And then there's the letters.'

'Letters?'

'She says she never sent me a letter, and I certainly never sent her one. Do you think … no, it's crazy.'

'Go on, son.'

'Her sister, Terri, in the year below us had a reputation for forgeries at school. If ever you wanted a sick note, a letter to excuse you from a PE class, Terri was the person you asked. It'd cost you, but she did a good job.

'Dad, what if Terri wrote the letters? She could've written the letter I thought was from Julia and forged my writing too – I'd written Julia enough cards when we were together. Maybe it was all an elaborate plan instigated by Julia's mother to split us up. Lord knows she never much liked the idea of me and her daughter together.'

'Son, it was a long time ago.' Louis' hat fell onto the path, the dried, dusty dirt coating the top of it.

Andrew reached down, brushed it off and handed it back to him. 'My daughter is out there somewhere. She even found Julia.'

Louis shook his head again and again. Clearly this was a lot to take in. Gingerly he stood up and Andrew took his arm, linked it through his own. 'I think I need to go home now, son.'

Andrew patted his hand. 'Of course.'

They negotiated the uneven pathway approaching Main Street.

'What the hell am I supposed to do, Dad? I have a daughter out there, somewhere. And apart from that, how am I supposed to tell my wife, the woman who so desperately wants to be a mother, about her? I've already created a life and she isn't a part of it. Tell me what to do.'

Louis kept walking, didn't turn his head. 'Damned if I know, son. Damned if I know.'

And they didn't say another word about it.

Chapter Thirteen
Gemma

Gemma, Darcy, Carmen and Sofia gathered in Gemma's lounge room the following weekend, no men allowed, bottle of Prosecco at the ready and another in the wine cooler in the kitchen. They'd done as promised and not left it too long between catch-ups and Gemma sensed they were avoiding baby talk. She'd had to wheedle details out of each of them about their offspring and eventually she'd confessed she and Andrew were looking into IVF.

'So, what happens now, Gemma?' Darcy pulled out a bag of Doritos and dumped it on the coffee table.

'We'll need to go in for tests.' Gemma sipped Prosecco, enjoying the fizz of the bubbles.

'So get yourself booked in.' This also from Darcy. 'You can't waste any more time.'

'Darcy, it's not one of your work projects,' said Sofia. 'The girl has feelings.'

'All I'm saying, and I'm sure Carmen will agree, is that your fertility declines rapidly with every year over thirty-five. You can't hang about.'

'It took us ages,' said Carmen. 'We tried for two and a half years to get pregnant with Jacob.'

'I know, I know.' Gemma relaxed back in to the plump cushions of the floral couch. 'I have all the facts and we'll sort it soon. Once Andrew and Louis have been into hospital and are on the mend, we'll get moving.'

'How's Andrew taking it all? How does he feel?'

‘He’s fine.’ But Gemma wasn’t sure about anything where Andrew was concerned. Something was bothering him and it felt as though it was more than the worry about Louis, the stress of trying for a family.

‘Fine?’ This from Sophia.

Gemma twirled the stem of her glass of Prosecco between her fingers. ‘I think it’s getting him down more than he’ll let on. Lately he’s shut off and doesn’t seem to want to talk as much.’ Had her marriage become more of a habit than a relationship where they shared everything?

‘I’m sure he’s only worried about you.’ Carmen topped up all four glasses, sucking in her breath as the liquid fizzed over the top of Sophia’s glass. Sophia put her lips to the liquid immediately and a hand beneath the stem as Gemma passed her a tissue to dry the vessel.

‘Men are different,’ Sophia continued as she balled up the tissue. ‘They keep it all in, try to be strong – at least your man does – but he’ll let you in eventually.’

When the girls left a couple of hours later, Gemma’s head felt light from the bubbles and the laughter and chatter that always left her somewhat elated. She was thankful to have friends to support her. Andrew was her best friend, of course, but when it felt as though he was hiding something, she needed other people to tell her she was being silly, paranoid even. In the kitchen she ran a sink full of warm water, squirted in the washing-up liquid and let the bubbles foam up before gently lowering the champagne flutes in as a knock sounded at the back door.

‘Come in,’ she called, and when Louis shut the door behind him, she placed the champagne flutes on the drainer and pulled off her washing up gloves. ‘What are you doing up at this time of night? I thought you’d be exhausted from this morning’s dialysis.’

'It did take it out of me, but I slept for a few hours this afternoon.'

Louis didn't stand, he made straight for the wooden chair closest to him and Gemma brought two glasses of water over to them and sat opposite.

'How's the nausea?' she asked.

'Better. It's almost gone.'

He definitely didn't look as peaky as he had on the drive home from the hospital. She'd read magazines while he was getting dialysis. Usually they chatted, laughed about inconsequential things, talked about the bossiest nurse they'd come across so far who Louis joked would put him over her knee if he wasn't careful. But today, he'd been too tired and had simply shut his eyes.

Now he looked so much better, although his forehead painted a different picture to the colour in his cheeks. He looked stressed. 'Did you eat the sandwich I left in your fridge for you?'

He nodded. 'Thank you.'

'My pleasure.'

'Have your friends gone?'

'Yes, you're safe. We weren't too raucous, I hope?'

'No, no.' He dismissed her suggestion.

'Do you want me to put the TV on? I think there's a film tonight, a James Bond.'

Louis smiled at her. 'Where's Andrew?'

'He stayed back at the shop. I don't think he realised the enormity of the task when he agreed to supply the mini chocolate eggs for the Easter Egg Hunt.'

Louis laughed. 'He'll love every minute of it, I'm sure.'

'You're not wrong there, he's about halfway done making them already.'

'It'll be a great day out for families.'

Gemma nodded.

'He told me, you know.'

'Told you what?'

'About trying for a family.'

'Ah.'

'I had no idea what was going on. You should've said something.'

Gemma hesitated. 'I guess I wanted to wait until I could share good news with you. I didn't want to moan away. You're the old man, it should be you moaning.'

Louis threw back his head and laughed. Gemma always could have a joke with him. He was a lovely man and in many ways like her own dad who she missed more than she thought possible.

'Not so much of the old man, thank you very much. So how are you, really?'

She shrugged. 'I'm coping okay, I guess.'

'And I suppose all your friends are pushing babies out like there's no tomorrow.'

It was her turn to laugh now. 'You make them sound like a production line. But yes, they're all making families, and Andrew and I … well, we're not. Some days it hurts more than others. You know, we're looking into IVF. Once the operations are out the way we'll get moving with it.'

'Sounds like a good idea. Go and get the help you need.'

'You're desperate to become a grandfather, aren't you?'

He smiled at her, but this time it didn't reach his eyes.

'It'll happen, eventually,' she said, finishing her water.

She and Louis talked some more about the shop, about the new Easter moulds Gemma had ordered in so they could make bunnies, chicks and eggs in a variety of sizes.

'What will you do with the window display?' asked Louis.

As soon as Gemma had seen the shop with its curved front window and the chocolate brown window shade jutting out from above, she'd fallen in love with it. She planned to change the window according to the time of year. Of course, given the delicate nature of chocolate and its sensitivity to temperature, she wouldn't put actual chocolate on display, but instead create something out of their packaging, branded boxes and ribbons. 'For Easter I've bought little yellow chicks – pretend – and I've made some papier mâché egg shapes to wrap in shiny paper for the Easter eggs. I'll put them in a huge straw basket with bows.'

'You sound like you're having fun with it.'

'I know. Initially it was Andrew's business and I wasn't going to be involved, but I love it more than I'd thought. And now the shop is only down the road I can pop in and do those things around my own work schedule.' She watched Louis, who was smiling. 'Sorry, I won't bore you with any more tacky details.'

'I'll be upset if you don't.'

She hesitated and then, 'At Christmas I'll have twinkly lights and pretend gift boxes with bows – I'll do the same for Christmas in July, for all the expats – and around Valentine's Day the window display will be a red theme with lots of heart shapes. I even thought I might cater for the racing carnival period, around Melbourne Cup Day. I know it's a quiet time, the lull before Christmas, but you never know.'

'Andrew's lucky to have you.'

This time she didn't smile. 'Do you think we'll be all right?'

'You and Andrew?'

'All of us.'

'Of course.' He covered his daughter-in-law's hand with his own.

'Did you have hard times like this, you know, when Penny was alive?'

At the mention of his late wife's name, Louis softened. 'We had our moments, everyone does. Hard times are par for the course, but the best marriages get through anything that comes their way.'

'I think he's hiding something from me.'

Louis was startled. 'What makes you say that?'

'He's never secretive, never shut off from me like this. I think it's about more than making babies, more than worry about the operation coming up. But I don't know what it is. Did he say anything to you, on the walk the other day around the lake? You were gone for a while.'

Louis took his water glass over to the sink and gently pushed it beneath the bubbles. Gemma watched him wash it using the same delicate touch he'd used to mould chocolates and truffles over the years.

'You know something,' she said.

His hands stilled and the cloth he'd been twisting inside the glass stopped moving. And then he carried on as though she hadn't even asked the question. Gemma watched as he left the glass to drain and reached for the red and white checked tea towel to dry his hands.

He was a loyal man, and if Andrew had said anything to him, he'd never tell her, no matter how close they'd become over the years. She expected him to sit down again and tell her something like, ‘talk to Andrew’, ‘you need to ask him, not me’. But he didn’t. He stayed opposite the sink facing the wall, staring at the glass splashback behind the taps, and then he spoke.

‘Gemma, I’ve done something terrible.’

Chapter Fourteen
Gemma

With two more weeks until the school holidays, Gemma was relieved. She loved her job, but the last few days since Louis had confided in her had just about finished her off. She hadn't mentioned anything to Andrew, she hadn't mentioned anything to anyone. She and Louis hadn't talked about it either. In fact, she'd avoided her father-in-law the best she could. She made dinners for them all but ate in silence, she disappeared for bubble baths more often than she really wanted, she volunteered to help out at the shop as much as she could, spending time getting the Easter window display looking exactly how she'd envisaged. It looked impressive now with brightly coloured papier mâché eggs, which nobody knew weren't the real thing, and it had drawn several customers inside to stock up on Easter provisions nice and early.

Gemma knew she needed to carve out a time to talk to Andrew. Louis was keeping secrets from his son and Gemma, unwittingly, had become his accomplice. All of a sudden their lives had become one big entanglement of lies. She was angry Andrew hadn't told her how, once upon a time, he'd got a girl pregnant. She was even angrier he hadn't told her the abortion he believed had taken place never had and that he had a child. She was angry on Andrew's behalf at what Louis had done, and most of all, she was damn angry at her body … angry it couldn't carry a baby like so many other women on this planet. Her body couldn't give her what she wanted and she hated it.

By the school gate, Gemma retrieved a cardigan when it fell from a child's bag as he ran past to meet his mum. 'Don't forget this,' she called after him. He thanked her and Gemma nodded to his mum, who hugged the boy and started their walk home.

Gemma did a double take when she saw Andrew walking towards her.

'You look worn out,' he said, kissing her on her forehead. 'You were out before me this morning.'

'I went for a walk.' Arms crossed, she didn't move. 'What are you doing here?'

'I finished up at work early. I think we really need to sit down and talk, Gemma.'

'No kidding.'

'What?'

'Nothing. I'll get my bag and I'll be right out.'

She collected her bag from the classroom, plus the pile of marking she'd have to do later, and when she saw Andrew's face again she fought the urge to scream and yell at him.

They walked home in silence, without holding hands as they so often did. Right now, Gemma couldn't bear touching her own husband. They walked down the hill, crossed Main Street and wound their way down to Myrtle Close. The minute Gemma put her things inside the door, she said, 'Not here.'

Andrew looked at her quizzically but followed her out the door again. They walked back to Main Street and then took the path down to the lake, where a swan glided across the surface of the water, cutting it and letting it reshape in its wake. They didn't speak until they sat down, side by side, on the low wall.

‘You didn’t tell me about Julia.’ Gemma looked from the surface of the water to her husband.

Andrew’s face fell as the sun hid and grey clouds loomed overhead. His back to the lake, he rested his arms along his thighs. He was wearing the jeans she’d bought him last month, the pair that fit him so well she’d joked he looked like a jeans model. He was still a very good-looking man, and for a chocolatier he was still fit, more muscle than anything else.

‘Dad,’ he said.

‘Louis told me, yes.’ It wasn’t all he’d told her either. But for now she wanted to focus and hear about Julia, about the baby. And she needed to hear it from her husband.

‘How could you keep this from me?’ She watched his shoulders sag. Rather than the anger she’d expected, he seemed relieved, as though finding the words all by himself was always going to be too difficult.

‘I only found out a few weeks ago. I didn’t know what to make of it myself.’

‘But why didn’t you tell me before now what happened when you were fifteen?’ She twisted slightly and dipped her fingers into the water of the lake. The cool water felt calming as she spoke. ‘You got a girl pregnant.’

‘I know.’

‘And you didn’t think you should tell me?’

‘I thought about it when we discussed starting a family, but I’d buried that part of my past a long time ago.’

‘Did you love her?’ Gemma spoke quietly, barely able to say the other woman’s name, which was crazy. How could she be jealous? But then again, it wasn’t really Julia she was jealous of, was it?

'I was fifteen. I think I did love her, as much as any fifteen-year-old boy can know what it feels like to be in love. When she told me she was pregnant, we were both as shocked as each other, but neither of us pushed the other one away. We knew we'd deal with it together.'

Gemma brushed her fingers across the spots of rain as they landed on the skin of her forearm.

'I studied harder and harder,' said Andrew. 'I knew that if we were going to keep the baby, then I'd need to work doubly hard to carve out a future for all three of us.'

Gemma's heart sagged at the thought of her husband planning a different future entirely.

'I worked hard which meant less time with Julia, and then one day I came home from my mock exam feeling pretty pleased with myself, convinced everything would work out, and my mum handed me an envelope. Inside was the locket I'd given Julia for her fifteenth birthday and with it a note saying … well, it said goodbye. It said we should both move on.

'I phoned her, I went round to her house but I couldn't get hold of her. I'd call late at night when my parents were asleep, I snuck out the window once, under the cover of darkness, and cycled over to her place on the dodgy estate where she lived. I knocked on the door, looked through the windows, but there wasn't anybody there. I got a second letter shortly afterwards, with a postmark from Ireland where her family was originally from, and she told me she'd had an abortion. At least, I thought the letter was from her. I had no reason to think otherwise.

'A few months later I sat my exams and we emigrated to Australia. And I never heard from Julia Mason again, until a few weeks ago.'

Five cygnets followed a swan across the lake to where two children were tossing the remains of a loaf of bread as high into the air as they could before running for shelter beneath the trees bordering the lake. But Gemma didn't care about the rain. She wanted to hear this, all of it.

Andrew stared straight ahead and gradually the line of his jaw softened. 'Apparently Julia got a letter from me telling her I didn't want a baby for our future, we were too young, we should go our separate ways.' He harrumphed. 'One minute she was there, the next she was gone.'

'You should've told me,' said Gemma.

He turned to face her, the rain soaking him through as it fell harder. A drop ran down his nose and off the tip. 'How could I? How could I tell you I already have the one thing you want the most? I already have a child, Gemma. And I knew it'd break your heart.'

She saw his pain and reached for his hand. 'It breaks my heart that you couldn't confide in me.'

He looked at their hands, together. 'I wish I had now. You know, I never wrote her a letter. I don't understand what went on all those years ago, I really don't.'

Gemma felt overwhelmed hearing the truth from Andrew. She wanted to cry as she saw the sadness on his face threaten to overpower him.

'What are you going to do?' she asked.

'I've got no idea.' He looked into her eyes. 'Our daughter went looking for Julia.'

Gemma tried to be strong when she heard those words tumble from his lips: 'our daughter'. She wanted so much to be the other part of that bond, the mother in the equation, but it wasn't her. Andrew's flesh and blood was nothing to do with her.

'Julia turned her away.'

The rain fell harder and they ran for shelter beneath the trees. Everyone else had fled. There was no longer a family feeding the swans or the ducks, or standing hoping the rain would pass; there was no longer a couple kissing beside the sign to Magnolia House where so many sealed their love with a wedding.

'How could she?' Gemma asked.

Andrew shrugged. 'I don't know Julia any more. I don't know why she did it, what she has going on.' He reached out and touched his wife's cheek. 'I wish we were talking about *our* baby.' He put a hand against her belly.

'Don't.' Gemma's voice caught, and a tear trickled down her cheek, mingling with the rain.

'I never wanted to hurt you, Gemma.' He lifted a hand to her face, but she pulled away.

'We should get home, get warm and dry.'

Back at the house they showered, together. There wasn't passion but a mutual understanding, a softening of their hearts as they realised they needed each other for this. And when they were dry and dressed, down in the kitchen warming soup for supper, it was time for Gemma to tell Andrew the rest.

She hugged her husband, wrapping her arms around his waist, careful not to touch the cooker as he stirred the soup with a wooden spoon. He smelled of soap, of fresh linen from the T-shirt he'd grabbed off the airer. His hair was still wet from the shower and had left a tiny damp trail across his collar.

'Andrew, there's something else.'

He turned to her, but at the same time she heard a noise behind her.

It was Louis. He'd shuffled in so quietly in those slippers, she hadn't heard him.

'This needs to come from me,' said Louis, his voice stronger than she'd heard in a while. 'Sit down, son.'

Louis motioned to the table and shuffled there himself, taking a seat opposite. 'There's something I need to tell you.'

Chapter Fifteen

Molly

Molly's parents took her to London's Heathrow Airport, and on the journey there, Molly looked up at the cobalt blue sky with the odd cloud plumping its way across, grateful for the clear spring day. Surely it was a sign this was going to go well.

The atmosphere was tense, the anticipation of what lay ahead on everyone's minds as they checked her in and had a coffee at a café. And when it was time for her to go, her dad hugged her tight. It was all the more poignant because they weren't the hugging type of family, especially when they lived so close to each other and saw one another all the time. The last time she remembered hugging her dad this tightly was when he'd picked her up from a party when she was seven and he'd scared her half to death. He'd shaved his beard off – the one and only time – and he'd looked so unlike Jeff Ramsey it'd freaked her out. He'd hugged her close to calm her down and since then he'd never shaved it off again.

Once Molly had passed through passport control and could no longer see the worry etched on her parents' faces, she relaxed. She lost herself amidst the duty-free, smelling perfumes dominated by the scent of a single flower, those with a strange woody base, others mixed together with the scent of vanilla, flowers and wood. She and Ben had agreed to meet at the gate an hour before their flight after liaising over Facebook and managing to book their seats at round about the same time, ensuring they were sitting together. Molly had told Ben she'd be wearing khaki cargo trousers, a black sporty T-shirt with pink piping around the sleeves, her dark hair would be tied up into a ponytail and she'd be carrying a red holdall as her carry-on. He'd replied flirtatiously to say she sounded pretty perfect, and he'd made some remark about the mile-high club which had at least made her laugh, but she'd told him off, and he'd reluctantly swapped the details of his appearance seeing as his Facebook photos weren't helping at all. Molly knew it'd be easier to text a photo of herself and for him to do the same in return, but for some reason neither of them suggested it. So she'd be relying on his description of himself: dark blond hair, black tracksuit pants, white T-shirt and he'd have a royal blue Adidas bag. Molly was pretty sure they'd find one another easily enough because by now, making her way to the gate with her bag of duty-free, she stuck out like a sore thumb. She was the only one who looked like they were absolutely shitting themselves about getting on this plane. Everywhere she looked people chatted, laughed, went about their business with control and poise and inside she was about ready to fall into a quivering heap on the floor.

Molly stood beside another gate where passengers awaited their flight to Dubai. She watched the luggage handlers standing out on the tarmac, unloading suitcases from a trailer and onto the conveyor belt running into the hold of the enormous Emirates plane. She moved to the window and watched another flight take off in the distance. There it went. Up, up and away in a straight line safely into the blue skies beyond. She watched another taxi down a different runway, turn a corner and then come to a stop. The heat from its engines made the air above the tarmac outside fuzzy, the vibrations from the rumbles could be heard and felt as the plane moved again, gathered speed, and took off in a different direction to the previous one.

Molly ducked into the nearest ladies' toilet. She couldn't meet Ben like this. She was sweating, her hands were clammy. She felt as though she was about to faint. It had all been so easy in theory, even that day the girls went to Malta and she'd only been at the airport as a spectator. Thinking about meeting her birth father had momentarily overshadowed her fear, but now she was actually about to set foot on a plane, she wasn't sure she would be able to go through with it.

Inside the toilet cubicle Molly told herself to take deep breaths – not easy when the smell wasn't the greatest. She reapplied her deodorant to freshen up and then emerged to the sinks where she washed her hands beneath the cold tap and pressed her palms to her cheeks to cool her skin. It felt nice. And then she went back outside and walked to the gate, more confidently than she felt.

She'd only been sitting at the gate for five minutes when she saw Ben walking towards her – dark blond hair and tracksuit, a royal blue holdall with the Adidas wording on it, exactly as he'd told her.

Never mind the fact her nerves had suddenly abated, Molly thought she'd need a forklift truck to lift her chin off the floor, because Ben was no seventy-year-old man using an online mask to meet women. He didn't look much older than she was, he had an athletic build with an air of breezy confidence.

And to top it off, he was cute as hell.

Chapter Sixteen

Molly

'Molly?' He scratched his chin, which was noticeably smooth. 'I'm glad to see you. I thought you might change your mind.'

'About meeting you?'

He nodded, smiled.

'Bit difficult when we have the same flight number,' she said.

'You could've switched seats at check-in.' He opened his blue holdall and pulled out a bottle of water. 'Did you?' His hands were steady, but his eyes had left hers as he waited for her answer, and she realised he was nervous about meeting her too.

'Of course not. If we hate each other we can go our separate ways at Singapore.'

'Yeah, well if you run away from me in Singapore don't expect me to flirt with you online any more.'

Molly was glad her immediate physical attraction to Ben had been just the tonic for the dreaded flight she would soon be on. Who cared if it never went anywhere? A bit of flirting never hurt anyone, especially if it could get them through a stressful time.

'So how are you feeling?' Ben screwed the top back on his water and slotted it inside his bag. 'I see you've already treated your fear with some retail therapy.' He eyed the bag of duty-free on her lap.

'Some perfume.' She knew she was blushing.

'Come on then, I'll give you a bloke's opinion. What, why are you grinning?'

'I've not really heard an Aussie accent before, apart from on the TV.'

'I think you're going to hear plenty where you're going.' Impatiently he motioned for her to show him what she'd bought.

Molly handed him the perfume. 'You can't smell it. It's still sealed.'

'Ah, good point. Looks all right though.'

Molly put the perfume back in the bag.

'What else did you buy?'

'Don't laugh, but I bought an adult colouring book.'

'I was reading a newspaper article about those the other day. They're supposed to quieten the brain or slow it down when you're anxious, something like that.' He nodded his approval and flicked through the book when Molly passed it to him.

Molly pulled out another bag. 'I nearly forgot to buy these.'

'Felt-tip pens…The colouring in could've been pretty tricky without them. Although I'm sure most airlines have kids' packs.' He winked at her.

Molly still hadn't told her parents about the arrangement to fly with Ben. They'd have worried all the more if they knew she was meeting a total stranger. She had visions of her dad insisting he had to get through passport control to check who his daughter was going to sit with for the next thirteen hours.

Molly's mind leapt when she saw the cabin crew filing past. Her heart thumped hard, everyone around her except for those staff disappeared into a blur. It was only when she felt Ben's hand on her arm that the breath she was holding slowly left her body.

'Keep looking at the crew,' he said. 'Look at how neat and tidy they are and how capable they look.

They're all smiling and chatting. They do this all the time. It's another boring day at the office for them, remember.'

Molly did as she was told, and it helped. Her breath went in and out, normally.

When the crew disappeared through the doors to board the plane first and the airline staff busied around the gate preparing to greet passengers, Ben said, 'It's almost time.'

'It's almost time,' Molly repeated.

Ben pulled out his phone from the front pocket of his bag. 'I think this is the perfect time for a selfie.'

'What?'

'Come on, we need a picture before you get on this flight. For the group,' he explained. 'Everyone knows today is the day and they'll be dying to know how you get on, so I'll post this before we board.'

To do the selfie Molly squeezed next to Ben. He had a familiar male smell she struggled to describe. Fresh, perhaps shower gel or the lingering scent of shaving foam. Whatever it was, she hadn't smelt it for a long time. Boyfriends had been few and far between and the closeness now made her giddy.

'Smile for the camera,' said Ben and she hoped he wouldn't be able to tell from the picture the effect he was having on her.

She put out her hand for the phone. 'I need to approve it first.' And when he dropped it into her palm, his fingers lightly brushed against her skin, sending tingles right through her.

The picture was good. They looked happy, excited, her dark locks against his dark blond hair, his blue eyes alongside her hazel ones. She gave her approval to post it on the Facebook page, well aware he was the first man who'd made her think about dating again in a long time. She'd had a serious boyfriend in her early twenties, but it had fizzled out when he left to go and work up North, and since then she'd never really gelled with anyone enough to progress further than a couple of dates.

Seriously, what was she thinking? Ben was a no-go zone … he lived on the other side of the world, for goodness sake!

'You're making me break my rule, by the way,' he said.

'And what rule's that?'

He wiggled his phone in the air after he'd posted to Facebook. 'I don't put pictures of me on the group page, but now everyone will know what I look like.'

'Good job you're leaving the country then.'

'I suppose it is.' He grinned. 'Although I'm sure we have a few members from Australia.'

'You might get a sexy blonde stalking you.'

'I don't go for blondes.'

His words hung in the air between them, but their antics had been the perfect distraction. Only now Molly looked over to see people jostling into a queue, as though the plane was going to leave without them.

'Ready?' Ben picked up his bag.

Molly nodded and they made their way over to join the end of the queue.

Fifteen minutes later they were on the plane, stopping and starting as they slowly progressed up the aisle while people climbed into their economy class seats and others tried to shove oversize bags into the overhead lockers. Molly followed Ben. She watched the way his shoulder blades moved and the muscles beneath his top as he made his way to their seats at the back of the plane. They'd have preferred seats nearer the front, which supposedly didn't get such a bumpy ride, but those had been taken so they'd chosen two seats on their own next to a window at the rear.

When they reached the correct row, Ben removed a book and a bottle of water before shoving his holdall into the overhead locker. Molly took out her own water, the colouring book and pens and pushed everything else into her bag, zipped it up and let Ben do the honours for her. 'Would you like the window seat or the aisle?' he asked.

'I really don't mind.'

'Take the window then. If you're tired you can lean against it and sleep.'

'I should've taken ultra-strong sleeping pills,' said Molly.

'Ah, but then, could you trust me alone with you?'

The butterflies already residing in her tummy were suddenly replaced by panic thanks to a thumping sound coming from beneath the plane. Immediately she was on edge.

'It's the bags being slung into the hold,' said Ben, as he waited for her to move across to her seat so he could sit in his.

Molly relaxed again, as much as she could when she knew before long they'd be up in the air. 'I can't believe we each have one of these.' She pointed to the TV screen in the back of the seat in front of her.

'Yes, we all get a TV.' Amused by her reaction, he told her, 'I'll even let you watch it for thirteen whole hours. As much screen time as you like.'

'Thanks, Dad.' She slotted her colouring book, pens and water into the back of the seat in front, and following Ben's lead, looked at her copy of the inflight magazine with the TV guide inside. There were plenty of movies she'd not seen, plenty she wanted to watch again. Her mounting excitement took her completely by surprise.

'What are they doing?' Molly watched the cabin crew position themselves along the aisle.

'Safety demo, nothing to worry about. You know about these, we've talked about them on Facebook.'

Molly focused. She watched the cabin crew all the time, listening to their every word. Other passengers didn't seem to be taking much notice. She wanted to call over to them and tell them to listen, this might save their life! She wondered how many of them had done this so many times they'd become blasé about it all.

The cabin crew were professional, well-presented and in control, and although Molly felt herself draw a big inward breath when they demonstrated how to do up a lifejacket, which made her think about the plane that had landed in the Hudson, and although she felt her palms sweat and wished she'd layered on more deodorant when they showed how to pull on an oxygen mask, she knew having someone sitting there beside her was the best thing right now.

Everyone around them fastened their seatbelts – Molly had had hers on from the moment she sat in her seat. She knew from talking to the group to expect strange noises, unfamiliar sounds as the aircraft did what it needed to do to get into the air into the first place and then stay there.

'All machines make noises, remember.' Ben must have seen her close her eyes, sit back in her seat and do her best to remain calm when the plane released its brakes and reversed from its parking space. As the giant aircraft moved it made whooshing noises, it sounded like something being sucked in, the engines groaned, there were weird whizzing and whirring noises.

Breathe, Molly, breathe.

'My mum's old washing machine used to move across the floor on its own,' said Ben.

Molly opened her eyes and looked across at him. 'I'm thirty, not five. You don't have to make up stories for me.'

'I'm not joking. It was a beast. I was scared of it. I wouldn't put my dirty socks in the laundry in case it got me.'

'Poor excuse,' Molly smiled. She looked out of the tiny oval window. They were still taxiing down the runway, slowly, calmly.

'So how are you feeling about meeting your birth father?' asked Ben.

Molly turned back to him appreciating his efforts to distract her. 'I'm not really sure, now I'm on my way.' Part of her had been on a high thinking she'd find him and get answers. The other part of her was worried he'd tell her to go away.

'I think you're doing the right thing.'

'Really? You don't think this is totally crazy?'

'Don't get me wrong, what you're doing is pretty out there and a bold move, but under the circumstances I can see why. You want answers and you're taking control to see you get them.'

'My family are worried,' she said.

'Do they mind you getting on a plane with a strange man?'

She looked at him and smiled. 'You're joking. I didn't tell them. A long distance trip they can cope with, doing it with a stranger would've been unimaginable to them.'

She turned back to look out of the window again, watched a plane take off in the opposite direction to where their plane was taking them. It was pretty uneventful.

Molly considered the likely impact of her sudden and unannounced arrival in Australia, and what it would do to Andrew Bennett. She was going to be one hell of a surprise. But she wasn't about to back out now.

Her thoughts shifted as she tried not to get too wound up about confronting her birth father. She thought about how happy Isaac would be now she was able to get on a plane. She'd make his wedding, and perhaps this flight could be the first step in having a whole new lease of life. She'd be able to holiday with friends, experience the big, wide world out there.

'I wonder if he's fat,' said Ben.

'What?' He'd distracted her from looking out over the wing as bits of metal moved and flapped, and engines produced steam as they prepared for take-off.

'I can't imagine a skinny chocolatier, can you?'

'He didn't look fat in his photograph.'

'What did he look like?'

She thought about it. The only words that came to mind were, 'he looks like me', but she didn't say it. When she'd first seen a photograph of him, she'd been shocked. Funny, you never expected to look like your birth father. Your birth mother, yes, but not the birth father. She wondered if it was different if you were a boy. Maybe then you assumed you'd look more like the male part of the puzzle.

'He's got dark hair, a little bit grey,' she answered. 'He looks normal.'

'Didn't have two heads then?'

She laughed. 'No, didn't have two heads.'

Her smile faded as the plane came to a standstill. ‘Why are we stopping?’ She peered over the top of the seat in front to see if there was anything going on.

Ben’s voice softened. ‘We’re not.’ And then the engines rumbled, long and deep, and it was like releasing a pinball from the flippers at the bottom of the machine as the plane sped off down the runway.

‘I’m right here, Molly. Right here.’ Ben’s voice came from beside her as she gripped her armrests and shut her eyes, her body pinned back in her seat.

Without thinking, her hand shot out to find his. She adjusted her grip as she felt the ground disappear from beneath the plane, felt the unsteady movement as they left the tarmac and the plane changed its angle to climb up into the sky. The higher the plane climbed, the harder she gripped, his voice with her every now and then assuring her she was okay.

There was a groaning sound, a slight jolt.

‘It’s the wheels tucking under the plane, out of the way,’ Ben explained, ‘and now the plane is levelling off.’

She could feel it. She was no longer plastered against her seat. She felt the plane lessening its angle as it found its place in the sky, and when she opened her eyes and released her grip on Ben’s hand, she realised they were straight. All she could see outside the window were the white fluffy clouds, moving past them like puffs of gentle air. It felt as though they were gliding, drifting. It definitely didn’t feel as though they were travelling at a speed she’d never before experienced in her life. It felt dreamlike, as though it was in her imagination, with nothing but the sound of air circulating around the cabin.

She looked at Ben. He was wincing and shaking his hand up and down.

‘What’s the matter?’

He turned over his hand, the hand she’d gripped hold of.

‘Oh my God, was that me?’ She looked at the indentations her nails had left behind. ‘I’m so sorry. Why didn’t you say anything?’ She put a hand across her mouth. ‘Are you sure you’re okay?’

‘I’m not going to start crying over a few marks. Let’s just say I’m glad your nails are reasonably short or we could’ve seen blood.’

Molly looked out of the window, more enamoured with flying than she thought she’d ever be. The take-off had been terrifying – the marks she’d left in Ben’s hand were testament to that – but now the noises of the aircraft had abated and the plane was gliding through fluffy clouds, without a care in the world. People sitting all around her were going about their business normally, watching the TV screens, chatting and laughing, blissfully unaware, or at least ignoring, how far they were from the ground.

‘I did it,’ she said to Ben, a huge smile on her face.

‘You sure did.’

The seat-belt sign went off and it wasn’t long before the cabin crew brought round small plastic containers of apple juice, orange juice and water. Molly selected an apple juice and opened up the colouring book to a forest scene with woodland creatures.

‘Had enough of talking to me already?’ asked Ben.

‘Not at all, but every time I hear a little sound my mind risks going into overdrive. I need distraction.’

Molly spent the next hour colouring the picture and all its intricacies: trees, squirrels, different flowers, a toadstool. They ate their first meal of the flight, Molly watched a movie when her eyes tired from looking at the colouring book and before long she braved taking off her seatbelt to make her way to the bathrooms.

'Word to the wise.' Ben moved to the aisle to let her past. 'Go in the one on the left. The right-hand side …' He pinched his nostrils.

'Thanks for the tip.' Molly steadied herself down the aisle, walking tall and proud. She couldn't believe this was her. On a plane! Right now she felt as though she could tackle anything.

When she returned to her seat, it was time for the big trolley to be wheeled out again. Feeding time seemed to come round quickly on these flights. This time it was roast beef with roast potatoes, baby carrots, peas, and a chocolate cake for dessert, plus a roll with butter, a couple of bite-size chocolates on the side, all in their miniature containers.

'I can't believe how much they feed you on here.' She sliced through a piece of beef using the plastic cutlery. Not the easiest task.

'You wait. On the leg to Oz you won't want to eat a thing. You'll be pushing it away from you.'

'How many times have you flown?'

'Twelve flights now. As soon as I got over my fear, or anxiety, or whatever you want to label it as, I wanted to get out there and see things.'

Molly smiled. 'I can't believe I'm sitting on a plane with a virtual stranger.'

'So let's get to know each other.'

She sliced another piece of beef. 'Okay. What do you do for work?'

'I'm a doctor.'

Molly rested her fork against the container as she swallowed the last piece of potato. 'No way.'

He laughed. 'Don't I look capable?'

'Of course you do. It's just … well, you look like a student to me, especially with the travelling thing.'

'I saved up enough to take time off work and travel. I'm not sure I'd ever get to do it if I didn't take the chance now, while I'm still young.'

'How old are you?'

'I'm thirty-two.'

'Old then.' She teased. 'Much, much older than me.'

'Oh come on then, what are you, a twenty-something?'

'Thirty.'

'Yup, so much younger than me.' He shook his head. 'Travelling is a lot of fun, but I'm looking forward to going home to Australia now. The time feels right.'

Molly could relate to that. It was the right time to get over her fear of flying, it was the right time to go and find her birth father.

'So what do you do?' Ben pulled off the foil covering for his dessert.

'I'm a midwife.'

It was his turn to be surprised. 'Weird how we're both in the medical profession. So where do you live? Oh come on,' he added when she didn't answer, 'I'm next to you on a plane and I'm flying back to my home country. As long as you don't give me a street name and number, I think you'll be pretty safe.'

'I live in Bath, Somerset.'

'Beautiful city. I went to a rugby match there.'

'Very cultural.'

'Not really. It was ten per cent rugby, ninety per cent propping up the bar. Although we did see the Abbey.'

'From your bar stool?'

He pulled a face. 'Point taken.' He went on to tell her about some of the more cultural things he'd woven into his visit to the northern hemisphere: the Aran Islands, Croke Park, Trinity College and Giant's Causeway in Ireland, then in England he'd been to Stonehenge, the Cheddar Gorge, Woburn Safari Park, Westminster Abbey, Covent Garden.

Molly finished up her chocolate cake but left the bread roll, unable to eat much more. Sitting down and sitting still for prolonged periods of time didn't exactly require much energy, and she felt as though all the food was collecting in her tummy.

'Where do you live, in Australia?' she asked. 'Which city?'

'I'm from Melbourne.'

She felt it was safe to admit where she was heading. 'I'm flying into Melbourne.'

His eyes lit up. 'I thought you weren't going to tell me any specifics.'

She smiled. 'First stop is South Yarra.'

'Nice place. Hotel?'

'Short-term apartment – cheaper.' She had the place booked for three nights to give herself time to recover from jet lag, time to digest what she was going to do. Then she'd hire a car, complete with a satnav, and make her way up to Magnolia Creek where Andrew Bennett ran his chocolaterie. Those few days would hopefully allow her feelings to settle before she went to find out whether he had any room in his life for her.

'Are you ready to tackle Melbourne's tram system?'

'I think so.' She was more than a little excited about getting on a tram for the first time. The idea of zipping around the city to go to the shops or see the sights – imagine going to work on one – fascinated her.

The cabin crew cleared away the trays of food and Molly put on another film. She could see Ben was watching quiz shows, playing the interactive *Millionaire* game show and tutting if he got one wrong. Her eyes were heavy, with London time closing in on midnight, and tired of the TV screen she rested a pillow against the window, smiled across at Ben and shut her eyes. She tightened her seatbelt when the plane bumped a little. She blocked out any scenarios about turbulence she'd heard, and as she told herself she was going to be fine, as she thought about her birth father and maybe meeting him face to face, she drifted off.

When Molly woke, the plane had nearly completed its descent and they were coming in to land. She smiled over at Ben, who looked like he'd been dozing too.

'Well done,' he whispered and she grinned from ear to ear.

Chapter Seventeen
Molly

Ben hoisted his bag over his shoulder and walked alongside Molly as they moved from the plane and through the passenger boarding bridge when they disembarked. Molly was tired and felt grubby, but she was buzzing. The adrenalin of knowing she'd got on a plane, without freaking out during the thirteen hours they were up in the sky, flooded her body. It had been a smooth landing, and the only moment she'd felt panic rising was when the wheels were on the ground and the rush of noise got so loud it was as though the plane was heading straight for something. But then it had quietened and the plane had leisurely crawled along the runway, into its designated bay, and the flight was officially over.

'How are you feeling right now?' A huge smile spread across Ben's face as they walked away from the gate.

She couldn't stop grinning. 'Pretty pleased with myself.'

Ben stopped and pulled his phone from the front pocket of his bag. 'Selfie time.'

'What? No way! I must look hideous.' The air in the plane had left everything feeling dry, tight and like she needed a damn good shower.

'Rubbish. You look fine, you look happy.'

She accepted the compliment but held her breath when their heads tipped towards each other so they could both get in the frame. As well as a shower, she desperately wanted to clean her teeth. She hadn't braved the miniscule cubicle on the plane to do it, but now she wished she had.

She watched the tendons in Ben's arms as he stretched out and positioned the phone and took the picture.

He checked it. 'No, wait, do it again. You're not even looking at the camera.'

Of course not. She'd been looking at his skin, his naturally tanned colouring, which seemed at odds after a visit to the northern hemisphere that had only just emerged from winter.

'Say cheese!' This time it worked, and he said he'd post it in the Facebook group.

Ben turned over his palm. 'I think my hand survived to tell the tale.' The marks she'd made had disappeared now. 'I think it's only fair to warn the next person you sit next to though.'

'Hopefully that won't be necessary.' She stopped, put down her holdall and removed her hoodie. The heat of Changi Airport left her no choice. 'It's boiling in here.'

'I can't wait to get some sun. I've had an Irish winter and an English start to spring. Bloody freezing.'

She laughed. 'And it's Australia's winter coming up. You didn't time it very well.'

'Yes, Australia's winters can be brutal,' he joked, taking out an immigration card from the middle pocket of his bag. Molly already knew she didn't need one as she was in transit. There was so much for her to learn! And besides, she'd managed to be asleep when they handed the cards out on the plane, something she never thought would happen.

They smiled at one another until they realised what they were doing, and awkwardly, Ben said, 'What's your layover time?'

'My what?'

He grinned. 'How long do you have until your next flight?'

'Three hours, so I'll stretch my legs, enjoy not being scrunched up in a seat.' *Clean my teeth and reapply my deodorant*, she told herself.

They were looking at each other again. Molly broke the silence. 'And you get out there and enjoy the sunshine and heat.' She wished she was joining him. He'd described Singapore to her during the flight and it sounded clean, neat, tropical.

'Best of luck,' he said.

'With the flight? Or with meeting my birth father and possibly facing more rejection?' The closer she got to Australia, the more real this was becoming.

'Both.' His eyes held hers for as long as they both allowed. 'I'd better go. My mate's meeting me at arrivals, and knowing him he'll have left his car in a no-parking bay or on double yellows.'

'Bye, Ben.' Molly turned to go, but he pulled her arm and spun her round to face him. He looked about to kiss her, but instead he pulled her into a hug. He smelt cleaner than she'd expected, given the long flight, and the scent of washing powder still clung to his top. Perhaps he'd secretly used deodorant on the plane and freshened up when she was asleep. She hoped she didn't pong too much as she hugged him back.

'It was great to meet you, Molly,' he said when they pulled apart.

'You too. Keep in touch.'

'I will, and I'll see you on Facebook. Get on there as soon as you can and have a chat with everyone, they'll want to know how you are. And if you find yourself at a loose end in Melbourne, we can always meet up when I'm back.'

'We'll see.' She really wanted to leap at the chance. Now she'd met Ben in the flesh, she knew she hadn't imagined the easiness of their banter, the feelings she'd begun to have despite hiding behind a computer screen.

When Molly walked away, she turned back once and Ben was still rooted to the spot. She waved to him and then he turned to go, and for the next few hours she didn't think much about having to get on another plane, she didn't worry about turning up to see Andrew Bennett. All she really thought about was Ben.

And she was still thinking about him as she boarded the second flight, this time on her own.

*

The flight from Singapore to Melbourne was better than Molly had thought it'd be. She had the window seat again, a spare seat next to her and then a woman who looked to be in her fifties sat closest to the aisle. The woman was Australian, and they made polite conversation – was it Molly's first time? where was she off to? – and it distracted Molly from a slightly bumpy take-off.

The woman eventually opened a magazine, and Molly took out her colouring book, turning to an ocean scene with shoals of fish, fronds of seaweed and oddly shaped shells. When the food came around, Molly smiled to herself. Ben was right. She barely touched a thing this time and started to realise why everyone moaned about airline food. It wasn't that it was so terrible; it was just that after sitting couped up on board, each meal became less and less attractive.

Halfway through the flight, Molly found herself listening attentively to any out-of-the-ordinary sound the plane made, and her mind was beginning to go to all sorts of places. She'd read a tip from someone in the Facebook group who said fearful flyers listen for any little noise, convinced it could be a life-threatening problem, so instead she put on headphones and watched a movie, even though her eyes were sore and dry from the air conditioning.

When the fasten seat-belt sign pinged on urgently and the plane bumped so much her tummy leapt up and down with it, Molly imagined Ben's voice in her ear saying everything was okay.

The turbulence was only mild, but Molly definitely wasn't as relaxed as she was during the first leg to Singapore and she didn't manage to sleep a wink. The descent was smooth, the landing bumpy, but before midnight local time they touched down in Melbourne, Australia, and Molly looked out of the window as the plane taxied along the runway. The lights from the aircraft flashed against the night sky, pooling all around them, and eventually they pulled into their allotted bay.

She was here. She was in Australia. And everything was suddenly becoming real.

Chapter Eighteen
Louis

He watched as Andrew's face drained of colour. In all his years, Louis had never seen such a look of disgust, fear, anger and regret, all rolled into one.

Andrew bashed a hand against the kitchen bench and the only sound to be heard was breathing. Louis thought it was his, but he wasn't sure.

Andrew picked up the bowls waiting for the soup he'd warmed for lunch and, one by one, slung them across the kitchen. He refused to look at Louis, and even though Louis understood, hadn't expected anything less, Andrew's fury still broke his heart.

Louis sipped from the glass of water Gemma handed to him and his breathing calmed. If he hadn't been sick, his breathing loud and sometimes laboured, he imagined his son would take a swing at him. He imagined those bowls would've been hurled his way rather than at the cupboards on the opposite wall.

And after what he'd done, he couldn't blame Andrew.

The tinkle of china and the gentle swoosh of the brush were the only sounds between them as Gemma swept up the debris from the floor, and they all waited to see what would happen next.

And then, Louis told his story from the very beginning.

Louis – 1985

'How was your day, love?' Penny Bennett shook out the sheets she'd already dried on the washing line out back at their home in a small village in Surrey.

'Busy.' He set down his bag, took out the cinnamon twist he'd brought home for them.

Penny looked up briefly before returning to the task of folding the sheets. As he always did, Louis went over to her and kissed her cheek. He patted her arm and went through to the kitchen to make them both a cup of tea. It'd been the routine, six days a week, every time he came home from the bakery where he worked as a pastry chef, for as long as he could remember.

It was a particularly mild winter's day for England, and locals were out in force, crammed into the local beer garden as Louis had driven past on his way home. Kids were skipping on the village green, and mothers were out walking with prams, trying to make the most of the weather before winter jumped out and reminded them that summer was a long way off yet.

'Are the kids around?' he asked as the kettle bubbled its way to the boil. 'It's awfully quiet.'

'They're doing their homework.' She seemed troubled.

'What's the matter?' Louis stirred the tea, tapping the spoon against the china cup as he always did.

'I'm worried about Andrew. He's not himself.'

'Girl trouble most likely.'

'You're probably right. But Julia seems like a nice girl, she's good for him.'

Louis harrumphed. 'He's young, Penny.'

‘I was only sixteen when we married.’ She didn’t wait for him to say she was right, or for him to refute her point. She smiled and then turned and took the pile of folded sheets upstairs to the airing cupboard.

She was right about one thing: she had been only sixteen when they married, he’d been twenty-five, but there was so much to do before you settled down. He didn’t want Andrew settling for anything less than extraordinary. He’d been lucky himself. He’d known from an early age that he wanted to be big in the world of food. He hadn’t narrowed down what field it would be exactly, but he’d spent hours as a small lad studying his mum’s recipe books, doing what he could in the kitchen – not a common occurrence in the late fifties and sixties. His father had been killed in the war and his mum had four children to raise, so they’d all become pretty adept at mucking in where needed.

By the time Louis was in his early twenties, he had a job at the local bakery, four days a week, baking bread and dealing with customers and using the accountancy skills he’d been pushed to acquire in school. He’d hated anything mathematical, but he’d knuckled down, eager to please his mother, and got qualifications to help him secure a job should he not be able to follow his dream of going into the cooking industry. He’d never had a girlfriend, not in the formal sense. He’d kissed a couple of girls in his late teens, after discos, behind the shelter at the bus stop. But nothing more.

And then, at twenty-five he’d met Penny. She’d been in one day to buy a loaf of bread, back the next day and the one after that. And on the fourth day of her coming into the shop, he’d asked her how big her family was. ‘There are four of us, and my brothers eat like horses,’ she’d giggled coquettishly. She was younger than him;

he'd seen her in a school uniform the other day. 'Well, you sure do eat a lot of bread.' He'd grinned, this time wrapping up two brown rolls in a paper bag for her. She went on her way.

Slowly Louis and Penny got talking more and more, and before long he'd asked her to the dance at the village hall and they'd started seeing each other: a picnic on the village green, a walk through the Surrey countryside. Her parents disapproved, which, he suspected, was part of the excitement. She was sixteen and wanted to experience life, and they laughed their way through countless weekends, through long summer nights and rainy autumn days.

Then, in the early winter of 1969, she'd kissed him longer than usual as they parked down the road from the cottage she lived in with her family. She'd kissed him for so long that in the end they'd run from the car, through the fields beyond her house and to the old barn that housed two old classic cars belonging to her dad. And it was there they'd both lost their virginity. It'd been tender, exciting, thrilling and a moment of weakness, but it had also been the moment everything changed for Louis.

'Louis.' It was Penny, calling from the laundry now. 'The back door's stuck again, I can't shut it.'

Things were forever going wrong with this house. They'd lived in it for thirteen years – the first two years of their lives spent with her parents in her childhood bedroom, all three of them crammed in together, as if being married in the first place wasn't enough to contend with – and Louis did his best to keep everything shipshape, but things broke quicker than he could fix them. The door had warped at the bottom, and whenever it rained hard and got wet and they opened it, it'd get stuck and take forever to wedge shut again.

Louis fixed the door, and by the time he came back to the kitchen, wiping the dirt from his fingers on an old rag, Andrew had come downstairs.

'How was school, son?'

Andrew looked to the floor. 'Good.'

'Doesn't sound it. You didn't get in trouble, did you?'

Penny's ears pricked up. She was a good mother, loving but firm, and their three children had discipline instilled in them but the right amount of childhood to balance it. 'What's happened, Andrew?'

Andrew couldn't look at either of his parents. His dark hair had recently been cut, and he could no longer hide behind the fringe that had flopped over his eyes until last week.

'It's Julia,' said Andrew.

His mother drew in breath. 'Is she all right? What's happened?'

Andrew scuffed a foot against the floor, his foot tracing the beige and brown hexagons on the old seventies carpet.

'She's pregnant,' he blurted out.

Penny slumped down at the table.

Louis looked at his son. 'You're sure? She's definitely pregnant, with your baby?'

'Dad!'

'Sorry, son, I didn't mean it the way it sounded.' His mouth was bone dry, he looked around for a water. He'd rather have a beer.

'She's seen a doctor. We're sure.' He chose to ignore the other implication.

Penny sat at the table in stunned disbelief, her tight fawn curls perfectly in place.

Louis' mind flashed back almost sixteen years to the kitchen of his own home, telling his own parents much of what Andrew was saying to them now. But at least he'd had a job, he was older, he had a foundation with which to bring a family into the world.

Louis and Penny barely slept that night and the next morning, when Andrew left the house for school without saying a word, Louis didn't make it into work.

'He can't get married,' Penny sobbed as she sat at the kitchen table. 'He's too young.'

Louis watched his wife with fondness. She was a good mother, the best mother he could ever have imagined her to be.

'We need to sort this mess out,' Louis decided. 'God knows what we'll do, but this can't happen.'

He picked up his keys and went straight over to Julia's house. He tried to talk to Julia's mother, Kathleen Mason, at the rundown cottage where she lived with her children, but Kathleen ushered him away. It seemed she was about as impressed with this latest development as he was.

The next afternoon, as Louis and Penny wrestled with what to do, Kathleen came to their home. She accepted the cup of tea offered by Penny, and all three of them nursed their china teacups with the rose pattern on them as though their lives depended on it.

'I want more for my Julia,' Kathleen said after a while, and Louis didn't miss the tears spring to her eyes. 'I married a man I was infatuated with. I was young and foolish. I had no qualifications, no prospects, and when Brian left us, it was hard. It was almost impossible to make ends meet. I struggled to put food on the table when my kids were babies, and I'm only just starting to get myself sorted. The house is falling apart at the seams, I miss my family in Ireland but can't even afford a ticket home to see my sister, who has cancer, and isn't expected to live through the year.'

Louis pulled out a chair and sat down, his cup still full.

'I don't want the same life for Julia, I don't.' Kathleen pulled a tissue from her pocket. 'She's too young to have a baby. If she has this baby, she'll never do anything else, you mark my words.'

Louis thought it sounded as though Kathleen had little faith in her daughter, but perhaps she was right. If Julia married Andrew and they had this baby, of course he'd help them financially to get themselves sorted, but his help could only go so far. He'd seen them together. They looked as though they were in love, but they were so young. Who knew what love was at their age? He certainly hadn't.

'Has Julia said she wants to keep the baby?' Louis asked.

'She hasn't said much at all. She's done a lot of crying, as though she thinks it'll make the problem go away.'

'I know Andrew would stand by her.' He was sure of it, but it wasn't what any of them wanted. But was it even their choice to make?

'I'd better get back.' Kathleen pushed out her chair, discarded the cup of tea she hadn't touched. 'Julia will be home from school soon.'

'We'll talk again,' said Louis. 'Tomorrow?'

'Maybe.' Kathleen didn't look back, and Louis and Penny watched from their kitchen window as she walked down the path and turned past the gorse bush and out of sight.

*

Louis couldn't get hold of Kathleen the next day or the day after, and Andrew shut them out the best he could by disappearing into his room to do homework, taking longer showers than usual, going out on his bike to goodness knew where until the late hours when the only thing to bring him home was exhaustion.

Four days after they'd first sat down with Kathleen Mason in their kitchen, Julia's mother knocked at the Bennett's door again.

'Julia is adamant she will have this baby,' she told them. 'She's sure she and Andrew will marry.' She didn't take off her coat.

Penny lowered herself into the floral armchair at the corner of the room.

'Maybe we need to get them both together, here, tonight, and we can all talk this through. No misunderstandings,' suggested Louis.

Kathleen pushed her hands firmly into the pockets of her red coat. 'I have another idea.'

And so Louis and Penny Bennett listened to this woman's suggestion, the way she wanted to tear apart the fifteen-year-olds and whisk Julia away from all of this, leave a life that had turned sour.

*

'You can't be serious!' Louis' voice boomed around the room after Kathleen told them her plan. Penny touched a hand to his knee, but he stood anyway, to get some height over this woman. 'She's your daughter, how can you be so … so—'

'So what, Mr Bennett? So caring for her future? So sure I want more for her than what *I've* ended up with?'

'This is sheer blackmail! And I won't stand for it.'

'Then you leave me no choice. Goodbye, Mr Bennett.'

Her red coat swung as she turned.

'Wait a minute.' Louis' hand made contact with her shoulder, and he held up his hands when she spun back again, anxious to show he wasn't a violent man. It hadn't come to that, at least not yet. 'Do you think Julia would thank you for this, if she found out?'

'She won't find out. Absolute discretion is part of the deal. You pay for my family's airline tickets out of here, back to Ireland, and I'll persuade Julia she needs to abort the baby. She'll listen to me eventually. And if you don't, then I'm afraid I'll go to the authorities and tell them Andrew had sex with Julia and it wasn't consensual. I'd say she was coerced into it. She's still a minor, and I think the law would take a pretty dim view.'

Louis sank into the chair. He couldn't believe what he was hearing. 'Even if I could prove you were wrong, you'd ruin him by doing that. You'd ruin this family. Are you telling me you're happy to do that?'

She had the good grace to look guilty. 'There's nothing about this situation that makes me happy, Mr Bennett, believe me.'

'So why be so ruthless?'

'I'm doing what I can to look after my children. We have no money, Mr Bennett. No money to return to Ireland, but when we get there we are to stay with my brother. He can find me work and it's the start of a new future. Please don't think I'm a terrible person.' She twiddled her thumbs anxiously. 'I want Julia to go to university, get a job, fall in love and have a family with the right person, when the time is right. This isn't personal.'

'Like hell it isn't!' When Louis' voice echoed off the walls, tears fell down Penny's cheeks. 'And you'd persuade her to get rid of the baby? You think she'll listen?'

He felt oddly protective over the unborn child. Much as he didn't want Andrew to be trapped into a marriage so young, and fatherhood before he was ready, he couldn't bear the thought of destroying a part of their family. But Kathleen left them with no option. She'd ruin them, she'd said as much. Blackmailing, to her, was her way of looking after her own family.

'Think about what I've said,' Kathleen continued, 'and we'll start making plans.'

The following afternoon, Kathleen returned to the Bennetts' home.

'You leave us with no choice,' Louis told her. 'We'll go ahead with whatever you suggest.'

Kathleen looked him straight in the eye. 'Julia and Andrew must know nothing about this. I've thought of the best way to do it, and they need to completely break away from each other.'

'And how do you suggest we do that?' Louis guffawed. All he cared about now was that Andrew would come out of this relatively unscathed.

Kathleen had thought it all through. She would put the locket Andrew gave Julia for her last birthday into an envelope with a short note, made to look as though it were from Julia, to tell him she'd decided to have an abortion. Julia's younger sister, Terri, was apparently a whizz at copying other people's handwriting. She'd been caught forging notes for skipping school and grounded as a result, and given enough incentive, monetary or otherwise, she'd do whatever she was asked. Louis was to give Andrew the letter and say Julia had delivered it.

Kathleen also took a page from an old school exercise book of Andrew's so Terri could copy his handwriting and pass the note off as authentic. Then, on the same day Louis passed Andrew the letter from Julia, Kathleen would pass Julia a letter from Andrew saying he was too young to be a father, and he was moving away from the area with his family.

'But we're not going anywhere,' Louis argued.

'It'll stop her resisting the move to Ireland if she thinks Andrew is leaving. Once I've given the letter to Julia I intend to fly immediately. Everything is ready for us. I just need—'

'The money,' said Louis, hands clasped firmly together in case he couldn't help himself and reached out to strangle this woman.

He pulled the chequebook from the wooden dresser at the side of the room. The piece of furniture had been his mother's, and she'd turn in her grave if she was here to witness what was going down this afternoon, but he couldn't run the risk of his son being prosecuted. And he wasn't sure he'd dare to call Kathleen's bluff either. She seemed as though she'd stop at nothing to get what she wanted, and deep down, Louis longed for his son to have every door open to him, every opportunity, and that included the opportunity for true love.

Louis wrote out a cheque for five hundred pounds, as they'd discussed briefly, signed it and tore it from its stub.

'I'm sorry it had to come to this,' said Kathleen. 'But you must understand, I'm looking after my family.'

Louis walked her to the door and waited for her to step outside. 'You make me sick to my stomach. You've threatened our family, lied to your child and leave me no choice but to lie to my own. Shame on you.' And he slammed the door so hard, the fresh coat of navy blue paint he'd only put on in the summer cracked all the way past the hinges.

*

Three days later, when Kathleen had waited for the funds to clear in her bank account and had purchased flights for her and her three kids, the plan had been put into action. Louis had wailed inside, cried through his entire body as his son read the letter from Julia, not suspecting for one minute the writing wasn't hers. Tears had sprung to his eyes when the locket had fallen out to the floor and Andrew grappled to pick up the last remnants of his girlfriend. And then Louis had learned how even fifteen-year-old boys weren't immune to hugs when the chips were down, and he clasped his son to his chest, holding his shuddering body that spoke of the unfairness of it all.

He'd wondered about Julia, how she was, how she'd coped with being whisked away to Ireland to start a new life, forced to get rid of a baby she wanted to keep, forced to sever contact with the boy she might very well be in love with. But they had to keep their promise. The thought of Kathleen's blackmail angered Louis no end, but the thought of Andrew getting in trouble with the law was worse. As a parent, the plan had seemed the only way out, and guilt and shame wouldn't allow him to dwell on whether there might have been another way.

Louis threw himself into work for the next few days. Andrew took to bed, sinking beneath his duvet. He had ridden his bike round to Julia's place twice, looking in the windows to check it hadn't all been some terrible dream, and when he found out she'd left the town, he was heartbroken.

After a fortnight of Andrew moping round the house and the effort each day of coaxing him into going to school so his grades didn't slip, Louis was standing at work making éclairs, chocolate torte and Danish pastries when he realised the family needed to fight back from this. He'd made this decision in the best interests of his son, and now he needed to honour his promise to himself that his son would get the most from life. He'd make this up to him in every way he could. And so that night, at home, Louis told Penny of his plans.

Louis' brother had emigrated to Australia a long time ago where he'd set up a café business in Adelaide. He'd been back to England three times since and always talked about the lifestyle, trying to persuade Louis to make the move. 'You won't believe the sunshine we get,' he'd said. 'It's summer for eight, nine months of the year. No more digging your car out of three-foot snow drifts to get to work.'

'What do you think?' he asked Penny after dinner. Andrew was looking better, the colour was back in his cheeks and he seemed to be knuckling down to his schoolwork. 'Andrew's exams are in a few months, and if we get everything in place, we can go as soon as they've finished, settle him into a secondary school over there.'

'I don't know, Louis. It's a long way away.'

'But think of the life we'd have. It'd be a fresh start.' Away from the dismal weather, away from any memories of what they'd done. 'I think we could all be really happy.'

And when Penny asked whether there was work for him over there, Louis knew she was with him on this. Emigrating to Australia would be the fresh start they all needed. And they could forget all about Kathleen and Julia Mason.

Chapter Nineteen
Molly

At one o'clock in the morning, Melbourne time, Molly's taxi pulled into the driveway of a small block of apartments. She'd called her parents from the airport to tell them the flight had been fine and she'd heard their relief from thousands of miles away. The rain, as different as the currency she was using, lashed down as she paid the driver. England had fine, drizzly rain, but here in the southern hemisphere the rain fell heavier, thicker.

She wheeled her suitcase to the door of apartment two and fumbled with the keysafe to retrieve the key waiting for her. She let herself in to the apartment and switched on the lights. It was March, and in Melbourne the outside temperature when they'd landed was fourteen degrees, which was quite respectable, but inside this apartment was cold, and Molly was desperate to have a shower and warm up. She put the chain across the front door. She rummaged through her suitcase and found the plug adaptor and her charger, and while she showered and washed away the smell of the plane, she powered up her phone. She wanted to open up Facebook and see if Ben had sent her a message, look at their photo again, but she'd resisted the temptation on the way to South Yarra, not wanting to use up what remaining power the device had left.

She stayed beneath the jets of hot water for ages, longer than she usually did. She washed her hair so it was fresh with the scent of fruit and coconut from the travel-size shampoo and conditioner she'd brought with her, and when she was dry she pulled on her thick cotton pyjamas, plumped up the pillows on the bed against the wall and relaxed into them, her phone now charged enough to log on to social media.

She opened up Facebook, and when she saw Ben's message, her heart leapt. She read it a few times, hearing about his friend in Singapore – apparently he'd parked at a taxi rank and there were a few people yelling at them as they threw Ben's luggage into the boot and left the airport – and then he sent her a few photographs of him in a bar with his friend, Seb, with iced beer glasses held aloft. Molly wrote straight back to tell him about the flight she'd managed to do all by herself, she briefly described the apartment to him, told him it was cold and raining and said she had a few days to be a tourist and get her head sorted before she took the next step.

When Ben didn't reply immediately, as he so often did, Molly realised it was the middle of the night where he was too. She flicked over to the group page and scrolled down to find the post she'd been longing to see ever since they'd parted in Changi Airport. His blue eyes looked out at her from the selfie they'd taken before the first flight and again from the second photo they'd taken after landing in Singapore. She couldn't help but smile, warm inside at what she'd achieved. It was a long, long road ahead, but she didn't care. She was on her way.

After she'd checked the corners of the ceiling in the bathroom, bedroom and kitchen area for spiders or cobwebs that could be home to anything large and Australian – Isaac's fiancée had told her some terrifying facts about redbacks, snakes and other wildlife she hoped she wouldn't encounter – she climbed into the bed. The sheets weren't soft like hotel sheets. They were stiff, as though they'd seen the washing machine too many times. But this was a bargain price compared to a hotel, and she'd needed extra money to hire a car and drive to Magnolia Creek, more money to rent a cottage up there rather than drive back to the city and enough money in case of an emergency.

Despite the less than plush bedding and the strangeness of her surroundings, the weight of jet lag weighed Molly down quickly and she fell into a heavy sleep. She dreamed of greenery, the rich shades of Magnolia Creek she'd seen in photographs on the internet. She dreamed of chocolate running down a hill near the cottages she was going to in a few days, she dreamed of Ben standing beside her as they watched a waterfall of chocolate and she heard his voice saying, 'It'll all work out, you'll see'. But she didn't dream of meeting Andrew Bennett. He may have been the reason she was here in Australia, but somehow there wasn't enough room in her head for him tonight.

*

Molly woke feeling as though she'd slept for hours. Wide awake at only seven o'clock in the morning, she guessed this was what they called jet lag. She climbed out of bed and looked out of the window. Sun. She smiled. She was here in Australia, and the weather was already helping to lighten the feelings she had stirring inside of her.

When she'd arrived at the apartment after the flight, she couldn't have imagined ever being hungry again. She felt as though she'd consumed the equivalent food she usually ate in a week. But now, she was ravenous. She quickly showered, piled her hair up in a bun and pulled on some fresh clothes.

Armed with a local map of the area, she navigated her way to Prahran markets where the scent of fruit mixed with the warmth of the outside filled her with joy. Row upon row of brightly coloured vegetables made her wonder whether she'd be able to carry everything she bought back to the apartment. She tasted cheeses on crusty bread, mushrooms served with tomato and apple chutney in tiny paper cups and dipped crackers into a fresh olive-based dip. The tastes exploded on her tongue and fuelled her desire to be here in this exciting new place, eager to find out more.

She texted her mum to make idle conversation when it was daytime in the UK, to assure her there was a sense of normality on the other side of the world, and on the way back to her apartment, she ducked into a bookstore and browsed for a while at travel guides showing Australian cities and amazing places she could visit. A world that was open to her now she was willing to get on a plane.

Back at the apartment, Molly cooked the mushrooms. She baked them under the grill as the stallholder had explained, and then tossed them with the chutney she'd bought from him. At his suggestion she'd bought spinach, and she threw a couple of handfuls into the pan with a little butter and served it with the mushrooms and toast cut up into little triangles.

Molly checked her Facebook again, and sure enough there was a 'howdy' message from Ben. She wasn't sure what made him say 'howdy' when he was Australian and nowhere near the USA, but with Ben she was beginning to realise he was someone who often did the unexpected. She'd done nothing of the sort, until now. She'd done everything she was supposed to do. She'd graduated from university, got her first job as a midwife, had every

Friday and Saturday night out with her mates, and the most she'd veered away from being conservative was to order takeout on a Tuesday night. She'd even done everything she was supposed to with Julia, and look how that had turned out. Her brother's wedding had started Molly thinking about making some changes, even if all it meant was getting on a plane, and now, at thirty years old, flying to the other side of the world to meet a total stranger was the first thing she'd ever really done outside the norm.

After chatting with Ben, Molly spent the rest of the day making the most of the new surroundings. She caught the tram to the city, loving the ting of the bell as they approached lights or warned a pedestrian who'd crossed the road dangerously. Ting, ting, ting went the bell – coming through! She loved it. She went up to the top of Eureka SkyDeck and dared to walk out on The Edge, the almost three-hundred-metre glass cube suspended above Melbourne city. Up there she felt invincible, like nothing could go wrong for her now.

She stopped for a hot chocolate at a quaint café in one of Melbourne's laneways, she checked out the famous domed structure of Flinders Street Station, dodging out of the way of commuters as they raced for their trains. She bought a woollen dress at the big department store in Bourke Street, crossing over a smaller road to go in the other side before realising she'd ended up in a different shop entirely. And when her jet lag caught up with her, she caught the tram back to South Yarra, watching out the window and gazing upon green spaces freshened up by last night's downpour.

Back at the apartment Molly boiled the kettle and made a cup of tea. She sat at the table and hopped onto Facebook again, ready to chat with Ben. He'd sent her a longer message this time, telling her all about his trip to Sentosa Island and Resort World. He'd sent her a photo of him and Seb on a ride called the Luge, his long legs bunched right up as he tried to fit on the thing. She'd laughed at his story about the most revolting nachos he'd ever tasted with warm, puke-like cheese and a runny salsa. He suggested she check out the impressive Crown Casino during her time in Melbourne, and he asked her how she felt about meeting Andrew Bennett.

Molly: I honestly don't know how to feel. The euphoria from the flight has kept me going till now, but I'm starting to get nervous about the whole thing.

Ben: You can't back out now!

Molly: I won't.

Ben: Good. And the offer still stands. I'll be back in Melbourne soon, and if you want to meet up, I'm all yours.

Molly: Goodnight, Ben, jet lag has defeated me today.

Ben: I'll take that as a yes! Goodnight, Molly, sweet dreams. x

She smiled at the 'x', and although she didn't reply with a kiss in return, she did go to bed thinking about him, her tiredness the only reason he didn't leap into her dreams.

*

Two days later Molly's jet lag had subsided a little, and with the sun in the sky, she collected a hire car and programmed the satnav with the postcode for Magnolia Creek Holiday Cottages.

This was it. She was really doing this.

Molly enjoyed the freedom on the drive, the space you didn't get in England crammed up on the motorways, going nowhere, pulling in and out of parked cars on tiny side streets that were the only way to get through some towns. She sipped from her bottle of water at her side and let the satnav do the thinking as the wind blew through the open windows and lifted tendrils of dark hair around the sides of her face.

The countryside was amazing, or was it the bush? She really had no idea in this foreign country, but whatever it was called, it was stunning scenery to drive through. She smiled at unfamiliar signposts and read words out loud: Murrindindi … what a funny word that was. But then, finally a name she knew as the road narrowed and the trees formed a canopy overhead.

A sign in big, swirly writing said: Welcome to Magnolia Creek.

She was here. She was going to meet Andrew Bennett.

Chapter Twenty
Andrew

'How could you?' Andrew repeated, over and over. He got to his feet, paced the kitchen.

Louis looked at the floor. 'I'm so—'

'Don't you dare say you're sorry!' Andrew's fists balled against his sides, his head hung as low as it could go. He leant against the kitchen bench for balance.

'I'll be upstairs if you need me.' Gemma had stayed while Louis told his story, but now she put a hand to Andrew's shoulder, and he briefly touched his cheek to her skin. He felt her grip holding him, holding him up from all of this, until she retreated from the room and the kitchen fell into silence.

'How could you do it, Dad?'

He'd trusted this man sitting at the kitchen table. He'd trusted him his whole life. This man he loved and respected; a man who'd betrayed him so brutally.

'You had no right to do it!' Andrew yelled. 'I might have been young, but I wasn't stupid.'

'I don't know what to say, son.'

'How could you pay her mother to get rid of our baby, part of your own flesh and blood?' Andrew spat.

'I did it because I thought she'd ruin you. She said as much.'

'But the sex was consensual.'

'She would've twisted it, maybe even persuaded Julia to say the same. God knows what the woman was capable of.'

‘All this time … all this time, I’ve despised Julia for not having the decency to face me and tell me what she had planned. And all along, she didn’t even do anything wrong.’ He thought about Julia as a teenager, giggling as they listened to the radio in his bedroom, her cheek as soft as silk against his as they both promised silently to never love another. He sat opposite Louis now, unable to stop himself worrying at how pale his father was, how weak. But no, this wasn’t about Louis today. This was about him. About Julia. About the child he’d never met.

‘I didn’t see I had any choice,’ Louis said quietly. ‘I had to give her the money or she’d have dragged your name through the mud and I didn’t want to take the risk.’

‘We could’ve tried.’ Andrew shook his head.

‘I didn’t want you to settle either.’

‘I’m not sure I follow.’

‘I didn’t want you to settle, like I did,’ he mumbled.

‘What are you talking about?’

Louis rubbed at his swollen fingers. ‘When your mum fell pregnant, there was no discussion about what we would do. What you did in those days was you got married and that was the end of it.’ When Andrew looked at him, he said, ‘I loved your mother, we were good together and really close friends. But I’m not sure I ever loved her the way you should. The way you love Gemma, like she’s a jewel at the bottom of the ocean, someone you found and keep looking at as though you can’t believe your luck.

‘Penny was younger than me, she was besotted, and we had a lot of fun when we first got together. But I’d already decided what I wanted to do, career wise, and I was going to go off to make my name in the world as a pastry chef in America or Europe.’

‘But you did all that, here in Australia.’

Louis shook his head. 'I should've been applying for apprenticeships instead of running around with a girl. I lost my focus and the next thing I knew, Penny was pregnant. I was in a job I didn't mind, but not an exciting job given my ambition. But it paid the bills and so that's where I stayed when I married. It wasn't Penny's fault, not at all, but when you were a baby I resented her for tying me down.'

'It takes two to make a baby, Dad.'

'I know it does.' His breathing sounded raspy, but Andrew didn't ask whether he was okay. 'I wanted you to fall in love,' he wheezed, 'have everything, including the one part of my life that perhaps I was missing. I was a horrible husband for a while, angry because I wasn't doing the things I wanted to do. I battled with it until my own father gave me a stern talking to. He told me I had responsibilities. He told me not to let them down. And I did love your mother. I learned what true love really was, right up until the day she died, but I had a life with tinges of regret that I'd never found a love that was so passionate it was all-consuming. A love I couldn't live without. You change a lot in your late teens and early twenties. It's the age you really start to learn about yourself, and believe me, it's much easier to do when you only have yourself to think about. My love with your mother grew out of mutual respect and friendship, but it didn't come naturally. I didn't want you to face the same battle.'

'I loved Julia,' said Andrew. 'I know fifteen is young, and maybe we wouldn't have stayed together anyway if she hadn't got pregnant, but you had no right to take the choice away from me. We both deserved to find out for ourselves.'

Louis nodded but stayed silent.

Andrew was mildly aware of the sounds from upstairs: Gemma flushing the toilet, using the sink to clean her teeth as she got ready for bed, waiting for him to find out what had happened. Waiting to see if he yelled, screamed at his dad, threw something else. He watched Louis, the elderly man who looked as though his world was rapidly falling apart around him, just as his had done all those years ago. The lines on his face always spoke of wisdom and experience, but right now all they looked like to Andrew were marks from the lies he'd told.

Andrew pushed back from the table, scraped both hands through his hair. 'This all feels like a hellish nightmare to me. I don't understand how any of you could rest easy after you did it … the money, the letters. It was all such a ruthless and sick plan. I can't believe you played any part in it.'

'I can't believe Julia had the baby,' said Louis, hands shaking. 'Kathleen assured me she wasn't going to let it happen. She was so sure of what she wanted for her child. If I'd have known, I–'

'You what? You would've taken her to the clinic yourself?' Andrew's voice went up enough to bring Gemma down to the kitchen in her pyjamas.

Louis met Andrew's stare for the first time. 'I don't know what we would've done had Julia wanted to keep the baby and you wanted to stand by her.'

'What you would've done? You would've stood by me, Dad, like any normal parent!'

'I wanted what was best for you!' Louis' raised his voice the best he could. 'What any parent wants.'

'Well, I hope if I ever become a parent,' said Andrew, 'I do a damn sight better than you.'

‘Andrew …’ When Gemma came into the kitchen, she touched him on the arm. ‘Enough.’ She went over to Louis who was struggling for breath now. ‘Slowly, Louis, slowly.’ She put a hand on her father-in-law’s back and held his hand with her other, trying to calm him.

Louis squeezed Gemma’s hand before continuing. ‘We did what we thought best. For our child. When you become a parent—’

‘Don’t you dare talk to me about becoming a parent! Thanks to you I never ever got the chance to be one. And by some cruel twist of fate, it’s not happening for Gemma and me either. God, I can’t believe this.’

‘I’ll go. Let you digest this.’ Louis stood up from the table, shuffled across the kitchen.

Andrew flew across the room, his face inches from his father’s. ‘I will never forgive you for this, never.’

Louis’ body shook, his hand on the back door. Andrew didn’t know if he’d ever look at his dad in the same way again. How he’d ever have the respect and love he’d once had for him. He wasn’t sure they could move on from this.

‘You broke both of our hearts that day,’ he told Louis. ‘We were fifteen years old and we were fucking terrified. And you were responsible. You. You were the reason for my unhappiness, for what Julia went through on her own, responsible for my daughter, who is out there somewhere probably convinced she wasn’t wanted.’

Louis pushed the door handle down to make his escape.

‘How can I give you a part of me knowing what you took away from me?’ Andrew yelled after him.

Gemma put a hand on his arm. ‘Andrew, don’t say anything you’ll regret.’

But Andrew wasn’t finished.

‘Your kidneys may be failing, but your sense of compassion disappeared back then when you ruined three peoples’ lives.’

‘Andrew!’ Gemma was desperate now.

‘No, Gemma.’ Andrew looked at his father. ‘I won’t do it. I won’t go through the pain of an operation to save you. You can go to hell!’

Andrew stormed out of the kitchen, away from the father he didn’t think he’d ever be able to respect again.

Chapter Twenty-One

Molly

Magnolia Creek was as picturesque as its name suggested. Molly drove along Main Street with its shops on either side, but with someone right behind her, she didn't have time to slow and look for Magnolia Creek Chocolaterie. She followed the signs to Magnolia House, a huge white structure with a veranda at the front, and drove round to a modest tarmac car park at the rear servicing a row of eight holiday cottages. It was such a beautiful day, and when she knew the mid-March weather back home would be fighting to grab a tenth of the sunshine she'd had in her short time here, it made her want to stay outside. In truth, she wanted to bask in the holiday weather and not have to tackle the reason she'd come.

Stepping out into the sunshine and a cool autumn breeze, Molly lifted her suitcase from the boot and stood for a moment beside the magnolia trees, which were naked save for a few burgundy leaves. This bushland setting was a complete contrast to the hustle and bustle of Melbourne's city with its trams, tall buildings and vibrant culture. The photograph of this place on the internet had shown the magnolia trees in full bloom with port wine leaves against the stunning whitewash of the cottages with their miniature verandas and tiny doorways, but even with the change of season, the cottages looked delightful. She took in the view of the lake as she walked over to the main house to check in.

Molly collected her key and went over to let herself in to cottage number six. The front door led into a dinky square hallway with a skylight fitted into the pointed roof. Off one side was a double bedroom and small en-suite bathroom, much like a holiday cottage in Cornwall, with seashells collected in an ocean-blue china bowl, photographs of sandy beaches strung together with old rope hanging on the wall by the mirror. The bed was made up with pale blue linen, fluffy ice-white cushions sitting on top, a white satin runner at the foot of the bed.

The lounge room was off to the left of the front door, and off that a kitchenette, which was modern and bright. All rooms in the cottage carried on the themes of sea blues and pearly whites, and she wondered whether all eight cottages were the same. Tea and coffee supplies had been added, two scones sat beneath a see-through cloche and Molly couldn't resist lifting it to inhale the fresh smell. And with her suitcase still at her feet, she spread one with the awaiting jam and cream and tucked in hungrily.

After she'd eaten, Molly wheeled her case into the bedroom and sat on the edge of the bed. This was certainly a step up from the basic and tired-looking little apartment in South Yarra. The window in the bedroom had been left open, and Molly checked for bugs, relieved to find the fly-screen covering the open gap to stop anything getting in. And when she saw the little basket beside the bed containing a selection of chocolates, her heart leapt. Little luxuries were a big thing in her book.

She unwrapped the first and tasted a hint of orange, and then she unwrapped another two, both milk chocolate mint. She threw the rubbish in the bin, and it was only as she reached for the fourth chocolate, that she noticed the inscription on the wrapping: Magnolia Creek Chocolaterie.

Her jaw stopped working as she wondered whether Andrew Bennett had been inside this cottage himself, whether he'd laid the chocolates in the delicate straw baskets for the guests.

Don't be stupid, Molly. Of course he hadn't.

But then again, he could've made them in the first place, his hands could've wrapped them.

This was driving her insane.

The sooner she got out there and did what she came here to do, the better.

*

Molly took a full hour to psych herself up to venture outside of her cottage. She showered, changed – twice – ending up in the same pale pink shirt and dark denim jeans she'd had on in the first place. She'd brushed her hair more times than a fairy princess, preened what little make-up she had on and hummed and hawed about whether to wear her flip-flops or more sensible attire for walking and exploring.

When she finally left the cottage and stepped off the miniature veranda at the front, the sun reflected off the lake and she pulled her sunglasses down. She followed the curve of the wall past the swaying branches of the surrounding trees, past Magnolia House where a redhead was stringing up fairy lights. She followed the path up to Main Street, but when she reached the top she started to feel afraid. She wished she'd logged on and got a talking to from Ben before this moment, but they'd messaged this morning and he was about to catch his flight from Singapore. She wondered whether they'd ever meet again. He'd offered to meet in the city. He seemed keen, and she had to admit, so was she. She was intrigued about him, this caring man who people looked up to in their Facebook group and all because of what? Because he'd got over his fear of flying and they wished they could too? He was a great mentor and encouraging to others and this thought warmed Molly as much as the sun on her back as she carried on walking. She'd trusted him right from the start and had no explanation as to why. They'd simply fallen into a friendship, and it felt right.

She paused opposite a shop undergoing renovations. She couldn't make out what the sign in the window said from here. She'd heard there had been bushfires last year, and when she looked to the right, she could see blackened trees, still standing tall, refusing to be defeated. This place felt strong, it had a presence, but it didn't make her feel any less nervous. She continued on her way and nodded a hello to a lady with bright red lipstick and dark wavy hair that caught the light. And when Molly reached Magnolia Gifts she stopped, still. She knew from her Google research that the chocolaterie would be the next stop.

Molly pretended to look in the window of the gift shop as a teenager emerged from the chocolaterie, licking at an ice cream. It looked like rum and raisin, her favourite. Behind her a blonde woman manoeuvred a wooden board outside and crouched down to write on it. She used several different coloured chalks, and when she pushed herself to standing, Molly saw she'd drawn a picture of an ice cream in a cone with a wafer sticking out one side. She'd written a list of flavours: cookies & cream, rum & raisin, strawberry, chocolate, honeycomb, mint choc chip. The woman turned, smiled and went back into the shop and Molly turned back in the opposite direction, bumping into the same dark-haired woman as before.

'Whoa, slow down there missy,' said the woman, smiling.

'I'm sorry, I forgot my purse.' Molly scurried past her and didn't hear what the woman said in her wake.

When Molly reached the lake again the fear subsided. She hadn't even made it to the entrance of the chocolaterie, let alone any nearer to Andrew Bennett. She could imagine it now. Going back home to the UK and saying to everyone, 'Hey, I spent hundreds of pounds on a flight to Australia, got over my fear of flying and it was so worth it … I could practically smell the chocolate itself. Hey, maybe next time I'll actually make it to the doorway and meet the man I went to see in the first place.'

Molly sat by the lake a while. She dipped her hand into the water. It was colder than she'd imagined. For some reason she'd never associated cold, or winter, with Australia. It always seemed to her to be a tropical place, with nothing but sun, sea and sand.

She climbed up onto the low wall, and balancing, walked most of the way round before she heard a voice behind her.

'Careful you don't fall in.' It was the woman she'd seen writing the sign outside the chocolaterie. Her neat, blonde bobbed hair swung gently when she walked, a wide, shallow straw basket looped over her arm, and she was very pretty as she smiled. 'Are you staying at the cottages?'

Molly jumped from the wall to dry land. 'I'm in cottage number six.'

'How long are you staying for?'

‘Until the Easter weekend.’ Molly wondered how many times she could get back onto the wall and walk back and forth without falling in. How many hours could she waste messing about before the chocolaterie was shut and she no longer felt as though she should be doing what she came here to do?

‘Well, welcome to Magnolia Creek,’ said the woman. ‘Did you like the chocolates?’

Molly noticed the contents of the basket, the looping silver Magnolia Creek Chocolaterie writing on each of them, the lettering standing out against the brown background of the wrappers.

‘It’s a new thing we’re trying,’ the woman continued. ‘My husband and I are attempting a little marketing ploy.’ She winked at Molly, who stood gawping in return. ‘You should stop by sometime, buy some souvenirs. Where are you from?’

‘England,’ Molly said in a small voice as it dawned on her that this was Andrew Bennett’s wife.

‘I’m sure the folks back home would love these.’ Thank God she didn’t ask why Molly was here. ‘I’m Gemma by the way. Ask for me by name if you do come in and I’ll make sure we give you some tasters.’

And off Gemma went, humming a tune Molly didn’t recognise and completely unaware of Molly still standing in the same place, fixed to the spot, too shocked to move.

*

In the evening Molly messaged Ben, but when he still didn’t reply, she gave up and went out for a walk. This time, she was definitely walking right past the chocolaterie. Or at least up to the doorway. There was no risk involved. This man had no idea who she was, and as long as it stayed that way for now, perhaps for a day or two, then nothing could actually hurt her.

Nothing could go wrong until she let it.

Molly turned the corner and her heart thumped against her chest. She got all the way past the gift shop and right up to the chocolaterie. And she breathed an enormous sigh of relief when she saw the sign on the door: Closed.

A rapping from the other side of the curved window suggested otherwise. 'Hey!' It was Gemma, crouching down, putting together some kind of Easter display with colourful eggs and bunting, and now she was positioning a basket with what looked like a giant egg in it, wrapped in shiny purple foil wrapping.

Molly reluctantly lifted a hand to wave back. She tried to go on her way, but Gemma came out before she made it past the doorway.

'Hi, remember me from earlier? Gemma,' she prompted.

'I remember.' Molly nodded, and then because Gemma's look begged the question, said, 'I'm Molly.'

'It's nice to see you again, Molly. I'll see you around?'

It was a question rather than a statement. She wished Gemma wasn't so nice. It'd be easier if she was a real cow because right now with her sparkling eyes, friendly smile and a certain innocence, she had no idea of the bombshell about to blow up in her life. 'I'm sure I'll come in the shop before long,' said Molly.

'Please do. We're a friendly bunch in this town.'

Molly said goodbye and continued on her way, nerves pervading every part of her. It could easily have been Andrew she'd bumped into just now, instead of Gemma. How would she have reacted then?

Walking along Main Street, Molly finally came to the town pub, Magnolia Tavern. It had the same Olde Worlde feel she was used to with English pubs, with a weathered brick exterior and its name hanging from two chains attached to the post out front. The beer garden was dotted with tables, and fairy lights were strung in the branches and already switched on, ready for the darkness to descend.

She pushed the door open, relieved a local's silence didn't fall across the entire room. A few years ago, before Isaac had met Claire, Molly and her brother had gone through a phase known as Boring Sunday Syndrome and each week had taken turns to drive out into the countryside, the satnav switched off, no navigation other than an impromptu 'turn right' or 'turn left' when they reached a crossroads. Their antics saw them discover pubs all over Somerset, some less welcoming than others. One pub in particular had been terrible. They'd pushed open the door, and the entire room had fallen deathly silent. Pints fell from open mouths, the chatter of women came to a stop, eyes burrowed into them as they bought two orange juices, downed them as quickly as they could, and escaped into the fresh air.

'Hello there.' The man standing at the beer pumps greeted Molly with a smile when she went in and sat down on a stool at the mahogany curved bar.

'Hi. I'll have a bottle of Budweiser, please.' She was relieved to see the familiar-looking brand in the glass-fronted fridge.

He deftly flipped the metal top from the bottle using the opener attached to the bar. 'I'm Chris, the landlord here. It's nice to meet you.'

'It's nice to meet you too, and I'm Molly.'

‘Just visiting, Molly?’

‘I’m on holiday, over from England.’ She welcomed the cool amber liquid of the beer as it rid her of some of the stress from her day, coming face-to-face with a member of Andrew Bennett’s family.

‘England you say?’ He leant against the bar, tea towel slung across his shoulder, deep brown eyes inquisitive as a landlord’s should be. You couldn’t be an antisocial bugger to work in a place like this … a love of people was surely a prerequisite. ‘I’ve never been there myself. My wife keeps saying we’ll go on a tour of Europe when we retire, but I don’t know, there’s plenty to see here. I’ve got visions of hiring one of those enormous campervans – a Winnebago – just me and the wife, travel round the edge of Australia taking a couple of months.’

Molly smiled, loving the way he talked so openly when they’d only met moments ago. He looked like he’d disappeared on his travels already, at least in his head. She wondered whether his wife was the typical woman, and instead of seeing the adventure he saw, she couldn’t see past the endless days of being couped up in a tin on four wheels, a bed that probably doubled as the dinner table and a toilet you had to empty periodically.

Chris beckoned to a man over in the corner who came to collect his drinks.

The man in question was good looking with dark hair, and he was tall. The tail end of a tattoo on his arm poked out from the sleeve of his T-shirt as he reached for the drinks left to settle beneath the pump before the landlord topped them up.

‘Where’s your brother, Owen?’ Chris asked the man. ‘I hear he’s back in town.’

‘He sure is.’ The man smiled. ‘He’s on his way.’

‘Good lad, that one.’ Chris nodded in Owen’s direction when he left to take the drinks over to a table with three chairs and the girl with red hair who Molly had seen earlier as she strung up lights at Magnolia House. She figured the brother would be claiming his pint soon.

‘And Rosie’s a lovely lass,’ Chris continued. ‘She moved here from the city last year and they live up at Rosie Cottage.’

‘Lovely name,’ said Molly. ‘Is the cottage named after her?’

‘It is,’ Chris smiled. ‘Owen looks rough and ready, fights fires in his spare time, but he’s an old romantic at heart.’

Molly smiled. ‘Do you know everyone in this town?’

Chris emptied a drip tray into a bucket. ‘Pretty much. Lived here my whole life. Fair dinkum,’ he added when Molly looked suitably impressed.

She giggled at the colloquialism. She intended to ask about the chocolaterie, but she didn’t have to say a word because Chris got there all by himself. He talked about Bella and Rodney Finnegan and how many years they’d been in Magnolia Creek, the school at the top of the hill where his daughter Stephanie had been a student and the fires that had come this way and destroyed so much of the surrounding bush.

‘The newest recruits are the Bennetts,’ he said.

Molly’s beer bottle paused before she drank the last dregs.

‘Can I get you another?’

‘Yes, please,’ she managed to say. She prayed he wouldn’t forget his train of thought.

He flicked the top off the bottle and placed it on the bar. ‘The Bennetts own Magnolia Creek Chocolaterie.’

He looked around, checked nobody else was within earshot. 'It's a dream come true for chocoholics like me. Don't tell the wife' – he patted a portly belly – 'she'd have me dining with rabbits on lettuce if she could.'

'You should go for the dark chocolate, it's got health benefits.' Molly sipped her drink. 'Tell your wife. And also tell her it's supposed to be an aphrodisiac.'

Chris laughed. 'I don't know about that, but it's definitely popular around here. The Bennetts seem like fine people too. And fine people always fit in well in Magnolia Creek.'

Chris looked up as the door opened. 'Ah, look what the cat dragged in! Welcome back, stranger!'

A raucous cheer went up, and Molly turned on her stool to face the newest customer tonight, but as Owen whistled to his brother and held the fresh pint aloft to get his attention, the only eyes this man had were for Molly. And Molly couldn't take her gaze away from him either.

'Molly?' In disbelief, Ben's eyes crinkled at the sides, his smile revealed a slight dimple in his right cheek. She hadn't noticed it on the plane. She'd been sitting to the left of him – maybe that was it – or else he hadn't smiled as big as this until now.

Molly hopped down from her stool and stepped towards him. He closed the gap and hugged her before pulling back, his hands on the tops of her arms. 'I can't believe you're here.'

'It's a bit crazy, isn't it?'

'When you said Melbourne, I never would've thought you'd be all the way out here. I thought you'd be in a trendy, beachy suburb somewhere.' He pulled a face. 'Wait a minute … are you stalking me?'

'I was here first,' she laughed.

His brother was looking their way, and Molly didn't miss Chris giving them the odd glance.

A faint layer of stubble lighter than Ben's hair covered his chin … she expected he'd had more fun things to do in Singapore than shave and keep himself shipshape.

'I still can't get over it,' said Ben.

'Stop gawping at her,' Owen called over. 'And get the girl another drink!'

'I suppose I'd better.' Ben didn't turn his body or his gaze away from her, and when the door to the pub creaked open again, she was too busy smiling at Ben to notice who had walked in.

Two men went up to the bar. One patted Ben on the shoulder in greeting, and it was then Molly realised who the other man was.

It was him. It was Andrew Bennett.

Molly went hot all over. Her throat felt as though it was closing up. Ben was asking if she was okay, but eyes wide, mouth dry, she bolted. She went out of the door, without a word to anyone, straight past Andrew Bennett and out into the cool early evening and beneath a few spots of rain, she simply ran.

She ran past the chocolaterie without a moment's thought, past the gift shop and to the end of the street where she stopped at a corner. She could see a fire station ahead but turned right to go round the back and down to the lake where Magnolia House and the cottages sat.

'Molly, wait!' It was Ben, behind her, shouting.

She stopped and doubled over, hands on knees. Heart racing, chest pounding, the black sky above her spinning as she stood tall again. She couldn't catch her breath, she felt as though she was going to faint.

A hand on her shoulder steadied her. 'Breathe, Molly. Breathe. In, out, in, out.' Ben's voice soothed her.

She tried to focus on his voice, let him lead her over to the gum trees marking the top of the path. And leaning against the trunk of a tree, she felt calm quiver its way through her as she breathed in, then out, over and over again. The dizziness abated, the pressure on her chest lessened.

'My God, you can run.' He put his hands gently on her shoulders. 'I hope you know I've left a pretty good pint of Guinness in there waiting for me.'

Molly managed a smile.

'You had a panic attack,' he told her. 'What happened back there? I know it's a shock seeing me, but—'

'That was him.'

'Who?'

'My birth father.' She closed her eyes, it helped her to concentrate on breathing normally. She'd never had a panic attack, not in all the time she'd been terrified of flying, not in life-threatening situations at work, never.

'Your birth father? In the pub?' Ben got to his feet. 'That was him!'

'Yes. Andrew Bennett.'

Ben sighed, and then he started to laugh and slumped against the tree next to her.

'It's not funny. It's the first time I've seen him.'

'It's not that.' He was still laughing.

'Then what?'

'He walked in with *my* dad. For a minute I thought … well, I thought …'

Molly laughed out loud, wondering if the swaying branches of the trees above would carry her whispers to the pub and tell Andrew Bennett all about her without her having to. She looked up at the stars starting to make their grand entrance in the sky. The moon crept out from behind the white pointed roof of Magnolia House.

Ben smiled. 'Of course, my dad is no chocolatier so I should've known, but let's just say we've had a bit of strife in our family regarding paternity. It's a touchy subject. I won't go into detail now, it's family stuff, but it could be why I was a bit more understanding than others might be, when you told me about your search.'

'You were adopted?' Molly asked.

'No, but there were family secrets and the truth took a long time to come out. The man in question, my brother's biological father, isn't likely to ever be a part of our lives. Something we're all grateful for. But the secrecy did make me wonder, when it came to your situation, whether this birth father of yours has his own story, a story that needs to be told by him, and only him. It's the reason I encouraged you to find him.'

'I still can't believe you're here, standing next to me,' said Molly.

'Neither can I. Small world, eh?'

Molly giggled, mostly from nerves.

'What's funny?'

'The look of panic on your face that we could be related.'

He blew air out from between his lips. 'Yeah, not funny at all. If we were related, it would mean nothing could ever happen between us.'

She laughed loudly this time. 'Never going to happen.'

Who was she trying to convince? Him? Or herself?

'That's what they all say. Where are you staying?'

She tipped her head in the direction of the lake and the holiday cottages beyond. She knew his dimple would be back now as she felt his smile on her, but she didn't look up at his face as they walked down past the lake, dark but ever present. She'd felt a pull to him even when they only knew one another online, then again after the plane journey he'd helped her through. And seeing him tonight had felt like coming home in a way she couldn't explain.

'You know,' said Ben when they reached Molly's cottage, 'you can't run a mile each time Andrew Bennett comes near. You need to let him know who you are.'

She leant against the white wood of the veranda. 'I know.'

Ben took out his phone. 'Sorry, it's Owen. He's getting impatient.' He declined the call.

'Do you know anything about him?'

'Owen, or the chocolatier?' He grinned.

'You know who I mean.'

'All I really know is that he's new to town.'

'But he knows your dad. They were chatting when they walked in.'

'It's a small town, Molly. Everyone knows everyone else. But if you like, I'll ask about him, you know, casually. See what I can find out.'

She smiled sheepishly. 'Thank you, Ben.'

'I'd better go and have that Guinness. Are you sure you won't come back with me? Rosie and Owen are a good laugh.'

'I can't, not with him in there.' She didn't need to explain who she was referring to.

He smiled. 'Then have a good sleep, Molly.'

'You too, goodnight.'

When he'd gone, Molly stood at the tiny front room window, the light off so she could watch him go back the way they'd come. Was fate trying to tell her something by having Ben turn up in the small town where her birth father lived? She smiled at the thought as Ben disappeared into the darkness, but the smile was replaced by a frown when she thought about what she still had to do.

Tomorrow, it was time to confront her past and face the man she'd really travelled across the world to find.

Chapter Twenty-Two

Andrew

Andrew arrived home from the pub and staggered up the stairs. He'd avoided Louis, avoided Gemma and found comfort in the amber nectar, tipping it down his throat as though it were water. He'd found company too, good company who knew nothing of the latest family saga. He and Michael Harrison had talked sport. They'd talked about the idea of a trip to Europe for Andrew to attend a chocolate conference, and somehow Michael must've sensed all was not right because, despite a medical background, he didn't once mention the kidney transplant.

Andrew fell into bed. Gemma was asleep already, but facing away from her he fell into a fitful sleep. He was awake at two, three-thirty and then again at five a.m., thirsty as hell. He went to the kitchen and downed two big glasses of water and then went into the study and turned on the computer. The only woman he should be thinking about right now was Gemma and how she was handling all this shit that kept getting thrown at her from a great height. But the only girl he could think of was Julia. All these years he'd thought she was a bitch for walking away, a traitor for aborting their baby without a care in the world. Since he'd discovered the truth, those feelings had morphed into something unrecognisable, a fireball of anger, hate, spite, bitterness and regret that he didn't have a clue how to control.

It took him an hour to write the message to Julia this time. He deleted sentences and rewrote them. He deleted whole paragraphs, added them in again, deleted them a second time. How could you find the words to tell someone how their parents had betrayed them, how they'd supposedly acted in their best interests?

The next morning, Andrew showered away some of the hangover. Emilio was covering for him at the shop first thing so it was a later start than usual, and in the kitchen at home he cooked two fried eggs, toast and mushrooms. No need to be healthy any more … he had no operation coming up. He was free to pile as much cholesterol into his body as he liked, put away as much alcohol as it took to numb the pain. When the eggs were cooked he even shook salt across the tops of the yolks, more making a point than because he needed the hit.

'What time did you get in last night?' Gemma didn't comment on his breakfast, which was a complete contrast to his usual muesli or wholegrain toast.

'Late.' He stabbed the square of toast he'd cut, dabbed it in the yolk and watched yellow explode all over the white plate.

'There's caramel mixture in the fridge,' said Gemma.

'Thanks.'

Gemma pulled out a fruit salad she must've prepared the night before. For Louis, Andrew assumed.

He said nothing.

Before she opened the back door, Gemma stopped. She came over to the table and pulled her pale grey cardigan tight around her torso. 'Can't you talk to him?'

Face like thunder, Andrew looked up at her.

She retreated and at the back door said, 'Think about it. He's your father. And he's dying.'

She let the screen door slam shut behind her.

*

The chocolaterie was quiet when Andrew arrived an hour later. Kids were in school, tourists were yet to surface and Andrew lost himself in the joy of his work, his first task to progress through the to-do list out back: white chocolate discs covered in multicoloured sprinkles, frogs in dark chocolate and milk, milk chocolate bunnies to make now it was approaching Easter and people prepared for the Easter Bunny's arrival. He also had the order for the Easter Egg Hunt to fulfil, and he was glad to be so busy. It took his mind away from his family, to a place it needed to be so he didn't do or say anything else rash.

Emilio came through from the shopfront. 'We need more hollow milk chocolate eggs. They're selling out early this year.'

'Good idea. Can you mark down dark chocolate eggs too? I think we'll need more before long. Oh, and you can take the chocolate discs from the fridge. They're ready for packaging.'

'I'll get right to it.' said Emilio.

Andrew felt the tension ebb out of him as he worked. His shoulders relaxed as he filled a jug of dark chocolate from the tempering machine and tipped the mixture into a mould of bunny shapes. He held the filled mould on the vibrating grill covering the machine, watched as the chocolate levelled out into place. He did the same for another three trays and set them all to dry.

Business was thriving. At least something was.

'Everything on the left-hand side of me is ready for packaging,' he told Emilio, who was wrapping up chocolate discs. Andrew had already assigned the lot numbers, essential for identifying the chocolate and the date it was made should any issues arise. He ran Emilio through the labels he'd already printed to ensure the correct one matched the correct chocolates ready to be packaged up.

Out front, Andrew refilled a shelf with long plastic tubes containing miniature chocolate koalas and kangaroos and checked supplies in the ice cream freezer at the front counter. Honeycomb was a popular flavour this year, and he'd be sure to reorder it within plenty of time. He liked to keep his customers happy.

'Good morning.' He greeted his latest customer, a young woman he'd seen last night at the pub, briefly. She had dark hair and was wearing a red and black checked shirt. He didn't usually notice such things, but Gemma had a similar one. Her cropped jeans and Converse shoes looked typical of a young tourist, and he wondered what it was like not to have a care in the world, to be out in the beautiful countryside able to saunter into a chocolaterie and browse.

Oh the simplicity of youth.

He filled another shelf with white chocolate discs and helped the local veterinarian choose between a chocolate shoe, chocolate handbag or a chocolate flower basket as a gift, and when he rang up the order, the same girl was still browsing. Or was she? Perhaps she was lurking and trying to steal something, but given the fitted jeans he wasn't sure where she was going to stuff any of these packaged chocolates, let alone stop the rustling of the cellophane as she tried to make her escape.

He clasped his hands together as he approached her. She was engrossed reading the label on the back of the giant koala. 'Can I help you?'

'I was just … er …'

'Sorry,' he held up a hand, 'didn't mean to startle you. I wondered if you were looking for anything in particular.'

‘Er … chocolate,’ she stammered.

His head tilted to the side. ‘Then you’ve come to the right place.’

Her eyes darted around. ‘Workshop,’ she added. ‘I was interested in the chocolate workshop.’

‘Oh, right.’ He went behind the counter and took out the diary for upcoming slots. ‘Well, our next chocolate lovers’ workshop is …’ he flicked over a page, ‘this afternoon, three-fifteen.’ He’d thought about cancelling it because Gemma couldn’t take the workshop, and given his hangover he wasn’t keen on running it. But that was no way to conduct a business. ‘There are four other people down. Would you like me to add you?’

She seemed reluctant to come forward, reluctant to speak. ‘Yes,’ she whispered from the other side of the shop.

‘If you come to the till,’ he suggested, ‘I can take some details.’

She was a striking young lady when she got up close: dark hair, rich hazel eyes as round as a film star’s.

‘Sure. My name … my name is Molly. I’m staying at the cottages.’ She pointed to the back of the shop and he knew she meant those cottages at Magnolia House, which pretty much sat directly behind but at a distance.

‘And do you have a phone number, Molly? A number I can reach you on if the workshop is cancelled?’

‘Is it likely to be?’

He shook his head. ‘Nope. Not unless something happens to me.’ He smiled, and she froze like a possum, big eyes wide, spotted running across the top of the roof as night fell.

She gave him her number.

‘You’re English,’ he noted.

She nodded.

'So am I.'

She cleared her throat. 'You are?'

'Moved here in my teens.'

She didn't seem keen to engage in further conversation so he said, 'We'll see you this afternoon.' And off she went.

Andrew went upstairs to the café. It was deserted up there, but he wiped down a few of the tables, mopped up a milk spill and replenished napkins from the supply in the cupboard beneath the till. He went outside to the balcony and looked out over the bush. The shopfront had grabbed Gemma when they'd first looked at buying this place, but for him, it was this. Looking out over the bush and the tip of the roof of Magnolia House, this was a dream location.

Back downstairs, he reordered honeycomb ice cream, and when he served another customer at the counter, he saw her again. Molly. She was standing out front, looking at the shop, peering up at the sign.

He shook his head. An odd young woman, that one.

*

Gemma had been in to the chocolaterie at lunchtime. She was occasionally able to take a break, if she wasn't on playground duty, and would walk down the hill to see Andrew. Sometimes they'd walk by the lake and sit in the sunshine, appreciate the calm before they both went their separate ways back to work. But today all she'd done was try to talk to him about Louis. It was the same thing, again and again, how she knew he was hurting but at the same time telling him what he already knew. His refusal to speak to his father was most likely going to kill him. But he couldn't look the man in the eye, let alone anything else. Gemma had taken over all of Louis' runs to and from the hospital to do his dialysis. It was an hour's round trip, and while he knew how unfair it was to his wife, he couldn't bear to relieve her of any of the pressure. If he sat next to his father in a car, he thought he might kill him with his bare hands, never mind by denying him a kidney.

'You've got fifteen minutes.' Stephanie poked her head around the corner of the room where the workshop was to be held that afternoon. Bella had signed up – Andrew knew she was bored with the café still out of action – and Rosie and Rebecca from Magnolia House were coming along too. They'd been talking about learning more ever since the chocolate fountain at the wedding.

Andrew lay out moulds on each table, a jug, flat trays with no edges, three small metal bowls filled with three types of couverture chocolate: milk, dark and white. He put out several tiny metal bowls filled with decorations: dried, crushed strawberry pieces, gold lustre dust, sprinkles. He positioned a laptop at the desk at the front of the room and ensured the media was up and running to do his presentation he'd named From Bean to Block, meaning how the chocolate from the cocoa bean eventually became the chocolate you bought in his chocolaterie.

When he looked up he saw his first attendee in the doorway. 'Bella, great to see you. Come in, pick a spot.'

'This is so exciting!' She squealed like a kid who'd finally got to go to Willy Wonka's chocolate factory. Her eyes lit up when she saw him taking a cold bottle of Prosecco out of the fridge.

'Complementary,' he explained. 'All part of the workshop.'

'I like the sound of that!'

Next through the door were Rosie and Rebecca from Magnolia House. Andrew smiled at the newcomers as he lined up four glasses. Gemma always laughed at him when he ran the workshops filled with ladies. Kids warmed to her, she joked, but the women warmed to Andrew. He was charming in an effortless way and had them eating out of his hand without even trying. She'd always said it'd been what won her over from the get-go.

When Andrew looked up again after fiddling with the laptop, Molly hovered nervously in the doorway. These English girls were different to how he remembered. He didn't remember many girls at school being this afraid of him. Or maybe he was getting old and had forgotten.

Molly came in and took up station at the table in the corner at the back.

'You're just in time, Molly.' He held the glass aloft and she nodded. 'Talk among yourselves, grab an apron from the collection hanging at the back and we'll get started.' He poured four glasses as the women engaged in friendly banter and when he handed them out, Molly didn't look him in the eye. She was so shy, with beautiful long eyelashes casting shadows across her cheeks beneath the bright downlights of the room.

The next hour was fun. The women quietened, listened, asked questions in all the right places. They were in hysterics trying the chocolates he'd selected, holding their noses as they put chocolate discs on their tongues and then letting go of their noses to let the flavour explode powerfully.

'Eurgh … coffee. I hate coffee!' Rebecca Martin reached for her Prosecco, and the rest of the room had erupted with laughter as she downed a great big gulp, even Molly who seemed to be starting to relax.

When it was time to decorate their truffles, Andrew gave Molly some guidance on how to apply the gold lustre dust. 'Dip the tip in the dust and sweep it over the chocolate, lightly. Less is more in this case. It's great for champagne truffles.' He winked at her, but she looked so uneasy that he left her to it and went over to Bella.

'Colourful,' he commented at the sprinkles covering some of her truffles. 'Matches your lipstick,' he nodded to the rest of the pieces covered in dried strawberry bits.

Rosie made a comment about being unable to enter *MasterChef* with her creations, and Rebecca had painted the gold lustre dust on so thick he wondered how it would taste when she bit into it.

Andrew topped up all four glasses for the ladies. It was the end of the day, and hosting this fun group he found himself more relaxed than he'd been in ages.

Stephanie appeared in the doorway and spoke in hushed tones, barely audible with the laughter filling the room. 'I don't mean to bother you, but your dad is here to see you.'

Andrew tensed. 'Tell him to go home. I'm busy.'

A bit taken aback and blissfully unaware of the turning tides in the Bennett household, Stephanie did as she was asked. Andrew took out cellophane wrapping and some small cardboard trays ready for the women to take their truffles home. But when he turned round, there was Louis.

Andrew said nothing. He looked up at his father, across at the women and then down again as he separated four cardboard trays and pulled out the roll of Sellotape to fasten them once the truffles were safely inside.

Louis shuffled forwards in his slippers. Andrew glanced briefly at him, and in those few seconds noticed his father was paler than last time he'd seen him and looked as though he'd shrunk a good six inches. Or perhaps that was how Andrew saw him now he knew his dirty little secret.

'What are you doing here?' Andrew snapped. His voice was as quiet as he could manage.

Louis took a moment, steadied himself against the table Andrew was working behind.

Bella was at Louis' side. 'Let me get you a chair.'

Andrew was angry, but didn't want to see his father fall. He nodded his thanks to a confused Bella, who pulled a chair over and then went back to the other women and her Prosecco.

'I need you to talk to me, son.'

Andrew said nothing.

'Andrew, you won't talk to me. You won't talk to Gemma. I understand you're angry, but—'

'No, you don't,' Andrew snapped. 'You don't get it, and you don't get to come here, to my place of work, the one place I can get some sanity, and force me to talk to you.'

Andrew adopted a jovial tone, left his father sitting at the front of the room and handed out the four boxes with instructions to carefully lay the truffles inside so they could be wrapped to take home. 'This is your party bag!' he called out to the welcome delight of the women. The only woman who wasn't so enthused was newcomer, Molly, who seemed more intent on watching the exchange between him and Louis.

'Dad, go home,' he told Louis as he separated out the sheets of cellophane. 'This isn't professional.'

Louis bowed his head. 'I don't know what else to do.'

Andrew nearly weakened. All his life they'd been close, they'd laughed, joked, batted out business strategies, talked chocolate and crazy concoctions late into the night over a bottle of wine. And he'd offered this man a kidney, a piece of him.

But he couldn't do it. Or he wouldn't. Even he didn't know which answer was accurate any more.

'Andrew, please, I'm begging you.'

'For part of my body?' Andrew's voice was fierce and he knew the need to keep the volume down was the only thing stopping him from roaring.

'I don't care about the damn kidney.' Louis' breath became shallow. 'I honestly don't give two hoots about it. But I do care about you. I do care about this family. And even if you let this come between us, do not let it come between you and Gemma.'

'You leave Gemma out of this. Now I've got work to do.'

He barely glanced at his father as Louis shuffled out of the workshop and through to the main shop. Instead he focused on showing the women how to wrap the box carefully in cellophane, then handed each a sheet and some ribbons. 'Make it look as beautiful as the truffles,' he said, unable to make eye contact with any of them.

Andrew zoned out of the chatter. His fun mood had gone the minute Louis stepped into the room, but he'd at least been reminded how none of this was Gemma's fault. And he'd been a bastard to her, letting her bear the brunt of his withdrawn moods, letting her take Louis to each dialysis session. She'd shouldered the worry of everything, and he knew how wrong that was.

And Louis was right about one thing. He couldn't let this come between him and his wife.

Chapter Twenty-Three
Molly

'You should've seen the way he was with his own dad.' Molly sat on the small, pale blue sofa running along the edge of the lounge room in the holiday cottage. She toyed with the conch shell on the coffee table beside her, smooth and pale on one side, spikier on the other. Ben sat on the deep blue rug on the floor.

'I can't believe you did a workshop with your birth father.' He shook his head. 'That's insane.'

Molly smiled. 'It was totally by accident.' And she explained to Ben how he'd come into the shop and taken her by surprise when she was browsing. Lost for words, her eyes had zoned in on a sign in the window advertising chocolate-making workshops, and the words were out before she had a chance to think about it.

'Imagine. The guy has no idea he helped his own daughter make chocolates.' Ben shook his head in amazement.

Molly put down the shell and covered her eyes. 'It was a stupid thing to do.'

'Why?'

'Like I said, I got to see Andrew Bennett in all his glory. Another lady told me there was some family argument going on, but she had no idea what it was about. But apparently the father, Louis, is on kidney dialysis, and he didn't look well to me. How can anyone turn their back on family like that?

‘It makes me worry about how he’ll react to me.’ She smiled at Ben. ‘I was warned about this from the agency. I was warned I couldn’t predict his reaction.’

‘Are you regretting coming?’

She almost said yes. ‘Actually, no. This way I get to see him as a person right away, with no pretence, no airs or graces, no effort on his part to make me believe he’s a certain kind of man.’

‘I think you’re starting to panic.’ Ben sat forwards. ‘You can’t really believe you’ve got him all worked out, surely? From that small part of the day, you figure you know exactly who he is?’

‘I suppose you’ve got a point.’

He dug her playfully in the ribs, which coaxed a giggle. Maybe she was over-dramatising the day, but Ben hadn’t seen the look on Andrew’s face. The look hinted at a simmering anger, something she’d not seen on any member of her own family. When they’d fallen out there’d been shouting, plenty of it, but then the air was clear. When words were unspoken they brewed for too long, and there was no chance for rage and frustration to subside. It was tantamount to disaster for everyone involved.

Molly handed Ben a can of Diet Coke from the fridge and grabbed one for herself. ‘Apart from the run-in with Louis, he did seem nice.’ Maybe she was misjudging Andrew Bennett. Maybe he was the good guy, and the frail old man was really a bit of an arse.

‘“Nice” is a word I use to describe my mum’s new Volvo, “nice” is a word I say when my brother’s girlfriend talks about hosting weddings at Magnolia House. “Nice” isn’t a word to adequately describe the first meeting with your birth father.’

Molly sipped from her can. 'Okay, so he was friendly. That better?'

'Much. Try some more … use your adjectives.' He grinned.

'Okay,' said Molly. 'He was polite – to everyone apart from his father. He was thoughtful.' She remembered him helping her brush on the right amount of gold lustre dust, tender in the way he used the brushstrokes, gentle in the way he handled the truffles. 'He was charming too. Bella was batting her eyelids at him.'

'I'd heard Bella was there. My brother works up at the fire station and she came in raving about her chocolate workshop.'

'So that's how you knew I'd gone there.'

'Yup. You should've told me, if only for moral support afterwards. Tell me next time?'

'I'm not sure I could go through it all over again.' She lay down on the sofa, a hand over her eyes.

'You flew ten thousand miles to get here, Molly. You *are* going to go through it again.'

Ben had brought homemade sandwiches over for lunch and handed one to Molly. They were huge doorstep wedges of fresh bread with tuna, lettuce, tomato and mayonnaise. He'd even added black pepper, and when she'd accused him of having his mum make them for him, he'd laughed and asked her how useless she thought he was.

When Ben headed to his shift at the hospital, Molly set off for a walk round the lake and down through the bushland bordering Magnolia House. She'd seen signs in town advertising the Easter Egg Hunt to be held here on Good Friday, the day she was due to leave, and it brought it home to her how little time she had left. She wondered how she'd feel by then, whether she'd be on good terms with the Bennetts or whether she'd run away from Magnolia Creek crying and screaming because it had all gone so horribly wrong.

Molly stepped over the roots of trees encroaching on the pathway – or was she encroaching on their territory? – and she walked down to where the path thinned. The sun shone brilliantly and gave the day its mild temperature. Autumn leaves littered the path, and she kicked through purples, yellows and golds, the rustly sounds of the season. She leant in to smell the creamy white spray of flowers on a fiddlewood tree. Its shiny, lush leaves showed no signs of dropping. She walked on further until the path opened out to an enormous field, the bush carrying on at the foot of it and up a hill the other side. It was hard to believe all this beauty sat less than two hours from the cosmopolitan lights of Melbourne.

When she turned to follow the white, worn wooden sign saying Main Street and rounded the base of the gum trees to follow a different path, she saw Louis, sitting on an enormous tree stump, which made him look tinier than he really was.

Molly scurried past and followed the path, slightly uphill. She didn't stop until she knew she was out of sight, hidden by surrounding mountain ash trees, foliage dotting the bases of their trunks. She put a hand against her chest as the same feeling as yesterday threatened to overcome her. Ben wasn't around to help her this time if she had another panic attack.

She rested against one of the trees. She shut her eyes, told herself to breathe, in and out, in and out, and eventually the feeling subsided and her chest relaxed. It still amazed her how she'd reacted to flying on the airplane without any of this panic, because in reality, the flight had been the easy part. She was about to move on, but curiosity got the better of her, and Molly turned and walked back towards Louis. She stuck to the edge of the track so he'd see her approach and she wouldn't scare him.

'Lovely day,' she said when he looked up.

A smile reached his eyes. 'It's beautiful.' He sounded more Australian than she'd expected when he dragged out the first syllable, and the 'T' came out more as a 'D', softened from his years out here. He'd been in the country more years than she'd been alive, but still she'd expected more of an English-sounding man.

'Are you okay?' She moved closer. He didn't look well. Not well at all.

Despite his pallor, his eyes shone out of him as though there was still hope.

'May I?' Molly gestured to the tree stump big enough for a family of four, but she wasn't sure whether this man – her biological grandfather – wanted company.

'Go ahead.'

She listened to his breathing, the little catches every time it went in, every time it came out.

'You were at the workshop yesterday,' he said.

'That's right.'

'I'm Louis.'

'I know.'

He nodded his head, lips pressed together. 'Yes, I suppose you do.'

They sat, side by side, looking out over the same area of bush.

'What was the row about?' she asked. The wind lifted her hair and when she shivered, goose bumps travelled up her arms.

'It's a long story.' He coughed and Molly put a hand on his shoulder, to calm him she supposed. 'My son is very angry with me.' He smiled, kindly. 'And you probably think you saw a strong, competent man being an arrogant bugger to his own father. Am I right?'

Molly nodded. 'Well—'

'It's not as simple as that. Oh, he was being an arrogant bugger, but he has every right to be.'

'Why?'

'I did something, years ago.' He stopped as though he'd suddenly remembered he was talking to a total stranger.

'Was it really that bad?' Molly asked. 'What you did?'

He closed his eyes. 'Oh, yes, it was bad.'

'And he won't forgive you?'

Louis shook his head. 'Maybe in time.' He looked out into the depth of the bush again, and after a while he changed the subject. 'So what brings you to Magnolia Creek?'

'I needed a holiday,' she lied. Thankfully he didn't add, 'why here?'

He asked her where in England she was from, and they chatted about places they'd both visited, the beautiful English countryside, the differences between here and there.

Molly shivered again. 'You should get home, it's getting chilly. Come on, I'll walk with you. I'm staying up at the cottages.'

'No, I'm fine here.'

'No you're not.' She glanced down at his slippers, but didn't want him to know how vulnerable she thought he looked.

If she didn't think the shock could kill him, she'd tell Louis who she was, but one step at a time.

She held out her arm.

'You're very kind, taking pity on an old man like this.' Louis took her arm as they walked slowly up the path to Main Street.

'You shouldn't go walking down there on your own alone,' Molly admonished. 'If you fell, you could be there for hours before anyone realised, and with the weather getting chillier—'

'You sound like my daughter-in-law.'

Molly smiled. She'd met Gemma and liked her. In fact, it seemed she liked everyone she'd met so far, and the only person she had doubts about was the one she was really here to meet.

Chapter Twenty-Four

Andrew

'I heard what happened at the shop.' Gemma put a cup of tea in front of her husband.

So much for coming home to make amends with her. This was likely to result in either a full-blown row, or at the very least a tense conversation.

'Who told you?' Andrew asked.

'Does it matter?' Gemma sat opposite, her fingers wrapped around a mug of hot chocolate. 'You can't go on like this. Neither of you can.'

'Louis shouldn't have come to the shop.'

'You won't talk to him here.'

'So this is my fault?' Andrew swigged his tea, wincing at the heat of it.

'I didn't say that.'

He looked up at Gemma, into those brilliant blue eyes. She was as beautiful as the day he'd first seen her, as lovely as the day he'd asked her to be his wife, in sickness and in health; for richer, for poorer. What about when the shit hit the fan? Here she was, putting up with all of this, and she didn't deserve to.

'I'm sorry,' he said, but even to him his words sounded weak. 'I'm sorry for everything.'

'You don't need to apologise.'

He reached for her hand and pulled it from the hot chocolate, squeezed it firmly in his own. 'I do need to apologise. In all of this I've only been able to see me, to see my father, to see what they did to me back then. I haven't once asked about you. And I'm sorry.'

Tears sprang into her eyes, and she wiped a finger beneath one and then the other, sniffed lightly and looked upwards to stop any more tears falling out. He reached for her other hand, gave it a squeeze too.

'I don't know how I'm supposed to feel,' he said. 'I can't see past what happened to be able to even think about what I'm going to do.' He held her hands a little tighter. 'I wrote to Julia, told her everything.'

'Has she written back?'

'Not yet. God knows what this will have done to her. I don't even know if she's on good terms with her mother, whether her mother is even alive.' He laughed briefly. 'Julia had a right temper on her sometimes. She threw a shoe at my head when I was late to meet her once. I think she'd been scared, waiting alone at the railway station, but I'd been held up at school and couldn't get away.' His eyebrows knitted to a frown. 'If her mother's alive now, then I'm pretty sure all hell will break loose over this.'

'I thought you were going to hit Louis when he told you everything.' Gemma gripped his hands tightly in return.

'So did I, and it scared me. I never knew I was capable of being that angry.'

'He's running out of time, Andrew.'

Andrew looked at the kitchen table, the knots beneath the varnish, the weathered corners and the chips that had happened over the years without even noticing. 'I know he is.'

'Did you mean what you said?'

His silence confirmed the answer.

'Andrew, you'd never forgive yourself if you let him wither away in front of you. Does seeing his pain every day really make up for the pain he caused you?' She didn't wait for an answer. 'I'm worried, Andrew. I love both of you so much and I know you're going through hell, but I know Louis, and I really think he was doing what he thought was best for you all those years ago.'

When a tear finally crept its way down Andrew's cheek and he sniffed, Gemma was there by his side. He'd never cried in front of her before.

Gemma wrapped her arms around her husband as she stood behind him. 'You're not a malicious man. You're kind, loving and you have a heart. Don't let this take all of that away.'

He held her arms against his chest.

'What are you going to do?' she asked. 'Are you going to try to find your daughter?'

'That's the other thing. Dad lied to me, but it kills me to know I've got the one thing you so desperately want. The child we *both* want.'

Gemma let go and came to sit on his lap. She rested her forehead against his. 'I don't think it's ever going to happen for us.'

The tears came from both of them. Tears for the past, tears for the present and tears for what might have been.

'We still have a chance,' he told her. 'We'll try IVF.' But he'd already seen the IVF leaflets tossed in the recycling with an empty box of muesli and knew she was giving up on their dream of a house full of kids.

'Will you try to find her?' Gemma asked, the topic of IVF shut down, at least for now.

'I honestly don't know.'

When they heard the back gate go, Gemma got up, dried her eyes.

'Is it Dad?'

‘Yes. He must’ve been for a walk.’ Gemma blew her nose into a tissue. ‘He shouldn’t be going without one of us. He’s not strong enough.’

Andrew didn’t say anything until Gemma had stood there watching through the window for another couple of minutes. ‘Go to him,’ he told her. ‘Despite what he’s done, I still want him to be okay.’ He pushed the chair back and left the table.

‘Andrew,’ Gemma stopped him. ‘Please think about the operation again, for all our sakes? You might not like him much at the moment, but he’s your dad and we know this is his best chance to be with us for the foreseeable future. He’s got another dialysis session in the morning. It’d be good to know I won’t be driving him to those appointments for much longer.’

When Andrew dropped down onto the bed upstairs and turned on his side, he wondered how he could go back to thinking of his father in the same way, the way he had before all this had been thrown into the mix.

*

Gemma must have taken his socks and jeans off for him and tucked him beneath the covers, because when Andrew woke the next morning, groggy from a sleep filled with dreams he’d rather not be having, he was only in a T-shirt and boxer shorts. He dragged himself to the shower, went downstairs for breakfast and left the house, all without waking his wife, all without seeing his father.

At the shop, Andrew adjusted the thermostat in the kitchen. The days and nights were cooling down now, and the ideal temperature was a prerequisite for perfect chocolates. He systematically made his way through his to-do list and lost himself in the job he loved. Two hours later, after he’d turned the sign on the door from Closed to Open, he carried the blackboard outside, and using coloured chalk he drew a picture of a cup with steaming liquid, purple chalk creating curls of steam, and wrote Couverture Hot Chocolate along with the price for the winter warmer, which should start gaining in popularity now the days were cooler.

He turned to walk inside but looked twice when he saw the young woman across the street. It was Molly. And she was staring at him, or the shop, he wasn't sure, but he raised a hand to wave to her. He was quite taken aback as she waved across to him and smiled. She was a beautiful young woman, and he was sure it wouldn't be long before she captured some man's attention.

Andrew went back inside the shop and continued with the order for the Easter Egg Hunt. This time, he used a little melted chocolate to fix together two halves of chocolate eggs he'd made earlier. It was an intricate job, required a delicate touch and a firm press to keep the halves together long enough so they'd set and not fall apart. But by lunchtime he'd made another hundred.

'Those can all be wrapped, Emilio.' He patted Emilio's shoulder and indicated the first few batches that were set by now. He liked Emilio, who had more expertise than he'd given him credit for when he first employed him. He had vision too, and Andrew liked that in his team. Emilio had come up with a good range for Halloween already even though they were way off the season, but it'd given him a chance to buy in some special moulds in readiness.

When Andrew replenished the white chocolate discs on the shelf towards the front of the shop, he looked up and saw Molly, again. But this time she wasn't alone. She was talking to Louis. They were sitting, side by side, outside the vet's surgery, and she was chatting away, her face tilted to the gunmetal clouds lurking in the skies above, announcing autumn was well underway.

He disappeared out back again, anxious not to be spotted, and there he pulled another batch of mint milk chocolate hearts from the fridge where they'd been finished off. The fridge was set to a special temperature – for cocoa crystals to form the correct pattern, the temperature was vital to avoid fat blooming, which resulted in the fat in the chocolate rising to the surface and ruining both the appearance and the taste. And once he'd done that he figured the coast was clear, so he pulled out a sandwich from the mini fridge in the office, along with a bottle of water, and went down to the lake.

At the lake, Andrew sat on the low wall surrounding the water and shivered, realising it wouldn't be much longer before he needed to remember a jacket when he was out and about. A light breeze flapped the paper wrapping his sandwich, and he watched as Rebecca Martin arranged chairs on the veranda at the front of Magnolia House, most likely in preparation for a wedding. She draped a white cloth over a chair and then pulled it into a bunch and wrapped a thick, pink strip of satin around the backrest and tied it in a bow. She did the same with each chair, and Andrew thought back to his own wedding with Gemma. They'd married in an old house in a Melbourne suburb beneath a gazebo in the gardens with all their friends and family there to share the day of hope and happiness with them. Gemma's father passed away a few months before, and so Louis had given her away. He'd looked so proud walking her down the aisle, handing Gemma's hand to his son, her long fingers outstretched, ready to become his wife and join his family and take on anything that came their way.

Giggling behind him alerted Andrew's attention, and when he turned, there was Molly again. This time she was with Ben, the youngest member of the Harrison clan.

Andrew smiled. Young love … there was nothing like it.

He picked up the sandwich wrapping he'd stuffed beneath his thigh so it didn't blow away and off he went, back to work.

A few spots of rain told him he'd timed it perfectly.

Chapter Twenty-Five
Molly

Molly and Ben stood outside the cottage. The clouds had started to release their first drops of rain, and Molly had surreptitiously watched Andrew Bennett walk away. The rain had started to fall more heavily, and they'd run to the shelter of the tiny veranda.

'You came here to do something, and if you're not careful you'll run out of time,' said Ben. 'It's a massive thing, but when you don't exactly live nearby, you have to factor that in. Otherwise you'll tell the guy who you are, and he won't have five minutes to get his head around it before you leap on a plane and disappear.'

Resting on his forearms against the wooden posts on the veranda, Ben looked out over the lake. Molly faced the opposite way, next to him, He was right, of course.

'I asked Dad about the family,' said Ben, continuing when Molly looked at him hopefully. 'He seems to think they're really nice, respectable people. And you liked the old man … what was his name?'

'I thought small towns were supposed to be close-knit, where everyone knows everyone else.' Molly grinned.

'Hey, I have an excuse. I've been away, remember, and my shifts since I got back have been a little erratic.'

'Okay, you're forgiven. His name's Louis, and yes, he seems very nice.'

'Despite the confrontation in the chocolate workshop?'

She sighed. 'As far as Louis knows, I'm just another tourist.'

'I hope the shock doesn't kill him.'

'Ben! Don't say that! Don't even joke.'

'Sorry.' He turned to face the little cottage, his back to the lake, and for a minute neither of them spoke.

Molly softened. She wanted to chat to him, she enjoyed it. It was easy. 'I've been posting Aussie pictures like crazy in the Facebook group. Everyone is so happy I'm here, finally seeing a bit of the world. Zara has been going to Stansted Airport – her nearest – to do the same as I did, spend a bit of time getting used to the sights and sounds. She wants to make it to Crete with some girlfriends.'

'She seems pretty wild.' Ben laughed. 'Did you see those photos of her and her mates on their last holiday to Devon?'

'Let's hope if she makes it to Crete she posts plenty of photos of scenery,' said Molly, 'and not body parts.'

The rain came down harder, and Molly was aware of Ben's body, the warmth from him standing next to her as the air around them cooled. It'd been an unexpected pleasure to have company these last few days when she was in a strange country about to do the impossible and turn up on her birth father's doorstep. Without Ben by her side, a sounding board in moments where she doubted herself, she was starting to realise how much more difficult this would have been. Discussing normal things like their Facebook group enabled her mind to quieten and prepare for what came next.

Ben checked his watch.

'Do you have to go?'

'Work calls, I'm afraid.'

'You're gonna get soaked.' Molly looked up at the heavens, black clouds overtaking the grey.

'I saw an umbrella in your kitchen.' He raised an eyebrow, and smiling, Molly went to fetch it for him.

'I'll need that back,' she said.

'Oh no, you don't. Get your cardigan, your handbag … whatever. You're walking me to Main Street where I've parked near the gift shop, and then you're going into the chocolaterie.'

Molly's smile faded.

'Come on.' He stepped off the veranda, put up the umbrella and wasn't about to take no for an answer.

Molly hesitated one second longer, but then grabbed her keys and a cardigan and dived under cover of the umbrella with Ben.

'I'll hold you up until you get there,' he told her, 'but then it's time you met the man you came all the way across the other side of the world to see.'

*

Molly left Ben outside Magnolia Gifts. He hugged her and climbed into his car and he drove away.

That was fifty minutes ago.

Molly wished she'd gone with him. She'd rather be at a maternity emergency helping out than feeling as useless as she did right now, lurking in Main Street.

She drew in her breath when the little bell above the chocolaterie tinkled and out came Bella.

'Molly, hi! Lovely to see you again. How's the holiday?'

Molly looked up from beneath her umbrella as Bella put hers up against the downpour.

'Great, thanks.' But when Bella looked about to engage in more conversation, Molly ducked into the chocolaterie and slotted her dripping umbrella into the stand by the front door.

He wasn't there. There was a girl with long blonde hair behind the counter arranging truffles in an empty section in the glass-topped display cabinet. There was another man browsing the selection of Easter eggs that coloured the shop with their gold, pink, purple and silver wrappings.

Molly's heart was in her mouth. She concentrated, imagining Ben's voice right there, telling her to breathe. But her heart pounded, her chest tightened. She grabbed her umbrella and ran out the shop. The scene with her birth mother at the forefront of her mind, she couldn't go through with it. She couldn't do it this time.

'Hey!' a female voice shouted. 'Look out!'

Molly stood back. She'd nearly taken the woman out with the spike of her umbrella. The damn thing was stuck and she couldn't put it up.

'It's Gemma,' the woman said. 'Are you okay?'

Molly stared back at the beautiful blonde woman about to go into the shop. She turned away and tried again, in vain, to force the umbrella up so it could do its job. She was getting drenched, her dark hair curling at the bottom and sticking to her face.

'I asked whether you're okay?' said Gemma. 'You don't seem it.'

And then there was a voice behind the woman, a voice she recognised from someone she hadn't seen. She'd been too busy trying to sort the umbrella out. 'I'm not up to this, Gemma.'

Molly turned round and saw Louis standing there.

'Lovely to see you,' he said. Or at least that's what she thought he said. 'You're getting soaked through.' He beckoned her to the shelter, but as the rain came down harder and harder, she didn't move.

'Come inside,' Gemma begged. 'Both of you.' She looked sternly from one to the other, and Molly found herself moving forwards. Her feet were sodden, her flip-flops squelched as she walked. Her jeans were stuck to her legs, her top hung heavy and drips ran into her eyes.

'You should throw that useless thing away.' Gemma took Molly's umbrella and tutted at the bent canopy. She dropped it in the umbrella stand. 'Let me go out back and get some towels, for the both of you.'

Molly looked at Louis and Louis looked at her, and the twinkle in his eyes was what set her off. Molly's laughter echoed all around the shop.

'She's treating us like we're naughty kids up at that school of hers,' Louis guffawed, a big sound from a frail old man.

Molly's face turned serious as Gemma returned with towels. 'Andrew is out back, Louis. Go and talk to him and I'll be there in a minute.'

Louis didn't move.

'Go, Louis.'

'Does he know I'm here?'

Ben's voice was there again, inside her head, telling her to get on and do it. But before she or Louis could move from the spot where they stood dripping onto the dark wooden floor of the chocolaterie, there he was. Andrew Bennett. Dressed in an apron, he was standing watching all three of them from behind the counter.

Molly had seen him before, of course, in the pub, at the workshop, on the street when she'd watched from a distance. But being close again now and knowing why she was here made her notice him in full light. The planes of his face – were they the same as hers? Dark hair like hers maybe, once upon a time, but now salt and pepper with flecks of grey among the dark, especially where it had been allowed to grow longer on top. The crease between his eyebrows told of frowning too many times. Molly was guilty of doing the same thing, especially when she was concentrating or annoyed. The only difference was her skin was too young to have a permanent mark etched already. She relaxed her expression to avoid the same happening to her.

'What's all this?' He walked towards them. His apron was filthy with smears of dark chocolate and a lighter variety, and for some peculiar reason Molly found herself wondering why, on all these cooking shows on TV, pastry chefs and those who worked with chocolate were always in crisp, white chef clothing. Was it all a gimmick? A game of make-believe?

'You two need to talk,' said Gemma, looking first at Louis, then at Andrew.

Before Andrew could open his mouth, Molly found herself saying, 'We do.'

All three turned to her.

'I'm Molly.'

Gemma, Andrew and Louis looked at her as though she were barmy.

'Molly Ramsey,' she added, but they had no idea, did they?

'Am I missing something?' Gemma turned to Andrew and then back to Molly.

Andrew looked confused, as did Louis, but as Molly locked eyes with Andrew one more time, looking into piercing blue eyes, at the softly curved top lip she knew hers was a mirror image of, Andrew Bennett saw what she did and when he opened his mouth, no words came out.

Andrew and Molly stared at one another. Gemma asked what was going on. Louis stayed silent.

'Do you two know each other?' Gemma looked worried, and Molly hated how she was about to blow this woman's world apart. She was nice, the sort of woman she wished was her birth mum rather than the woman who'd told her to go away.

Next to them Louis' breathing became heavier.

'It's you.' Andrew looked at Molly.

'It's me,' she said.

Chapter Twenty-Six

Andrew

They say shock affects your body in many ways. The body doesn't get enough blood flow, and it can't function. You get dizzy, become light-headed, have difficulty breathing. All of this and more was happening to Andrew right at this moment, and he had no idea how to feel, what to say, how to react.

Molly.

His daughter.

Andrew had never been this shocked. Not when his father told him they were emigrating to Australia, not when Gemma had her first miscarriage, not even when Louis told him the web of lies they'd woven back when Julia was on the scene. And not even now when Gemma left. One minute she was standing there next to him in the chocolaterie, the next she was running out of the door, unable to cope with this girl who'd suddenly turned up in their lives.

'I'll go, leave you two to talk.' Louis touched Molly's arm, smiled warily and without another word shuffled towards the door of the chocolaterie.

Andrew had no idea what Emilio had overheard, but his employee was there now, at Louis' side. 'I'll walk Louis home,' he told Andrew. 'I'll see you in the morning.' He turned the sign on the door to Closed as they left.

Only metres separated Andrew and Molly, and for a while neither of them moved, neither of them spoke.

Eventually, Andrew went to the door and locked it, pulled the chain across. And then he motioned for Molly to follow him upstairs to the café where they wouldn't be disturbed, where customers couldn't peer through the window to see if they were still open.

By now the rain had stopped and the sun was brave enough to appear in the sky, and they went out onto the veranda. Andrew grabbed an old towel to wipe down the chairs at a small round table, and Molly tentatively sat down. He stood, sodden towel in hand, watching her toy with the phone in her lap.

Without a word, Andrew went back inside and made two mugs of hot chocolate. He added whipped cream to the top of each, finishing the drinks with chocolate sprinkles. And when he'd run out of things to do to delay the inevitable, he joined Molly outside. He set down the mugs and sat opposite.

Andrew was the first to speak. 'Beautiful out here, isn't it?'

A friendly kookaburra assumed his position at the far end of the wooden railing and laughed in a way that coaxed a smile, albeit very small, out of Molly. Andrew knew, he'd only quickly glanced sideways at her, but it had been enough. They both stared out into the wide expanse, the mountain ash trees able to hide a million secrets in their density.

When he felt brave enough, he turned to Molly. 'I didn't know.' He took in the eyes the same shape as his, her mouth sitting in the same relaxed manner, the cheekbones structured in the same way as Julia's had been all those years ago when she'd sat next to him in maths class and smiled at him for the first time. 'I didn't know anything about you,' he said.

Her hands shook when she tried to lift the hot chocolate. The small chocolate disc he'd put beside the cup had melted against the hot vessel and gone all gooey, and when she got it on her fingers, she put the mug down and licked the mixture off.

'So my birth mum never told you she was pregnant?' she asked.

'I knew she was pregnant,' he began, worried that anything he said could jeopardise things between them, creating an obstacle in an already unruly path. 'But I only found out recently that Julia had gone on to have the baby, *our* baby. You.'

He was making right mess of this. He couldn't even get his words out straight.

Molly toyed with the teaspoon beside her mug. 'You thought she'd get an abortion?'

'It wasn't what I wanted at the time, but I was told that was what was going to happen.' His anger reared its ugly head again, but he didn't want it to. Not right now. 'Julia left without seeing me, without telling me anything to my face.'

'Sounds about right.'

His heart broke at the pain behind Molly's words. Julia had told him she'd refused to see Molly, but it hadn't meant as much to him as it did now, with Molly sitting right in front of him, the hurt written all over her face.

'It must've been a shock,' said Molly.

'One hell of a shock,' he clarified.

Her chair scraped back, but she didn't go anywhere. All she'd done was put a bit of extra space between them. Perhaps they both needed it for now.

Andrew stirred his hot chocolate as the cream disappeared gradually into the hot liquid. To anyone watching, they would've looked like father and daughter enjoying a chat, relaxed in the bush setting with their luxury drinks. But between them and the kookaburra, they knew it wasn't the case.

'Why didn't you write to me? Let me know you were coming?' he asked.

Molly took a while to answer. 'Because my biological mother turned me away. I wrote her letters, and I waited for months. I was *so* patient, but she still didn't want to get to know me or tell me anything about what happened when I was born. I decided I wanted to see you for myself, without giving you warning. I didn't want you to make excuses in your letters or emails. I wanted to see you, face-to-face, and rather than prolong the agony, I decided I'd rather have you slam a door in my face if you didn't want to see me. At least then I'd be able to move on and I'd know.'

He couldn't stop looking at her. 'So you flew all the way here from England.'

She nodded, and when her eyes glistened over she looked down into her cup and stirred the remaining cream through the liquid until it'd gone.

'You did something very brave,' he told her.

'It sounds crazy to everyone else, I know. But I had to do it. When Julia pushed me away, it hurt more than you could ever know.' She stopped, gathered herself, her bottom lip wobbled, but she kept it in check. 'I never wanted to hurt that much again, ever.'

'Listen, Molly. Before we get into this … can I ask you one question?' His eyes begged her to give him a chance. His mind tried to focus on the moment, not even think about Gemma, about Louis, about Julia, about anything else other than the two of them.

'Go on,' she said.

'Were you happy?'

'When?'

'In life. Were you happy in life? Did you end up with a family who loved you? A family who wanted you?' He brushed an ant away as it braved crawling onto the table's surface.

'I was, and I am, very happy.' Her voice was soft, and when she spoke his shoulders melted with relief. 'My family are the best people in the world.'

'Brothers? Sisters?'

She nodded, smiling, and it was a joy for Andrew to see. Here in the moment with anger, sadness, questions, she still saw the family she'd been loved by and raised with.

'I have a brother, Isaac. We're very close.'

'Was he worried when you told him what you wanted to do?'

'Yes, very. I'm loyal to each of them, but they understand my need to find out where I came from. And just because I'm finding out more about myself doesn't mean I'm betraying them. To a lot of people it means that, but not to us.'

'You must have a strong bond.'

'We do.' Her lips pressed together conclusively. 'And my family are behind me completely. They'll be there to pick up the pieces if I get hurt again.'

He couldn't begin to imagine what it must've been like for her. Julia hadn't gone into detail, but he knew she'd told Molly she didn't want to have a relationship with her, she couldn't cope. It was Julia's choice, but a tiny bit of him hated her for not giving their daughter a chance. None of this was Molly's fault.

'And you think that's what I'm going to do?' he asked. 'Hurt you?' She looked straight at him. 'Is that what the chocolate workshop was about? You wanted to check what I was like before you got too close?'

'No, you caught me off guard. I was watching you from a distance that day, and when you spoke to me I got so flustered and blurted out the first thing that came into my head.'

He laughed. 'Julia used to do the same. She was confident, much more so than me, but when she got flustered she was totally different. You know, she asked me out, not the other way round?' When Molly smiled at him he said, 'She was talking to me outside the maths lesson, and when I turned to go on my way, she called after me, "maths homework". She didn't admit it for three weeks, after getting together at the local library no less than six times with our text books, but it was her way of asking me out on a date.'

'I hate maths, too. I'd ask a boy to help rather than struggle with it myself.' Molly relaxed enough to finish her mug of hot chocolate. 'Thank you, that was delicious.'

'My pleasure.' He tapped his top lip. 'You've got froth on your lip.'

Embarrassed, she wiped it off. 'How did you suddenly find out about me?'

'Julia messaged me on Facebook. I have a page for the chocolaterie,' he said when she raised an eyebrow in the same quizzical way he knew he did. 'We got talking and the truth came out. All of it.'

'Do you mean the truth about me?'

He gulped down the rest of his hot chocolate. He didn't use a spoon like he usually would to get the rich chocolate from the bottom of the cup. 'We were young, neither of us thought to question anything.' He stood up, turned on the veranda and rested his hands against the white, tired paint he'd promised they'd redo come spring. 'At fifteen you question the world to a certain extent, but some of it you still believe in. Well, Julia and I did anyway. We never thought to question our parents.'

'I don't understand.' Molly moved over to where he was.

He looked ahead, out into the forest of greens, some dark, some light, some shiny, others plain. 'We were lied to by our parents, they split us up and Julia went off to Ireland. I came with the family to Australia.'

'Was that what the row with Louis was about?'

Andrew nodded. 'He said he didn't know what else to do.'

'You know, I've talked with him a few times.'

'I've seen you.' Andrew faced her and smiled, keeping a respectable distance between them.

She didn't look at him. 'Whatever he did back then, he's no monster.'

Andrew noticed the way her eyelashes shaded her prominent cheekbones. He didn't want to talk about Louis, not now. 'You look a lot like Julia, you know.'

'Do I?' She looked up at him.

He nodded, looked away briefly, uncomfortable in their sudden familiarity. He had a sudden flash of memory of the warmth in Julia's eyes, the way he'd sunken into them when she looked at him.

'I saw her so briefly when I turned up on her doorstep,' said Molly. 'I didn't have a chance to think about whether I looked like her. She couldn't wait to get away from me.'

'It would've been a shock. I know she's still hurting.' He wasn't going to make excuses for Julia and he was upset with her, but he didn't hate her. She would've been in an impossible situation back then, and he didn't see the woman who'd told Molly to go away. He saw the terrified fifteen-year-old, pregnant and abandoned – or so she thought – by her boyfriend.

'It's different for a birth mother,' said Andrew. 'She carried a child inside her for nine months, and I can't imagine the pain when it came to such an abrupt end and she gave her baby away.'

Molly mellowed. 'It must've been very hard.'

'In a way it's better I didn't know until now,' he told her. 'I'm not sure I could've coped knowing you'd gone to another family, knowing we were going about our lives as though none of it had happened.' He paused. 'You must have a lot of questions.'

Molly's phone chimed, but she ignored it. 'It's probably Ben.'

'Ben Harrison? I've seen you with him. How do you two know each other?'

Molly grinned. 'I had a slight – okay, massive – fear of flying. Anyway, my brother is getting married in America in a few months and he wants me to be there, so a year ago I joined an online support group for those with the same fear.'

He shook his head. 'There's so much we don't know about each other.'

'This was the first flight I've ever taken,' said Molly.

Part of him beamed with pride that she'd got over this huge obstacle in her way to get what she wanted, what she thought she might need. Molly told him all about her time with the online group, how she'd warmed to Ben straight away and how he'd flown part of the way with her. He'd laughed as she told him about the nail marks she'd left in Ben's hand after the first take-off.

'And neither of you had any idea you were about to bump into each other in Magnolia Creek?'

Molly shook her head. 'Ben and I were both protective of our identities and careful not to share specifics. You never know online, do you? And I never probed once we met because I was focused on the reason for me coming to Australia in the first place.

'You say I must have lots of questions, but I don't really. I thought I'd have a million things to ask you, but I feel a bit numb. Does that make sense?'

'Perfect sense. I felt the same way for days when I found out about you. I couldn't even think straight. After I'd read Julia's message and found out about your existence, I swished my mouth with some clarifying lotion of Gemma's instead of the mouthwash.' Molly laughed and the tension abated. 'It tasted revolting!'

'I'm sure it did.'

Andrew snapped back to reality, having been lost in the easy repartee. 'It's not just me trying to get my head around this,' he explained.

Molly nodded. 'I know you have your own family to consider.'

He scraped a hand across his jaw.

'If this all blows up in my face, then I'll deal with it,' said Molly. 'But I had to take the chance and I'm sorry if this makes things difficult at home for you.'

'Can you do something for me, Molly?'

Her eyes searched his beneath the darkening sky as the sun began its retreat behind another cloud. 'Of course.' She gulped.

'Promise me you won't apologise again for coming into my life,' he said in earnest. 'I'll never be sorry you've turned up the way you have.' He didn't realise until he said it quite how much he'd longed to have contact with his daughter. Ever since the day he knew of her existence in the world, his life was destined never to be the same again.

Chapter Twenty-Seven

Andrew

As they felt a few spots of rain, they retreated inside and sat next to one another on the worn yellow sofa – another item due to be replaced as the business grew. They talked about Molly's childhood. She had a few pictures on her phone of her mum, her dad, her brother … the family she had now, including photos she'd added especially for this moment to fill in some of the gaps for him. Andrew warmed to the thought of her being so close to her family, but each time he looked at photographs of the past – her first bicycle with tassels hanging from the handlebars, her sixteenth birthday and the cake her mum had made, her graduation ceremony with Molly in a mortar board, sandwiched between two proud parents – he saddened a little bit more. These were moments he'd been cheated out of by their lying parents, moments he could never get back for himself.

Oh, the unfairness of it all. It made him wonder how many other birth fathers were out there and had been forgotten about, kept in the dark, lied to.

He loved hearing about Molly's career so far, her tales of her job as a midwife. She spoke with passion; she had the same sparkle in her eye and persistent smile on her face that he had when he spoke about the chocolate business. In turn, he told her all about how he'd come to own the chocolaterie, their move from the city to the country.

'Do you have any children?' Molly asked then. 'Or, any *other* children?' she corrected herself.

'It's hard to know what to say, isn't it? Do I say "daughter" when I talk about you, do I call myself your "father"? I don't really know what my position is.'

Molly didn't say anything.

'No, no other children.'

'Can I ask why?'

He noticed he still had his apron on, spattered in chocolate from his day's work. 'It hasn't happened for Gemma and I. I'm not sure it ever will.'

'Oh,' she said quietly. And then, after a while, 'I must have been a big shock to Gemma.'

Truthfully, he felt stuck between these two women and he had no idea what the solution was. Gemma had a lot of weight on her shoulders and Molly turning up out of the blue must've been the final blow. She'd never run off, avoided a confrontation. Gemma was strong, she tackled things head on.

'A shock,' he said, 'but I hope eventually she'll accept it. We've never kept secrets from each other, especially not secrets of this magnitude.

'But don't you worry about us, Molly.' As he reassured her he chuckled to himself. He sounded so … father like! 'We'll get through this, I'm sure we will. It might take Gemma a while to come round, that's all.'

'I hope so. Gemma seems lovely.'

'She's very special.' He nodded. 'Why are you smiling?'

Molly looked around the top floor of the café. 'This … everything … you. It's all so normal.'

'I wouldn't say that,' he grinned.

'When you search for your biological family, you're warned you might uncover things you'd rather not know. You worry you'll find them so far from the ideal you'd imagined, that you wish it'd stayed in your head, a figment of your imagination.'

'And what did you dream we'd be, before you searched for me and Julia?'

'It's so silly now.'

'Try me.' When Molly looked up he was still taken aback by how much she resembled Julia. How had he missed it when they first met? Or maybe she only looked like Julia because he was looking at her in that way, taking in her flawless young skin, the dark hair curling at the ends like Julia's had.

'Okay,' Molly continued. 'I'll admit I definitely had an ideal when I met Julia. I had this image of her in my mind. And apart from any physical similarities, she'd take one look at me and be unable to stop. She'd open her arms the minute I landed on her doorstep, pull me inside and tell me how she'd done nothing but think of me over the years and how her life had been nothing until I knocked on the door.

'See, told you it sounded silly.'

'It doesn't at all. But Julia was always pretty determined, even back then when we were fifteen. The problem is, we don't know what has gone on since.' He let his comment settle.

Molly smiled. 'When I was really little, I had this crazy notion my birth parents would still be together, madly in love, waiting for me to get in touch. They would, of course, be ready to shower me with gifts – a magnificent bedroom, a pony, as many sweets as I wanted.'

They both smiled at her dreams.

'I was a happy child and I never once wanted for anything, but eventually curiosity got the better of me. Over the years, before I traced her, I'd built Julia up to be this angelic woman, this person who was missing a piece without me, but when she pushed me away I didn't think about *you*. And I don't mean it spitefully.'

Molly explained about the man who'd been refused access to his newborn at the hospital. 'You don't do a job like midwifery without it affecting you emotionally. It's impossible, and anyone who says they can completely detach themselves is lying. I felt for the man, really felt for him, and it got me thinking about you. It made me realise there was another part to the story, another piece missing.

'If, in the end, you don't want to be involved with me in any way, then I'll know. Dealing with rejection would be hard, but I know I'd find it easier than dealing with uncertainty.'

'I'm so sorry, Molly.' Andrew shook his head. 'Being turned away by Julia must've been awful.'

She looked up at the ceiling, eyes glistening with tears. 'I can remember everything about that day with such clarity, even the sound of a dog barking nearby, the smell of home-cooking when she opened the door. And I remember standing there, my hand on the pointed iron railing, and she told me she wanted nothing to do with me.'

Molly pulled a tissue from her pocket and turned away to dab below her eyes. Andrew's hands lifted slightly as he thought about putting his arms around her, but he drew them back. He couldn't. He wasn't ready.

'Could I trouble you for a glass of something cold?' Molly asked.

'Sure.' He couldn't have got up much faster, grateful to have something to do with his hands, something to break the moment. Behind the counter he found two small bottles of orange juice, and he took his time opening each and pouring them into the awaiting glasses. Molly looked like she needed as much time to gather herself as he did.

‘So given my birth mother won’t tell me what happened back then,’ Molly began when Andrew returned with the drinks, ‘will you?’

He downed half the glass and set it on the table. ‘I only found out recently myself. I’m still dealing with it.’ He wanted her to know. She had a right to know. But the other part of him was reluctant to paint Louis in a negative light. Molly may have been afraid at what she might find when she found her birth father, but now she was here he didn’t want anything to frighten her away. A couple of days ago, he’d been wrestling with what to do. Should he trace her and introduce himself? Should he leave well enough alone? But now, he knew. If she walked away because of what their families had concocted together, it’d tear him apart.

‘I need to know, Andrew.’ Her voice pleaded. Her hands tugged at the bunched up tissue between her fingers.

Hearing her use his name brought it home to him how far apart they still were, and would be if he didn’t let her into their lives. He finished his orange juice and sat back in the sofa. And then he started from the beginning.

‘I met Julia in the summer of 1983. She was like a breath of fresh air …’ He told her everything from the times they studied together, him helping her with her maths, her helping him in return with his history, a subject he had no passion for and one taught by a teacher he had no affinity with.

Molly asked him all about Julia. ‘What were her hobbies back then?’ ‘What did the two of you talk about?’ ‘Where did you go together when you dated?’

And for Andrew it was like a film reel had been rolled up and shoved away in a box in the back of his mind for a very long time, but finally someone had found it in the attic, unravelled it, and he'd been allowed to share in the pleasure and pain of his life all those years ago.

'We were so in love,' he told her. 'Every night after school we'd do homework, we'd take long walks. She'd watch me play football, I was often at the side of the hockey pitch watching her game. We were inseparable.'

He told her more about the time they'd dated, going to the movies together, out for ice creams, when he gave her the special necklace for her fifteenth birthday and then the day she found out she was pregnant.

'We didn't have much of a chance to talk about it. I'd always been close to my dad, not so much Mum but definitely Dad, and I thought he'd be more supportive when I told him. I can still remember the look on his face and I've not seen it since. It wasn't disappointment, it was as though he truly was gutted, like he'd lost a big part of him, which I couldn't understand at all.'

'So how did I end up being put up for adoption?' When she asked, Molly sounded as though she'd detached herself from it being her. It was as though this was someone else's story and she was gathering facts ready to sort through in her mind.

Andrew wanted something stronger to drink. A beer or a big glass of red wine, something to take the edge off repeating the story that still sickened him to the stomach. He couldn't look at Molly. He was so ashamed of his father. And when he told her, she didn't speak, not for several minutes. Each of them let the story settle, the secrets of the past, the lies that had been told.

'Did you never suspect Julia had had the baby?' Molly asked.

He pondered his own gullibility. ‘It was a different time back in the 1980s. Not like today with emails, Facebook, the internet giving you everything you want to know. Back then it was a phone call or a letter to keep in touch, and with Julia being whisked away so quickly and my parents barely pausing for breath before we emigrated, there was never the opportunity to find out anything more. I had no reason not to believe what I’d been told.’

Molly shook her head. ‘I don’t understand how your parents could do it.’

‘I honestly don’t know either,’ said Andrew.

‘I guess it was a different time.’

‘Yeah,’ he said. ‘A different time.’

The rain had stopped and they moved out on to the veranda again. They both needed the crispness of the air, the chill to batter their senses that were left in shock. There was a smell of fresh rain as it dripped from leaves, dampness all around, seeping into their skin.

‘It’s beautiful out here. Australia is an amazing country.’ Molly joined Andrew at the edge of the veranda. Down below they watched as a fawn rabbit hopped into denser foliage.

‘It certainly is. I can understand why Dad brought us here, and I guess I should be grateful.’

‘But you’re not.’ She wasn’t asking a question.

‘How can I be now I know what he did?’

Molly brushed the drips on the veranda railing with her fingertips until they were no more. ‘Is he really sick?’

Andrew drew in his breath. ‘He has kidney disease. Dialysis four times a week.’

‘It’s pretty gruelling. I’ve got friends in the renal unit and I’ve heard stories about patients who wait and wait for organ donations.’

‘I think the wait is about four years,’ Andrew confirmed.

‘He doesn’t have that long, does he?’

Andrew shook his head, and in his mind he didn’t see the monster he’d pictured the last few days; he didn’t see a man who’d lied to him, who’d been the reason this girl hadn’t known him before today. He saw a vulnerable, seventy-year-old man who still loved his family.

He bowed his head. What would Molly think of him if she knew he’d denied Louis the one chance he had at living?

‘Can I ask you a question?’ Molly’s hands wrapped over the wooden railing.

‘Go on.’

‘How did you really feel when you found out about me? I don’t mean now. I mean back then, when you were only a teenager.’

‘When Julia got pregnant I was fifteen. I didn’t know how I was supposed to feel, but we were so in love and I guess I was scared, but at the same time a small amount of happiness dared to burn inside of me. When I thought she’d aborted our baby, I was devastated. I was angry she could do such a thing, that she could keep it a secret, that she hadn’t let me have a say at all. Over the years my anger mellowed and I tried to put it behind me. I didn’t think much more about it until Gemma had her first miscarriage.’

‘I didn’t realise—’

‘She’s had four in total, so having a baby is the impossible dream right now.’

They let his words settle in the air between them.

‘The more I wondered about you,’ said Andrew, ‘the guiltier I felt. There I was wondering what you looked like, where you lived, whether you were like me, when Gemma was fighting a battle that shouldn’t be hers alone.’

‘It must be stressful for both of you.’

‘I want you to know, Molly, that I never wanted to get rid of you, not even at fifteen years old. I wasn’t even given a choice, no say in anything, and it eats me up inside to think you might hate me for everything that’s happened.’

She put a hand out and touched him lightly on the arm. ‘I’ve had a good life. I’ve been loved and never wanted for anything.’

Andrew sniffed, wiped at his eyes. He looked up to stop any tears creeping out, the same way he’d seen Gemma do enough times so she didn’t fall apart. ‘I wonder, now, where I’ll fit into your life. You have a “dad” … the man you grew up with and don’t get me wrong, I’m so happy for you. But I don’t know who I’m supposed to be.’

‘I guess the only thing we can do,’ said Molly with a smile, ‘is see how it evolves.’

‘I’m the fourth part of the triangle,’ he said.

Molly pulled a face. ‘Now I think I must take after Julia for my maths skills, but even I’m pretty sure a triangle has three sides.’

‘I’ve been looking into adoption online, ever since I found out about you. There’s the adoption triangle – birth parents, adoptee and adoptive parents – which seems simple. But I’m not sure how much of a look in the birthfather ever really gets.’ Did he sound too dramatic? He didn’t mean to. ‘I’m just trying to figure out where I fit in, after all this time.’

‘I know.’ She met his gaze. ‘You know, I hadn’t really thought this far. I hadn’t thought any further than knocking on your door, introducing myself and having you either slam it in my face or invite me in. But this …’ She pointed to herself and then him, back again. ‘I hadn’t thought about this and what should happen after.’

‘Can I assume you’ll want to stay in touch, when you return to England?’

She fiddled with her phone gripped between her hands. ‘I know I don’t want this to be the end.’

He swallowed, relieved. ‘How long are you in Australia for?’

‘I’m not leaving until Good Friday.’

His shoulders relaxed. He’d had visions of her saying ‘tomorrow’ or ‘in two days’ time’ and it wasn’t long enough. At least some time gave them a chance at building a foundation. ‘This is a pretty shit time for my family,’ he said honestly. ‘We’re going through a lot of stuff right now.’ He needed to go to Gemma and find out how she was feeling about this. He couldn’t face Louis yet, but he needed to be with his wife.

‘Listen,’ said Molly, ‘this is a lot for one day. I’ll go and if you give me your phone number, perhaps we can meet again tomorrow or the day after.’

‘That sounds like a good idea.’ They exchanged numbers and made their way downstairs. ‘I’m glad you came.’

‘I’m glad too. I’ll see you again.’

When he held the door to the chocolaterie open for her, he watched her walk away down the street towards where she’d turn and head to the cottages.

He hadn’t missed the way Molly’s fingers had trembled as she tapped his number into her phone. When she spoke, she sounded so together, but it was clear she was vulnerable beneath the confident exterior.

Andrew wanted this to work out so badly. He wanted peace in his own family, he wanted to somehow become a part of Molly's life. This wasn't one of those cheesy TV programs where everyone came together for a group hug and stuck together from thereon in. This was real life. And real life could be very different.

Chapter Twenty-Eight
Gemma

Since that afternoon at the chocolaterie, Gemma and Andrew had barely spoken. He'd wanted to talk the minute he returned, after Molly had gone back to her accommodation. But Gemma hadn't been ready, and when she came inside from Louis' annexe, she still didn't feel as though she could face it.

'Gemma, talk to me,' said Andrew. 'We can't block each other out.' He tried to pull her to him in the kitchen, but she backed away.

'I can't, not right now,' she snapped.

'Okay, calm down.'

'For God's sake, Andrew!' Her yell startled him. 'I'm taking Louis to dialysis four times a bloody week! I'm working at my job plus yours to cover the extra Easter demand, I'm battling with a husband who won't save his dying father, I can't have a baby of my own because for some reason my insides kill them all before they get a chance to live. And to top it all off, *your* child is here, come to find her *father!'*

She took a deep breath. 'So no, Andrew. I won't calm down.'

He looked strung out, the same way she felt.

'I know you're hurting.' He slumped against the sideboard. 'And I know a lot of it is my fault.' She didn't disagree. 'But how the hell am I supposed to make it better?'

They stood for a while until the silence began to torture her. She had to get out. Fast.

In the hallway, she pulled on her shoes, and without another word she left the house, slamming the door behind her.

*

An hour later and Gemma was back to find Andrew fixing the leak beneath the sink in the laundry she'd told him about weeks ago.

'Don't you have better things to do?' she asked.

His head banged against the top of the cupboard as he jumped at her voice. 'I didn't hear you come in.' He rubbed his forehead as he got to his feet. 'All fixed.'

She followed him into the kitchen. 'Sorry I stormed off.'

He pumped soap into his palms and washed his hands. 'It's a lot to take in.'

'Yeah.' She leant against the sink as he finished up and dried his hands. The walk to the end of the street, all the way past the fire station, past the railway station and following the cycle trails all the way back to near Myrtle Close had allowed the anger that had boiled over to settle into a simmer.

Andrew stood next to his wife, the tips of their fingers touching. 'In all of this,' he said, 'I've never stopped worrying about what it means for you.'

'You haven't?'

'Of course not.'

She'd let herself take on too much, something she often did and failed to realise until it was too late. But she'd never been any different. When she was little she'd do the ironing, baskets of it, refusing to let anyone else help, and then she'd make the dinner, again insisting she was happy to do it when all the while she was thinking it'd be nice if someone else lifted a finger.

‘I should’ve insisted you employ someone else at the shop in the busiest times,’ she told Andrew. ‘And I should’ve made you drive Louis to his dialysis, talking to one another or not.’

She could see how much Andrew was hurting. She could see it in the way his shoulders slumped, in the way his head hung. But she needed to let him know what this meant to her. This wasn’t about one event, one person. It was about everything bundled into one huge mess she was struggling to handle.

‘I think I’m jealous,’ she admitted sheepishly.

‘Jealous?’

‘I know. Ludicrous, isn’t it?’

‘Jealous of Molly?’

‘Yes.’ She covered her face with her hands. ‘There you go, I’ve said it. As crazy as it sounds, I’m jealous of Molly.’

Andrew sat at the kitchen table and waited for Gemma to follow. ‘It’s not crazy at all.’

‘She’s your daughter, the child I’ve never been able to give you. You two have this bond and the start of a relationship that I’m not part of.’

‘Gemma, we’re a team, me and you. Molly comes into my life and she comes into yours, simple.’ If only it was as easy as it sounded.

‘Did you two talk much?’

Andrew looked at her, eyes misted over. ‘She’s lovely.’

‘She is.’ Gemma couldn’t disagree. ‘I suppose she had a lot of questions.’

‘I think the questions will come in time, for both of us. She knows she freaked you out by turning up here.’

Gemma hated to admit it, but Molly was spot on. She had no idea how she was supposed to feel or how she even wanted to feel these days.

'It's a big shock, Andrew, and I haven't had much time to get used to the idea. You have a child, who up until today wasn't real to me. You had no idea where she was, or whether you'd ever be in contact with her.' Gemma shook her head. 'I never for one moment envisaged her turning up like this.'

Andrew recounted some of his conversation with Molly. She knew he was trying to put her mind at ease, trying to convince her to rethink this turn of events as a positive, not a negative. He looked shattered, but instead of the anger that'd sat behind his eyes for the past few days, there was a kind of peace with the knowledge he'd gained.

'Molly knows I have family to consider,' said Andrew, 'and I think she'll give us the space we need. I'll call her soon and meet with her again. She's only here for a while, and I'd like to get to know her before she leaves.'

Part of Gemma wanted to push this girl away, not let her into their lives, but she wasn't cruel. She forced a small smile. 'You should. She hasn't done anything wrong.' And when she said those words, she almost convinced herself she wasn't blaming this girl for anything, wasn't worried Andrew would become more invested in fostering a relationship with Molly than he was in repairing the damage with his father and wife. She told herself she wouldn't end up resenting Molly for being the child she could never have.

But telling herself one thing and actually believing it was more difficult than she'd thought.

‘I want you to come with me, when I meet her again,’ Andrew brushed his lips lightly against her cheek.

‘I’d like to meet her. But not yet.’ Gemma stroked his hair. ‘You need to get to know her as a person, and I’d feel as though I were intruding. It’s a private thing, for you and her.’ And something Gemma would never be a part of, even if she was physically with them.

She sighed. ‘Can I heat through some chilli for you?’

Andrew got up, planted his hands reassuringly on her shoulders. ‘You stay right there and let me do it.’ First, he took down two glasses and pulled out a bottle of red wine from the sideboard in the kitchen and poured two generous measures. ‘And you can drink this.’

She smiled at him, thankful for the glass of red smoothly trickling its way through her insides. It would give her the courage to bring Louis’ name into the conversation.

‘Louis is shocked she turned up,’ she said tentatively.

Andrew kept his back to her as he stirred and reheated the chilli in the pan on the stove. ‘I don’t want to talk about him, not tonight.’

The way he said it told Gemma they had a long road ahead of them. But they were restricted in time. Louis didn’t have a whole lot of that, and if Andrew didn’t back down soon, there would be no relationship to repair.

Louis would be dead.

Chapter Twenty-Nine

Molly

'So, how do you feel?' Ben plonked himself on the sofa next to Molly. They'd been texting non-stop the last few days since Molly had met Andrew Bennett for real. Ben had been working flat out at the hospital on the night shift, and there hadn't been much time to meet up until today.

Molly leant back against the sofa, aware their shoulders were touching. Ben had come straight from another shift, and his clothes had a faint, familiar antiseptic scent, but it didn't bother her. It was comforting, something familiar in a world that had pretty much turned upside down over the last few weeks.

'Honestly?' she asked. 'I still feel numb, like it didn't really happen. It's like my imagination did all the work, and I'll wake up tomorrow and find I've got to go and do it all over again so I know it's real.'

Molly giggled.

'What's funny?' he asked.

'Do you remember on the plane, asking me whether Andrew Bennett was fat?'

He pulled a face. 'I'm not sure where this is going. He looked pretty fit to me.'

'Exactly, and when I was with him at the café contemplating what to say next, all I kept thinking was how fit and well he looked, not an ounce of fat to be seen. Deep, huh!'

Ben smiled. 'I guess it's funny when you think of it that way. But funny things come into our heads at the strangest times. It's like people who get the giggles at funerals. It happens. The rest of us can't understand, but maybe they're thinking of something completely different, to take their mind off the reality of the situation. Otherwise they'd go the other way and fall apart.'

'I suppose you're right.' She yawned when she saw the time on the baby blue clock nested on the shelves above the television.

Ben nudged her arm. 'I know I'm not exactly scintillating company after work, but I'm not that bad, am I?'

'Sorry.'

'Wait … It's not you, it's me?'

Molly laughed.

'I'm glad you finally did it,' he told her.

'I think the Bennetts are going to be hard to get to know. The wife ran off when she realised who I was, the father and son aren't talking to one another because of the lies the family told years ago and Louis might die before I get a chance to know him.'

Ben sat back too, tilted his head to look at the ceiling like Molly, their eyes fixed on the same hairline crack running from the light fitting to the far corner. 'And you thought you had problems when you were scared of flying.'

Molly sighed. 'You're not wrong there.'

'How did you leave things with Andrew?'

'We said we'd text or call, but I think both of us need space.' She hoped he wouldn't take so long that it was time to leave the country before she'd got to know him even a tiny bit.

'How about tomorrow morning we get you away from Magnolia Creek, go and have fun, no stress?'

‘Sounds like a brilliant plan to me.’

He stood up, unable to hold in his yawn any longer. ‘I’ll pick you up around eight-thirty in the morning.’

‘See you then.’ She smiled as he turned and made his way to the door. She saw his reflection in the window, and he was smiling too. ‘It can’t be a date though. Remember I leave in less than three weeks, and we’ll have to go back to being online buddies.’

‘Suits me,’ he shrugged.

Somehow she got the feeling he wasn’t as serious as she was.

*

The next day Ben did as promised and picked her up bright and early. She hadn’t heard from Andrew again, but she checked her phone every few minutes as Ben drove out of Magnolia Creek. She turned her head as they went past the chocolaterie, wondering whether he was in there, whether he was thinking about her.

‘Has he contacted you?’ Ben asked as they cruised away from town.

‘He hasn’t.’ She hesitated. ‘I’m sure it’s a lot for him to think about.’ She caught a waft of the manly fresh shower gel Ben must’ve used. ‘Where are we off to?’ She needed a distraction from thinking about Ben and how good he smelt, how amazing he looked, not just today but every day they’d met up.

‘Well, whenever I could use a break, I head to the beach.’ Ben joined the freeway. ‘Fresh, salty air clears the head. So we’re on our way to Albert Park. It’s a little suburb with an amazing beach, a row of trendy cafés. You’ll love it.’

Her spirits lifted. She’d not been to the beach since she’d arrived in Australia, and beach went with the territory. She pushed her phone into her bag and put it down at her feet where she wouldn't be tempted to check it again.

An hour later and they were following the smaller roads to take them to Albert Park. They crossed tramlines, the windows open to feel the change between freeway air, suburban air and finally beach air when they reached the main road running parallel to the water. Palm trees were spaced evenly, framing the road on either side, a pier jutted out into the water, roller-blading couples and friends cruised up and down the paths. A strip of grass separated either side of the road and enormous, hotel-like properties overlooked the ocean and lined the side of the road farthest from the water.

Molly was mesmerised by the beauty of the area. She sat taller in her seat to focus on the golden sands and the sea with its frothy white edging as the waves came in to shore. Ben slowed, looking for a parking space, but it seemed they were among the many who'd decided it was too beautiful a day not to be beside the ocean.

He turned into a side street. 'I'll park by the lake and then we'll walk down this way. You got your walking shoes on?'

Molly looked down at her white Converse trainers. 'Yup.'

A tram came to a halt in the middle of the road, and Ben pulled up before he was level with it. Once passengers had disembarked and were safely on the pavement at the other side and the tram trundled on its way, they continued.

'This is Albert Park Lake,' Ben announced when they pulled in to a car park. 'Home of the Grand Prix.'

She nodded, impressed. 'It looks too peaceful.'

'It's completely transformed every year,' he told her as he pulled into a vacant space. 'You wouldn't believe it now, would you?' He leapt out and went to feed the meter.

The water glistened, framed with a backdrop of city buildings in the distance. Molly and Ben walked side-by-side, clockwise around the lake. They'd agreed to do a lap first before heading to the beach and right now, Molly couldn't imagine anywhere more beautiful.

Following the path around the lake's perimeter, Ben said, 'This is almost as relaxing as the beach. More so in some ways.'

'It's away from the crowds,' Molly agreed.

'Do you sail?'

'I would've liked to learn, but it's one of those things I never got around to. I did windsurf once.'

'Yeah?'

'Lots of fun.'

'You stayed on the board?'

'Eventually. It took a bit of practice. I learnt on a lake, and I think it's the only reason I managed to stay upright as much as I did. The water was a lot calmer.' She followed Ben along a thinner winding path, past a small building, until they were beside the water once more. The temperature was perfect. It had rained during the night, more than a gentle pitter-patter on the cottage roof, and she'd thought today was going to be one of those days spent in warm clothes and a waterproof, but as soon as she'd woken and seen the sun streaming through the gap in the curtains, she knew she was in for a great day. There was a slight breeze, but the sun refused to bow down to the autumn season and it kissed Molly's skin as they followed the path around the water's edge.

'I've never been into water sports,' Ben told her as he watched the teenagers in the boat sail past skilfully, not too close to the edge, aware of another sailing boat close by. 'I do, on the other hand, love to ski.'

'Ski?'

'What, you think all Aussies can do is barbecue and lay on the beach and tan?'

She grinned, because she'd pictured exactly that. 'Do you go over to New Zealand? My brother tells me the skiing there is amazing.'

'I've been a couple of times but not for a while. The most recent skiing has been in Victoria.'

'As in Victoria, Australia? You're kidding.'

'Nope. You can drive from Magnolia Creek to Mount Hotham in less than three hours.'

'No way.'

He seemed amused by her surprise. 'The ski season is June to September, our winter.'

'I can't believe I never knew that.' Molly shook her head and laughed. 'I never, ever thought you could ski in Australia. It seems to go against what we expect Australia to be like.'

'Have you ever skied?'

She shook her head, and as they meandered around the lake with the sun on their backs at first and then shining directly in their faces, Ben told Molly about various skiing expeditions, one of which had resulted in a broken leg.

'I was showing off,' he admitted. 'Trying to impress a girl.'

'Sounds about right.' She grinned to show she was jesting. 'Does it ever snow in Magnolia Creek?'

'Very occasionally. Usually we get a ground frost and it can be a bit icy, but generally we get away with only having the dark, the damp and the rain.'

A black swan glided through the water, and Molly could all of a sudden imagine how this could become the setting for the Grand Prix. The lake wasn't a uniform shape and the roads surrounding it had bends, curves only the most skilled drivers would be able to negotiate at high speed. She wondered what happened to the wildlife. Did the swans hide out somewhere? Were they rescued and kept safe during the event?

'What's that building?' She pointed across the road as they came full circle to where they'd parked.

'It's the Aquatic Centre. It has an awesome Olympic-size, outdoor swimming pool. Maybe we could go sometime.'

Molly's heart both leapt and plummeted, the former because he wanted to see her again, the latter because this wasn't going anywhere. But one thing had worked today, his plan to bring her away from Magnolia Creek and get some distance from the Bennetts. She hadn't even inhaled the salty sea air of the beach yet, but she felt totally relaxed and hadn't given a second thought to checking her phone.

Completing their circuit of the lake, they made their way down to the beach where the salty sea breeze coming off the water wrapped around them with every step they took. She removed her Converse trainers and followed Ben onto the sand, letting the granules massage her feet as they walked, weaving past people enjoying the last few beach days of autumn. They admired some serious sandcastle construction from two twin boys armed with spades, forks and different shaped buckets.

'So,' said Ben, pulling his hoodie off over his head. Molly didn't miss the glimpse of his stomach as he did so, the line of dark hair running down, the toned muscles, which spoke of activity and a healthy lifestyle. 'How are you feeling?'

When Ben gestured for her to sit down on the hoodie, she did so. He sat down too, although they were incredibly close given the size of the clothing. She was nervous all of a sudden, an unexpected feeling she hadn't experienced much with Ben until now.

'About the Bennetts?' she asked for clarification.

'The reason you're here, yes.'

Looking out over the ocean, brave kite surfers battled the rougher conditions down towards St Kilda. 'Ever tried it?' She nodded to one guy as his red and black sail caught the wind, his body below straining against the force as he glided across the water.

'I don't think it's my thing.'

She laughed. 'Windsurfing was hard enough. That looks impossible.'

'Stop avoiding the question anyway,' said Ben.

'I'm not avoiding it. I'm simply choosing not to answer.' A refreshing spray from the ocean flecked her face when the breeze blew the right way. 'I'm not sure how he feels.'

'Andrew?'

'This is a big shock for him, not to mention the rest of the family, and with his father sick … God, I really don't know. I mean, it was my choice to do things this way. But if it's all going to fall apart at the seams, I'd rather it happened sooner than later.'

'Do you think it'll all go wrong?'

Molly shrugged. 'There's a flicker of hope it'll all work out, that he'll want to get to know who I am and become a part of my life, no matter how big or small. But at the same time, I'm looking at it negatively, trying to prepare myself for the worst.'

Ben drew his knees in to his chest and wrapped his arms around them. 'I think it was right for you to get out of Magnolia Creek for today.' He grinned at her. 'The last thing you want to do is become some weirdo stalker.'

As Molly relaxed, a smile spread across her face.

'Give him a couple of days,' advised Ben, 'and if he doesn't get in touch, give him a nudge and see where he's at.'

They watched the kite surfers some more, admiring their skill, and when Ben stood and held out a hand, Molly took it and he pulled her up. For a moment she was so close she could feel his breath in her hair, the warmth coming from his chest beneath the black T-shirt.

'Come on, let's walk.' Ben moved from the dry sand to damp and then wet as they got closer to the shoreline.

'Hey, I didn't know you had a tattoo.' As Molly's toes sunk into the wet sand she looked across at Ben and spotted the tail of a design peeping out from the sleeve of his T-shirt. He pulled up the sleeve for her to see it fully, the outline of a rose with the slightest shade of red. 'What's the significance?' she asked.

'My brother Owen started it and then it was a brotherly, solidarity thing. Long story, maybe I'll tell you someday. You know, as a friend.'

Molly knew she was blushing and kept walking, swishing her feet through the white foam that covered her toes, went away again and then came back for her moments later. 'Are you close to your brothers?'

'I am. We've had our brotherly ups and downs but it's great being one of three. What about you and your brother? You said you were close.'

‘We are. Isaac has always been there and he’s one of my best friends. I’ll miss him when he moves out to America.’

‘The world’s a smaller place now.’ Ben grunted as he misjudged the tide’s return and it wet the bottom of his jeans. ‘You’ve got emails, Facebook … all sorts. It’s harder to miss people now.’

‘I don’t know.’ Molly was unconvinced. ‘Sometimes it’s worse, seeing things you miss out on. I can’t even begin to imagine what it’ll be like when Isaac posts photos of his adventures and we can’t nip to the pub and chat about them over a pint.’

‘Well, when you do meet up, now you’re over your fear and everything,’ he joked, ‘it’ll feel like you only saw him the day before. Trust me. I was away for a while and my brother Owen flitted here, there and everywhere until he found a steady girlfriend, and then Tom is knee-deep in fatherhood, but when we all meet up, it’s like we’ve never been apart.’

Molly wondered whether, eventually, it could be like that with Andrew. If – and it was a big if – he decided he wanted to form a relationship, would they be able to pick up where they’d left off? Would this holiday be a good start and enough of a foundation to sustain a relationship over a long distance until they could meet up again?

The fresh air made them hungry, and they made their way to Albert Park village where Molly couldn’t resist ducking into the little bookshop.

‘You should’ve bought something,’ said Ben when they left empty-handed.

‘I can’t. I’ve got a suitcase full, and I don’t want to make it any heavier.’

‘One book won’t hurt.’

Her look told him of course it would. 'I don't want to risk going over the baggage limit.'

'You'll be an experienced flyer before you know it, and you'll bring only the bare necessities, allowing for shopping in the country you're going to.'

They walked on until they came to a café, with silver chairs and tables spilling out onto the wide, curved pavement. Leaves skittered across the footpath, dry and crunchy from the season. 'I'm starving,' said Ben, eyes glued to the menu already. 'Let's eat and then we'd better get back to the car before the money runs out and I get myself a little souvenir of my own. Parking ticket,' he explained.

They both ordered the Eggs Benedict, something Molly had only ever tried once at a restaurant in Covent Garden more than a year ago. And now they were sitting, Molly sneaked a look at her phone.

'Has he texted?' Ben didn't miss a thing.

She shook her head, embarrassed he'd seen her checking.

'Don't be disappointed. We men don't like to rush things.'

She pushed the phone back into her bag. He was right. She'd had a while to think this through, all her life in fact. But Andrew had only known about her existence for a matter of weeks. She had no idea what this was like for him. Julia had known about her existence for thirty years and look how she'd reacted.

Molly suddenly had no clue as to how this was going to pan out, and as she tucked into her eggs, she knew it wasn't only Andrew she had to think about now. There was Ben. He was starting to mean more to her than an online acquaintance, someone to laugh and chat with. He was there for her, helping her through this when they barely knew each other, and there was an undeniable connection.

How would she leave things with him when this holiday came to an end?

*

When they arrived back in Magnolia Creek, Ben pulled up on Main Street and Molly thanked him for taking her away from it all, even if only for the day.

'It was great to get some headspace,' said Molly.

'I told you, the ocean cures all troubles.'

'I'll try to remember that.' She hovered awkwardly beside the car. If Ben was a friend, she'd lean in and kiss him on the cheek right now. If he were a friend she'd give him a hug and tell him she'd see him soon.

'Are you sure I can't interest you in a swim over at my place?' he asked, breaking the silence.

She smiled, wondering whether he was thinking about what she looked like in a swimsuit. She was definitely wondering what he looked like without his T-shirt. 'Maybe another time. I think I'll go back to the cottage, lie down a while.'

'Fair enough.'

'Are you working again tonight?'

'Nope. Night off for me.'

She was about to be brave and ask whether he wanted to join her for a takeaway dinner, when she looked up and caught the eye of the blonde woman walking past, a straw basket looped over her arm. Molly froze. She didn't know whether to raise a hand, smile or completely ignore Gemma, but when Gemma waved and muttered a hello before scurrying across the other side of the road, she didn't have a chance to do anything except let her mouth fall open.

'You okay?' Ben's gaze followed Gemma and then fell back on Molly.

Before Molly could answer, she looked up to see the next person coming along the pavement.

'Good afternoon, Molly.' This time it was Louis, and his words came out quite clearly. 'You're looking well. The Australian sun must be doing you good.'

Relieved at his interest in her compared to Gemma's obvious need to escape her presence, Molly muttered, 'You're looking well too.' She sounded so lame!

Louis shuffled on his way, and Molly was still looking at him when he turned back.

'And Molly,' he said. 'Remember, time is a great healer.'

Ben came to Molly's side as she watched Louis continue along Main Street. 'Are you okay?'

She nodded.

'Do you want to rethink my offer?' he asked. 'Not many more swim days now it's autumn, but I know the heating in the pool has been on all day. Owen's forever over at my parents doing laps, keeping himself fit. Sickening really.'

She smiled. 'I'll run down to the cottage and get my swimsuit.'

Chapter Thirty

Andrew

Andrew's hands shook as he scrolled down the contacts in his phone until he reached Molly's name. He'd almost called her the morning after they'd met for the very first time. He'd nearly called her each day after too. And now, upstairs at the café, standing on the veranda outside looking over the mountain ash trees, he finally pressed Call and waited to hear her voice. His mind had been a kaleidoscope of feelings the past few days, mish-mashed from what he knew, from the past, from the present. What could he possibly say to Molly? What could he tell the girl who'd come all this way for answers; answers he wasn't sure he could give. And hanging in the back of his mind was whether pursuing a relationship with Molly would destroy his marriage to the woman he loved. He felt as though he was facing an impossible choice: Molly or Gemma.

*

'Thank you for coming.' Andrew led Molly into the office at the back of the shop. A group of elderly tourists had commandeered the seating area in the café upstairs in the time it had taken Molly to walk from the cottage to his place after his phone call.

'What's that?' He nodded to the bright orange bag she was clutching.

'I was on my way for a swim.'

He sat on the desk chair, and Molly took the other seat. 'Anywhere nice?'

'Ben's family has a pool.'

'I'm sorry. I didn't mean to ruin your plans.'

She smiled, cautiously. 'You didn't. This is more important.'

He moved his desk chair back a little so this didn't feel like an interrogation or an interview.

'I'm sorry I didn't call before today,' he said.

'I get it, you know.' At last she looked at him. 'This is a big thing. Everyone told me I was playing with fire turning up on your doorstep.'

'And you didn't think so?' He reached for her arm when she stood up as though she was going to leave. 'I'm sorry, that came out wrong. I didn't mean I wasn't happy you'd turned up. I suppose what I was trying to say, or show you, was how determined you are. Julia was the same.' He added the last comment as though it could explain away a lot of things, but he wasn't sure whether it did really.

'I think she still is, given she won't see me or talk to me.' Molly relented and sat down again.

'Julia was sometimes too stubborn for her own good.' A flicker of guilt passed him by as he remembered an ex-girlfriend, glad Gemma couldn't hear him even though he had no desire to resurrect the past relationship. 'One day we'd been out blackberry picking, and we took the quick way home, cutting across a field where there were several horses grazing. One of the horses caught my eye. It was ebony, gleaming beneath the sun, the most impressive horse I'd ever seen.

'Anyway, I got closer to the animal wanting to feel his coat for myself, but its ears were laid flat, the whites of its eyes showing. It was scared, but Julia thought I was being a wimp. She teased me and insisted she'd stroke the horse first if I wasn't going to. I kept telling her not to but she went ahead and did it anyway.'

'So what happened?'

'The horse turned around and bit her in the stomach.' He chuckled. 'I think you could hear the screams all across the village.'

Molly laughed but soon turned serious. 'I think the worst thing was how unprepared I was. I had this vision of Julia opening her arms to me eventually.'

'Real life rarely goes the way we plan though, does it?' he philosophised, aware of his own far from idyllic domestic situation. These days, the cosy world he called home constantly spun on its axis and Molly turning up had only made it spin faster.

'No, I guess not.' She held the orange bag on her lap and toyed with the handles. 'Part of me thought that if I could get on a plane to come and meet you, then no matter what happened, I'd survive it. It kind of made me feel invincible, to be taking control.'

He thought about what she'd said. 'How do your parents feel about all this? Have you talked to them since you arrived in Australia?'

'I have, and they're supportive, if a little worried.' She'd called her mum late last night and reassured her that everything was fine, she was taking it slow. She'd almost burst into tears the second she heard her mum's voice, but she'd kept it under control, not wanting to worry them across the miles.

'How's Gemma?' Molly asked.

Her question made him sit up straighter. 'How does she feel about you, you mean?' She nodded. 'To be honest, I really don't know. You're not seeing the real Gemma, or at least the Gemma who was here before all of these family issues began.'

'What's she really like?'

'She's usually able to size people and situations up at a glance, take control, adapt and work out strategies to make everything easier. She's strong, but struggling to have children has battered her out of shape.' He smiled awkwardly. 'Sorry, very bad analogy there. I think everything happening at once has started to take its toll, and finally I see she needs support as much as the rest of us. Trouble is, she's usually so strong it's difficult to recognise the early warning signs. She's been coping with taking Louis to hospital too. Something I could easily rectify if I got over myself.'

She returned his smile, and he briefly saw the fifteen-year-old Julia, scared and unsure. 'My appearance won't have helped,' said Molly.

'Don't take it personally. Easier said than done, but in her heart she doesn't wish for any hurt to come your way.'

'Do you wish I'd given you more warning? Written first?'

He thought about it for a moment. 'Actually, no. Sometimes you can overthink a situation, and by doing so you get nowhere.'

They talked some more about Molly's visit to Albert Park with Ben, but he tried not to pry too much. This was obviously a blossoming romance even though Molly described their relationship as a friendship. He could see it was more by the way she needed to control her smile when she spoke about Ben, the way her eyes were downcast as though thinking about him and talking about him at the same time made it too difficult to do anything else. In this moment, Andrew felt like a father, an overprotective father wondering whether Ben Harrison was good enough for his little girl, and the feeling took him by surprise.

‘You must be pretty angry at Louis,’ Molly noted.

He drew in his breath. ‘That’s putting it mildly.’

‘I saw him this afternoon, and Gemma.’

‘Oh?’

‘Gemma could barely look at me, she crossed the road. I feel so bad this is coming between you.’

Andrew ran a hand through his hair, tugging hard at the roots as though it would help.

‘It must be hard for her to know what to say.’ Molly smiled. ‘Louis spoke to me … he was wearing slippers, in the street.’ She pulled a face.

Andrew laughed. ‘Dad won’t wear something that doesn’t feel comfortable, so he’s been living in a pair of slippers or his runners since his feet are too swollen for shoes.’

Louis shouldn’t have been out walking on his own, and Andrew hoped he’d only gone as far as Main Street and then turned back for home. They weren’t speaking, but his chest still clenched at the thought of his dad walking somewhere, unable to get back to them because he’d taken a turn.

‘He can get really tired,’ Andrew explained. ‘He’s exhausted at times, especially on the same day as the dialysis. He often sleeps it off the second he’s home. But other days he’ll be up and about, determined not to let it get the better of him.’

‘And Gemma takes him to dialysis?’

‘She does. We were sharing until—’

‘Until he told you everything,’ Molly concluded. ‘What about a transplant?’

Her question startled him. ‘There’s a long waiting list.’

‘You know, family members are often a match. There’s always live donation.’

Oh God, how had he got into this conversation? 'I'm not a match.' The words were out before he could stop them. This was about him and Molly, father and daughter, not about the wrongs of his father, the secrets and lies he'd kept.

'I might even be a match,' said Molly.

'Oh no, no way.' She could well be, but he'd never, ever let her do it. 'Please don't even entertain the thought, Molly.'

Anxious to escape any talk of transplants, he said, 'I'm angry at Dad for what he did, but he's a good man deep down.' Admitting it out loud was more for Molly's benefit than his own, but it made him take pause. 'He knows how wrong he was and he also knows – maybe this wouldn't have been the case all those years ago – that he can't push away a member of his own family. I imagine he'd be thinking perhaps he could make amends, through you. He'll want to get to know you, Molly.'

She seemed pleased at the thought.

They sat in the quiet of the office, the breeze blowing through the open window, the whir of the computer on the desk. The sounds of the chocolaterie seeped through the door – Stephanie calling to Emilio to fill another online order, Emilio asking for packaging for chocolates destined for the shop floor.

Molly put her bag down and scooped her legs up onto the chair, hugging them to her. 'Tell me more about life in Australia when you were younger. I'm fascinated. It must've been so different.'

He told her about the first year in the country, making friends, all the usual schoolyard shenanigans from fighting with other boys to trying a cigarette and hating it. He told her how he'd studied a Hospitality degree in

Melbourne and was set to do hotel management, but then during an apprenticeship as a pastry chef at a hotel in the city, his passion for chocolate grew. He'd studied under Louis, working in the family chocolate business, and then he'd met Gemma and decided to go it alone under the banner of Magnolia Creek Chocolaterie.

'Do you need to get going?' he asked when he heard her phone bleep.

'Ben,' she said. 'Sorry, I'll text him to explain where I am.'

When Molly had finished sending her message, Andrew asked her to tell him more about her childhood, more about her life now. She recalled school days: the time she'd taken her guinea pig into school for show and tell and it had died on the table, literally; the childhood scrapes she and Isaac had got into; the time she broke her arm playing leapfrog.

'I'll miss Isaac when he moves to America,' said Molly. 'Mum and Dad are heartbroken, but they know they have to let him go.'

The room fell silent until Andrew asked. 'Where do we go from here?' and instantly regretted it. It sounded like he was taking charge in a business meeting, working out an agenda.

'I don't really know. I guess some of it depends on Gemma,' she said tentatively. 'I don't want to come between you. The last thing I want to do is cause trouble. But if she doesn't want me in your lives, then moving forwards will be difficult, all round.'

'You're too understanding.' He smiled. 'Julia always said I was too soft, you must get that from me.'

Molly's phone bleeped again. 'I'd better be going.' She hesitated. 'Thank you for inviting me here today.'

'I enjoyed it,' said Andrew, conscious they still weren't entirely relaxed in one another's company. There was still a slight awkwardness, unspoken words hovering somewhere in the air, refusing to be caught for now.

*

The chocolaterie was closing, and Andrew switched the tempering machines in the kitchen to standby so the remaining chocolate inside would keep until he switched them all back on in the morning. Outside the sky had turned a gunmetal grey, clouds puffed in the distance and Magnolia Creek was quietening, preparing to say goodbye to another day as the light faded.

'Gemma?' Andrew unlocked the front door to the shop when his wife appeared in the doorway and tapped gently on the glass. 'Is everything okay?' She was usually at home at this time, tired after a busy day teaching.

She kissed him on the cheek.

'What's that for?'

'Because I haven't kissed you in nearly a week.' She followed him out into the kitchen where he rinsed a few moulds and dried them with kitchen towel.

'It's understandable,' he said.

'Andrew.' She stilled his hands and he put down the mould and the tissue. 'I don't want this to come between us. We've got so much going on.'

He smiled, reached a hand up to stroke her cheek. 'You're amazing, you know that?' This was the Gemma he'd fallen in love with. The woman who saw problems as temporary glitches, nothing they couldn't bounce back from.

She looped her arms around his neck. 'I know.'

When he grinned, she leant past him and plucked a wonky white chocolate disc from the tub on the top shelf where they kept any rejected chocolates, unsuitable for display. She plucked another and put it in Andrew's mouth as he pulled her to him.

'I saw Molly today,' she said.

'So did I.'

Gemma pulled back. 'You did? Did you speak to her?'

He nodded, couldn't help the smile. 'We talked for a while.'

'And?'

'It went well, really well.' He told her what they'd talked about, downplaying how awesome it had felt, how elated he still was even though she'd left a while ago.

'How did you leave things?' Gemma asked.

'We'll talk again. It's a shame she lives so far away.' He searched Gemma's eyes for any indication of whether she would ever be able to accept this new person in their lives. Molly was close to Gemma in age. Only seven years separated them, and Andrew wondered, if Molly were younger, would it have been easier for Gemma to accept Molly as his child?

'Make the most of the time you have with her,' she said.

'I intend to.' He went to kiss her, but she pulled away. 'What?'

'Talking of making the most of the time you have …' She raised her eyebrows.

'Oh don't, don't start on about Dad again.' He went into the office to turn off the computer and Gemma followed him.

'If I don't say it, nobody else will, least of all him!' Her voice was strong, determined, angry even.

'Leave it, Gemma.'

'No! I can't leave it!' She eased off and sighed deeply, leaning against the doorjamb. 'I didn't come here for a row. God knows we've been strangers in our own house for the last few days ever since Molly turned up. I'm not suggesting you forget all about what Louis did, but he's sorry for what he's done.'

Andrew conceded. 'I know he is, but I can't get past it. I can't.'

Gemma moved towards him, stood on tiptoes, rested her forehead against his. 'Try. For his sake.' But Andrew pulled away.

'I don't want to talk about it any more.'

'Well, hard luck!' Her voice grew louder as she tried to get through to him. 'You have to talk about it! Did you know he's getting worse?'

Her words stopped him as he pushed his phone into his bag and picked up his coat.

'Today he got out of breath coming from the annexe to the house. He fell into a chair the second he got there.'

'Molly says she saw him out walking today, you know, when you ignored her? When you felt the need to cross the street?' It was a low blow, but he was angry, couldn't help it.

'I'll ignore that remark because, right now, it's not about me or my feelings. For your information, Louis had been holding my arm right up until I saw Molly and told him I couldn't do it, I couldn't act like I was happy she was here, in our lives all of a sudden. I couldn't look at her and not hate her for being the child I can't give us.'

'You hate her?'

Gemma hesitated. 'I'm not sure I can have her in our lives.'

'This is about you! You're not even trying to see it from my point of view, or from Molly's.'

'We've got enough going on in this family right now.' Gemma couldn't look at him.

'And Molly is a part of this family. Like it or not.' He dug his heels in. Someone had to. He'd lost Molly once, or thought he had when the families had pushed him and Julia apart, and he didn't want to lose her again.

'You're too stubborn for your own good, Andrew. Your dad will die if you have your way.'

'I don't want him to die!" He bellowed back at her.

'You're refusing to give him your kidney when you're the perfect match. You may as well sign his death certificate and be done with it.'

Gemma turned on her heel to leave and bumped straight into Molly.

'I'm sorry,' said Molly, looking from Gemma to Andrew. 'The door was open.' She hooked her thumb behind her towards the front door. 'I left my swim bag.' She stepped forwards and picked up the orange bag. 'We didn't swim, too cold. I thought I'd come and get it,' she stammered.

'Molly, I—' Gemma began.

'No need to explain.' And with that she was gone, and all Andrew could do was look at Gemma. Anger and resentment coursed through his veins.

It was an impossible choice. If the two most important women in his life couldn't make peace, he'd lose both or either of them. And if he let the past dictate the future, he'd lose his father too.

His family was about to snap like a brittle chocolate square, wafer thin, but with an inside he didn't like the look of much at all.

Chapter Thirty-One
Molly

Molly ran straight to the Harrisons' house. She'd spent so long talking with Andrew that afternoon that the autumn temperature had crept up on them, and they'd already decided not to swim, but she'd run back to the chocolaterie, before it closed, to get her bag in case they wanted to swim tomorrow.

Ben was still sitting out in the cabana at the foot of the garden, past the pool, when she arrived.

'I couldn't bear the thought of being in the cottage on my own,' she told him after she'd explained what had happened.

Ben grabbed two beers from the outside fridge. 'So Louis could die, and his son could be the reason?'

'Looks like it.' Molly slumped at the bench beneath the cabana, which housed everything needed for a good party: the barbecue, the fridge, the stunning pool with a backdrop of the bush or the back of the house, depending on which way you were facing. 'When we talked this afternoon, he told me he wasn't a match.'

Ben whistled in surprise and took a swig of beer. 'Lying to you isn't exactly a good way to start a relationship.'

'You think?' Molly knocked back half her drink as they listened to the water glugging from the solar system, the gentle chugging of the pool cleaner as it skimmed dirt from the blue tiles below the water.

'Andrew Bennett is as bad as his father if he thinks lying is the way to deal with things,' said Molly. 'That's exactly the reason he's as angry as he is. Why didn't he tell me the truth?' She was angry at being lied to. Here was yet another twisted story from the Bennett family.

'Perhaps he thought you'd think badly of him,' said Ben.

'I think badly of someone who can't tell the truth.'

When he noticed she'd necked most of her beer already, he didn't even ask before he went to the fridge and brought back another. He cracked open the top and handed it to her.

'Thank you.' The first beer had already calmed her down. She ran her fingers down the second bottle, watching as the brown glass darkened when her skin warmed the vessel.

'Look at it from his point of view,' Ben suggested diplomatically. 'If he'd told you the truth, you would've thought he was heartless for saying no to his dying father, am I right?' She didn't answer, confirming his assumption. 'It probably went under the banner of things-to-tell-my-long-lost-daughter-eventually.'

'I suppose you're right.'

Ben nudged her. 'Go and see him tomorrow, talk to him. My family kept secrets over the years and if you ask me, it makes matters worse. Owen found out my parents had hidden something from him his entire life and it very nearly blew up in their faces.'

'Are they okay now?'

'Everything is great now, better than before. But I realise how easily it could've gone the other way.'

'Yes, Doctor Ben.'

'Hey, don't mock. I'm a good doctor. But this isn't medical advice. It's common sense.'

'Gemma hates me, you know.'

'The wife?'

She nodded and filled him in on everything else she'd overheard.

'It sounds like the Bennetts have a lot going on.'

'I don't want to come between them,' said Molly. 'I don't know. Maybe in her position I'd feel the same.' She rested her arms on the table, the beer bottle pressed between outstretched hands. 'This is the sort of thing that makes me wonder whether I'm mad to get involved. I mean, I'm happy in England. There I am with a great mum and dad, a pretty awesome brother – don't tell him I said that – so why, oh, why did I want to screw it all up?'

'Because you're human, Molly. You wanted to know where you came from and you decided to give this man a chance to know about you. You gave him the benefit of the doubt.'

Their eyes met for a moment until Ben's gaze focused on her bag. 'We could use the spa.'

'What? It's cold out.' Already she'd pulled on the cardigan she'd brought from her place.

'It's heated.'

She shook her head. 'I dunno. Feels weird, sitting in a bath … with you.' She tried to make a joke, nervous at the intimacy of the proposed situation.

'It's not a bath.' He laughed, and looking at his profile Molly saw the Ben who was a little mischievous when he wasn't being sensible. He had tiny creases at the corners of his eyes when he laughed, creases that were there face on but looked different from this angle, and she tried to ignore the way his lips made contact with his bottle of beer, the stubble on his chin and neck as he swallowed the liquid.

'Look, my parents aren't around,' he said. 'We have the place to ourselves and barring my brother making an unexpected trip to the back garden, which I highly doubt now he's all loved up with Rosie, we're safe. You can get changed inside in the bathroom. Come on, what do you say? It's a great way to unwind after a stressful day.' He hooked an eyebrow and she knew she couldn't resist.

In the downstairs bathroom inside the Harrisons' house, Molly pulled on her midnight blue tankini, adjusting the bottoms correctly, ensuring the top was covering everything it should. When she emerged, wrapped in a towel, she looked up at the Harrisons' home. It was a beautiful house with a garden she couldn't imagine having in her wildest dreams. The pool and the spa were something else, the tended rose beds all inspiring and the view of the bush looked as though it could make you forget anything else existed outside the walls of the home. It was certainly a huge contrast to her flat back in England and the house she grew up in, a modest semi-detached in a quiet town with neat, boxed front lawns and uniform driveways. But it seemed nobody had the perfect life, not even the Harrisons, judging by what Ben had told her.

Molly clutched her towel to her body and made her way back down to the pool. The blackness of the night had wrapped around Magnolia Creek quickly, but even in the dark she could appreciate the contours of a man's body. Ben had taken off his shirt, and she watched him as he unhooked the fasteners of the spa cover. He was defined but not in an over-the-top way, and the rose tattoo looked in place, as though it was part of him rather than something that had been painted on.

When he looked at her, she could tell he was making an effort to keep his gaze at her eye-level and she hadn't even dropped her towel. She scooped her dark hair into a high ponytail, using the band on her wrist, and climbed in to the spa.

'Sit on the far side.' Ben dragged the spa cover away and stowed it at the edge of the pool. 'It's the best position to look at the stars, although the moon must be hiding.'

Molly lowered herself into the water on the far side, facing away from the house, and Ben pushed a button, sending the bubbles into life. The gentle hum of the spa was paradise itself, and the water lulled Molly into an unexpected sense of calm.

Ben put one leg over the side of the spa, but before the other leg followed he tutted. 'I can't believe I almost forgot. Can I get you another drink?'

Molly settled on a glass of wine this time, too blissed out to even think about Andrew, Gemma or Louis Bennett. Right now she could've been anywhere in the world, on holiday, enjoying the company of a man who understood her more than anyone else for miles around.

He clinked his beer bottle gently against her glass of white. 'To new friends.'

She met his gaze briefly and took a sip.

'See, sharing a bath with me isn't so bad, is it?' he said.

'No, I don't suppose it is.'

'And you're starting to relax, I can tell.'

She rested her glass on the side of the spa, careful to place it so it wasn't in any danger of falling off. She shut her eyes. 'I'm not even going to mention the "B" word for the rest of the evening.'

'You mean the Benn–'

She opened one eye and shut it again when he nodded his understanding.

'This place is gorgeous, Ben.' She kept her eyes shut. 'You're spoilt living here.'

'It's only temporary.' His voice came from the seat on the other side of the spa, facing the pool. 'Now I've done my travelling stint I'll be moving into a cottage up past the fire station.'

Molly opened her eyes. 'You've bought somewhere.'

'I have, but it was a hole when I bought it. Owen renovates properties for a living, so he helped me see past the ugly exterior and the interior, which looked more like a squat.'

'Had someone been living there?'

'Not recently, which is why it'd been so neglected. But it worked out well as I couldn't afford to buy anything renovated. Aussie prices are sky-high, even out here, but the cottage is a decent twenty-minute walk to Main Street, and it needed work doing and was a deceased estate, so I got a good deal. Owen did the work much cheaper than anyone else would've and what's more, he's done it properly. He's very particular.' He laughed after another sip of beer. 'He's so … what's the word? Pernickety?'

'Great word.'

'More polite than saying he's anal.' He grinned. 'Growing up he was no different. One Christmas, all three of us boys got a magic set. When our parents cleared out the loft a couple of years ago, we found Owen's. I don't even know what'd happened to mine or to Tom's, but I expect they were trashed after a few years and then thrown away. Owen's, however, was still in its original box, completely intact, not a single piece missing. I mean, who does that?'

'Pernickety people.' Molly had shut her eyes again. 'He seems nice, your brother.'

'He's a top bloke. I think Rosie helped to mellow him out. She was a surprise to all of us. Owen has never been one to get serious about a girl, and there was a mix up when my parents went overseas. They had a contract with an official house-sitter – Rosie – and then Owen turned up and refused to leave. Somehow, God knows how, they coexisted in the house and eventually they got it together.'

Molly smiled, totally blissed out until Ben spoke again.

'It's hard to believe you're only here temporarily,' he said. 'You'll have to come back and visit again.'

One eye open, she said, 'Maybe.'

'Maybe as in you don't know if you want to see me again, or maybe as in if the Bennetts accept you?'

She frowned, not knowing what to say.

'Sorry, I forgot we weren't mentioning the "B" word.'

'It's fine, I don't really have the luxury of blocking them, much as I'd like to, and sit in this spa all night. Those stars are amazing.' She looked up as one winked at her and a sliver of the moon appeared from behind a cloud, the silhouette of trees masking any more of it.

When Ben moved to her side of the spa, his leg touched hers beneath the water, and she was suddenly aware of their near-naked bodies, side-by-side, gazing up at nature's beauty. His leg touched hers again, and she wondered whether he felt it, whether the water had moved his body her way and he hadn't resisted.

'It's a beautiful night.' She sank a little lower into the warmth of the water.

'You're beautiful,' said Ben.

Molly looked at those stars, kept her mind where it had to be. 'Ben, we've been through this.'

'Ah, the long-distance thing again?'

'It's not long-distance, it's stupid-distance. How can anyone from the UK get involved with someone who lives in Australia?'

'I bet it happens all the time. I bet there are backpackers, even now, tonight, looking at the same moon and stars as we are, both from opposite sides of the globe, having this same debate.'

'Yeah, and they're probably all wasted, and what seems like a good idea tonight won't be in the morning.'

'Maybe you can't control who you fall for.'

'Ben—' She didn't get a chance to say anything else because all of a sudden it wasn't his leg touching hers that was the problem. His hand had reached around and cupped her cheek, and his face moved closer to hers until their lips finally touched. And she didn't want it to feel this good, but it did. She'd been strong up to now, but tonight she knew they were only doing what she'd thought about ever since she'd first seen him at Heathrow waiting for her. And Molly was no longer preoccupied with her fear of flying, now she was scared of something else. She was scared of getting in too deep in an impossible, never-going-to-happen relationship, with someone on the other side of the world.

Her eyes conveyed the feeling to Ben when they pulled apart, the taste of him still on her lips.

'Stop fighting it, Molly.'

'But—'

He silenced her with another kiss, and this time she didn't let it end so quickly. His hands tugged through her hair; she felt the dark tendrils escape in his eagerness. She ran her hand up his arm, the one with the tattoo, knowing exactly what it looked like, and finally getting to feel the skin of this man she'd let get so close so quickly. He trailed kisses down her neck, spluttering as he tried to kiss lower and the bubbles jumped up into his open mouth.

'That'll teach you!' Molly grinned in delight.

He moved in to try again. Molly was pinned back against the spa but sat taller to lift the top of her body from the water, letting his kisses go lower this time. She ran a hand through his dark blond hair as the stubble on his chin scratched pleasantly against her chest. He moved the straps of her tankini top so they fell off, and he kissed the top of her shoulders, his tongue circling. And then he met her mouth again. She knew she should stop, and she felt vaguely out of control when, instead of telling him this was a bad idea, she climbed on top of his lap, sitting over him, kissing him all the while. His hands planted on her hips, pulling her as close to him as he could. Her hands framed his face; she looked deep into his eyes, eyes that told her this wasn't a game.

'I wish you weren't leaving,' he said. But Molly put a finger across his lips. 'I do,' he said again, teasingly licking the tip of her finger so she couldn't silence him any longer.

Her head tipped back as he kissed her along her collarbone. 'Ben, we should stop.'

'Probably,' he said.

Back in control, she looked at him again, her body curled over his, her hands forcing him to meet her gaze. 'It'd be different if this could go somewhere, but we have to say goodbye in two weeks and I don't want to catch the twenty-four-hour flight home pining for you.' She'd be doing that anyway, but she didn't want it to be any worse than it had to be.

‘I’ll be pining for *you*, Molly Ramsey.’ He accepted the situation and pulled her into a hug. ‘You big tease,’ he laughed, nibbling playfully at her ear.

‘I know, sorry. Heat of the moment.’ She clambered off, and they sat side by side, the moon appearing from behind the trees as though watching them. They sat for quite some time, both contemplating the boundaries they’d overstepped in their friendship, the boundaries they both wished never existed and that breaking them made perfect sense.

‘My fingers are shrivelled.’ Molly let Ben wrap a towel around her when they eventually climbed out of the spa. He pulled her to him once she was encased in the soft material.

‘So are mine,’ he said. ‘Thankfully nothing else is.’ His eye raise made her laugh. ‘Sorry, I forgot we can only be friends.’

She kissed him lightly on the lips. ‘Stupid-distance, remember. Not long-distance, stupid-distance.’

‘Ridiculous-distance,’ he said.

‘Absurdly-long-distance,’ she replied.

‘This could go on all night if we’re not careful. Come on, get changed and I’ll walk you back to your place. I promise I won’t even try anything.’

Part of her wished he would.

Chapter Thirty-Two
Gemma

'Try to keep the paint in the pot, or on the paper,' Gemma instructed her class. For the last few days, she'd kept herself busy with teaching, volunteering to take extra-curricular activities, taking piles of work home with her when she didn't always need to. She'd gladly taken Louis to each and every dialysis appointment, relieved to get out of the house and away from Andrew. The tension was palpable following the day at the chocolaterie when Molly had walked in on them, and she and Andrew had barely exchanged three words with one another since.

Today the kids had been asked to paint based on the 'Home' theme, and so some had painted their own houses, another had painted a picture of his back garden equipped with swing and monkey-bar set and another had painted the fire station.

Gemma stopped next to Megan. 'Do you live right near the fire station?'

The little girl shook her head. 'No.'

'But you think it's pretty important?' She guessed the fire station was in the forefront of many peoples' minds given the recent bushfires. Owen Harrison had been in yesterday to give a fire safety talk to the kids. He'd had them enthralled with his natural sense of adventure, the animated way he spoke. And the teachers were even happier than the kids. He was pretty easy on the eye.

'My grandad was a volunteer,' said Megan.

‘He must’ve been very brave.’ She let Megan get on with her work of art and walked round the next few tables until she came to Ellie, who had only painted long green strips across the bottom and was flicking droplets in numerous different colours. Usually a teaching assistant worked closely with Ellie, but she was out today with a bad case of the flu and they hadn’t been able to find a substitute. Gemma had thought she’d be able to handle it but now realised Ellie was having trouble focusing.

Gemma did a quick scan of the room, but all the other kids were enraptured with the task, and the paint looked as though it was going to and from the correct places.

‘Remember how we said this was the “Home” theme?’ When Ellie didn’t answer and the brush showed no signs of stopping, Gemma covered her hand with her own. ‘Ellie, eyes on me.’

Ellie stopped and looked at her teacher.

‘That’s better,’ said Gemma. She turned to the back table and grabbed a fresh sheet of paper. ‘I’ll put this first one to dry on the rack. You’ve got some lovely autumn colours there, but now let’s think about what you can paint to show me where you live.’

Ellie didn’t tear her eyes away from the original piece of artwork, suspecting Gemma was going to drop it in the nearest bin, but when she saw Gemma hang it on the rack as she’d said, Ellie turned back to the plain sheet. Gemma did another scan of the class, told Jacob to stop messing about and knew she had a few minutes one-to-one with Ellie.

‘Right, Ellie. What comes into your head when I ask you to think about where you live?’

Ellie bit gently on her bottom lip as she always did when she was thinking. 'Mummy and Daddy, Cooper and Ebony.'

'Ebony?' Gemma already knew Ellie had an older brother called Cooper.

'My dog. She's a black Labrador.'

'Right, that's a great start. Now, close your eyes, and where do you see Mummy, Daddy, Cooper and Ebony?'

She did as she was asked. 'In our backyard, playing.'

'Now paint what you see.' Gemma guided Ellie a little more. They talked about trees in the garden, a rusty swing, her dog running to catch a stick, and Gemma left the little girl powering ahead with the task. She was coming out of her shell more and more, and although different to the other kids with her mild autism, she was doing better in the mainstream classroom than anyone had predicted.

As Gemma walked around the classroom, she wondered whether, if she closed her eyes, her picture of 'Home' would look the same as it had a few weeks ago when Andrew and Louis were as close as could be, when she and Andrew still talked about having a family – when she and Andrew talked at all for that matter – and before Molly came on the scene. She looked at Joe, a little rascal but cute to boot; she watched Katy, hair never staying in her ponytail and whose clothes got muddy the second she stepped into school; she watched Millie, the little girl who blushed whenever she was asked a question in class. She wondered then how they had come into the world. Had their parents gone through the same struggle? Or had it all been plain sailing for them?

As the class came to an end and Gemma supervised the hanging of the artwork, the clearing up of paint pots, the washing of brushes, she realised what she needed to do if any of this mess was ever going to be sorted out. And she knew she should do it sooner rather than later.

*

Gemma knocked tentatively on the door to the cottage opposite the lake. No answer. She lifted her hand to knock again, but before she had the chance, Molly opened the door.

'Hi.' Molly was wrapped in a towel.

'I'm sorry, you were in the shower. I can come back.' Gemma turned and stepped off the tiny veranda.

'Would you mind?' Molly stayed tucked behind the door so nobody could see her. 'Give me five minutes?'

'Of course.'

Gemma gave her twenty. She felt terrible putting Molly on the spot, but she couldn't let this go on any longer. Despite her nerves at the thought of a confrontation, she had to face the girl for all their sakes.

'Come in,' said Molly when Gemma knocked at the door once again. She gestured to the sofa. 'Please, sit down.'

Gemma sat on the edge of the sofa in the lounge, anything but relaxed.

'Can I offer you a tea? Coffee? Something cold?' Molly rambled.

'I'll have a tea, please.'

'Milk?'

'A little, but no sugar. Thank you.'

Gemma sat rigid while she waited for Molly to go into the kitchen and make the drinks.

Molly reappeared with two mugs, each with a string and a label from the teabag hanging out the side. She set them down on the rectangular coffee table on top of the sky blue china coasters and pulled a little blue china teapot-shaped teabag drip tray from her back pocket.

'I didn't know how strong you like your tea.' Molly explained. 'Mum always makes builder's tea, Dad on the other hand makes tea so weak it's practically like water. I've learnt people can be quite particular about how they take theirs.'

Both women stirred their drinks, squeezed the teabags and discarded them onto the special tray.

'I'm sorry for the way I reacted to you when I first found out who you were.' Gemma was first to speak. 'I've been in a state ever since you turned up and made everything so … real.' She stirred her tea unnecessarily. She suspected that, had she had her own children, the shock of Molly's existence wouldn't have been so brutal, so raw. But for a moment, she'd let it change the person she was. 'I'm also sorry for everything I said.'

'There's no need to apologise, really.'

'I disagree.' Gemma set her mug down on the table, clasped her hands in her lap and faced Molly. 'I'm not usually an angry person, and if I am I'm never spiteful. I manage my feelings, but everything seems to have happened at once in our family and to be honest, I've not been coping as well as I might.'

When Molly looked at her, Gemma saw a flash of familiarity, but she couldn't place why. She didn't look exactly like Andrew, at least not in her opinion. It wasn't Molly's eyes, or her nose, or anything in particular. It was more Molly as a person, her presence, which exuded something Gemma could only describe as Andrew-ness.

'You remind me of Andrew.' Gemma smiled, watching Molly's face. She looked happy, took it as the compliment it was meant to be.

'He says I look a lot like Julia too, my birth mum.'

Relieved Molly had finally spoken, Gemma nodded. 'He told me the same thing.' She hadn't seen a photo. He'd asked if she'd wanted to – there were a few on Julia's Facebook apparently – but it was a step Gemma wasn't quite ready to take.

'Molly, I don't know what it is, but there's something about you that makes you very much a part of the Bennett family,' Gemma explained. 'I want you to know I'm not a complete bitch.'

Molly spluttered as though her tea had gone down the wrong way. 'I don't think that at all.'

'Not even a tiny bit?' She smiled.

'I really don't. I was warned this sort of thing could happen, but after Julia turned me away, I decided I had nothing to lose by turning up here.'

'Still, I said some pretty unpleasant things, and, well, quite honestly I'm embarrassed.'

Molly rested her cup on the table. 'You've come here and apologised. You don't need to feel bad any more.'

'You're a good person, Molly.'

Both women looked at one another, and it was a few moments while the mutual understanding settled between them.

'Louis spoke to me in the street that day,' said Molly.

'He's a good man. Despite everything, all his faults, he's a good man.' Gemma finally shuffled back so she could lean against the sofa. 'He's pretty sick. I honestly don't know how much longer he'll go on.'

'It must be awful. And he's on dialysis four times a week now?'

Gemma smiled. 'Andrew told me you're in the medical profession. You must be clever … you got that from him, and you got his compassion.'

The compliment sat well again.

'Louis has four sessions a week,' Gemma explained, 'and a while ago Andrew was tested and found to be a good match to be a live donor. He took it all in his stride. Louis had refused to let him help until he started to get worse and Andrew gave him a serious talking to. And then—'

'And then I happened,' Molly concluded.

Gemma looked across at Molly as she leant back against the sofa. 'He had a message out of the blue from your birth mum. It knocked him sideways. And then Louis told him everything.'

'It must've been terrible to know he'd been lied to.'

'When Andrew found out exactly what Louis had done, he went ballistic. He was so angry. They've always been close and this was the ultimate betrayal. I don't think I've ever seen Andrew so mad. I really thought he'd hit Louis.'

'Was that when he told Louis he wouldn't donate the kidney?'

Gemma nodded. Molly sounded calm, much calmer than Gemma felt. Maybe she was still enough of an outsider. Nothing was close enough to hurt her as much.

'How long does Louis have?' Molly asked.

Gemma shook her head, tears welling up in her eyes.

'Wait there,' said Molly, heading off to the kitchen. In less than a minute, she was back with two wine glasses and a bottle of Prosecco. 'Sorry, no champagne flutes in this place so these will have to do. I figure we need something stronger.'

Gemma wiped beneath her eyes. 'Oh, God, would you look at me.' She took a glass as Molly wiggled off the top of the Prosecco with a telltale 'pop'. 'I didn't mean to fall apart on you. Usually I'm quite a together person.'

Molly filled Gemma's glass and then her own. 'Can I ask you a personal question?'

'Is that why you're plying me with this?' Gemma lifted her glass to her mouth and took a sip. 'To lower my defences, get me talking?'

'Not at all.' Molly smiled. 'I wanted to ask how you really feel about me being a part of Andrew's life. I don't want to come all this way, meet him and then say goodbye. That can't be it.'

'I agree. It can't be it.' Gemma paused. 'And even though our family has its problems, we're not bad people. It was an incredible risk to turn up on our doorstep. Imagine if we'd been some sort of crazy family, bogans who welcomed you with open arms but for all the wrong reasons.'

Molly smiled. 'I did do a bit of digging on the internet before I came so I'd seen photos, read up about the business. I figured it was worth the risk, and I like to think I'm a pretty good judge of character.'

'You picked well with Ben Harrison.'

'Ben?'

'I've seen the way you two are with each other. Chatting away like nobody else exists … reminds me of when Andrew and I got together.'

'It's a bit of a fling, it's not going anywhere.' Molly told Gemma how they'd met, how they'd flown together from England. 'We've spent the last few days together, as friends, and it's made the trip so much easier.'

'I don't know much about the Harrisons, but they seem a lovely family,' said Gemma.

Molly filled Gemma in on their trips to Sassafras, the city restaurants they'd been to, another trip to St Kilda beach. In return Gemma talked about their move here from the city and giving up the fast-paced life for Magnolia Creek.

'We wanted to raise a family somewhere a little calmer,' said Gemma.

'Do you think you will? Raise a family.' Molly looked into her bubbles.

'I hope so, I really do.'

Molly filled Gemma's glass and her own again. 'Do you think you can change Andrew's mind about the operation?'

Gemma shook her head. 'A month ago I was so sure of everything, but now, I really couldn't tell you.'

'He'll never forgive himself if Louis dies.' Molly's voice was small, and Gemma knew she'd underestimated how much Molly was already invested in this extension of family.

'I know he won't. But what can I do?'

Molly swigged the remains of the second glass of Prosecco. 'I might sound out of line here, but I think he likes me. Louis,' she added when Gemma pulled a face. 'I think maybe we start with him.'

'What do you mean?'

Molly winked. 'I think we need a plan.'

Chapter Thirty-Three
Molly

A low mist had settled on Magnolia Creek, bringing with it the feeling of an approaching winter. Molly finished her toast and cup of tea, cleaned her teeth and checked her appearance again in the bathroom mirror. Yesterday, she and Gemma had hatched a plan, or at least a way forward out of this mess for the Bennetts. Andrew wasn't going to come around about Louis on his own, and he wasn't going to come around by being nagged constantly.

When someone old was found to have done something bad in their past, it always seemed so unimaginable to Molly. There they were, grey hair, stooped posture, papery skin … how could an elderly person have ever done anything wrong? She was struggling to see anything but the good in Louis.

She pulled on a cardigan, picked up her bag and grabbed the key to the cottage. Louis didn't have a dialysis session today, and so this morning Molly was going over to the house to see him, maybe even take a walk along Main Street if he was feeling up to it. She'd not been to the Bennetts' home and she was nervous now, but last night she'd discussed with Gemma how forming a relationship with Louis might help Andrew to see his father wasn't only defined by the lie he'd told all those years ago, the actions he'd taken, but by the many other parts of him that Molly didn't yet know. By seeing Louis form a relationship with his granddaughter, maybe it would pacify Andrew and enable him to see the positives as well as the faults with his father.

Molly went the back way to the Bennetts' place, following the clearly marked trails. An eerie grey mist still lingered over the bushland and hid the tops of the mountain ash trees, the gum trees Molly knew were there, somewhere. She followed the path running parallel to the trees all the way up to main road and took the first turning off to Myrtle Close. She knew Andrew was most likely at work, and she hadn't heard from him in days so she didn't want to bump into him in the street. She'd been disappointed he hadn't contacted her, but Ben had distracted her well enough and she knew she had to grant her birth father this space for the time being.

'Molly, come on in.' Gemma opened the door and the smell of home baking hit her head on. 'It's cold this morning, where's your coat?'

'I'm British, remember. This isn't cold.' Molly pulled the door shut behind them.

'Good point.'

Molly lowered her voice. 'Is Andrew here?'

'No, he's at work. I didn't mention this to him.'

'Do you think he'd flip?'

'Probably.' She led Molly through to an oak-panelled kitchen.

'It's a bit early in the morning for baking,' Molly's tummy rumbled when her eyes fell on the loaf tin on the cooktop.

'I don't sleep well these days,' said Gemma. 'And especially not today when I knew you were coming. I'm a bit nervous about it.'

'Me too.' She watched Gemma carefully turn the loaf out onto a board. 'What is it? It smells divine.'

'Banana bread.'

‘Oh, I love banana bread, especially fresh.’

‘This one’s my own take on a traditional recipe.’

‘What’s the secret?’

‘I guess I could tell you, seeing as you’re family.’ She grinned mischievously. ‘I throw in a handful of chocolate chips, another of cranberries. It makes the loaf really moist.’

‘Oh my God, my mouth is literally watering.’

Gemma cut the loaf into thick slices. ‘It’s Louis’ favourite, but he can’t eat it anymore. The diet he’s on is pretty restrictive.’ She arranged a few slices onto the pale green plate she’d taken from the cupboard and then covered them in cling film. Then she passed Molly a second plate from the kitchen table.

‘What are these?’

‘They’re blueberry muffins for Louis, made from a specially adapted recipe. He’s got plenty of tea supplies over there in the annexe, so you’re all set. I told him to expect you.’

‘And is he okay with me visiting?’

Gemma planted one hand on her hip. ‘Are you kidding? He’s over the moon. After everything that’s happened, he would never have been the one to approach you apart from the odd hello and informal chat.’ She paused and then, ‘This goes to show Andrew, and anyone else who may doubt him, that Louis is kind. He’s gentle, has family values. He made one mistake, that’s all.’

Molly nodded. ‘I’m sure we’ve all made mistakes and I’m only just thirty, there’s plenty of time for me to stuff up yet.’ She wasn’t nervous any more, now she knew Louis was enthusiastic.

She followed the path from the house to the annexe as the mist gave way to fine rain. She didn't have to knock because the door opened before she even got there.

'Molly, welcome! Come on in.' Louis had a sparkle in his eyes she hadn't seen before. And despite his pallor, his spirits overcame any physical demands. 'I'm glad you came.'

Molly noticed his hands were a bit swollen and unsteady. 'I'll take these straight to the kitchen shall I?'

'Be my guest.' He pointed to the back of the annexe.

It was a modest home, the right size for one and decorated tastefully in shades of beige with chocolate brown furniture. She looked around and peered more closely at the photos on the kitchen wall. 'Andrew?' she asked, pointing to the one of a young boy in a school uniform: black blazer, pale blue and black stripy tie, black trousers.

'His first day at secondary school,' Louis confirmed. 'Tea?' He lifted a cup from the mug tree on the worktop.

'I'll make it.'

'Nonsense.'

'Come on, I insist. Are you having one?'

'No tea for me, thanks. As part of my delightful diet I need to restrict fluids. Bloody awful mess, my body is.'

Molly made the tea and asked where the side plates were. She took Louis a blueberry muffin and then went back for her own and joined him at the kitchen table, square and perfect for two.

'Winter's on its way.' Louis broke off a corner of the muffin.

'I bet you've forgotten what a real winter is like, you've been here so long.'

'True,' he said.

'I love the snow, especially the first snowfall of the year when it blankets everything in white. The crunch when your foot first steps into it. I don't miss the aftermath though, with the slush and wondering whether summer will ever come.'

Molly popped a piece of banana bread into her mouth and her eyes rolled heavenward. 'This is amazing.'

'Gemma's a marvellous woman.'

'She sure is,' Molly said, taking another piece. 'I understand this was your favourite.'

'Banana bread and me go back a long way.' He chuckled. 'But the muffins are pretty good too. Can't complain.'

'She's an amazing cook.'

'She is.' He paused. 'You know they've been trying for a family for a long time now? Gemma has been through a lot, but she's strong. And so is Andrew. Neither of them will turn their back on you, or on each other.'

He sounded so confident.

'You'd be good with grandkids,' she told him.

He smiled. 'I hope I'm not doing too badly with the one I've got already.'

Shocked at the candid remark, Molly opened up to this man, her biological grandfather. She told him all about the day at the hospital when a father was denied access to his newborn baby, how that day had changed her way of thinking.

'I'd never thought about finding my birth father before then. I guess I spent so much time obsessing about my birth mother, I didn't think about the other piece of the puzzle.'

Louis sighed. 'It's different. Perhaps it shouldn't be, but it is. A birth mother carries a baby for nine months, feels it kick, hears those newborn cries.'

'I'd always assumed the birth father wouldn't really have an emotional attachment, especially if he didn't even know his baby was ever born. Oh, God, I'm sorry. I didn't mean—'

'Don't apologise, Molly. There's no need. I did the wrong thing and regret it with every part of my being. But what's done is done.'

He was right, of course. 'I sometimes wonder what would've happened if Julia had agreed to see me.'

'Andrew hasn't told me much about what happened when you contacted her,' said Louis, kind eyes looking back at her. 'But I know she wouldn't talk to you, not properly.'

'I was so angry with her. I'd spent a long time being patient and it seemed so unfair. I wonder if she'd have come round had I left well enough alone. But I'm not sure she would've done. She seemed to have made up her mind, and I've heard nothing since.'

'So you took matters into your own hands when it came to finding Andrew.'

Molly finished her slice of banana bread. The rain was coming down harder now, pelting against the window and she cradled her cup of tea in her hands. 'I decided I wanted to know rather than tentatively try to make contact, risk misunderstandings, risk him never contacting me again.'

'It was a big step.'

Molly grinned. 'Do you know I was terrified of flying?'

'Then I'm even more impressed,' Louis smiled. He'd only eaten half the muffin, surprising Molly as Gemma had already told her it was his favourite.

'You're not enjoying it?' She nodded to the plate.

'I've not got much of an appetite these days.' All of a sudden he seemed weary. 'It's the kidney dialysis, takes it out of me.'

That and the disease, Molly knew.

'I can go after this,' she said, sipping more of her tea. 'Let you sleep.'

'No need.' He patted her hand. 'But let's move to the lounge and I can sit back, put my feet on the stool.'

'Good idea.' Molly stacked their cups and plates by the sink and joined Louis in the lounge, where he'd taken the armchair in the corner, obviously a special one for him. It had a tartan throw over the back, and he pulled it down across his knees. She noticed his legs moving beneath it. She moved closer and, one by one, lifted his legs onto the ottoman in front.

'Thank you, dear. I'm not as strong as I once was.'

'You're welcome.' Molly sat on the armchair next to him. 'Tell me more about Andrew,' she requested. 'I want to know what he was like before he met Gemma, before he was a successful chocolatier. He's told me snippets, but I'd like to hear more.'

Louis relaxed into the armchair as he recounted the past and his son, all the way from the first time Andrew fell off his bike and had a concussion to the time he got braces on his teeth and vowed he'd never smile again.

'I think I had him laughing by the end of the day,' said Louis.

'It's very different now,' Molly explained. 'Nowadays all the kids *want* their teeth straightened. I was so jealous when a girl in my class got braces, everyone was. Perhaps it's a rite of passage. Maybe it shows you're growing up.'

'Well, let me tell you, he hated it.' He cleared his throat. 'His teeth were perfectly straight and the braces long gone by the time he met Julia. He was smitten from the get-go. They became inseparable, everywhere he went she went and vice versa. But we had no idea they were … having relations.'

Molly smiled at Louis' inability to include the word 'sex' in his description. It reminded her of the generation gap between them.

He looked down at his hands, clasped together in his lap. 'When Andrew told us Julia was pregnant, it was a shock. But I also saw the past replaying itself.'

'What do you mean?' Molly sat forwards in her chair.

'Andrew's mother and I …' He hesitated. 'We were kids, messing around really, and one thing led to another and we conceived Andrew. We got married soon after and when Andrew told me about Julia, I didn't want the same to happen to him.'

'You didn't love your wife?'

His face softened. 'In those days, if a girl was pregnant, you got married, end of story. But it isn't as simple as asking whether I loved Penny or not.'

'I'm sorry, I—'

Louis waved his hand to stop her. 'Love for us evolved. It came out of friendship, respect, a lifetime together. But if she hadn't got pregnant, I don't think we would've ended up together. We had fun, got on well enough, but there was never a spark to make me feel we'd be together forever. We had a good life and built a family. I had the business and threw my heart and soul into it, but I wanted my children – Andrew included – to have everything.' He smiled at Molly. 'When you have kids, you'll know what I mean. You want them to have the world at their feet, to know no bounds, to never be constrained by anything.'

The rain pelted harder against the windowpane. 'But it sounds like Andrew was happy with Julia, from what he told me,' said Molly.

'He was, but all we saw were two fifteen-year-olds who would be forced to grow up quicker than they should, forced to clip their wings and stay put rather than spread their wings and fly away.'

'But if he was happy—'

'I know it sounds as though we were callous back then, but when Julia's mother threatened to go to the police, it made sense to do as she suggested and get those two apart. Let them carry on and lead normal lives, settling down when the time was right.

'I don't know what you think of me, Molly.' Louis refused to meet her gaze. 'But I want you to know I'm not a monster.'

She moved closer and covered his hand with her own. 'I know you're not a monster. I wouldn't be sitting here otherwise.'

'I felt guilty for years,' he continued. 'We'd conspired between ourselves to rip those two apart, to get rid of the baby. God, if Julia had gone ahead with the abortion, you wouldn't … you—' He broke off and tried to push himself up from the chair, embarrassed his eyes had filled with tears.

Molly found the bathroom, gave him a few moments alone, and then brought tissues back with her. Louis was still sitting in the same chair, against the backrest now. She passed him a tissue, and he wiped beneath his eyes.

'You may not think I'm a monster, but I bet you think I'm no man, not with my crying and all.'

‘I think you’re human,’ said Molly. She waited for him to compose himself. ‘What made you run away to Australia?’

Louis’ smile reached his eyes. ‘It was something I’d been thinking about for a while and the timing was right, so I think what happened was the encouragement I needed to stop dreaming and start doing.’

Louis told Molly all about the plans for Australia and Andrew’s time at school. ‘The kids had a few issues settling in but none we didn’t iron out after a few short weeks. And after a while, Andrew stopped mentioning Julia, he stopped looking so miserable, and gradually he got on with his life.’

Louis began to look drained, and Molly knew it was her cue to leave.

‘Thank you for coming to see me today, Molly,’ he said, when she stood up.

‘It was my pleasure. I enjoyed talking to you.’

‘Will you come again?’ He tried to push himself from the chair, and Molly stepped forwards to help him.

‘Of course. How does tomorrow sound?’

She helped him up and he linked her arm, patted her hand. ‘It sounds perfect. But for now I need to sleep.’

Molly helped him to the bedroom. ‘Do you want me to ask Gemma to come over?’

His eyes were already shut as he pulled the duvet cover over his body. ‘I’m fine, thank you, Molly.’

Molly closed the curtains for him, took her umbrella from her bag and let herself out of the annexe. The plan had been to get close to Louis and show Andrew the man was more than the lie he’d told for years. He was also a man who knew how to love, how to accept, how to forgive and move on. But as Molly walked down the path towards Gemma and Andrew’s back door, she wasn't so sure this plan was a good idea. She was getting attached; she was emotional, weakened at the tug she'd felt between herself and Louis. And very soon she'd have to leave this town behind and return to England. And life would probably go on as though she'd never been there at all.

Chapter Thirty-Four

Andrew

'What are you doing home?' Gemma was drying up a large saucepan when Andrew came through the door. He'd hoped she wouldn't be there; he'd hoped he wouldn't have to battle the tension that constantly hovered between them. Not today. His thoughts were on Molly for now. He still hadn't had the guts to call or text her, and he knew he was running out of time before she left the country.

He dropped his keys on the bench. 'I forgot the extra Easter moulds I'd stored up in the loft. I need them to start making the raffle prize for Good Friday.'

It was small talk, but at least it was talk.

'I think I should go and see Molly, clear the air about the other day.' He tested the waters to see if Gemma's anger rose, but it didn't. 'I need to apologise.'

Gemma turned to him and smiled, but his eyes went to the window when he saw a purple and white polka dot umbrella heading down the path from the annexe. She didn't need to tell him who it was because the back door opened soon enough.

'Molly?'

'Hi.' She looked from Gemma to Andrew and back again.

'Molly and I have talked things through,' said Gemma.

His relief was palpable, and he looked at Gemma, conveying his thanks to his wife for being a far bigger person than he had been these last few days.

'Here, let me take that.' Gemma stepped forwards and took the umbrella from Molly who was shuffling from one foot to the other, awkward and unsure. 'I'll put it in the laundry sink.'

Andrew pulled out an old towel from the bottom drawer in the sideboard and mopped up the water pooling by the back door.

'Sorry,' said Molly. 'There's water all over your floor.'

'Don't be silly.' Andrew gestured to the table, and when Gemma reappeared she pulled three cups from the cupboard.

'Tea, coffee or hot chocolate?' Gemma asked.

'Hot chocolate for me, please,' Molly smiled.

'Me too.' Andrew watched his daughter, still mesmerised by her, firmly imprinting her face on his mind, knowing she'd soon disappear again. 'How was Dad?'

'He's fine. He looks tired, but he's well and he's in good spirits. He told me lots of stories about when you were younger.' She looked at Andrew. 'I heard all about the braces, I'm afraid.'

He couldn't help but laugh. 'Those braces, the bugbear of my teenage years. Like train tracks, they were!'

Recounting some of the other anecdotes Louis had shared with her helped all three of them to ease into conversation. She recalled Louis' tale of a camping trip to North Devon when their tent had blown down in a gale and Andrew had slept through the entire thing. Louis had dragged him from his sleeping bag, bundled him into the car and they'd driven home.

'I was so confused!' Andrew took a mug from Gemma. 'I'd gone to sleep beneath canvas, and when I woke up I was in my bed, my Transformers lined up on the shelf opposite, the bucket of Lego in the corner.'

Gemma handed round a tin of biscuits, but Molly declined. 'I've already had banana bread. At this rate they won't let me on the plane home due to excess baggage … and not the variety that goes in my suitcase!'

The atmosphere relaxed to something closely resembling normal. And that hadn't happened around there for a long time.

'I messaged Julia this morning,' Andrew told Molly and Gemma. He was afraid of ruining the moment, but he was also aware of keeping the channels of communication open, the importance of honesty. He knew nothing of Julia's circumstances now, whether she'd married, whether she had more children, whether she was happy. And that was what had propelled him to get in touch again. He had had a support system, and although he'd been wronged, he also knew how lucky he'd been.

'Does she know I've come to find you?' Molly asked.

'She does. There've been too many lies over the years. I wanted to be upfront. I want us all to be upfront from now on.'

'Has she written back?' Molly clasped her hot chocolate as she waited for the answer. She had the same long, slender fingers Julia had, the same neat fingernails, unpainted but well looked after.

'No. We haven't exchanged many messages, and I don't expect she will for a while.' Molly turning up had made him revisit his fifteen-year-old self, and in doing so he'd realised how much hurt he had buried since they'd left England. Julia had probably been doing the same for years. 'I don't know Julia now. I knew her then, but so much time has passed. All I'll say to you, Molly, is that hopefully, given time, she'll come round.'

Molly didn't look convinced.

'I'm not sure what her home life was like, even back then.' Andrew sipped his hot chocolate. 'She was always out and about with me. We hung out at our place mostly, never hers. She got on well enough with her mum, but I got the sense she never really trusted her, never really knew where she stood with her.'

'I can't imagine that,' said Molly.

'You have a good relationship with your parents?' Gemma held Andrew's hand beneath the table, and he squeezed her fingers reassuringly when she asked the question.

'They're the best. I've always known about my adoption, but working as a midwife raised questions. My parents were willing to answer any queries I had, help me trace my biological roots.'

Molly told Gemma and Andrew more stories of her growing up, the scrapes she and her brother got into, about his upcoming wedding in America.

'I don't think any child would ever say they were glad to be given away, but at the same time, I'm not sorry I ended up with the family I have now,' Molly explained to them both.

'I'm glad you all found each other.' He watched Molly. She'd stopped drinking her hot chocolate. 'What's wrong?'

She shrugged.

'Come on, out with it. Everything out in the open, remember?'

Molly drew her breath. 'I'm wondering what happens now?'

'With us?' Andrew asked.

When Andrew looked at Gemma and saw acceptance in her eyes, the way her head nodded ever so slightly, he said, 'I'd like to keep in touch.' His words sounded so weak. 'I'd like to get to know you properly, Molly. I want you to feel as though you're a part of this family.'

She seemed taken aback.

'I've scared you now, haven't I?' He scraped his chair back and leant forwards, forearms on his knees, unsure of where this left either of them.

'You've surprised me.' Her voice was small, but he could hear warmth in it. 'In a good way.'

When Andrew looked up, Gemma had reached across the table and was squeezing Molly's hand in her own. Both women were looking at each other, both realising the tendrils of family extended in many ways, so many directions.

'Molly, there's an Easter Egg Hunt, on Good Friday, at Magnolia House.' Andrew's voice brightened. 'Magnolia Creek Chocolaterie is supplying the chocolate eggs, it's going to be a crazy day, but it'd be really great if you could join us.'

'I'd love to.'

'We'll be having a raffle, a great prize organised by Gemma, there's—'

'Andrew, she said she'd come.' It was Gemma's voice.

He hadn't registered because he'd been rambling, nervous at the next step.

'I'll come, but on one condition.' Molly's voice came out small.

'What's that?'

'You think really carefully about Louis.' She had his attention now. 'You said you want me to feel a part of this family?'

Gemma and Andrew exchanged glances.

'I meant it,' said Andrew.

'Then I believe you should put the past behind you. Stop seeing Louis as one-dimensional. He lied back then, made mistakes, but I want you to give him a chance. Give *me* a chance to get to know my grandfather before it's too late.'

When Molly went on her way to meet Ben, Andrew and Gemma sat in the kitchen pondering her last request. Her words had taken Andrew by surprise. She'd arrived in town and until now had been polite, a little unsure of herself and had made no demands on him or his family. But today he'd seen how she'd inherited Julia's determined streak, and it wasn't a bad thing.

Gemma was the first to speak. 'She's r—'

'Don't … don't say it.'

'She's right though, and you know it.' From the wobble in Gemma's voice, she was bracing herself for a showdown, for him to argue back, but this time he couldn't.

Deep down Andrew had always hoped he'd reach this point. Always hoped he'd see reason, and realise that if he let his father die without even trying to help him, he'd regret it for the rest of his life. He'd have to live with the knowledge that one mistake had cost Louis not only his son's respect, but ultimately his life.

'I'll call the hospital this afternoon, make an appointment to go in and discuss a suitable date,' he told Gemma as he pulled her into his arms. This was one less thing for her to worry about. It was one less weight on her shoulders.

'That sounds like a great idea.'

Andrew pulled back. ‘Have I told you lately how amazing you are?’ He tilted her chin up towards his face with his fingers.

‘Tell me again, I like hearing it. You know, in case I forget.’

He laughed and kissed her firmly on the lips, a closeness they hadn’t shared physically or mentally in weeks. ‘I love you, Gemma.’

‘I love you too.’

‘Thank you.’

‘For what?’

‘You know what,’ said Andrew.

‘No.’

‘You do, but you want me to say it. So I will. Thank you for giving Molly a chance, thank you for giving me a chance to get to know her in the short time she’s here. Thank you for supporting Dad and letting me know how unreasonable I’m being.’ He kissed his wife for longer this time. ‘And in a few weeks, when this is all over, when I’m fighting fit again and Dad is back to his old self, how about we start getting this baby thing sorted.’

‘This baby thing?’

‘Yeah I know, sounds simple and it’s not. But somehow, Gemma, I feel as though everything is going to work out fine.’ He took her hand and led her up the stairs. ‘And there’s nothing like good, old-fashioned practice, of course.’

She followed him, giggling, all the way up to the bedroom.

And in that moment, he really did believe everything would work out fine. They’d had their challenges, had their obstacles. Maybe they were about done?

But life had a funny way of taking the Bennetts by surprise.

Chapter Thirty-Five
Andrew

At the hospital Andrew had been declared fighting fit and ready for the transplant, which would be scheduled as soon as possible. But right now he had the order to fill for Good Friday. He'd already made the ten thousand mini chocolate eggs, all wrapped in different coloured foils – pinks, purples, silvers, gold. He'd avoided wrapping any in green, figuring he'd give the kids and any adults helping them at least a fighting chance in finding them in the lush green grounds of Magnolia House. The mini eggs were boxed up and ready to go, but now he needed to make the huge milk chocolate egg and the individual chocolate bunnies to go inside.

He took down the moulds for the bunnies – this variety of chocolate was sold in the shop anyway, so he'd make six of each for this prize: six white, six dark, six milk. He'd wrap each, again in multicoloured foil, and before he used melted chocolate to secure each half of the giant egg together to look like a whole item, he'd fill it with the wrapped bunnies.

He checked the thermostat in the kitchen at the shop. Perfect. The autumn rain had cooled temperatures but not so much they needed the heat on, just enough to work at the room's natural temperature today. Starting with the dark chocolate tempering machine, Andrew filled the mould, moving it from side to side until rich, thick, glossy chocolate filled every space.

Andrew had been over to see Louis after Molly left the house yesterday and he'd told him about his change of heart. At first Louis had protested and told Andrew he wouldn't take the kidney. Stubborn old goat. But Andrew had placated him with talk of Molly, telling him the feelings he'd had since she'd come into his life. Feelings which, up until now, he'd kept closely guarded. Andrew knew he needed to learn how to forgive. He wasn't sure it came naturally to anyone, but he didn't want to give a kidney to appease any guilt he'd feel if his father died, he wanted to give him the kidney for the right reasons. And to do that he needed to talk to his father and see the good in him, not just the bad.

When Andrew knocked on the door of the annexe yesterday, Louis had taken a while to answer. Molly had told him his dad was sleeping, but he'd given him a few hours before he'd come over. It'd given him time to collect himself.

Louis stepped back. 'Come in,' he'd said softly, and shut the door behind his son.

'How are you feeling?' Andrew ran a hand through his hair to rid it of the fine rain that still hung in the air outside.

'I slept for a while,' Louis said matter-of-factly and walked through to the lounge. 'I feel better now.'

It took his dad longer to sit in his favourite chair than usual.

'Did you have a good chat with Molly?' Andrew asked when Louis was safely in the chair. He hadn't offered his help, the determination on his dad's face warning him off, as though he didn't want to put Andrew to any more trouble than he already had.

Louis' face thawed. Whatever he'd worried about, whatever he'd thought Andrew was about to say, he seemed glad at what he'd heard. 'She's a lovely girl. A really lovely girl.'

Andrew smiled. 'I know.'

'She's like Julia.' Again, when Louis mentioned Julia's name it was as though he were waiting for a specific reaction, a launch into the same slanging match they'd had days ago.

'She is,' said Andrew.

'And to think—'

'Dad, enough.'

'Enough?' When Louis looked across at his son, it was as though they'd switched roles. It was as though this old man, shorter in stature than Andrew, was the child and Andrew was the grown-up following the right way to do things, educating the other.

'I didn't come here to fight, Dad.'

Louis' legs shuffled restlessly, and his face contorted.

'You okay?'

'I'm fine, a bit of pins and needles, that's all.' He looked more squarely at his son. 'Why did you come?'

'I came to tell you …' Could he really use the word forgive? 'I came to tell you I understand why you did what you did back then, why you lied. I'm not saying it was right, but I can see how you felt you had no choice.'

Neither of them said anything and the silence stretched into five, ten minutes. Andrew wondered whether Louis was waiting for him to say the word 'forgive' but he wasn't there yet. He hoped in time he would be. Molly had forgiven both him and Julia for creating a life and signing that life over to someone else, albeit unwittingly on his part; Gemma had forgiven him for not telling her about Julia and the baby they'd made together. Forgiveness was one of the most powerful emotions he knew, and Andrew would do his damnedest to get there, eventually.

‘I’ve phoned the doctors.’ Andrew broke the silence, shuffling one seat closer to his dad and watching for his reaction. He saw shock, regret even. ‘I told them I’m willing to go ahead with the live transplant. I’ll need to have the necessary checks again, and we’ll find out more tomorrow when I take you for your dialysis.’

Louis eyes filled with tears. But he didn’t let them spill over. He was still the father, Andrew was still the son. ‘I can’t let you do it.’

‘What?’

Louis shook his head. ‘I don’t deserve it, son.’

‘I should never have pulled out in the first place.’

‘Yes, you should. I did something so dreadfully, dreadfully wrong. And I’m sorry.’

‘I know you are, Dad.’ Andrew’s voice caught. ‘But don’t refuse me this. I want to help.’

They both sat in stunned silence for a few minutes until Andrew pulled out a packet of playing cards from the bureau at the side of the lounge and challenged Louis to a good old-fashioned game of poker. Shuffling blue slippers or not, the man was a master at the game and beat him every time, and many an evening in his teenage years had been spent bonding with his father over a few games.

‘Loser gets to forfeit a kidney,’ said Andrew, and locked eyes with his dad.

All Louis did was nod, and he picked up the playing cards, shuffled them and dealt, ready to go again.

Of course, today was no different. Louis beat him quickly and efficiently.

Now, at the chocolaterie, Andrew smiled as he rested the final bunny mould on the vibrating plate over the tempering machine and watched the milk chocolate settle perfectly. He set them aside to cool as Stephanie called through to the kitchen to say they needed more dark chocolate bunnies for the shop. Apparently they were selling like nobody's business out there.

'Knock, knock.' It was Gemma this time, a big smile on her face. 'Can we come in?'

Andrew wiped a couple of moulds clean and noticed his father behind Gemma. 'Pull up those chairs.' He gestured to the corner, strangely nervous with all eyes on him. 'I'm under the pump so I'll keep going if you don't mind. Lunch hour?' He looked to Gemma.

'Yup. I walked home to check on Louis and we thought we'd come and say hello.'

He smiled. He knew exactly what she was up to. Even though he'd already worked this through with Louis, Gemma needed to see it with her own eyes.

Gemma brought the chairs over and unstacked them, positioning one for Louis and one for herself, and then she grabbed two requisite blue hairnets to match Andrew's, one for her, one for Louis, and they sat and watched.

'I miss the smell as much as the taste.' Louis inhaled the sweet air all around them, the life of a chocolatier, which had surrounded him for more than forty years before he'd retired.

Andrew worked well under pressure, but he was suddenly aware of his audience. Louis never criticised or picked fault, he knew his son was more than capable, but they were only just finding their footing after the fallout, and it made Andrew nervous.

He worked and chatted simultaneously with Gemma and Louis. They laughed about the ten thousand eggs Andrew had made and wrapped, giggled when he told them he'd dreamed about those eggs on more than one occasion. They talked about Molly and how lovely she was, how it would be great to share Good Friday with her. They gossiped about Molly and Ben.

'Long-distance romance is tricky,' said Gemma.

Andrew retrieved moulds from the fridge, turned out the Easter rabbits that were set. He took out sheets of coloured foil from the stock cupboard and began to wrap, feeling therapy in his actions. He smiled to himself, shook his head.

'What is it?' Louis must've been watching him.

'I worry about her.' Andrew looked to Gemma, but he saw nothing but happiness across her face, probably glad he could finally be in the same room as his dad without wanting to strangle him. 'Is that weird? I've only known her a couple of weeks.'

'Not at all,' said Louis. 'It makes you a father.'

'Yes, I suppose it does. Although her dad is the one who should worry. Plenty of men can father a child, but he's been there parenting her for thirty years.'

'Andrew, I—'

'That wasn't a dig at you, Dad. I'm simply stating facts. What's done is done, and at fifteen I don't think I'd have made a particularly good parent anyway.' He wrapped the fourth bunny, carefully folding the edges so they didn't tear, careful to protect the bunny and keep it fresh, then the fifth and a sixth, and he set them all aside on a tray and popped them out of the way.

'Where's the enormous egg?' Louis asked.

'It should be ready.' Andrew went over to the fridge. 'I had to move around some of the shelves in the fridge to get the thing in there.' He opened the door and took out the ginormous half egg in its mould.

'It's enormous!' Gemma squealed, leaping up. 'Is it ready to turn out?'

Andrew tentatively felt the edge of the chocolate. 'I think so.'

'Wait there.' Gemma scarpered over to the sink and washed her hands. 'Let me help, it's huge!'

'Great project to get, son,' said Louis.

Andrew looked at his dad, held his gaze. 'Thanks, Dad.' It had been a stroke of luck getting the order for the Easter eggs. Apparently before Andrew had opened up the shop in town, the idea of doing the hunt at Magnolia House had already been discussed and talks had already taken place about finding a suitable supplier.

'Andrew?' It was Stephanie from the shop. 'Visitors for you.' She popped her head around the corner of the kitchen.

'Send them through.' His hands were on either side of the mould, ready to turn the half egg out onto the benchtop with Gemma's help. He put a thin metal sheet over the top of the chocolate so the dome was on the bottom, and with one hand firmly on the metal and the other beneath the dome of the chocolate and Gemma mirroring his actions, they counted to three and flipped the chocolate over. Placing the metal sheet on the benchtop he said, 'Fingers crossed.'

He slid the metal sheet out from beneath the mould and gently began to lift the plastic from the chocolate.

'Whoa! I don't think I've ever seen that much chocolate.' This from Ben who'd come out back with Molly at his side. They were holding hands, Andrew noticed, until Gemma handed them each a hairnet and they pulled them on.

'What do you think?' Andrew asked, proud Molly had witnessed the unveiling. 'It's going to be the raffle prize. I'll make the other half now and then put those bunnies,' he nodded to the tray full of foil-wrapped pieces, 'inside.'

'So is this egg hunt for adults too?' Ben asked Molly.

Molly touched Ben's chest with her hand. 'You big kid!'

'How are you, Molly?' Andrew used kitchen towel to wipe out the mould ready for the other half of the ginormous egg. He'd wrap the first half carefully so the air didn't attack it before he had a chance to let the other half set.

'I'm good, thanks.' He'd already turned away to carry on with his work, but he could tell by her voice she was smiling. 'Silly question, but why don't you have two moulds?'

'We did but the other broke last Easter. I forgot to replace it but it's on order and should arrive any day now.'

Knowing Louis, he'd want to help Andrew right now, but his body was weakening more by the day, hands not as strong as they once were and legs not as sturdy to hold his shrinking body above him while he worked. Instead, Louis disappeared into deep conversation with Molly about all things chocolate.

Andrew filled a jug at the tempering machine and when the liquid reached the top he turned and poured it into the mould, lifting the vessel and tilting it so the chocolate coated all sides. He refilled the jug and used a brush to add more of the mixture and ensure the chocolate achieved the required thickness, and as he finished he looked over at the family gathered in the kitchen with him and a lump formed in his throat. A few weeks ago he'd known nothing of Molly, he'd not known his father as he'd been back then, back in England. He watched the scene, with four additional people wearing their identical blue hairnets, and he knew he didn't want this moment to end.

'You okay?' Gemma left the conversation and came to his side. 'Andrew?'

He knew he had tears in his eyes and gave himself a moment, the warmth from Gemma's body melting against his own.

'I'm happy,' he said. 'I've got family around me.'

Gemma gave his arm a squeeze and left him to it. But next up was Molly.

'How long will it take to set?' she asked.

Tears all gone and a big smile on his face, he said, 'A while. But I've got the fridge to speed things up.'

'I thought you weren't supposed to put chocolate in the fridge.'

Andrew pushed the mould to the back of the benchtop. It was too heavy to lift to the top shelf where they usually cooled their chocolates. 'You mustn't put chocolate in a regular fridge,' he explained, 'but our fridge is set to a special temperature.'

Andrew had a captive audience with Molly and explained how cocoa crystals needed to form correctly for chocolate to be perfect. He explained how chocolate hardened and contracted, shrinking away from the edges of the moulds so it could be tipped out easily. He talked about the busiest times at the shop and the novelty chocolates they made for every season.

'Some of these chocolates are awesome!' This from Ben who was flicking through the trade catalogue Gemma had given him. He pointed to a motorcycle made from dark chocolate before leafing through more pages. 'I should get that one for Owen.'

Molly pointed to one of the Halloween creations. 'What's that?'

'Eurgh. It's revolting.' Ben pointed to the dog turd made out of chocolate. 'Although maybe my brother would like it.'

Louis laughed. 'I came up with the idea. Kids – boys mainly, but some girls – think it's hysterical.'

'I bet they do. It's the sort of chocolate me and my brothers would've loved to surprise our parents with,' said Ben.

'I don't think I could eat it,' said Molly.

Gemma pulled a face. 'Me neither.'

Andrew met Louis' gaze as Molly and the others sniggered over the magazine, and both men found themselves nodding. It was only a small movement of the head, barely detectable to anyone else, but nevertheless there. It was a nod of acceptance of everything that had passed, everything that had happened. The future was what mattered now, and Andrew felt a rush of what he could only claim as forgiveness.

The family went upstairs to the decking outside for lunch. Andrew and Ben helped Louis up the stairs, slowly but surely. This was one family gathering Louis wasn't going to miss out on, and Andrew didn't want him to either.

Gemma ran home and raided the pantry for bread rolls, the fridge for cold meats. Ben went to the Harrisons and brought back a selection of cheeses and crackers and some fruit, and Andrew sorted out tea, coffee and soft drinks for everyone. They pulled tables together out on the decking. The rain had dissipated and, with a good wipe of all the chairs and the tabletops, they were able to set lunch up outside overlooking the bush in all its beauty.

One thing Andrew loved about chocolate was the way it brought people together. Most people loved chocolate in all shapes and sizes, and today he'd worked in the chocolaterie, relaxed in his familiarity as his family gathered around and watched, asked questions, discussed processes, laughed over funny creations. It was everything he'd dreamed his life would be, and sitting next to Molly for lunch, he was devastated she lived on the other side of the world.

'Are you straight back to work after the holiday, Molly?' he asked, willing himself not to get overly emotional.

'I have four days when I get back.'

'To allow for jet lag?' he asked.

Ben unwrapped another portion of Brie and offered it round. 'That, or in case she got the fear.'

'The fear?' Andrew asked.

'My fear of flying.' Molly grinned, not in the least bit riled by Ben. 'And I think I'll be fine.'

'But you won't have me by your side.' Ben was clearly smitten. Andrew wondered who would struggle more with Molly's departure: Ben or him.

'Dad, can I get you something else to eat?' he asked Louis, sure he was encroaching on Ben and Molly's time together. Young love, especially when the two people involved didn't realise that was what it was, was all-consuming.

'No, I'm good thanks, son. My appetite is pathetic really.' He looked over at Molly. 'I'll miss her when she leaves.'

'Me too.'

'Gemma has adjusted well.' Louis watched his daughter-in-law pouring a glass of lemonade at the other end of the table as Molly drew her into whatever she was talking about with Ben.

'She's doing okay.'

'I love her as though she were my own, you know.'

'I know you do, Dad.'

'And Molly is a keeper … she's wonderful. Hold onto her.'

'I intend to.'

'Remember, son. Life isn't black and white. It's colourful, like everything you create in the chocolaterie … life is crumbled raspberries, gold lustre paint, hundreds and thousands. Life is rarely anything but complicated. It's glorious technicolour.'

They stared at one another until Louis said, 'I did a terrible, terrible thing—'

'Dad, you don't—'

'No, I do need to say it. I did a terrible thing, but don't let my mistake become your mistake. Don't let anything come between you and that girl, whether it's geography or your own need for a family. Gemma will be by your side every step of the way, I know it.' Louis patted his hand. 'Would you mind if I went home now? I'm tired.'

It was as though he'd been gearing himself up for his speech and now he was done, he could rest easy.

Andrew popped his last piece of cracker and cheese into his mouth and readied himself to help Louis down the stairs. Louis lifted a hand to say goodbye to everyone, and Ben came over to shake the old man's hand. 'It was nice to meet you,' he said.

'Good to meet you too,' said Louis.

Molly hovered awkwardly but then stepped forwards, and for a moment Andrew thought she'd shake Louis' hand, but she didn't. She put her arms around his father and hugged him, carefully, as though he might break if she squeezed too hard. Louis was taken aback, Andrew could tell, but he was also clearly pleased at the gesture, especially when he gave him a wink that made him smile as though he were a little boy again being praised for getting top marks in a test.

'I'll walk you home, and then it's back to school for me,' said Gemma.

Andrew looked to Molly and Ben. 'Feel free to stay here as long as you like, I'll be downstairs.'

'Thanks,' said Molly. 'I'll come and see you before we go.'

Andrew helped his dad down the stairs, Louis stopping more than a few times, Gemma continuously asking whether he was okay.

'Do you need me to help him home?' Andrew whispered to Gemma when Louis sat down and she went to retrieve her bag from the office where Andrew had put it for safekeeping.

'We'll be fine, thanks.'

When they went on their way, Andrew checked the chocolate mould and it was setting nicely already. He opened the door to the fridge and then lifted the mould carefully to carry it over. But before he could slot it onto the shelf, he heard Gemma, screaming Louis' name over and over again, yelling about an ambulance.

The mould crashed to the floor, and chocolate went everywhere, as the plastic shattered into a million pieces.

Chapter Thirty-Six

Molly

'I feel so useless.' Molly's body sagged against Ben, who was sitting behind her. In a few short weeks, her family had grown with Louis, Andrew and Gemma, and the thought of losing one of them was unimaginable. At the hospital Louis had been rushed away, Andrew and Gemma had gone with him and Ben sat holding Molly's hand. She gripped him tight, afraid to let go.

Molly and Ben had been upstairs in the chocolaterie, looking out over the beauty of the bush, enjoying the autumn sun on their faces, when they'd heard screams. They'd run downstairs to find Gemma yelling, telling everyone to hurry. Ben had run straight to the front door of the shop to help Louis, who was lying on the ground outside. Stephanie was at his side, Gemma was panicking and Andrew watched on as though he was some kind of ghost at the side of the room, hovering like this wasn't really happening at all. Molly had taken a couple of steps closer, her body moving slowly, her mind nowhere near catching up. She remembered Stephanie coming over and putting an arm around her. She remembered Bella Finnegan crossing the street outside when she saw the commotion, Owen and Rosie standing outside, hands across their mouths in shock, Emilio still in his brown apron with the business logo, waving arms frantically and standing in the road to flag down the ambulance.

‘Can I get you anything?’ It was the first time Ben had stroked her hair so tenderly, the closest she’d felt to him, even more so than the night they’d shared the spa.

‘I think I need to phone my mum and dad,’ she said.

Ben squeezed her hand as she stood.

Molly floated down the corridors, through the maze of the hospital, not hearing any sounds, barely seeing anything apart from the green dimly lit exit signs as she made her way outside to make the call. She didn’t register the nurses who looked her way to see whether she was okay, she didn’t take in the little girl who called after her to tell her a tissue had fallen from her pocket. All she saw was daylight shimmering at the front entrance, pulling her outside.

She dialled the number without even checking the time.

Her dad picked up the phone. ‘Molly, what’s wrong?’ The time difference must have given her identity away.

And all Molly could do was cry.

Chapter Thirty-Seven

Andrew

Andrew watched Louis, lying in a bed that looked too big for him, stared at his skin that seemed to be the only layer left of Louis Bennett. The smell of antiseptic was rife in intensive care. Hands were scrubbed, including his own, each time they came in here. It was quiet save for the sound of machines and hushed voices. Louis wasn't conscious, but Andrew told himself his dad would pull through. They'd go ahead with the kidney transplant and everything would be okay. Louis would live in the annexe until he was well into his nineties, shuffling along the pathway every evening in his blue slippers to join them for a meal.

But deep down he knew it wasn't true.

Andrew closed his hand over Louis'. A monitor next to the bed kept an eye on his vital signs, wires led from it to his body, attached by sensors. But Andrew didn't see any of the technical details. He simply saw Louis, the man he'd had his whole life, the man he hoped he'd get a chance to share more of his life with.

'Dad?' Andrew's voice came out in a whisper and Louis didn't answer, but Andrew was convinced he'd felt his hand move beneath his, if only a fraction.

'You can fight this,' Andrew insisted as Gemma came into the room and sat down beside him. 'You have to.'

'Andrew.' Gemma's hand lifted to her husband's shoulder and squeezed it reassuringly. 'Why don't you take a break, grab a cup of coffee. I'll sit with him.' Her voice fell softly on his ears.

'No. I'm staying.' He'd spent weeks being furious with Louis and avoiding him. He wasn't leaving his side now.

'I'm sorry I treated you so badly.' Andrew spoke as though they were on their own in the room and Louis could hear everything he was saying. 'I didn't know how to deal with what had happened, I didn't know how to forgive you. But I know now that what you did, you did for me. You were right. At fifteen years old neither Julia nor I knew a thing about being in love, we knew nothing of what it took to be a parent and the commitment involved.

'I can't rewrite the past, Dad. None of us can. But we can control our future.'

He rested his head on Louis' bed, his forehead against the coolness of Louis' forearm. 'To be a parent you need to be strong, you need to be there, you need to put your child first, and you did. You did that for me. And I've had a good life, a really good life, and I found Gemma.'

He felt Gemma's hand against his back. 'Molly's here,' he told Louis. 'Your granddaughter is here, waiting for you. Even after everything that's happened, she wants to be a part of our family, and watching you two today was one of the most special experiences of my life.'

A nurse checking the charts and the machine left them to it. Andrew had barely registered her presence.

'I'm going to get a coffee,' said Gemma. 'I'll give you some privacy.'

Andrew nodded and when she was gone he carried on.

'I think about Julia, you know. I wonder how her life turned out. It's hard enough for me to know a child of mine was given away, a child I never knew about. I can't even begin to think about what it felt like to grow Molly for nine months when she thought her boyfriend had abandoned her, when she was taken away to live in Ireland without her friends, everything that was familiar to her.'

Andrew let his head rest for longer, feeling every slight twitch in his father's body. Maybe he'd imagined movement, maybe he hadn't. But he felt comforted being here, he felt close, he felt he could make peace between them.

Andrew smiled now. 'You know, I think I might make it over to Europe one day. I'll visit all those places we talked about … the Swiss chocolate shops, the Belgian chocolate places. I have the perfect excuse when Molly lives in England.'

He watched his father's hand, lifeless beneath his own. Maybe he really had imagined any movement.

Louis' eyes were shut, but Andrew looked at them as though they were open when he said, 'I forgive you, Dad. For everything that happened, I forgive you.'

He sat in silence, holding Louis' hand until Gemma returned.

'Any change?' she asked.

He shook his head.

'Molly's asking to see him again.'

It was the first time Andrew had smiled. And like any concerned father, he'd already adapted to worrying about Molly, happy Ben didn't appear to have left her side since they arrived.

Molly appeared ten minutes later, the smell of antiseptic coming with her from her washed hands before she was allowed into intensive care.

'How is he?' She sat next to Andrew.

His voice came out small. 'Same as before.'

Molly tentatively put her hand on the bed next to Louis.

'You can touch his hand,' Andrew assured her. 'You never know, he might be able to hear us.'

'It feels weird. I've only spoken with him a couple of times.'

'I bet you don't talk to expectant mothers for long before you're holding their hand, helping them through labour.'

'Good point.' Molly reached out and jumped as her skin made contact with Louis' and Andrew knew it was because of the temperature. Louis' hands were cold, small, weak and such a contrast to anyone who was walking around freely right now.

'Do you think he'll wake up?' she asked.

'I hope so.'

Andrew wondered whether she'd been crying. The glow on her cheeks reminded him of Julia. In the winter time, when it was freezing and her head was all warm and beneath a woolly hat, Julia always did have the rosiest cheeks, and more times than he could remember he'd reached out his hands and put them either side of her face to warm them up. Funny, he'd forgotten about it until now.

Molly asked all about the plans for the Easter Egg Hunt, presumably to take both their minds off the gravity of the situation, and Andrew happily complied, telling her all about the morning of the hunt when they hoped and prayed it wouldn't be raining so they could go and scatter the wrapped chocolate eggs over the lawns of Magnolia House.

'The kids are going to love it,' said Molly.

'I think your Ben is going to like it too.'

Molly looked coy. 'He's not *my* Ben.'

'He is.' Andrew pushed. 'Enjoy it.'

'He was unexpected, that's all. I haven't had a serious boyfriend in years, I've been too busy having fun, working, going out with friends. I can't believe it's happened here, on the other side of the world.' She turned to him. 'But who knows what the future holds, right?'

They chatted some more about her family and her phone call with her parents earlier.

'I bet you've got them worried.' Andrew was already in the worry zone when it came to Molly. He couldn't imagine how much that would be heightened had he been her dad for the last thirty years.

'We talked for ages. Dad called me back on my mobile, Lord knows what the phone bill will be.' She smiled. 'I needed to hear their voices.'

Strangely enough, he wasn't jealous. There wasn't room for jealousy if he was going to be a part of Molly's life from now on.

'I've texted mainly, given the time difference,' she told him. 'This was the longest chat we'd had. It got a bit emotional.'

'It's a big thing,' said Andrew, his hand gesturing first to her and then to himself. 'Us, I mean.'

She nodded in agreement. 'I leave on Good Friday. How can I leave when Louis is like this?'

For the first time Andrew put a hand on Molly's arm and gave it a reassuring squeeze. 'We'll all miss you,' he said.

They talked more about her family, her brother and the upcoming wedding over in America. Molly told Andrew all about the bridesmaid dress she'd be wearing – silver, strapless, with beading which shimmered beneath the sunlight, and he knew she'd look stunning.

'Dad and I talked of visiting Europe one day, but we never got round to it.' Andrew looked at Molly now, her hand still covering Louis' as though one of them needed to hold on to him constantly for him to stay with them. 'I think I'd like to start with England.'

'I'd like that.' She smiled at him. 'There's an amazing chocolate shop in London, with the best name: Choccywoccydoodah.'

He laughed, relaxed for what felt like the first time in ages. 'What a fantastic name. Dad would've loved it.'

'I'm sure he would've heard of it. It has the most amazing, flamboyant creations. I'll tell you what …' She paused, unsure of herself. 'When you come over, we'll go. We'll make a day of it and go round London visiting Choccywoccydoodah and other chocolate places. You can see how they do it in the northern hemisphere.'

His mind grabbed hold of the words 'when you come over'. This was the start of a special relationship, and he felt glad she was letting him into her life.

The hours ticked by and as the skies outside grew dark, Andrew's tummy rumbled. 'Molly. Would you like to get something to eat? There's a café not far from here, and it's open until seven o'clock. Would you like to join me? Ben's welcome to come.'

She hesitated.

'Oh, you don't have to,' he said, suddenly unsure of himself. 'I didn't mean to put you on the spot.'

'You didn't.' Molly smiled. 'But I'd love it to be just the two of us.'

‘Sounds perfect,’ he said.

*

‘I’ll take this over hospital canteen food any day,’ said Molly after they’d sat in the café and chosen the All Day Breakfast with extra sides of spinach and mushrooms.

‘Gemma had a sandwich earlier, said it wasn’t bad.’ Andrew poured two glasses of water from the carafe in the middle of the table.

‘I like Gemma,’ Molly told him.

‘She likes you.’

Molly looked at the table but eventually met his gaze. ‘I’m glad. It makes it easier.’

‘It certainly does. She’s a good person. I’m sorry you walked into a bit of a minefield, what with everything the family has going on.’

‘It is a minefield, but then again, so are a lot of families. I’ve got friends whose parents had a bitter divorce, other friends who detest their siblings, a colleague who no longer speaks to her own mother. I think you guys are pretty normal.’

‘We’re not so bad once you get to know us.’ Andrew smiled.

They chatted and laughed as they ate, and by the time they walked back to the hospital, the temperature had dropped ten degrees and the sky was blanketed in darkness, stars twinkling above them.

They sauntered along slowly, enjoying one another’s company.

They only broke into a run when Gemma’s phone call came through.

Chapter Thirty-Eight
Molly

Molly sat on the front pew between Andrew and Ben, among the people she'd known only a few short weeks, as they said goodbye to a man she'd taken seconds to like, moments to respect and understand.

While they'd been at dinner in the café, only a short walk from the hospital, Louis had suffered a second, catastrophic heart attack. Gemma had been with him, and by the time Andrew and Molly reached his bedside, he was gone. There were no nurses or doctors calling for help, nobody pushing on his chest to do compressions and revive him. A nurse was gently peeling away the sticky white circles that had been allowing the wires to send signals to the machines to monitor his vital signs; the machines were silent. Gemma was crying, but Andrew froze on the spot, stunned. Even when his wife hugged him, his eyes had been fixed on Louis and he couldn't look away.

'It was a beautiful service,' Bella told Gemma now as they made their way outside the chapel.

'I'll miss him.' Stephanie sobbed onto Gemma's shoulder. The Bennetts had only been in the community a short while, but Molly could see the impact they'd had, knew the impact they'd had on her alone.

'How are you holding up?' Ben was by her side.

'Thanks for coming.'

'Hey, where else would I be?' He tilted her chin up so she looked him in the eye. 'I know this must be an impossible day for you.'

Molly crumpled. 'I only just got to know him.'

Ben pulled her to him and held her as she cried, quiet tears that were no less powerful than those of anyone who had known Louis Bennett for years.

Despite the sombre mood at the chapel, the wake at the pub was filled with celebration of Louis' life. Andrew, dressed in a black suit and tie, cleanly shaven, looking so different to the Andrew Bennett who was so often covered in chocolate as he created new masterpieces, recounted stories he knew about his dad, times when he was growing up and he'd clashed with Louis. This man in front of her now was a man Molly was proud to call her father – not her dad, she already had a dad who'd been there since she was a baby, and that would never change – but a father she was tied to in a different way and one she felt glad she'd got to know.

Molly wasn't angry with Julia any more. If any good came out of Louis' passing, it was that all of them had learnt about forgiveness. The Bennetts, and Molly, all had a deeper understanding of what the word really meant. And Molly was grateful. Julia had named Andrew on her birth certificate. She was glad too that Julia had contacted him and told him of her existence, because in some way it showed Julia was dealing with things in her own, albeit slow, way. But most of all she would be forever grateful that Julia hadn't gone through with the abortion in 1985. Molly was glad she'd been given a chance to live.

Chapter Thirty-Nine
Gemma

'It's too early,' Gemma groaned when the alarm went off. She nudged Andrew, who turned over to face her and squinted when she turned on the bedside lamp. Even the sun was still sleeping somewhere beyond the moon.

She kissed Andrew gently on the mouth. 'Don't go back to sleep,' she urged as she got out of bed and pulled on her dressing gown, ready to go downstairs to make a cup of tea for them both. It was five o'clock, but they had too much to do to even think of having a lie-in. Today was the day of the Easter Egg Hunt at Magnolia House and somehow the laughter and excitement of it all was helping the pain of losing Louis a week ago. The funeral on Friday was still fresh in their minds, but this was a big distraction today and Gemma hoped it would help Andrew cope.

But it was also the day when Andrew would have to say goodbye to Molly, and Gemma knew it was at the forefront of both their minds as they prepared to start their day.

Downstairs, Gemma put the kettle on. She dropped a teabag into each of the awaiting two mugs and as she waited for the bubbles to boil rapidly and settle again, she wiped the kitchen window with the back of her hand so she could see out to the garden. It was still dark but in the moonlight she could just about make out Louis' annexe. She shivered and felt the familiar lump in her throat. She still wasn't used to him being gone, knowing she'd never see him shuffling from his door to theirs, or hear his voice call out in greeting to make sure he wasn't interrupting. Neither she nor Andrew had set foot in there since they'd got some of Louis' clothes to dress him in for the funeral. She knew what it would be like … the curtains were drawn, the place would be unaired. They would see signs of Louis all around.

Pouring boiling water onto each teabag in turn, she knew they'd have to get out there soon and sort through his things. There was most likely food going off in the fridge, a rancid carton of milk, bread with telltale green fur lying in the pantry. It'd be hard, but together they could do it.

Andrew's footfall on the stairs announced his arrival five minutes later. He'd already had a quick shower, and when he leant in and hugged his wife as they stood side by side looking out of the window, his skin held a warm, citrus tang and a droplet of water fell from his hair onto her cheek.

'How are you feeling?' she asked.

'Much the same,' he sighed. 'I miss him. And I'll miss Molly when she goes.'

She reached a hand up to his cheek. 'Let's do this thing today. Let's do it for Louis, and let's do it for Molly.'

'I love you,' he told her. 'Now, can I interest you in a bacon sandwich?'

'Sounds good.'

'We might need a good breakfast if we're going to cope with hyper kids descending on Magnolia House.'

'I can handle kids, it's my job, remember?'

He winked. 'You're a natural.'

It broke her heart a tiny bit more when she felt the familiar pang of longing, the desire to have children and complete their family.

After breakfast they took the remaining boxes of mini chocolate eggs and the raffle prize – the new mould had arrived safely and Andrew had made the second half of the giant egg yesterday – over to Magnolia House as the sun rose to its optimum position in the sky. With no sign of rain even though winter was just around the corner, there was a warm glow across Magnolia Creek and it looked set to be a perfect day.

Magnolia House was all ready for the Easter Egg Hunt. There was a face-painting stall all ready and set up to go. There was a stall with a sign indicating it would be selling baked goods – breads, cakes, slices of sweet desserts – there was a wine stall run by Chris from the pub who was busy lining up bottles, there was a lucky-dip stall, a hot dog stand and a burger stand.

'We have a few helpers today,' said Rosie, leading them to the main room where Gemma saw boxes of their eggs stacked up. And there waiting for them were Stephanie and Emilio, Bella and Rodney Finnegan, Ben and Molly, Owen, and many other faces Gemma was starting to get to know.

'We'll get these eggs scattered in no time at all,' said Gemma, and armed everyone with a box each. The helpers filed back out of the front doors where Rosie delegated areas for each of them to start. Rosie, Owen, Molly and Ben would take the farthest part of the field, working their way past the cottages and to the grass area on the left. Gemma and Andrew would take the area to the side of the lake, which would be vigorously monitored today with so many eager young chocolate lovers. They didn't want to risk any child thinking there was chocolate hidden in the waters beneath and fall in.

Bella and Rodney ensured the eggs were well positioned around the garden to the right of Magnolia

House, Emilio would take the hedges bordering another field and Stephanie would take the centre strip. The task of scattering the eggs was a lot of fun and Gemma could hear laughter, especially from Molly, Ben, Rosie and Owen in the fields the farthest away. She'd wondered how much they were getting done, but they got through their delegated boxes quickly enough and came back for more, and when the task was completed everyone willed the skies up above to hold their own, at least until mid-afternoon when the event would come to an end.

As the time crept towards twelve o'clock when the Easter Egg Hunt was due to kick off, the approach to Magnolia House gradually filled with vehicles and Main Street was choc-a-block with traffic queuing right back to the edge of town. Gemma hadn't seen a setting so busy since the last time she'd been to the Easter Show in the city.

'This is crazier than I expected.' It was Andrew at her side, a huge grin across his face as the people kept on coming. Teenagers accompanied siblings, primary school children gabbled excitedly, all waiting for someone, anyone, to yell, 'Go!'

'It's manic, isn't it?'

'You love it.' He watched his wife and she linked her arm through his own.

'I do. I can't deny it.'

'You're not content with just me, are you?' He was half serious, but there was humour in his voice and Gemma nudged against him.

'I love you to bits, Andrew Bennett. But I want a family. I need a family.'

She turned to him until a small child bumped into her legs.

'I'm so sorry.' It was the mother, flustered and running after her child.

'No worries, no worries at all.' Gemma crouched down to the same level as the little girl. 'And what is your name?'

A timid voice came out. 'Bea.'

'What a beautiful name.' Bea had the cutest little button nose, the rosiest cheeks, and chestnut hair pulled into a tidy plait. 'Are you ready to find those eggs?'

The girl shook her head and the mother said, 'She was running away. That's why she bashed into you. I think the whole thing is a bit crazy for her. She's so little she's afraid she'll get trampled.'

'Well, we'll have to fix that, won't we?' Gemma told Bea to wait there a moment. She went inside and came out with something behind her back.

'Ta-da.' She put a pair of long, white bunny ears onto Bea's head like a headband. 'How would you like to wear those? You're a good ten inches taller now, much less likely to be trampled on,' she winked.

'You're so kind. Thank you.' The mother scooped Bea up into her arms and joined the crowds congregating ready for the off.

Gemma turned to Andrew, who had watched the entire exchange without saying a word.

He kissed his wife on the cheek before they looked around them, and he said, 'Louis would've loved all this.'

'He would.'

Another couple of kids came up to say hello to Gemma, or Mrs Bennett as she was formally known, and when the voice over the speaker announced the start of the event, squeals erupted and the hunt was on.

Carmen, Sofia and Darcy had driven up from the city, kids in tow, and they all commented on how happy Gemma looked despite recent events. And she was. She missed Louis, they all did, but she felt as though today marked a turning point in their lives and it would only get better from here.

An hour into the big event and Ellie, the little girl in Gemma's class, ran up to her with a delicately woven basket in her arms, puffing and panting from all the running. 'Look how many colours there are!' Her eyes were bright, she was buzzing.

'Ellie, how are you? And what a gorgeous basket.'

'My daddy bought it from the gift shop,' she told Gemma as Ellie's dad came up from the field beyond. Ellie wouldn't have done the hunt on her own like many kids would, full of confidence and invincibility. Ellie was cautious among crowds, wary of new situations, which was one thing they worked on at school. Whenever they had a class trip Gemma made sure Ellie knew what to expect, talked through any concerns she may have. If there was a visitor in school, then Ellie would know about it in finite detail so she could process it her own way before it happened.

'Hello, Mr Sedgeway.' Gemma greeted Ellie's dad and reached out, shook his hand.

Mr Sedgeway smoothed down his daughter's hair as she cuddled up against him, still gawping at the massive haul of colourful eggs in her basket. 'It's nice to finally meet at last,' he said. 'Ellie speaks very highly of you.'

'She does?' Gemma smiled.

'We were worried about having her at a mainstream school, but you've taken away our concerns. So thank you.' He nodded to Andrew in acknowledgment and took Ellie inside to have her face painted. She promised to come outside afterwards and show Gemma, see if she could still be recognised.

'Hello, Mason.' Gemma waved over at a little boy with chocolate around his mouth. 'He's in my class,' she told Andrew.

'You're popular.' They sat together on the wall surrounding the lake, most of their hard work done for the day.

'Have you seen Molly?' Gemma asked.

'She's over there.' Andrew smiled and looked over to the veranda of the big house. Molly and Ben were deep in conversation, nursing a can of drink each. 'I said hello and we agreed to meet up after this has all finished.'

'How's she feeling?'

He shrugged. 'She's not said much.'

'I'm glad she got to meet Louis,' said Gemma. 'He really liked her. And I think Molly gave him closure on the secret he'd kept hidden for so long.'

Andrew nodded. 'I told him I forgave him. I don't know if he heard, but I like to think so. And his visit to the shop and the family lunch at the chocolaterie, the day he collapsed, is something I'll never forget.'

Gemma squeezed his knee with her hand, and they sat there quietly, contemplating. Andrew still felt guilty for the way he treated his father, guilty that he hadn't managed to persuade Louis to have the transplant before either of them even knew about Molly. But the doctors had been very clear. Whether or not he'd agreed to the transplant earlier, Louis' heart attack had been something nobody could've foreseen. The outcome would most likely have been the same whether it had happened before the surgery or after it.

Andrew turned to face her. 'We'll make an appointment with the doctor. I want to give you a family, and I'll do anything to make it happen.'

'Anything?'

He nodded. 'Anything.'

'Then don't book an appointment.'

His expression changed. 'What?'

'I've been thinking.'

'Always dangerous.'

She smiled. 'I've watched you with Molly, this girl you didn't know until she was well into adulthood. I've spent time with Ellie, a girl who has additional needs and blossoms when they're met.'

'What are you saying?'

She hesitated. 'What I'm saying is how about we forget IVF, or trying so hard to conceive naturally? Clearly my body is not happy to give us what we want, but there must be hundreds of kids out there who need people like us. We're good people, we deserve to be parents.' She reached up and touched Andrew's face. 'When I think of little Ellie, lost in the system with foster families for such a long time, I want to reach out and do something for any other child in the same position.'

Andrew drew in his breath.

'What do you think? Is it a possibility?' She crossed her fingers in her lap.

'Do you think we'd be eligible?'

'We could find out.' Gemma tried to keep her eagerness in check. She'd been thinking about this for a few weeks, mainly since Molly came into their lives, but saying it out loud made it feel real, and she was excited.

Andrew looked over at three little boys, two of them scrounging in the dirt by the roots of a tree to find the eggs the youngest boy had dropped. The third boy was crying, his face was covered in mud. The other two handed him eggs as they were found, each time putting a little bit more happiness on to his face.

'I'm in,' said Andrew, eyes only for his wife now.

Gemma's eyes filled with tears. 'Really?'

'One hundred per cent. I'm in. Before Molly came along I would've been scared I couldn't parent a child who came from somebody else. But Molly has made me realise it doesn't matter at what stage you become a parent, there are no rules. You pick up the job from the moment it starts, whenever that is. For Molly and I …' He paused, looked over at his daughter talking animatedly with Ben. 'We didn't meet until now, but I get the feeling we won't suffer for it.'

'So we're doing this?' Gemma clasped her husband's hand.

'We're doing this.'

Chapter Forty
Molly

Molly sat next to Andrew on the steps of her veranda at the cottage, overlooking the lake as darkness fell over Magnolia Creek. A crescent moon cast enough light across the water to see ripples as a duck sneaked across its surface.

'There were more than a hundred families here today,' he began, 'ten thousand eggs, and Bella reckons we've raised upwards of seven thousand dollars, what with the stalls inside Magnolia House too.'

'Wow, that's amazing. Everyone had such a great time. Me included.'

'I'm glad.' He looked at the water. It had already reformed since it was disturbed, returning to the flat surface as though the duck had never been there at all. 'What time's your flight?'

'Midnight.'

'Will you be okay? It wasn't so long ago you were terrified of flying.'

'I'm hoping I sleep. At least that's the plan.' She fiddled with the edges of her cardigan, pulling it more tightly around herself. Andrew smelt of chocolate sitting here beside her, and she wondered whether it was only from today, from his clothes or whether she was imagining it because chocolate was what she associated him with. From now on, every time she ate chocolate she would think of Andrew Bennett, her birth father.

'Are you sure you don't want a goodbye committee at the airport?' Andrew teased.

She was glad he was making jokes, at least pretending to make light of a heavy situation. This was harder than she'd thought, and she wanted to think of him happy rather than the turmoil of the past few weeks since she'd turned up on his doorstep.

'No, Ben will take me. I don't need a big send-off.'

'It'll be hard to say goodbye to him,' said Andrew.

'I'm trying not to think about it.' She smiled and they both focused on the stars above.

'You've got a good night for flying at least. Where do you change?'

'Changi Airport. Same as the way here.'

'Then it's back to London, eh?'

'Back to London.'

They sat in silence for a while until Molly spoke. 'I like the idea of you and Gemma adopting.' He'd told her that afternoon as they stacked up the empty boxes from the eggs and carried them back to the shop for the next time they were needed. 'Actually, I think it's pretty cool.' She nodded and broke out in a smile.

Andrew grinned. 'I'm not sure I've been described as "cool" in many years, if ever. But if that's what you think, then I'm glad.'

'You'll be a great parent.' She hesitated. 'You *are* a great parent.' When Andrew looked at her she said, 'I don't blame you for anything, you know. And I don't blame Louis, I don't blame Julia. It is what it is. Or … it *was* what it *was.*'

The shaft of moonlight graced the water in front of them, but nothing else moved save the trees whispering their goodnights.

'I know you'll be busy, with the business,' she said tentatively. 'But would you come over to England soon?

I'm not sure I want to wait too long before we spend more time together.'

When he turned to her, he had tears in his eyes. 'You try and stop me,' he said. 'I'm proud to call you my daughter. I know I'll never replace your dad, and I don't want to. But I'm glad you found me. I'm glad to make you a part of our family.'

She put a hand over his. It was the closest they'd been physically, and she squeezed the flesh beneath hers. 'I'm glad I don't have to wonder about you any more. Somehow my family understand me and we fit. But I've heard of so many children who aren't quite so lucky and spend their whole lives looking for meaning, for part of them. It wasn't like that for me, but there was always a yearning to know. And now I do. And I really like what I've found.'

She looked up at the moon, willing the tears to stay away. 'I'm worried this will all fizzle out. I'll leave the country and I'll be a girl who visited you once, a distant relation who goes on the Christmas card and birthday list.'

When Andrew started to laugh, she looked at him for answers.

'Can you see Gemma letting me get away with that?'

Molly laughed too, harder than she'd thought possible tonight. 'Actually, I can't.'

The laughter dissipated, and then Andrew said, 'I'm not going to let it turn into that kind of relationship. Gemma and I are hoping to adopt and we're thrilled. But don't for one moment think the family I'm going to have is *instead* of you. You're a part of it now, and I'll want you to get to know your new brother or sister. They'll need someone to watch out for them.'

'I like the sound of being a big sister.' She met his gaze, and the words settled around them until Molly checked her watch again. 'Ben will be here in less than an hour, I should finish packing. I have to check in at some crazy time, hours before the flight.'

Andrew nodded, and she knew he was crying and so she stayed there, beside him, close enough to still get the occasional waft of chocolate carried on the same breeze, which was lifting her hair around her shoulders.

Molly had no idea whether she would hug Andrew goodbye, whether she would shake his hand or if they would simply say a verbal farewell. But all of a sudden, he made the decision for her. He stood, held out his hand, and when she let him pull her to her feet, he wrapped her in a hug they held for a few minutes, a hug that encompassed all the feelings of the last few weeks. This other man, all of a sudden, had a solid position in her life. He threatened nobody else, no other relationship, and only added to her completeness.

Molly held back her tears, forced away the gut-wrenching feeling of saying goodbye when they'd only just said hello.

'Goodbye, Molly.' Andrew nodded, accepting what was about to happen. 'Email or phone when you're ready.'

'I will.' Her voice fell into the cool night air, and she retreated back inside the cottage, not daring to watch as Andrew walked away into the darkness.

*

'You'll never cope without me.' Ben lifted Molly's suitcase onto the conveyor belt at check-in. It was nine o'clock in the evening, and even at this time, Melbourne's Tullamarine Airport was heaving.

Once Molly had her boarding pass, they made their way to a café.

'Do you want anything to eat?' Ben grabbed two bottles of apple juice.

Molly shook her head. 'I'll wait at the table over there.' She was beginning to realise what people meant about airports. They were exciting places, the places where dreams started, the world opened up to travellers. But they were also the places where goodbyes happened, where hearts were broken, where tears were shed.

Molly had cried after saying goodbye to Andrew earlier. She was glad she'd held it together in front of him and glad she'd cried as much as she was going to before Ben arrived, but she knew she looked bad. Her eyes still felt puffy, her head ached.

'So.' Ben opened her apple juice and passed it to her. 'How are you feeling about flying again?'

'Fine.'

'Liar.'

She smiled up at him as he sat opposite. 'I've had so much going on. I've not had a chance to really worry, but I'm getting a bit nervous now.'

'Got your colouring books?'

'And pens,' she told him before he asked the obvious.

'You might sleep.'

'Maybe.'

'Have you been onto the Facebook group?'

'Not today.'

Ben took out his phone.

'Oh no, no photos, I look hideous!'

'Don't worry, I'm checking myself in.' He tapped away at his iPhone screen. 'I'll say I'm with you, you've had a great time and you'll be in touch. They're a great bunch of people, they'll all want to know what's happened over the last few weeks.'

Molly sipped her apple juice as he tapped away at his screen. 'It's a bit weird how most of us have never met.'

'Two of us have.'

She held his gaze. 'They have.'

Ben put his phone on the table and reached across to hold her hand. He'd had his hand on her knee on the drive here, but she'd been quiet, not wanting to talk, looking out the window at the lights whizzing by on the freeway from cars on either side, from overhead. So many emotions were whirring around inside her right now, including feelings about Ben and where they went from here.

'I'm glad it all worked out for you, Molly.' Ben squeezed her hand. 'Come round here already would you.' He rolled his eyes and pulled her to standing and round to his side of the table.

'I thought you'd never ask.' She didn't care they were in an airport café, that there were people around, when she leant in and kissed him. The warmth of his lips was familiar, exciting and sad all at once, and she rested her forehead against his.

'I wish I was getting on the plane with you.' said Ben.

'You've only just got home.'

He shrugged. 'Things can change.'

Molly put her hand to his lips. 'Things change all the time. A year ago I never would've thought I'd be here, at an airport, in Australia, having met my birth father.'

'It is pretty awesome.'

'I wish Louis was still alive.'

Ben pulled her close. 'I know you do. At least you had the chance to know him. He was pretty sick. I think you timed your visit perfectly.'

They stayed in the café talking about the Bennetts, talking about her family, Ben's, the nightmare of a long-distance relationship.

Ben rubbed a thumb across Molly's bottom lip. 'I want you to stay.'

'I wish … well, I wish we could be together, but my home is there, Ben.'

He nodded, accepting. 'Come on, we'd better get you to passport control.'

They gathered her things and made their way from the café to the point where they'd have to say their final goodbye.

'I do need to ask a favour though,' said Molly. 'And it's a big one.'

'Go on.'

'My brother gets married in Connecticut in a few months' time, and I don't have a date.'

Ben laughed, and they came to a stop at Passport Control. 'Then we'd better do something about that, Molly Ramsey. It looks like I'm going off on my travels again real soon … America, here I come.' He looked at her more seriously, took her face in his hands. 'And after the wedding, we'll see what happens.'

'We'll see what happens,' she said. A holiday romance wasn't at all what she'd been looking for, but some things happened for a reason. And perhaps Ben Harrison was that reason.

'You'd better go,' said Ben, tension visible in his jaw, in the way he took in a deep breath as though preparing himself.

Molly burst into tears, her third emotional goodbye in the last week taking its toll.

‘It’s not goodbye.’ Ben held her tight. ‘It’s “until next time”.’ He wiped the tears from beneath her eyes with his thumb.

‘Until next time,’ she said, and turned, leaving Melbourne and a small piece of her heart behind.

Epilogue

'Your family tree must be overgrown by now,' said Ben, loosening his tie and top button. He pulled Molly onto his lap.

It was a bright, sunny July day in Connecticut, and the temperature was well up into the thirties. Molly pulled at the bodice of her dress to ensure it stayed in place, but she couldn't stop smiling at Ben, who was her date at Isaac's wedding, looking devilishly handsome in the outfit he'd chosen. She had a hard time keeping her hands to herself in public, not to mention in front of her family.

'My family tree is enormous,' she said. 'I have extra aunties, uncles, cousins, living all over the world. And you know what?'

'I'm sure you're going to tell me.' He toyed with the dark ringlets of her hair hanging down from the up-do held in place with a diamante tiara.

'I intend to meet every one of them eventually.'

'Please tell me I don't have to do the same.'

'We'll see. Come on, let's dance.' She led him into the crowd assembled for Chubby Checker's 'The Twist'.

The marquee was bursting at the seams, full of family, full of love and laughter Molly hoped would never end. They joined in, but when the music slowed and men pulled women close and vice versa, Molly leant her head on Ben's shoulder.

'I'm glad you came,' she whispered into his ear.

'I wouldn't miss it for the world.' He looked into her eyes. 'You're becoming an accomplished traveller now.'

'I think I may even be enjoying it.'

She'd taken the flight over to America with her parents, and they'd both been surprised at how she'd handled herself. Even with minor turbulence in the last hour of the flight she'd stayed calm, not panicked, shut her eyes and let it pass. She didn't have another trip to Australia planned, with all her holidays taken for the year, but Andrew was coming over next week to meet her parents. Her parents had coped with Isaac's move better than she'd expected, and after they'd finished dancing and Ben had begged to escape into the fresh air, she joined her dad at the bar.

'How are you doing, Dad?'

He nodded. He had a beer, probably the same one he'd been on all night, not being much of a drinker. He turned and looked over at his son. 'He's happy.'

Molly looked at Isaac, dancing with his mother-in-law. 'They're a nice family.'

'They are.'

'Just because he's coming over here to live doesn't mean he'll forget you, Dad.'

'Oh, I'm not daft, pet, I know he won't. Like I know I'll never be replaced by Andrew.'

Before tonight he hadn't voiced any concern about Andrew Bennett's relationship with his daughter. He'd let Molly sort through her own feelings first, hadn't tried to influence her actions as she searched for answers. But now, it felt good to hear how much he cared. And she was glad her Dad knew his place in her life and that it would never be threatened.

'You'll never be replaced.' Her smiled reached her eyes.

‘I was worried for a while.’ He was joking, but it reinforced how difficult this had been all round. And sometimes Molly knew she was guilty of forgetting that.

‘You look happy,’ Jeff Ramsey told his daughter.

‘I am. And how’s Mum taking Isaac’s departure to America?’ Molly nodded over to her mum, who was the most relaxed she’d been in ages, kicking up her heels and owning the dance floor.

‘She was in bits when he first told us his plans, then again when you told us you were looking for your birth parents.’

‘Dad, I—’

‘No need to say anything, Molly. She would never have told you kids anything to make you change your minds, because deep down she knows you have your own lives.’

‘But after what Gran did to her, leaving her to sort everything out when she left for Canada. It must still hurt.’ Molly waved at her mum, who was none the wiser about this conversation. She was far too busy chatting away with her new daughter-in-law.

‘It hurt for a long time, and there’s no doubt about it, your gran could’ve handled things better. But your mum is excited for you, and for Isaac, whatever the future holds.’ He looked over at Ben, who was at the entrance of the marquee. Isaac had escaped his mother-in-law’s clutches, and he was now chatting away happily to Molly’s date. Molly had no idea what was going to happen with Ben, but part of her reached a sense of contentment that this would be about the two of them, and her parents would give their blessing however it turned out.

‘Thanks, Dad.’

‘She’s even signed up to a discount airfare website for deals so she can holiday wherever she likes. I think secretly she’s wanted to travel for years but never got the chance. Now she has the perfect excuse! She even said that if you moved to Australia, and Isaac is in America, then we could go and live halfway between.’

‘And where would that be?’

‘Hawaii.’

Molly laughed whole-heartedly. She could imagine her mum dancing the hula in a grass skirt, cocktail in hand, as she spent the kids’ inheritance.

‘Nice,’ she said.

‘I’m looking forward to meeting Andrew and his wife.’ Her dad was sincere and she was proud.

‘They’re lovely people.’

‘I hope they bring some chocolate.’

‘Dad,’ she admonished, giggling as they looked on at the throng of people dancing.

‘I like Ben. He seems good for you.’ Her dad clearly wanted everything out in the open tonight, and Molly was enjoying every minute of it. ‘And a doctor no less. I’m impressed. And he’s better than any other boyfriend I’ve met.’

‘There haven’t exactly been many. But yeah, he is.’

‘So what’ll happen with you two? Australia and England takes long-distance romance to a whole new level.’

‘It does a bit.’ Molly sighed. ‘I don’t know. He says he’ll come over for Christmas if we’ll have him.’

Her dad nodded, seemingly impressed.

‘Molly?’ he said after a while.

‘Yes, Dad.’

‘May I have this dance?’

‘I thought you’d never ask.’

*

Andrew held Gemma's hand as the cabin lights dimmed on the second leg of their journey from Hong Kong to the UK. He sat back in his seat and looked out over the wing of the airplane, the lights flashing intermittently against the inky sky as they cut through deep grey clouds floating past the tiny windows.

Andrew and Gemma had filed the necessary paperwork with the adoption agency, and because they understood it could take some time for their plan to reach fruition, they'd decided to take off to Europe while they could. Andrew felt as though he'd only just started in his relationship with Molly. They were so new to one another, and he wanted to keep his promise to make her as much a part of his family as any other child he may have. He was looking forward to meeting Molly's parents, although anxious of what they might think of him, wondering whether they'd harbour any ill feeling. From what Molly said they wouldn't at all; they were nothing but grateful she'd been let into their lives, but the worry still lingered and he suspected in some ways, it always would.

He pulled the grey and red blanket over his lap. Gemma was asleep already, and when he tilted his head towards hers, her blonde hair tickled his nose. She was his life, and watching her go through the paperwork for a possible adoption, he'd fallen bit by bit in love with her all over again. She was going to make a wonderful mother.

He looked out to the darkened sky as they glided through the air as though they weren't really moving at all and he thought about Louis. His secret must have eaten him up over the years, and even though he'd only known Molly for a short while, he couldn't ever imagine doing anything like that to her. It made him realise the desperation Louis must have felt to go ahead with such a plan.

Andrew thought about Julia too. He hadn't messaged her in a while. Julia knew Molly had shown up, but since he'd told her, she'd not written back. He expected she was shocked, trying to work this out in her own mind. He'd leave it a few months, but then Andrew knew he wanted to contact her again, not to ask what she was going to do about Molly, not to rake over what happened, but to ask how she was. And to let her know more about Molly and the life she'd had.

Andrew leant back and closed his eyes, and by the time he opened them again, the sun was rising in the sky and they were coming in to land.

The past was over. The future was here.

THE END

Acknowledgements

I'd like to thank a lovely lady called Mary from VANISH in Melbourne. In 2009 she started a search for my own birth mother and her encouragement, support and hard work was invaluable.

Writers need to research even when they are writing fiction and I thank everyone who was willing to be interviewed about the adoption process and their experiences. You all enabled me to write a realistic story from the heart, with layers of emotion that may otherwise not have been possible.

A huge thank you to mother and daughter team, Lucy and Andrea, of Creighton's Chocolaterie, in Leighton Buzzard. I had a fabulous day with you both, watching you create the most amazing chocolates and talking to me about what it's really like to be a chocolatier. And of course, let's not forget the purchases I made before I went home. They were delicious and I've been recommending you ever since!

Thanks goes to Belinda Holmes, my lovely editor, whose expertise helped me deliver the best story to my readers, and to Stephanie Box whose editing and proofreading skills are second to none. Also a big thank you to Berni Stevens for designing a cover I absolutely adore. You ladies are awesome!

I know I say it every time, but thank you to the other members of The Write Romantics, ten writers who came together via the Romantic Novelists' Assocation (RNA) and who are always there to discuss ideas and concerns, celebrate achievements and deal with any obstacles. It's a pleasure being part of such a wonderful group.

Writing can be a lonely occupation but one that is eased with support from family and friends, so my final and biggest thank you goes to my husband and my two children, without whom I would be lost.

Helen J Rolfe.

What Rosie Found Next

One house, two strangers, one very big secret...

A shaky upbringing has left Rosie Stevens craving safety and security. She thinks she knows exactly what she needs to make her life complete – the stable job and perfect house-sit she's just found in Magnolia Creek. The only thing she wants now is for her long-term boyfriend, Adam, to leave his overseas job and come home for good.

Owen Harrison is notoriously nomadic, and he roars into town on his Ducati for one reason and one reason only – to search his parents' house while they're away to find out what they've been hiding from him his entire life. When he meets Rosie, who refuses to quit the house-sit in his parents' home, sparks fly.

Secrets are unearthed, promises are broken, friendships are put to the test and the real risk of bushfires under the hot Australian sun threatens to undo Rosie once and for all.

Will Rosie and Owen be able to find what they want or what they really need?

Handle Me with Care

Does true love come along more than once in a lifetime?

Maddie Kershaw doesn't think so. She lost the love of her life in the 9/11 attacks, and since then has hopped from one casual fling to the next. But when she delivers an erotic cake to a one-hundredth birthday party by mistake, she meets Evan and starts to believe in second chances … until she realises there's a risk of getting hurt all over again.

Evan Quinn is serially single, yet when he meets Maddie he feels an instant connection, so much so that he confesses on their first date that he may have testicular cancer. Was it a mistake to tell her? He wants Maddie more than he has ever wanted any other woman. But he doesn't want her pity.

With the odds stacked against them both, finding love won't be easy. But beneath the Australian sun, a Happy Ever After could be worth fighting for.

The Friendship Tree

Is running away ever the answer?

Tamara Harding left the UK to join family in Australia, but more importantly, to put ten thousand miles between her and her ex, Bradley Cox. She is soon drawn in to the small community of Brewer Creek where she becomes the coordinator for an old fashioned Friendship Tree – a chart telling people who they can call on in times of trouble.

As she vows to start over, she meets Jake Manning – and life gets more complicated than she could ever have imagined. Jake is the direct competitor for the family business, and a man with a dark secret, and Tamara struggles to fight her attraction to him as she deals with secrets of her own and an ex who refuses to give up.

When danger descends on Brewer Creek in the form of Jake's own past, Tamara soon realises the Friendship Tree does a lot more than organise fundraising events and working bees; it has the power to unite an entire town. But will Tamara see past the complications and allow herself a happy ending with Jake? Or will she run away again?

Printed in Great Britain
by Amazon

76915537R00215